## MOTHER AND DAUGHTER

"How was lunch with Dad?" I asked, passing Ellery's open door.

"Like always." She sighed. Strewn across her bed were the pictures we'd taken on Memorial Day. "Can't you see what these pictures say about me?" she said. "Can't you see that I failed at the one and only thing I could do better than Claudia? Look at me in those snapshots! A little shadow, a little zero. A broken arm because I couldn't even get my horse under control. I wouldn't have been surprised if I turned out in black-and-white next to Claudia. Just look at her hair, her face! And the way she plays the harp!"

"Let's not forget, Ell. You could have stayed with *your* harp lessons. You might have been just as good."

"In your dreams! You just don't get it, Mom!"

"Listen, Ellery. I had a size-nine shoe when I was twelve years old. My sister had a three. I think I have an idea."

"And Daddy doesn't want me the way I am. No! He goes, 'As soon as your arm heals, we'll see if we can get you tennis lessons.' And then he's talking about getting me started on the violin, since I hated the harp and piano. And then he's telling me he's going to send me to Paris to learn French without an accent. So, does he want a new and improved version or what?"

"He just wants the best for his daughters, Ellery."

"I'm not the best. That's the problem. Nowhere near. I'm not fit to be 'the doctor's daughter.' " Ellery lowered her voice to a whisper. "I'm just the doctor's *other* daughter. . . ."

# TWO DAUGHTERS

Marlene Fanta Shyer

KENSINGTON BOOKS
Kensington Publishing Corp.
http://www.kensingtonbooks.com

KENSINGTON BOOKS are published by

Kensington Publishing Corp.
850 Third Avenue
New York, NY 10022



All Kensington Titles, Imprints, and Distributed Lines are available at special quantity discounts for bulk purchases for sales promotions, premiums, fund-raising, and educational or institutional use. Special book excerpts or customized printings can also be created to fit specific needs. For details, write or phone the office of the Kensington special sales manager: Kensington Publishing Corp., 850 Third Avenue, New York, NY 10022, attn: Special Sales Department, Phone: 1-800-221-2647.



First Printing: April 2002
10 9 8 7 6 5 4 3 2 1

Printed in the United States of America

# Prologue

The four of us—dressed in new outfits, assiduously glamorized, with hair meticulously arranged, belts, collars, and bow tie in place—sat gathered in front of the fireplace for the first photograph. The young reporter thought it would be on the cover, but in any case, certainly the piece would be full-color and run several pages. The magazine was a new one, *Southern Connecticut Life,* and each month, a prominent family was to be featured. Last month's headline story was the state senator in Hartford, the month before, the handicapped president of Connecticut State College; the flagship issue did four pages on Paul Newman and family. And now, the Ehrlichs. The reporter was a young, intense light-skinned black woman with corn rows, hunched over a tape recorder, fiddling somewhat nervously with the buttons. She sat in a pop-eyed trance as we answered her questions, pronounced with the slightest lilt of the Caribbean patois. She prodded Peter about his charity work in Bridgeport; she and the photographer would proceed up there later in the week to snap him caring for the patients in the state-of-the art geriatric clinic.

"Dr. Ehrlich, what do you see as the future of animal organs used to replace defective human ones?" "How do you feel about DNA tampering?" "What are the greatest medical strides we're likely to make in the next decade?" "Do you envision life appreciably prolonged within this century?" "What is your opinion of the low-iron theory?"

"Mrs. Ehrlich, I understand that you not only have your own antiques appraisal business, but that you make time for traveling, that you're raising two teenage daughters, and you've also been instrumental in raising funds for the Crandall General Hospital Coronary Care Unit. Can you tell our readers something about the hospital addition and also about your own background? How do you see the role of doctor's wife changed in the last twenty years?"

"Claudia, do you plan to make a future for yourself as a harpist?" "How long have you studied?" "Ellery, I understand you really enjoy equestrian sports. Does that include dressage?" "Have you had many lessons?" "Do you own a horse?"

It went on like that for forty-five minutes, with the photographer snapping us together on the couch, Claudia at the harp, and Peter, glasses on his nose, at his desk. He took a photo of Ellery on the stairs and one of me standing in front of the 1890 Wooten's patent desk on the stenciled floor of the front hall. The reporter said we all looked tremendously photogenic.

She shook our hands one by one when she was through, and the photographer thanked us and preceded her out of the house and to their car. In the doorway, the reporter said she felt she'd gotten all the material she needed, and appreciated our openness and cooperation. I asked when the story would appear.

"It's slated for either the October or November issue. Should run four, five pages." Then the young woman looked past me into the house. "A lovely home, Mrs. Ehrlich," she said, in that melodic, island way, and I had a quick change of perspective, saw us as if I were looking through her serious, seen-it-all eyes. It must have seemed as if we were a throwback to some gentler time, when what we had was as common as the clematis climbing up walls and fences all over this neighborhood. Did we seem too smug, untouched, above it all? I had the feeling I wanted to apologize: for my beautiful ceiling beams and expensive armoires, for the Waterford, for social injustice, for everything.

At the last minute, as she was getting into the car, and as I thanked her again for the interview, she unexpectedly turned and asked me my definition of happiness. I was caught unawares, but told her I'd decided long ago that happiness was simply the absence of unhappiness.

She turned to Peter. "And you, Doctor?"

Peter looked past her, over her head, (focusing it looked as if) on the rooftop across the street. Slightly embarrassed, he turned to give me a sheepish smile. "My family," he said. "My top-notch family."

# Chapter One

Could I guess that one random mishap on an afternoon in May would irrevocably change four lives? The small accident had a duration of maybe ten seconds, just a blip on the screen of our family life that should have passed without repercussions. A little something happened. A big something followed, in small, unpredictable steps. Now here we are, each of us blighted in some way, our lights dimmed. And although we're still a family, we've disbanded. The secure, best life, the one we'd been living, is gone forever.

Claudia was sixteen that spring, and Ellery was twelve. I got the call when I was out at a waterfront estate checking the authenticity of an eighteenth-century fall-front desk the owners claimed once belonged to De Witt Clinton. As soon as I got back to the office, Annie Wickes, my friend and partner, told me to call my husband at the emergency room at the hospital, but not to get upset. "He said it's Ellery, but not to worry. I think she was thrown, Libby. Want me to go with you?"

I told Annie I'd be okay and rushed back to the car.

It felt like I'd broken through ice when I pushed the key into the ignition. I'd encouraged my younger daughter, but why had I? Weren't there enough hazards out there for little girls? Peter was right; the possibilities of injury were limitless.

Ruptures, neck, spine—I heard sirens, saw stretchers, pictured oxygen tubes in her little-girl nostrils. Stopped at a traffic light, my breathing was short and fast. Peter had warned me, but in the end, he couldn't deny the girls anything. And it was more than that. A large part of him wanted them to compete. Glowed when we walked on packed dirt through the smell of manure to watch the competitions. The blue ribbons brought out the blue in his green eyes. He came around. She always wore the best, the most reinforced helmet, after all. "Great job, Ell. I want to get you next to Fast Forward—there, put your hand up on his flank—there you go! Now, take off your helmet, let's get another shot, maybe closer up."

Our navigator had a destination, and we were following his course. The harp teacher came for Claudia every Wednesday, and Ellery, outfitted in gabardine pants and four-hundred-dollar boots, leaped over wooden obstacles on the backs of Mr. Hoof, Walnut, and Fast Forward, her favorite. And Peter took photographs.

It was late in the afternoon, one of those glorious poet's days in spring when I pulled into the complicated parking lot, with its zebra gates, ticket machine, one-way signs, and crammed spaces. I couldn't find a slot for my car and squeezed the steering wheel until my palms hurt. Then, I began thinking that somehow it was retributive, I was responsible for this accident.

Getting it for having it too good. I was being punished for favoring Ellery just the slightest, tiniest bit: Ellery, born seven weeks prematurely, frail for the first two years of her life, had this edge with me. Claudia took her first steps on her first birthday, Ellery didn't begin walking until twenty months. She was late with talking and teething and learning colors. Over the years, we consulted experts and swallowed reports: "Trouble understanding language on an inferential level. Flat in her interpretations. Naive. Sensitive, too literal." I saw her as still wobbling slightly, always a half-step behind, forever trying to catch up. Still, in this family, it had felt not like half a step, but more like half a length behind.

Over the years, the gap had narrowed. Encouragement, force of will, maturity; the recipe for progress was unclear, but slowly, steadily, she was catching up. We had this soul-to-soul rapport, were mother-daughter psychic mirror images. She was named not after the mystery writer but after my initials, L.R.E., which stand for Libby Reid Ehrlich, the acronym being Peter's suggestion, since we'd named Claudia after him. (Claude Peter is the way it reads on his birth certificate, after his father.) It was as if naming her after me put my personal genetic stamp on the child, but that wasn't really it. I always felt she needed more than Claudia. Claudia was not only quicker, but less fragile and less moody. Claudia won at games and stepped forward to claim whatever she wanted, was inevitably first in line, and spoke up to the world when things were wrong. Claudia refused to have her hair cut, and it poured down her back in spiraling bunches the color of a straw basket. She was running her fingers through it constantly, irritatingly, making it noticeable. And herself. When we were at the club, people came up to whisper to me, "Your daughter is beautiful." "They both are," I'd say sharply, especially if Ellery had overheard. Ellery's hair was stick-straight like mine, falling from her head as if it were being pulled down by a vacuum cleaner.

Or, I might be being punished because of what happened three years ago when we hired a builder named Trevor Eddy to modernize an upstairs bathroom and tear out a hall closet to make room for a telephone booth for the girls. I'd seen one in *Better Homes and Gardens,* all etched glass and stained mahogany, inspired by a nineteenth-century Lannier wardrobe. Trevor Eddy copied it brilliantly, down to the brass door hinges and antique hardware, suggested an uncomfortable little seat to keep conversations short. The Confucius of contracting, Peter called him.

Could I be being punished now for one misstep, for which I've felt a remorse as permanent as moth holes in a winter coat? As I pulled into a space and leaped out of the car, I promised myself nothing like Trevor Eddy would ever happen again, if my little girl were spared.

"I'm Mrs. Ehrlich. My daughter?" I have dreams like this, where people don't listen to pleading, prayers, but keep doing paperwork. It seemed to take long before the nurse acknowledged me, looked at the clipboard, the row of names. I'd interrupted her in a conversation with another nurse. Around me, people sat in plastic chairs connected into rows, looking uninjured. There were magazines on tables and no visible signs of trauma or pathology, until a stretcher was wheeled in and there was some commotion. I spun around. It wasn't Ellery. It was a black man, moaning.

Simultaneously, Peter appeared. The sweat was lining the sides of his cheeks in shiny tracks.

He grabbed my arm. "Oh, sweetie, you're here. I just called your office again. It's a broken arm, that's all. A fractured humerus. A small crack in the ulna. No picnic but thank God, thank God when you consider what could have happened here." He mopped his forehead with his handkerchief, then his cheeks, his chin. "Some new maneuver she tried, and the horse suddenly reared, then did a U-turn. She fell into a swampy bog, between a rock and a pile of sawed trunks. . . . It could have been, well—oh, let's not think—" Peter's bow tie was askew and his hair looked ruffled, the way it did when he woke up in the morning. He pulled me along, into a corridor, to some sterile examining rooms. His voice lowered. "Sweetie, you look worse than Ell does. Are you okay? She's been examined head to foot. She got her period, and she's got severe cramps on top of everything else, that's all. That's what threw me off, all that girdle pain. I thought at first there might be some internal injuries, but it's not much more than superficial contusions. Of course, she's shaky as hell."

I hung on Peter's sleeve; we were blocking the progress of the stretcher on which the man—blue-black under the fluorescent light and still moaning—was now being wheeled into an examining room.

"You look paler. You want a Xanax, sweetie?"

"No, I'm fine now."

"You sure, Libby?"

"She must have been scared to death. And, her first period! She was having what she called a stomachache yesterday. I thought it was too many purple plums. Remember when I got sick after eating all those plums?" I practically fell all over Peter. The whiteness, the chemical smells, the stretches of linoleum floor, the orderlies in sea green—even the air felt sick and bloated.

"Where is she?" I leaned on Peter's arm. I hate hospitals. The green room for cemeteries, my mother calls them.

"Albertson just came in. I called his office right away. He called me back, said he just came off the plane from London. I said, 'Never mind, Al, just get down here.' He's putting on a cast right this minute. I trust him completely, jet lag or no."

I was so grateful for Peter at that moment. I remember thinking how lucky, how downright providential that I'd met him. All around me I saw women married to men married to their work, their golf clubs, their other women. The Connecticut sun must have shone down auspiciously on me that day at the beach when someone brought him over to look at the cut I'd gotten from a piece of beach glass.

I was born and bred in Westport, recovering that summer from a broken engagement to a hometown banker who loved boats and the Civil War, but most of all himself. My ambition was to visit every country in the world, then settle down to raise children and basset hounds and collect antiques. I don't know why basset hounds, except that they looked how I felt since my broken engagement: perpetually sad. My father, a commercial artist, had died and left behind not much more than his collection of photograph collages, debts, and a long, sweet letter of apology. I'd had to leave college and was working at every miscellaneous thing in the offices of a trio of angry lawyers, one or another of whom threatened to fire me every day, and I gave my mother half my paycheck. She said she'd race me to see who could "get well connected" first. She went to Florida, found a retired chef named Rudy, and won. My sister had already escaped to California.

It was a year and three months later that I met Peter. He wasn't interested in antiques, didn't much care about seeing the world, and preferred cats to dogs. It didn't matter; he was the world's idea of a catch: six-foot-one, a doctor, charming, a doctor, ambitious, a doctor. And not just a podiatrist, not just an internist. He was a cardiologist, with all those syllables, all that prestige. I got his attention, I won his affection, and sunshine is all I saw. I revised my dreams, and the same sun had been shining on us ever since . . . despite the early years, the black-bordered memories I've managed to bury so deep. It's as if they'd never happened at all.

My husband works with two partners, one new and eager, the other about to retire, and as far as Peter is concerned, not a minute too soon, since the old man is beginning to make mistakes. The younger doctor, Solow, is sometimes too harried and not compassionate enough. Peter is the star of this little medical group, and also the subtle luminary of this community. Times have changed, and priests, ministers, and politicians have been knocked off their pedestals, right and left. So have physicians, but in this town, there is still enough awe to place a healer into a high human category, especially one like my husband, who has never had a single malpractice suit filed against him (unlike his partners, who have over the years racked up a few near and real deaths between them.) Peter is The Doctor here in Crandall, Connecticut, affiliated with Crandall General and St. Anthony's. He does pro bono work in Bridgeport as well, working with the indigent in the public clinic twice a month. Once, during the baboon heart controversy, Ted Koppel interviewed him on network television. He spoke with quiet, impressive authority, but in real life, his voice booms when it wants to boom, and is soft when he speaks to very old ladies or children. Our children, in particular.

We are all careful to keep his secret.

"What happened to *her*?" Claudia breezed in with her boyfriend, Ess DiBuono, in tow. He has a way of swaggering, and walks across a room as if he were pacing it off. Ess stands for *S*, which stands for Salvatore, which Ess hates. He is a Danbury boy, who delivers pizza, drives a limo, works in construction, cleans boats, walks dogs for a vet, but never seems to work very hard, and has achieved a local reputation for bravery by saving a corgi from drowning on some Vermont lake when the ice-skating pond gave way in January. According to Claudia, Ess had waded in, right up to his chin, and pulled out little Humphrey Bogart, wrapping the dog's shaking body around his neck. The dog's owners, a well-to-do

Shelton couple, presented Ess with a check for an unbelievable twenty-five hundred dollars. On Claudia's wrist was a gold cuff he'd bought for her with some of the spoils. The rest went for a very used black van and a gold nose ring matching the row of gilded circles in his right ear.

"Hey, what happened to Ell, what happened? Some guy give her a hard time or whut?" Ess had a way of freezing in midsmile, as if he wouldn't allow himself anything as explicit as a facial expression.

"What happened to her?" Claudia echoed, turning to me.

"You guys don't want to ask me? Am I here or what? I got thrown off my horse. I broke my arm. I have two factures."

"Fractures."

"Fractures, I meant fractures. Didn't I say fractures? Anyway, they act like I'm not here," she said, but she'd had an evening of parental indulgence, and Peter had, in fact, just run out to Baskin-Robbins for Raspberries 'n' Cream ice cream. And Kotex. ("Every month for the rest of my life! It's filthy!") Her eyes were still bloodshot from crying.

"I broke my collarbone when I was in fourth grade. It was like, forget it," Ess said. "My father took a snapshot of me in my collar. I wanted to send it to the child abuse center so I could be their poster child."

"Ess." Claudia dimpled.

Ess's determination never to show teeth reminds me of old Buster Keaton movies. "How long you gonna be in your crate?"

"Not long. Maybe just until school lets out."

I looked over her head at Claudia and shook my head. "I'm afraid it's likely to be, hmm, I don't know, longer than that, Ellery."

Her eyes, which I didn't think were capable of one more drop of moisture, filled up again. "One minute

I was on Fast Forward's back, like, in complete control, the next minute—*whshsh*"—Ellery waved her good arm in an arc, let her hand fall over the edge of the couch—"it's good-bye summer."

Claudia took her hand and ran the back of it across her sister's cheek. "Hey, come on, Ell, you'll be okay. We'll be around. We'll hang out. Think of the TV you'll catch up on. MTV four times a day. Without guilt."

Ess was standing behind her, palms on her shoulders. He shot another one of his almost smiles at no one in particular. "Makes it worth it, huh, Ell? No more lift that bale. Next month, you play your cards right, you break the other arm." Ess seemed always available, always here. He rested his chin on Claudia's hair. "Yeah. And look at the bright side. If it'd been the horse, they woulda shot him."

We were lying in bed that night, still wide awake after the eleven o'clock news. Peter had given Ellery first one, then, with some hesitation, a second codeine painkiller, and she'd finally fallen asleep. A little accident had happened and we'd been spared all the horror my imagination had conjured up. I reached out and put a hand on Pete's pajama-covered shoulder. Married life, the ozone of the master bedroom, a husband's familiar and friendly smell . . . I took in the open-weave curtains I'd had made last year, the green glow of digits on the clock radio. There was the messy stack of magazines and papers I intended to read in a big basket I meant to go through, very soon. And in the corner, Peter's brass valet, on which his jacket, pants, and bow tie hung, looking a bit like a voyeur. Our bedroom. Safe. Home.

Peter had forgotten to take off his glasses and did so now, folding them and putting them on his night table. He keeps a tumbler there, half filled with water, in case he gets thirsty or needs an aspirin during the night, which he never does. He has his eccentricities and I have mine. I sometimes don't open mail for days. I just let it sit there and pile up and the hell with it. And I draw the line at picnics. I hate them. No one can get me to go sit in the grass or the sand and eat egg salad. And I sometimes get it in my head to bake at the Stephen King hours of two or three in the morning. Why not? It just sometimes comes over me. I've also been accused of daydreaming and inattention. When my mind wanders, I irritate everyone. So, Peter and I tolerate each other's foibles, and on good days, find them amusing.

"So, what are we going to do with Ellery this summer? She'll be so *bored*, especially with Claudia away in Spain," I said to Peter, after a moment of silence.

Our former live-in housekeeper, Lupe, the one before Marguerita, had invited Claudia to spend the summer at her husband's family's home in Bilbao, from where she could visit the islands of Majorca and Ibiza, learn Spanish painlessly, and inundate herself with tapas and El Greco. Claudia was thrilled. Peter immediately bought a Spanish language audio tape and remarked that it would be a far cry from last year's teen trip through New England.

"Well, sweetie, I was thinking. We can take her with us, when we do the Czech Republic."

I saw us trying to get a twelve-year-old interested in cathedrals and guidebook walking tours. I saw us scrapping Prague and Karlsbad and heading for Euro Disney. "She's not going to want to go. She's twelve years old. She'd hate hanging around with us, looking at old cemeteries."

"Even so, she'd learn something new."

"Don't you think we need time alone, Peter?"

"These are precious years, Lib. She shouldn't waste her time hanging around here."

Peter and his girls. He's like a baker embellishing a tiered masterpiece with frosting, rosettes, whipped cream, and candied flower petals. His daughters are destined to become Pulitzer prize-winning confections.

"And same goes for Claudia. Did she practice today?"

"I doubt it, I really do."

"Let's get on her case tomorrow. She goofs off all the time. And that kid with the rings in his head. Jesus, when did he grow a braid? I thought the ponytail was bad enough. Listen, am I being too critical? Why can't she find someone with a first name we're allowed to pronounce?"

"He's crazy about her."

"Crazy is the word. Do you suppose they're doing it?"

"Pete, we've discussed this one zillion times. I thought we agreed we were going to get off it."

"Probably, Lib. They probably are."

I wished Peter would lower his voice. The girls were asleep, but maybe not. I lowered mine. "Whatever they're doing, they *are* using condoms."

Peter's head turned slowly toward mine.

"I found a packet in her room."

Peter made a sound like a squeak.

"Jesus. You found a condom!"

"Pete, she's in the majority. I mean, in her age group."

"Claudia and that—oh, pigtailed shit. His chin recedes. Can that be fixed? Forget I said that. You actually found a condom!"

"I'm sure he's a decent boy. Pete, we sent her to sex education classes. They learn how; then they all do it."

"Well, all right then, let them! Not that we have a choice. Look, maybe it's not such a bad thing if they're screwing. Safely, I mean. It's a natural thing. Lust is very healthy. I'll bet adolescents who have sex are healthier than those who don't. I wouldn't be surprised. Oh, God! Claudia going to bed. With that . . . human wreck! No,

I take that back. Let me tell you, Lib, it may be healthy, but if it's your own daughter, you can't imagine!"

"Oh, but I can! Of course I can!" I thought about it every time I saw them together. And plenty in between.

"Let them have a good time, but . . . did you check the brand? Is it a safe brand?"

"I don't remember the brand. I wouldn't know one condom from another."

Peter sighed. "She has only one life."

My own mother had virginized me for years, a hand-me-down from *her* mother, but these were wanton years, for God's sake, and I wasn't my mother, after all. "We can't lock her up, Peter."

"Of all the guys around here to pick to do it with! It's not the way I imagined it. Not that I imagined it at all."

"I know, Pete. I think about it and think about it. Then I try not to think about it."

"When did you find it?"

"What?"

"The fucking condom."

"A great adjective. A few days ago."

"Why didn't you tell me then?"

"I knew you'd be upset."

"You're always protecting me."

"I was upset myself. Six Tums."

"Why are you always protecting me?"

"Pete, g'night, dear."

"I can't sleep, Lib. Claudia fucking."

"You will. Think of blue skies and white clouds."

There was a very long silence, then Pete turned toward me. The mattress creaked as his body shifted. Under the covers, he edged up my nightie and moved his hand on the outside of my thigh. He always begins that way. I imagined the noise as traveling through the paint, plaster, the laths of the walls.

"We did it last night, hon."

"Does that mean we can't tonight?"

"In our age group?"

"Tomorrow night then."

"Yep. If they can, we can."

We kissed good night. Peter snapped off the light. It struck me that half the time if he wanted it, I didn't. When I wanted it, he didn't. I imagined this to be emblematic of being parents instead of just lovers. I thought—again—of Trevor Eddy. When I'd like crazy wanted it.

Peter's mother stepped out of her car as if she were being followed by an entourage. She is a grand master at bridge, but looks neither studious nor sedentary. Today she was in navy and white, down to the earrings and spectator shoes. The navy bag had a white trim and somewhere she'd found bracelets of alternating navy and white enamel. She was once a Ford model and has scrapbooks of herself photographed in ball gowns, bathing suits, and Wac outfits, and one very famous image sitting in a Jeep, on the cover of *Liberty* magazine. Her professional name was Darley Vine, and she married Peter's father after a brief marriage to a local country doctor in Tennessee. (One look at Darley and it is clear that she is not intended for dirt roads or gingham checks.)

Since Peter's father died, she has found somewhat of a career teaching bridge on cruise ships. She is always off on one voyage or another, to Alaska, the St. Lawrence Seaway, around the tip of South America. Peter's father's photos and Civil War artifacts are all over her town house in Rowayton, but she can't fool me; she doesn't miss my father-in-law. He would begin drinking Friday at six and never stop until he passed out Sunday night. Monday morning, sober and starched, he'd kiss her good-bye and head for the hospital to make his rounds as if he'd spent his weekend in a hammock sipping lemonade. Peter once called him an early twentieth-century artifact, a disciplined drunk. Otherwise, Peter did not talk about him. Ever.

Now Darley stepped out of the car and lifted out a shopping bag. She seems to feel that her price of admission to our house is gift merchandise, and has never come without an assortment. Out of the shopping bag came a box of bakery cookies, a bottle of zinfandel she'd won as a bridge prize, a blank videotape for Claudia, and a monster jigsaw puzzle for Ellery. Niagara Falls. "She's going to have time now, aren't you, sweetheart? The Countess is going to help you, since she got her new prescription Varilux specs." It was her hairdresser's idea to call herself the Countess—she looked far too young to be called "Granny," he'd said—and so she'd become "the Countess," an appellation I was sure she secretly felt defined her well.

Darley slipped on the new glasses so that we could admire the gold frames, settled herself on the couch in the den, and clucked about Ellery's broken arm, her sister, Meggie, sick with dementia in a nursing home in Virginia, and the numerologist aboard the Sagjaford, who'd predicted a shadow would be passing over her life this summer. "Tell me exactly how it happened, Ellery. When your father called me I was sewing on a button and I swear to you I stuck myself with the needle. What bad luck! And right before summer! Sweetheart, was the pain really horrid? It doesn't hurt now, does it?"

I brought out tea and the cookies Darley had brought and we eventually moved out to the terrace—without Ellery, who had before very long excused herself to closet herself in the upstairs phone booth. Ellery now had a heavier than usual telephone load; her friends were zeroing in with sympathy and dutiful requests for medical updates. It was the spring most of her girlfriends seemed to be named Jennifer, and I could never get them straight.

Darley was halfway through her cup of tea before inquiring as to Claudia's whereabouts.

I had, of course, told my mother-in-law when she arrived that Peter would be home as soon as he was finished with hospital rounds and that Claudia had gone shopping.

"She went out to buy a bathing suit. She thinks she's going to swim on Memorial Day, but I doubt it. It's never warm enough."

"Is she still involved with that boy?"

I looked at my mother-in-law's curled red lip. A cookie crumb had stuck to the cherry Life Saver lipstick. Was it my fault Claudia was involved with Ess? Without saying so, she made it seem like I'd invented him, maybe even put the rings in his pierced nose and ears and braided his hair.

She went on. "He may be a fine young man, but . . ." She shook her head and closed her eyes, saying it all. "Not that it's your fault," Darley continued, while I poured tea.

"Claudia is sixteen years old, Darley. The attitude these days is a bit more relaxed." I was working hard to keep my hand and voice steady.

Her sigh was a sound deep and profound, the resistant hum made by a woman brought up in a time of rubber girdles and running boards, structure and decorum.

"I know it sounds far-fetched, but Claudia and that boy, well, and then, poor Ellery; things are going out of control. I know it could have been worse, but somehow, I wonder if the riding accident couldn't have been avoided."

I took a sip of tea before speaking. "Avoided. How?"

"I mean, going to a more reliable riding academy. Being thrown like that for no good reason. It's a terrible thing."

"It wasn't the academy, Darley. It was the horse."

"Hell, Libby, dear, the caliber of the animals, isn't it the same exact thing? Don't they examine them, or screen them, or something?"

"Horses? They're not Hondas, Darley. They have brains and hooves. They can sometimes be unpredictable."

"It's all a question of supervision. I think it's what's happening to our society altogether. There is not enough supervision *anywhere* anymore. I'm not even comparing it to my time, but look at the Japanese. They have rules, they have regulations. Those Japs . . ."

"The instructor was right behind Ellery." *And I am right here behind the girls like the Greek god Argus, who has one thousand eyes, of which five hundred are watching at any given time,* I didn't say.

"Don't you see how everything is breaking down, dear?"

"Not in Crandall," I said too quickly. "Well, hardly."

Darley waved her hand through the air, possibly to brush away a fly, probably wishing to brush the subject away. She was allergic to confrontation and tended to change the topic when it looked as if she might be losing ground. "These cookies are delicious. They melt in your mouth." She sent a wan smile sailing at me over the teacups.

I nodded, watching her lick the crumb off her lip. It took a minute to get back my equilibrium. After all, she'd been thrown into this decade of disintegration against her will, while in her heart, she was still back there wearing middies and planting victory gardens. I let it all go. "There's this little bakery with a French flag in the window right in town, La Something or Other." I said it mildly. She'd meant no harm. It was just her white-glove, prewar, be-good way.

A minute or two later we were discussing something the French lady in the bakery had mispronounced. With

Darley it had always been up and down like this. I maneuvered out of the rapids and into more tranquil waters. She forgot, ate another cookie. We were friends again.

It was Memorial Day. Peter had a new camera, a Nishika. It took 3-D pictures with four simultaneous lenses, and when the photographs were developed, they had depth, looked as if one could step into them. We flagged down a boy on a bicycle to take our picture in front of the blaze of flowers bordering the house, and Peter took forever to adjust the camera so the boy would only have to snap the picture. ("Daddy, we could have our pictures *painted* in the time this is taking!" Claudia intoned.)

She had painted an American flag on Ellery's cast and we took it out of its canvas sling and clustered around her. Ellery had fidgeted earlier when I'd fixed her hair by pinning it back with a red bow, bit her lip, looking totally whipped. A broken arm *and* a hair bow; she couldn't possibly go into town looking "unbelievably grotesque," couldn't. She softened when I replaced the bow with a scrunchie and promised to let her get a perm, so her hair would curl like her sister's. She turned sweet and thanked Claudia for lending her a sweater that buttoned in front so she could slip in her plastered arm. When we stood smiling into the camera, my girls looked radiant and wholesome, and my heart filled with pleasure and gratitude. Here we all were in the sunshine, Ellery had been spared life in a wheelchair, and the day and the future were ours.

Some things never change; in Crandall, the American Legion groups still march, as do the Rotary, Scouts, Kiwanis, and the Ancient Order of Hibernians. In this town of twisting streets filled with trees dating back to wars fought with cannons, Victorian houses with front porches, a garden club and ladies' bowling leagues, they were recently joined by the Tri-State Gay and Lesbian Coalition, Mothers Against Drunk Driving, the Lambs of Christ, and Connecticut Christians Against Drugs. Against a backdrop of quaint shops, the post office built in the early nineteenth century, and the eighteenth-century Episcopal church, pom-poms shake, batons twirl. The music surges and there are whistles and applause; in formation, traditionalists yield as contemporary life bulldozes its way in.

Now Peter and I linked arms and I leaned against the sleeve of his windbreaker. What is it about a parade—drums, flags, percussion, little girls and boys marching a bit out of step—that brings a tear to each eye? In the shadow of Old Glory, Peter curled his hand over mine. We waved to acquaintances and were stopped at least half a dozen times to answer questions about Ellery. "And my sister painted the flag on the cast," she recited, and Claudia would move the sling to give a viewing and take a little bow. I could see Ellery's face posed to hide that she didn't mind being the focus of attention. Her little sighs reeked of satisfaction.

A patient of Peter's appeared suddenly, grasped his arm, and told him he felt much better, but still wasn't able to march with the Knights of Columbus this year. Peter put a hand on the man's shoulder, gave it a squeeze. "A family like yours, you should be waving from a float, leading the parade," the man said, looking us over. Peter was beaming, like the time he got the call from Koppel's people at ABC.

A minute later Claudia nudged Ellery. "Oh, my God! Don't look now, but will you look at that!"

At the edge of the march, dark hair in a topknot, a round-faced girl with silver rings on every finger was leaning over a stroller to replace a pacifier that had fallen out of her baby's mouth.

"That's Brandi Glynn. She was in my math class freshman year. All she wanted was to lose enough weight to become a cheerleader. She would eat a head of cauliflower for dinner and drink Diet 7-Up, like gallons. Now look!"

"Where's the daddy?" I tried to remember if we knew anyone named Glynn.

"You mean *who's* the daddy! She wouldn't tell. Brandi's father keeps rifles in the garage and she was afraid he'd go out and blow him away."

"Blow him away?" I was thinking, *God, she's beginning to sound like Ess.*

"Yeah. She was thinking abortion, but they're Catholic. Y'know, like *really*. She'll never be a cheerleader, that's for sure."

Peter shook his head. "God, these kids. The kid's life is ruined. It sure is a new world."

The tone, the look on his face, was so reminiscent of his mother's, that it came over me. I had to, absolutely had to, challenge him. "Ruined? I'm not sure it's ruined. A baby is not the Ebola virus, after all."

"Adorable! Isn't he adorable!" Ellery cooed. "Isn't he cute, Mommy?"

Claudia gave a disdainful sigh. "Pink hat, Ellery. Got it? It's a *girl*."

"Babies having babies—it's almost as bad as the Ebola virus." Peter was talking out of the side of his mustache, like a movie detective.

The last word. He always had to have it.

The girls moved off a bit, found friends clustered in groups not far from where we were standing. Out of the corner of my eye I saw Ellery surrounded by girls, boys in team jackets bunching around Claudia. She hardly saw the parade. She pushed her fingers through her hair. Did it again. Threw back her head as if she were pointing to something in the sky with her chin. A convertible pulled up alongside the curb. It was painted silver, chipped here and there, overflowing with arms, legs, denim. "Hey, Claudia! Want a ride? Hey, Claudia, move your ass over here!" Peter had turned away, I was relieved he didn't see it. She had a talent, it was like perfect pitch, something you were born with. The mystery to me was, with so many choices, why Ess?

The waitress in the Crossways Diner recognized Peter, called him Doctor. He read her name off her name tag and told her she looked like Gwyneth Paltrow, but prettier. It was a little kidding around he always did with waitresses, flight attendants, clerks, the young ones. It was like the glass of water next to his bed, unnecessary, and once I got to the point of opening my mouth to tell him it was amusingly obsessive, but stopped myself in time. For the sake of accord, I just let it go on irritating me.

We always took it for granted that we'd be recognized now and then, and once long ago, during the bad time, Peter had suggested a move to Westport. For privacy. We went so far as to look at some houses. Actually bid on one, a Victorian not far from town. Crandall is no better or worse than any of the other waterfront communities in Connecticut, except that we'd been here for eighteen years, had joined the Crandall Yacht and Tennis Club, and could find any address without looking at a map. I was entrenched in my antiques appraisal offices with Annie, and was greeted by name on the street. Crandall had become home. Finally, Peter decided he had enough privacy right here, could drive to Greenwich for his Tuesday night meetings, and we dug in our heels and settled in to stay.

We ordered pancakes, except for Claudia, who wanted cottage cheese, a salad, oil and vinegar on the side. She had bought no bathing suit last week, had gained two and a half pounds, and refused to go back to the mall until every ounce of the weight was off.

She was watching with hungry eyes as Peter doused his pancakes with blueberry goo out of a glass dispenser and began digging into his stack. Claudia's salad had arrived oily with dressing and had to be sent back to the kitchen. She was nibbling on a bread stick she'd found under the rolls in the basket of bread the waitress had set in front of her. The gold cuff Ess had given her gleamed on her arm.

"Ellery and I are going to catalog all our family photographs," she said listlessly, her eyes wandering. I followed her gaze. The counter boy.

"Nice."

Claudia's tone turned motherly-sisterly. She looked at Ellery. "And Ess and I are going to take you to Playland, at least once. You can't do the Whip, but you can do some of the easier rides, even with a broken arm."

Ellery's eyes sparkled. "Yes, I could. I could do most of them. Even the Dragon Coaster."

"Do you feel a bit better about not going to riding camp, honey?" I asked. It was a mistake.

The sparkle in her eyes gave way to a shine that spoke of a spillover.

Peter and I exchanged looks.

"She'll be fine, by August. She can go then," Claudia insisted. So much kindness heralded something that was not good.

"We'll see, sweetheart," Peter shook his head, and as he was pouring on more syrup, Ess walked into the diner.

He was wearing cutoff jeans and a black T-shirt that was printed with a blurred eye chart under unblurred white letters: BEER DRINKERS' EYE CHART. "Ess!" Ellery saw him first.

Claudia's head swiveled as he swaggered his way

toward our booth, the smile-no-smile expression frozen in place. A Natalie Cole song Peter had given Ellery twenty-five cents to hear burst out of the little table jukebox.

"Came in to see if anyone needed help cutting their sunny-side ups," he said. Peter put down his fork and turned halfheartedly around to squint at Ess and his shirt.

Claudia put her napkin to her mouth to wipe away a random drop of lettuce moisture. "I thought you were working today!"

"Parade break," Ess said and leaned up against the back of Peter's side of the booth, one arm familiarly extended across the backrest. "I saw the family buggy out front on my way to the vet's, and I'm not in that big of a hurry to clean dingleberries out of sixteen dog runs, pardon my French."

"Would you like to join us?" I asked, wondering if he'd actually followed us, and although the question was clearly spoken in a polite-society tone no one could construe as enthusiastic, Peter threw me a look.

"No time this time, but thanks, Mrs. E. I just wanted to wish my favorite nuclear group a happy dead veterans day." And then he leaned over Peter and touched the top of Claudia's head. "Hey, you. I gotta surprise in my pocket. Wanna guess what it is?"

Peter leaned away from him, subtly moving toward Claudia.

"What? Tell me! You *didn't?*" The remains of her bread stick stopped in midair.

"Oh, didn't I? I did! Got 'em off the guy I was telling you about, works down at the marina, owes me a favor."

"I don't believe it!" Claudia's eyes enlarged, glowing as if a flashlight had been trained on them.

Ess patted the pocket of his jeans. "Right here," he said, and he sucked in his stomach. "Those babies are right here. I'm keepin' them warm."

"What?" Ellery asked. "What babies?"

"Wanna see 'em?"

Peter started to say something, changed his mind. He squeezed his fork and looked up at Ess, who had reached into his pocket and was now digging deep.

Ellery was straining forward, her cast like a wrapped gift on the table. "What are they?"

Ess extracted two pink tickets and held them V'd over Peter's head like rabbit's ears. "Ricky Martin. July twelve. Up at New Haven."

Claudia bounced as if the booth had hit a bump. "Ess!"

"July twelfth? But you're not going to be here July twelfth," Peter and I said in concert, like we'd rehearsed for a week.

"Oops!" Ess took an exaggerated swagger step back from the table. "Double oops!"

Peter's head swiveled toward Claudia. "You're going to be in Spain, Claudia."

"You didn't tell them? Hey, Claud—"

"Tell us?" My husband and I looked at each other. "Tell us what?"

"I decided. Um, I decided I'm not going to go. I've changed my mind. I'm going to stay at home with Ellery instead."

Ellery's eyes grew big. So did Peter's. It was the little bombshell I'd almost expected. As Natalie Cole sang on, I remembered Claudia rushing to the telephone to relay the news of Spain to her friends, her enthusiasm for learning new idioms in the Spanish-English phrase book, the call she'd made to share the tidings with my mother in Delray. Peter stared down at the half-stack of uneaten pancakes and wiped the corner of his mouth with his Crossways Diner napkin, which, in honor of the holiday, was printed with stars and stripes. "What are you saying?" I saw the split-second movement of his lips, the twitch that looks like a preparation to kiss. It's involuntary, that nervous pucker I know so well, almost imperceptible to most, but a radar signal to me.

"I know how you think it's a good idea to go, but Ellery is obviously staying here, so you'll need someone to take care of her when you go to Europe."

"Well, guys, I better be off." Ess, having stuffed the pink tickets back into his pocket, backed off quickly, like a string was pulling him. "I'll call tonight, Claud. Have a day, everybody!"

Peter waited until the black T-shirt had disappeared through the glass doors. Then he shook his head in a cartoony, disbelieving way. "You're not old enough to take care of Ellery when we go away, and if you don't go to Spain, what are you going to do all summer?" He kept wiping the corners of his mouth, which he'd long since dried of the shine of syrup.

"I'll work. I'll get a job."

Peter may be the only man living in the state of Connecticut who does not feel it's necessary for his children to hold paying jobs. His old-school father forced him to work from the time he was fourteen, and Peter felt he gained nothing whatsoever from flipping hamburgers on a grill at country clubs along the Long Island Sound shore. He felt he could have been learning polo or a language, or taking advanced courses in trigonometry. With both of the girls, there also seems always the issue of safety. Peter does not like his children rubbing shoulders with shadowy people, people like Ess. A vacation far away from Ess was the biggest bonus he saw for Claudia in Bilbao. "What kind of a job do you think you could possibly get, Claud?"

Claudia ran her fingers through her hair and thanked the waitress, who was putting a new salad in front of her. "I could get a job in the library," she said.

Now, an expression crossed Peter's face that is a duplicate of one of his father's—sort of a squint between disdain and discomfort. Mostly, though, he looks like

Claudia, who has his eyes, the same fish-tank green we never seem to capture well enough in Kodacolor. His hairline has receded, especially in the past five years, but those eyebrows, darker than the straw-basket hair, are as abundant as Claudia's, and occasionally move together as ominously.

"It's so per*verse.* I don't have one single friend who isn't allowed to drive, isn't allowed to get a job!" Peter's rule of no driving until age seventeen comes from years of seeing the results of vehicular accidents in the hospital emergency room.

"Dad, why can't she stay home?" Ellery put in. They close ranks like that, just the way Peter and I do.

"Ellery, honey, please stay out of this." Peter was still being very gentle with Ellery, but his voice had turned hoarse, as if a cold was just around the corner. The waitress appeared at that moment to ask if there was anything else she could get us from the kitchen.

"No, we're fine," my husband said, mustering his cordial distinguished-doctor smile.

"Enjoy," the waitress said.

"We will." The last word.

"I talked to Claudia," Peter said, much later. He had put his half glass of water on his night table and turned on CNN, and kept turning his head to catch the interview with the new baseball commissioner. "She's adamant. She's not going. It breaks my heart to have a daughter who is beautiful and gifted throw time away as if it were sand in her shoe."

"She's throwing our time away, too."

"It's that Cro-Magnon delinquent. How are we going to leave them here unsupervised?"

Unsupervised? Shades of Darley! "He's not a bad kid. And she's very trustworthy. I've been looking forward to this. . . ." I closed my eyes. I wanted Peter to turn off the discussion of the richest prize in golf tournament history. I wanted him to please turn off the set and talk to me about our vacation. He stared intently at the screen, the remote control on his chest; I waited for the commercials.

"Don't you want to go?" Our next-door neighbors, the Bergins, had gone last summer and showed us videos. They'd called the Czech Republic the pinup of middle Europe. I'd been checking Internet travel items since February.

Peter took the remote control off his chest and aimed it at a commercial for floor wax. His glasses were sliding down his nose and he had never looked more middle-aged, more like his own father when he was sliding into tanked sleep or in his easy chair. The woman squeegeeing the floor turned mute.

"We need this, Pete."

"Sure. I need a rest, boy, do I need—"

"I mean, for us."

"Lib, yes, I guess."

"We have to dig us people out of us parents."

"I suppose."

"We never really make love anymore."

Pete's head swiveled back to me. "What are you talking about? We did it last night."

"We had sex. We rolled around in this bed very quietly in the dark and I came and then you came and I went to pee, then you went to pee, then you turned out the light and said, 'Good night.' But I don't call that making love."

A blank, Orphan Annie stare.

"In fact, it was *pffft*—like, it came and went so fast, I hardly noticed."

Peter continued peering at me over his glasses. I wished he wouldn't keep looking like that; I kept seeing his father's avuncular face, a boozy pink, like the face of a latex doll. I wanted back the sexy, cool stud I'd married twenty-one years ago. I wanted back those five carefree in-heat years we'd had before we had Claudia. Even though he was getting plastered in those days, he'd put on the stereo and maybe take some Polaroids of me in centerfold poses. We worked up to it in dim light, then little by little I could let loose and scream down the place like I was going to heaven. Which, most of the time in those days, I was.

"I think we should have unbridled, crazy sex again."

"Well, sweetie, we're not twenty anymore."

"But we could be."

"In Middle Europe?"

"Yes. Free of the responsibilities, the walls that aren't thick enough, away from the girls. Out of here. A different bed in a different room, a different language—it definitely helps. Don't you remember how nice it was in Portugal last year?"

Peter's sighs meant different things. This one was ambiguous. "How long has this been bothering you, sweetie? You never brought it up before." Sometimes Peter was the important cardiologist, sometimes the strong parent, and always he was the family navigator, but occasionally, he reverted unexpectedly to being an insecure child.

"Since—I think since Ess."

"What?!"

"I think of them having such a great time, like we did once, and now you and I, we're . . . just plodding away half the time like ratchety oldsters."

"Plodding away? Ratchety?"

"Let's forget semantics. You know what I mean."

"I always know what you mean. That's what all those married years do for us. Knowing what's up in your head, knowing the sentences that are going to come out of your mouth."

"Really."

"Don't get defensive, sweetie. It's comfortable."

"You mean predictable."

"Marriage has to be a comfort zone that allows for other things to be exciting."

"Other things? What things?"

"Life. Our children."

He took off his glasses, folded them, and put them on his night table next to his water glass. He said we'd figure out a way to go and then he kissed me good night. Before shutting off the set, he took one more look at the Indianapolis 500 winner, who had completed the course in 3 hours, 4 minutes and 59.148 seconds. "Good night, sweetie," he said. "We'll do it, I promise."

# Chapter Two

It was Father's Day, our first barbecue of the season, and I'd overmarinated the fish, which was falling apart on the grill. White rhododendrons, lilacs, forsythia, pink and red bleeding hearts ringed the patio, purple clematis climbed the lattice screen that hid the driveway, the hedges and trees gleamed in every neon shade of green, sparrows and jays hopped above us in the branches of our listing oak tree, and sitting and staring at us from the low brick wall that divided our property was the Bergins' orange cat, Moxie.

Back from Panama, Darley, sunglassed and straw-hatted, was sitting under the umbrella in a wire-mesh chair, neck to toe in peach. She had brought the girls straw hats, hard candies for me, and a bottle of aftershave for Pete. Her face, half in sun and half in shade, was powdered and blushed. She was talking about her sister, Meggie, now very near the end. As Peter handed her a tonic with ice, she poked at the lemon on the rim of the glass. "There is no bond as close as the one we have with siblings."

"I don't know about that, Countess." Peter and his sister, who is in the paper business with her husband in Vancouver, hardly speak more than twice a year. My only sister and I used to talk on the telephone every few weeks, but she is a partner in a California vineyard and seems much more into grape clusters than family, and the sibling connection gets more diluted each year.

Claudia was moving around the table, putting salad into the bowls, which I had told her not to do until we were ready to sit down and eat. She had piled her hair up on her head, fastened it with combs and clips, and was in shorts and a cotton blouse with long billowy sleeves that kept threatening to dip into the lettuce in the bowl.

Ellery appeared on the patio, wearing the straw hat Darley had brought on the back of her head, looking wan and at low ebb. Since her accident, she'd been hanging around the house after school, staying inside and working on the new jigsaw puzzle. It looked like one of those impossibly frustrating ones, where all the pieces look alike—white foamy water cut into interchangeable-looking shapes. Peter had bought her a new computer last Christmas, and when she wasn't poring over Niagara Falls or the TV set, she now spent time in her room playing video games. Her Jennifers were for the most part preparing for a summer away somewhere—in camp or on teen trips or visiting relatives out West—and Ellery, being left behind, seemed afflicted with a generalized ennui, a sort of mono of the soul. Her shoulders were still slender to the point of being right-angled, but her breasts were already the size of shallow teacups, which seemed to have happened practically from one day to the next; when the braces came off her teeth, her breasts suddenly extruded. She had in fact recently become self-conscious and stopped wearing T-shirts, had taken to blousy man-tailored shirts, even before the plaster cast made anything that slipped over her head impossible.

"I've gotten most of the sky, Countess," she said now, and dragged a chair out of the shade into the patch of sun next to her grandmother's umbrella, kicking off her sandals and turning her face to the sun.

"Did you put on sunblock, Ell?" Peter asked, glancing over after putting the fish on the platter next to the grill.

"Yes, Daddy!" Ellery sighed, just as Ess arrived, appearing in the yard from out of nowhere, taking big, important steps, wearing a green T-shirt that said, TOMORROW IS ANOTHER DAY TO WASTE and carrying a paper cone filled with tulips for me. I saw Claudia touch her hair and push the back of her blouse tight into her shorts, caught her expression, the stony face suppressing some high-octane charge. She must have learned to freeze her features from Ess.

"I was beginning to think you'd gone to Philadelphia or someplace." She ran into the house to put the flowers in a vase, and also get a drink for Ess.

"Happy Father's Day, Dr. Ehrlich. Whatever you put on that grill, I could smell it all the way down on the highway." Ess peered at the platter of fish Peter had covered with foil. "Bluefish, I bet. I can smell the fins."

Peter sliced a piece of cheese and put it on a cracker. He handed it to Ess. "Try again."

"One fish, two fish, salmon, swordfish?"

"You're getting warm. Tuna."

Ess went to greet Darley. "How are you, Mrs. Countess? Perfect weather for a tuna barbecue, right? Not for the tuna, though?" Darley forced a smile. When he leaned over, raising his voice just slightly in case she had a hearing loss, I thought he looked much older and more sophisticated than his eighteen years. I'd never asked Claudia what his parents did—she considered that question the pinnacle of bourgeois snobbery—but I admit I was curious. I tried to picture his home and family, but kept seeing Ess as he might be in thirty years: order sheet in one hand, Samsonite attaché case in the other. Insurance, stocks, soft goods, time-shares. He'd win trips to Hawaii, incentive prizes like microwave ovens and tickets to the Academy Awards.

Peter had uncovered the fish, and was circling the platter with lemon wedges, between taking sips of his San Pellegrino.

Darley applauded, oohed, and said it looked "four-star," and we took our seats around the tempered-glass table Ellery had set with straw mats and canary yellow napkins. Moxie, smelling the fish, had leaped down from the wall and arrived under my feet. She began rubbing her body against my legs. Her tail was vertical and her purr sounded like the whir of a dishwasher. I leaned over to stroke her fur.

"Poor baby. She's hungry." Ellery always thought small animals were either hungry, lost, or cold.

Moxie suddenly and without warning leaped onto the table, almost knocking over Darley's glass of iced tea, and landing between the salad bowl and the dish of sour cream Ellery had put out for the baked potatoes. Darley cried, "Oh, my God!" and covered her mouth with her napkin.

Peter put down the bread he'd started buttering. "Claudia, please pick up the cat and take her next door, ask the Bergins just to confine her for an hour or two, will you, sweetie? She's going to be driving us crazy right through dessert—"

"Here, Mox, here, Mox—" Claudia jumped up, scooped the cat up with both hands, and gave him a hug. I thought of our own cat, Laszlo, who'd died of very old age last year and who sometimes still appears in my happier dreams.

"I miss Laszlo." Ellery was reading my thoughts.

"Laszlo's gone to heaven to be with Elvis Presley." Ess took a monster bite of buttered bread.

"We had a cat named Walter when we were growing up. He liked me better than Meggie," Darley said.

Peter patted his mother's arm. "And he loved eating white grapes and spitting out the seeds."

Darley picked up her glass of iced tea and put it down without taking a sip. "We each only have one set of memories, darling," she said.

Claudia was back without the cat a few minutes later. "I gave Moxie to Mr. Bergin," she said. "He was washing his car, and guess what? Moxie is pregnant!"

Ellery snapped to attention. "Pregnant!"

"And Mrs. Elfenbein was there. Just leaving, it looked like." Claudia's fingers were poking her hair, which had begun falling out of its clips and combs here and there, giving her the look of a disheveled milkmaid.

"Who is Mrs. Elfenbein?" Peter asked.

Ellery took a sip of her iced tea. "She's just one of those local real-estate aliens."

Claudia let out a whoop. "Aliens!"

Ellery blushed. "Agents, you mean," I corrected.

"Right. Agents. I meant agents. I was only *kidding,* Claudia."

"The Bergins've been our neighbors for umpteen years."

"Twelve years," Peter said, smashing his potato with his fork. "They moved in the year Ellery was born. I happen to know that because we had them to dinner and Ellery screamed through the whole thing: three courses of baby wails.

"Remember?" Peter asked me.

I didn't, but I did remember the pinking shears Sarah Jane Bergin borrowed two years ago. Had she ever returned them? I tried to recall other things she'd borrowed over the years. Eggs. Five dollars. Baking powder. The world atlas. Nothing ever came back. Sarah Jane was the creative type, flighty. Basically, I liked her husband better.

Darley let out a sigh. "What a shame if the Bergins are moving. You'll miss them, won't you?"

"They were always sweet to the girls. On the other hand, I think she still has my pinking shears."

"How'd you get through all these years without pinking, Mom?" Claudia dimpled.

"Moxie pregnant! Maybe we could get a kitten free!" Ellery cried.

"This family should be laminated," Ess said, his mouth full of bread.

Dessert was an ice cream cake from Baskin-Robbins that had HAPPY FATHER'S DAY written across the top. I stuck a Roman candle in it and Claudia lit it with a twelve-inch barbecue match. We watched it sparkle itself out. The girls presented Peter's gift from Lord & Taylor and watched as he took his time undoing the ribbon and lifting the lid off the burgundy box, unfolding the tissue and lifting out the croc-patterned leather belt.

"Ta-da!" Ess said he'd meant to bring the video camera to record this moment, a father receiving a weapon to use on his daughters from the future victims.

My gift was next. The bow had fallen off the gift wrap, and I thought the package looked forlorn.

"A book? It feels like—Lib! Let me guess! About conquered diseases?"

"That was last year."

"Right."

I watched him tear off the paper. "Hey! Leave it to the pragmatist. Good choice, Lib!"

Darley leaned forward in her chair, hands curled around the handles of her pocketbook. "Peter? My glasses are at the bottom of my purse. Is it a disease book? You loved the leprosy one."

"Not this time. It's a Fodor travel guide to eastern Europe. Hey, thanks, sweetie." He blew me a kiss and began examining the back cover.

"I almost forgot you were going! When are you going?" Darley asked. She rocked back in her chair, never letting go of the handles of her bag.

"July." I watched Peter, now flipping open the pages, and felt unaccountably edgy.

"But wait a minute. If Ellery doesn't go to camp—well, who is going to stay with the girls?" Darley asked. Now she looked as anxious as if she were contemplating a jump into a fireman's net.

"We've been talking about getting Marguerita to move in here for two weeks. She's a very steady girl, and she seems reliable."

"Marguerita? Is that the new *cleaning* lady?" I pictured the word *supervision* rolling under my mother-in-law's chin like a subtitle in a foreign film.

"She's worked for us for almost three years. She's Lupe's niece."

Darley had met Marguerita here at least three times. The fact that she could accurately memorize fifty-two cards dealt out at a bridge table but not remember meeting Marguerita, who had spooned gravy over her turkey at Thanksgiving and served her roast beef and eggnog for two years in a row at Christmas, baffled me.

"Doesn't she speak only Spanish?" The penciled eyebrows moved together. At any moment she might pitch forward in her chair and wind up on the lawn. I hoped.

"She's getting better at English. She can say, 'Low in fat and high in carbohydrates.' Claudia is teaching her."

"Ess!" Claudia lovingly pushed his shoulder.

"We're going to give Marguerita a crash course in calling 911." I'd actually had to talk Peter into Marguerita, pointing out that after all, the Bergins would be right next door and Ellery and Claudia were not wild teenagers; they were homebodies, old-fashioned, and definitely trustworthy.

The girls were clearing the table. "If you don't go to Spain, dear, what are you going to do this summer, Claudia?" Darley, relaxed, was back in her seat under the umbrella now, but looking slightly faded. She said she couldn't remember a better barbecue, a more perfect day. She said the same thing every year.

"I don't know yet, Countess," Claudia was trying to carry too many things in at one time. I opened my mouth to warn her she'd drop something, but thought better of it. One never knew how she would react; with Claudia it could be genial compliance one moment and bombs bursting in air the next.

"She's going to summer school," Peter said again. He'd rolled up his sleeves and was brushing the barbecue grill with a wire brush. I wished he'd let the dirty jobs go. Marguerita could do them. The grease would never come out of that Italian cotton shirt or those chinos.

"I haven't made up my mind, Daddy!" In one sentence, Claudia's voice jumped from alto to soprano and back to alto again. The glasses stacked too high in Claudia's hand looked ready to topple. Ess was at her side trying to take some out of her hand.

Peter's face looked intense and I could see drops of perspiration form on the back of his neck. "Nothing that says you can't do both."

Ess had found Claudia's hat and planted it on his head. "Maybe karate? Always handy for self-defense. One never knows when it will be needed around here!"

I saw a shadow cross Peter's face. He squeezed the little wire brush in his hand as if it were a lemon over a piece of fish and went on scrubbing. "Don't you celebrate Father's Day with your own dad, Ess?'' he asked pointedly, without looking up or changing his pleasant tone.

"Daddy!" Claudia's voice was in shock.

I felt sorry for the boy. His skin was glowing pink and a tiny bead of perspiration appeared at his hairline.

Ellery stopped wiping the table. With her hair curled, she looked a bit older, and very serious. "Daddy, he was only kidding." The "Daddy" came out like stainless steel.

"There's eight of us. My father would hardly notice if I was there or not." Ess turned to look at Ellery, and I saw him wink at her. "Unless he's setting us up for a square dance."

Peter's expression didn't change. He leaned closer toward the grill to examine an individual spoke, and acted as if he hadn't heard Ess at all.

"That kid really gets on my nerves," he said to me as soon as we heard Ess's van pull out of the driveway. The girls were inside, presumably putting things in order in the kitchen, and Darley, Peter, and I were watching our black squirrel bounding across the lawn.

"He chews his ice cubes. If I'd chewed an ice cube, if I'd *dared*, Mama would have sent me away from the table. Or if I'd sprawled on the ground barefoot, for that matter. And that ring in his nose. Oh, my."

"Darley, I can't very well send someone else's eighteen-year-old son away from the table." Surely Darley knew if I had a choice I would replace Ess with any number of nice-boy types with better manners. She'd raised two children herself; hadn't she learned that supervision could go only so far?

"He looks older than eighteen to me," my mother-in-law said. There was the implied *tsk-tsk* in her voice, and I looked at Peter, hoping for some moral support.

As I'd predicted, grease had spattered his striped shirt and darkened the right side of his pants with vermicular stains. He said nothing.

"I predict Ess will be just a nostalgia piece by the time the summer ends," I said firmly.

Peter intently began scrubbing again. "Although I'm too old to be an optimist, I guess I'm too much of a father to be a pessimist," he finally put in.

"Darling, let me remind you that when you were five years old, you planted a cherry pit in the yard and ran out the next morning to pick the cherries off the tree."

"Ah, another twice-told tale!" Peter stopped scrubbing to smile at his mother. "That was long before life had happened to us, Mother. That was even before you became a countess."

We were sitting in the living room with our coffee, and Claudia had finished warm-up scales and "Ode to Joy." Peter was sitting in the shield-back rocker with his back to the window, and looked as if I'd just slipped him a sedative. He had a sleepy, good-life expression, with his hands folded in his lap and his eyes half-closed. Ellery was hunched over her puzzle on the bridge table next to him.

"For the rest of my life, I have to have short nails. I can never have long nails or a French manicure as long as I play the harp." Claudia looked at her hands, which she had dropped into her lap.

Ellery looked up from the puzzle. "Why are you always worrying about your nails, your hair, your body?"

"It's Father's Day, girls," I reminded them.

"Thank you, Mother," Peter said.

Claudia sighed and leaned forward toward the harp again. She looked celestial with her hands on the strings, the light streaming over her hair, her shoulders, the puffy sleeves of her blouse. She played "Greensleeves" with only one or two tiny mistakes. The watery, mellifluous melody floated around us, rippled across the ceiling and up the walls, encircled us in our chairs, lifted and fell and lifted again. When she'd finished, we applauded robustly. Ellery said, "If I could play like that, you think I'd worry about my f-ing *fingernails*?" Darley said, "Bravo! Wunderbar!" and I sniffed away what could have been the beginning of a tear gathering in my eye, a tear of unadulterated joy.

Mondays and Tuesdays at the office tend to be busy, probably because people who've spent a bundle at weekend auctions call to have their newly purchased antiques authenticated. Annie Wickes is not only my partner, but also my good friend. She's the one who talked me into going into the appraisal business. We kept running into each other at auctions, which is how we met. I did have the "leanings," as she put it—not only the eye, but the spirit and interest in anything old, and specifically, anything American and old. She said, forget credentials, I had perfect pitch in old stuff. I did then take courses, drove twice a week into New York City, passed a day-long test at Parsons and got a license, which now hangs under Annie's on the wall. It is the first thing you see when you come into the office, which is on the second floor of a frame building on the Post Road, right over a frozen yogurt shop that used to be a needlepoint shop that used to be a fish store.

Annie and I do business here, but we also drink coffee, ingest tuna sandwiches and the frozen yogurt sold downstairs, and get on each other's nerves, give each other moral support, beauty advice, an occasional manicure. Annie also seems to have a biochemical need for gossip. She lives other people's lives intensely, as a way, I guess, of exiting her own.

Annie's husband, a graduate of Holy Cross, bounced

in and out of her life after they lost their only child, who died during a routine tonsillectomy at age seven. Never a word about suing the anesthesiologist or the hospital. "Taken by the angels," Annie has said, not a trace of bitterness in her voice.

She is just a year older than I am, but is already veering to the grandmotherly. Brownish hair in a department-store perm, a deepening vertical crease between her eyebrows and the beginnings of a dewlap—it is a pretty face giving up.

"A Mrs. Reingold called," she said, as soon as I walked in today. Lately, Annie's eyes seem smaller, peeking through puffy pockets behind her glasses. "She's got a house on Westview." Annie was squinting at the pink message slip in a funny way. Westview is one of Crandall's premier streets. The houses are on high ground, built on lots no smaller than four acres on a road famous for its ancient trees and distinguished residents. "And she wants to speak to *you*." I could not miss the emphasis.

"Why me? I don't know her. Why not you?"

"Biedermeier through and through, and she said she preferred to deal with the doctor's wife." Annie looked at some point on a far wall, not into my eyes.

"Well, I'll return the call, but I'll make it clear—"

Annie cut me off. "I hate to admit this, but I sit here, week after week, watch you at your desk, and I wonder, how did it happen? I mean, a husband who's a top-banana doctor and doesn't run around, two good girls, a house full of antiques, and look at you! Hair without frizz and narrow hips. Who'd you pay off?"

"Oh, Annie, don't talk hips. I think I just gained—"

"The world looks at you and sees quality control! And where am I? It doesn't matter that I know Biedermeier better than any German to this lady, and she's not the only one. I'm not an important doctor's wife, the local luminary."

"You don't really think that my being Peter's wife means absolutely anything in the appraisal business?"

Annie's eyes went to half-mast. "Are you being nice or naive? Being a doctor's wife in Crandall, even in this day and age, is being nobility."

"Oh, now, come on, Annie."

"Get real, Lib. You walk in sunshine. I walk in shade. Those are the facts. I pray not to feel envy. What I want to know is, I'm the one who goes to Mass every day, so how did *you* get on God's short list?"

The phone interrupted and it was Peter on his car phone. Annie went to her computer and pretended not to be listening. "I'm going to be late for dinner, Lib." Through the static, the fade-ins and fade-outs, I discerned my husband's agitation. My first thought was: Claudia. Or, Ess. "Lucas Greavy fell asleep in the middle of a consultation with a patient this morning. Wife of the state senator. Just closed his eyes and dropped off like it was a lullaby while she was reciting her symptoms." Not Claudia. Not Ess. I relaxed as Peter let out a grumbling, staticky expletive. "The patient actually had to shake him awake."

Lucas Greavy is Peter's older partner.

"He woke up, knocked over a glass paperweight on his desk. It shattered and the patient claimed a splinter flew into her leg."

"Unbelievable! Is she going to be all right?"

"Minor cut. The bleeding scared her."

"So you're going to stay late?"

"Looks like."

"But Pete, it's Tuesday."

"I'll go to my meeting tomorrow."

"But you never skip."

"Sweetie, I said I'd go tomorrow."

"Tomorrow's Wednesday? You've got the endodontist six o'clock, remember?" I lowered my voice. "You already put it off twice, I called for you last month, changed the appointment—"

Peter's voice was stonier. "So I'll go Thursday."

"Well, that's fine." I listened to the telephone silence for a moment.

"It's just been a bad day," Peter's voice faded in and out and I could barely hear him.

"I'll put dinner in the oven."

"Fine. See you later."

"Are you all right, Peter?"

"I'm all right."

"Really?"

"Oh, Lib, for Christ's sake."

It wasn't that night, it was later in the week. Peter was still in a terrible mood. His younger partner, Solow, wanted Lucas Greavy out, and Peter was for giving it a bit more time, hoping the decision to retire would come from the old man himself. "Solow is thirty-three years old. He's all facts and figures and too young to have room for a heart or a soul in his head. And just three months ago he prescribed Cardioquin to a patient with an ulcer who was taking Maalox. We had a real scare with her—she got serious ventricular fibrillation—but it looks like he's already forgotten that!" I felt Peter saw himself as right behind Dr. Greavy, possibly already—at only fifty-one—perceiving in himself the first symptoms of sluggishness, forgetfulness, the faltering step. "One episode of dozing off—well, I'm not ready to put the man on an ice floe, Lib." Peter was doing a great deal of thinking aloud.

Now it was, "What's to become of Greavy? His work is his oxygen!" And, "He doesn't even play golf!" There was often a silent withdrawal at dinner and through the evening. Solow wanted instant action. For Peter the problem translated into tense silences and headaches.

The lip twitch. He put in extra time in the small gym we'd installed in the basement. The NordicTrack had a squeak that carried up to the second floor through the heating ducts and woke me mornings. The decision that Peter had to make seemed like an extra, menacing guest in the house.

We were in the den, it was after dinner, and no one was seriously watching the talking heads on CNN. Pete absentmindedly glowered at the new bathing suit Claudia had just pulled out of a shopping bag. "It's something you have to see on," she said defensively, pulling it out of its tissue-paper nest and stretching its meagerness in every direction. Ess, it turned out, had gone with her to offer his opinion, and this little navy blue number, with its missing pieces of fabric and gold stars across breasts and pubic crest, was his choice. Peter was deep into his own thoughts. Not too long ago he used to object to Claudia's skimpy beachwear, but we seemed light years away from those days now. I'd been instructed to write down the name of the condom brand if I ever spotted another one in the house. Pete had also tried to broach the subject of safe sex with Claudia, but she'd cut him off instantly. She said there had been so many videos on AIDS in school that she was already a walking encyclopedia of cautious, wary, defensive sexual behavior. She'd plunked down on the arm of Pete's chair and asked if there was anything she could teach *him.*

Ellery, holding a bag of nacho chips, stepped into the room.

"Hey, Ell. Look what Ess bought me." Claudia pulled out another wad of tissue, in which there was a long slender box of the size that might hold a fever thermometer. "You will never, ever guess!" she said.

Ellery moved in, all eyes. "God, you are so lucky. He keeps buying you presents. He never stops!"

"He's not rich. Just generous."

"I'll never find a boyfriend that spends it like Ess does. I'll never even find a boyfriend!"

"Oh, yes, you will, Ell. You are going to knock them dead in a few years!"

"In your dreams."

"No, you are going to be beautiful."

"Why do you say that when you don't mean it?"

"I mean it."

"Give it up. We know who has the looks in the family. And we know she knows she has the looks."

Peter aimed the remote control at Ellery. "I wish this worked on tuning out sibling rivalry," he said.

Claudia, with theatrical flourishes, opened the box and slowly pulled out what I thought at first was a crystal-bead necklace but turned out to be a glittery rosary. It had large and elaborately faceted diamondlike beads and a dangling gold crucifix.

I noticed that Peter subtly jumped to attention, straightened himself in his chair, and looked at the beads hanging from Claudia's fingers as if they were poison sumac.

"That's a funny gift for a non-Catholic."

"Ess said he was going to have it blessed for me next week."

"What for?"

"Daddy, he takes his religion seriously."

"But it's not your religion."

"Of course not."

"So?"

"So, I sometimes wish it was."

Peter looked exasperated, but it might have more to do with Ess than Claudia wanting to be a Catholic. Peter's father was half-Jewish, and his mother changed her faith with each marriage. Churches we figured were for weddings, funerals, and listening to *The Messiah* at Christmas. And Peter hates religious prejudice.

"If you want to become anything other than a Presbyterian, when you get to be twenty-one, you can get yourself dipped."

Peter smiled.

"Dipped! You have no respect for Ess's faith." Claudia was swinging the rosary left to right, right to left, as if it were a dowser over a spring. "Just once you should go to Mass. Try it. All the DiBuonos go every week, they sit together and pray together. It's beautiful."

Annoyed as I was, deep in my own agnostic's heart, I was all ears. Incense, the family in a pew, confessions, organ music, faith, prayer, redemption. It all spoke loudly of order, tradition, and solidarity.

"Are you going to keep it?" Peter wanted to know.

"Of course she is!" Ellery piped up. She looked as shocked as if he'd suggested burning a witch. "Why wouldn't she keep it?"

"She's not a Catholic."

"If she marries Ess, she might become one."

He'd turned away, so I couldn't see Peter's face, but I saw it in my mind's eye, slack and losing blood.

"A little gift from the mall, is all it is," I said. I wanted him to see it as teenage ephemera, here today and gone tomorrow, like Claudia's past crushes, like Ellery's cracked humerus and her devotion to nachos.

"Right. A little gift that cost Ess two hundred dollars," Claudia said.

Later that week it was decided that this summer Claudia would study French conversation. Harp lessons would be suspended until September, but not dropped. She sulked a bit, called us unfair and a pair of Back Numbers, muttered things under her breath—everyone else was allowed to drive and had great, wonderful, fantastic summer jobs!—doors slammed. Finally, she simmered down. She'd still have three weeks at the end of August, the beginning of September. Ess would teach her how to drive. All was not lost.

Ellery wanted to sign up for French conversation classes with her sister, but the course was not open to junior high school students. Ellery, hunched over Niagara Falls, out on the patio with nachos and a glass of Snapple in her hand, or up in her room playing video games, looked forlorn and discarded. "I hate my hair!" she said. "I'm sorry I curled it. I'm going to let it grow as long as Claudia's." And she went on to name the other things about herself she hated: her nose, her breasts, her chin, and her teeth, which we'd paid four thousand dollars to align.

What magic combination of words could I use to set the little one onto the path of self-confidence already pioneered by the big one? What psychotherapeutic legerdemain would even these two girls out? Gone were days when I could plan a clambake or a treasure hunt and count on restored cheer, but the illusion that some maneuvering was within my power stayed with me. Supervision. Super vision. I woke mornings to the sound of the NordicTrack and my mind whirred, trying to think of what would set things right, make the girls—and us—happy this summer.

# Chapter Three

I was pulling the car out of the driveway about a week later when Sarah Jane Bergin came running out of her house and flagged me down. Sarah Jane is a lapsed shoe designer, with a very fit, second wife's body, and is always dressed in aesthetic getups that scream fashion industry. Today there was a gauzy top, Indian print bottom, and wrapped belt reminiscent of the Middle East, along with elaborate sandals in three shades of pink. Now, she is simply Barry's wife, seemingly thrilled to be growing old and borrowing things in Crandall, Connecticut. Sarah Jane talks fast, as if someone would cut her off if she didn't get it out fast. "Libby, I've been wanting to call you," she said. When people say, "I've been wanting to call you," but haven't, and haven't returned a million borrowed items and haven't mentioned the fact that they'll be putting their house on the market and moving away, I am not inclined to want to throw rose petals of greeting at them. "We saw a house we fell in love with in Weston, and made an impetuous bid."

It is known she has been visiting fertility clinics and

swallowing Chinese herbs despite Barry's clearly stated unwillingness to start another family. His grown children have taken the need to see another stroller or hear another spelling bee all out of him, he has said, and Sarah Jane let it drop once that Barry doesn't talk about his children to his wife, or about anything much, but seems to put all of what is left of his strength into washing his car.

"The Realtor thinks we have to do a little remodeling before we sell." She told me about the yuppies who were coming up in their Saabs and Volvos and turning up their noses at sixties kitchens and vinyl floor tiles. Then, as I was climbing into my car, she asked me the name of my "wonderful contractor. The one who did your upstairs renovation?"

I hesitated. "That was three years ago."

I didn't mention that to this day—out of habit—I crossed the street in town if his van was parked on my side. I pronounced his name.

"Trevor Eddy," she repeated, and said she'd write it down.

I felt confident that seeing the white truck with the green wrench logo in the driveway next door would no longer touch me in any way.

"Wait, Lib, wait," she called after me, as I moved off, "could I borrow a couple of postage stamps? I forgot to buy a roll and I need to put some checks in the mail today. . . ."

He was a graduate of Penn State and the grandson of a Portuguese ambassador. Some time before, he'd reinvented himself, reversed his name—Edgardo Tresorio—Wasped it, created an image to fit into Crandall, talked like a Ph.D., looked and sounded as if he should be stepping off a lecture platform instead of out of a van. He never wore a T-shirt, never. No jeans, the uniform of his profession, either. This walking GQ figure wore chinos and crisp plaid shirts—a man who'd decided to slide out of the corporate class into the fulfillment of working with his hands, and now did not quite belong in either the boardroom or in blue-collar taverns. That's where he conducted business, when he wasn't at the lumberyard, or at home in Fairfield, where he lived with his wife, an art teacher named Dee.

Little by little, as the plaster dust flew and new tiles went up, we would have to confer about the telephone booth, moldings, electrical outlets, recessed lights, and towel bars. At ten o'clock every morning—to this day I see him with a mug in his hand—Trevor joined me in the kitchen for coffee and conferences. We talked about this and that, whatever was in the news—the Olympics, an oil spill, there was something about Andy Warhol's cookie jars, as I remember—and it meandered into the personal, his giving up smoking, his father, shot and killed by friendly fire in the Korean War, his life with Dee, who'd had a bout of cancer and recovered but lived just to wait to die ("It's all she thinks about.") . . . and we talked about me. He kept asking what I thought of trivial things. Parrots: Should he get one? Marian McPartland: Had I ever heard her play? The cartoonist, Booth: Didn't I think he was funny? Ginger liqueur: Had I tasted it? Sleep: How much did I need? With Trevor, I felt like one of those paper flowers that blossom out of tiny shells when they are dropped into a glass of water. I became a new person, full of color and texture. I kept stopping to look at myself in the mirror. I'd never looked this vibrant, this rosy. Soon this new me veered over the edge and into daydreams in which I was roughly handled, crushed against the rough bark of trees in some movie-set primeval forest. I sometimes woke up with my arms and legs wrapped around my pillow, my head buzzing with innovative sexual scenarios. I wore perfume to the supermarket and tried to decipher the song lyrics on soft-rock stations on my car radio.

Charm bracelets were not very popular that year, but my mother had given me one and kept adding charms on every occasion. One day a gold four-leaf clover fell off it as I was pulling it out of my jewelry box. I walked out into the hall and got Trevor off a ladder, brought him this little enamel clover with a diamond chip in the center, and asked if he had pincers in his toolbox that would secure it to its link. He fixed the bracelet with a tweezers-like tool he had and put it on my wrist. His fingers seemed like sausages fiddling with the little clasp, but he touched the spot on the inside of my wrist where one feels one's pulse, and let his thumb rest there for a second. His eyes took aim, fired at mine, and it was all over. Psychologically, I crumpled and fell.

He approached me the next time in the mud room, pulled out his wallet, and showed me a picture he'd torn out of a magazine. A cruise ad, it was, the model in red. He said she looked just like me—she didn't, was twenty years younger and as many pounds lighter—and told me he took out the picture every night to look at just before he went to sleep. Then he took hold of my elbows and I pushed him away and we knocked over the umbrella rack, he backed off, and that was that. A few days later he put his hand on my hair, and I didn't move away. He ran his finger down my cheek, let his hand rest on my shoulder, and I just stood there feeling the back of my neck go hot, fixed on the spot like I was waiting to be photographed. He kept touching my cheek, not talking. It was in the upstairs hall. I let a kiss pour in some kind of plasma, let him proceed as if I were dying and he were giving mouth-to-mouth resuscitation. He knew wrenches and bolts. He knew joists and lathes. He knew lips and tongues. His thick fingers tangled my hair. I let it go on. It was like a professional demo; he had the technique of a virtuoso. I was curious to know exactly how he would continue if ever I let him. I was scared out of my wits, embarrassed to death and, at the same time, conscious of the hot and cold damp that was creeping up my scalp from the back of my neck. From the launching pad of the open neck of my blouse, his hand took off. He had warm, rough, outdoor-work fingers. The pictures on the walls behind him blurred and receded, the fleur-de-lis of the wallpaper began to spin. I led him into my bedroom while Claudia and Ellery were at school, and I pulled the shades, one by one. Then, in the midday dusk, we made love on the cushioned four-chair-back Baltimore 1805 settee. Some kernel of ethics made me edge him away from my marital bed, although Trevor grabbed a pillow from our four-poster to put under my hips. Peter's pillow. Afterward, I couldn't stand to be in the same room with him without wanting to do it again, so I stayed out of his way until the renovation was finished. I was paranoid, afraid even Lupe, then our cleaning lady, would see it written all over my face.

The day he left I spent half the morning looking for a four-leaf clover in a certain patch of grass in our backyard where I'd seen some earlier. I wanted him to take away something I'd given him, but searched without luck. Instead I asked Trevor to get the pincers out of his toolbox again, this time to take the four-leaf clover off my charm bracelet as a keepsake. It was the hokey gesture of an infatuated woman, but he took it and solemnly, wordlessly put it into one of the celluloid pages of his wallet.

I dreamed about him off and on for two years. I wished I could eradicate the memory, wanted to delete not so much the event, but what it was in me it got going. I asked myself the question, *Why?* and came up with different answers, none of them a valid justification for infidelity. Was it a vengeful act against Peter, who had disappointed me? A moment of weakness in a wash of desire? A wish for a dangerous detour in a marriage that was running too smoothly on automatic drive?

On one of our winter island vacations, I'd watched a woman swim far from the security of the beach and lifeguard into waters that were treacherous, known for riptides and possibly shark-infested. She ignored the whistles of the lifeguard and his waving arms, kept swimming out until she was just a bobbing dot in the distance. I thought of this woman from time to time, finally striding out of the surf, sleek, wet, and triumphant. She'd experienced a near-the-edge thrill and come out unscathed. That need for a bit of danger, that was in me then, too.

So, while no single cause was justification for letting ethics and fidelity evaporate in another man's arms, it was for a potpourri of reasons—and a confluence of circumstances. Above all, it was temptation that had come at *that* moment, packaged too beautifully, too brilliantly, in the person of Trevor Eddy. When we made love it was that near-the-riptide thrill, everything on the line, this stranger knowing me without knowing me, the bits of fantasy behind my closed eyelids, a lull, then the crashing imaginary ten-foot surf; I was drowning in all of it. He took me out of my life, that was the thing, but I hadn't counted on the guilt that followed. Then, I couldn't seem to forget the way he spoke my name, or those renegade hands, or the weight he gave to everything I said, and for years I saw his face everywhere, looked away when I saw his white van, embellished with the logo of a hammer and wrench over clover green lettering: TREVOR EDDY HOME REMODELING.

"Mommy!" I'd slept intermittently through the thunder, but Ellery was wide awake. She still wasn't sleeping well. Sometimes she couldn't find a comfortable position; occasionally she rolled over onto the cast and the pain in her arm woke her. Tonight, it was the storm. "Can I come into your bed?"

Peter was asleep but stirring. "Isn't Claudia home yet?" I whispered.

"Not yet."

I got out of bed and told Ellery we could go to her room and I'd sit on her bed until she fell asleep. We padded out together, and I quietly closed the door behind us. I could hear rain splashing against the windows and drumming on the roof. "Listen. It sounds like stars are falling," Ellery whispered.

"You're not afraid of thunder in your old age, sweetheart?" I asked as she climbed into her four-poster. As she swung her legs up onto the cotton quilt, her T-shirt rode up and I caught a glimpse of the dark patch between her legs. When had that happened? Wasn't it just last Christmas that I'd walked in on her when she was in the shower? She'd still had the smooth and petal-like innocence of a child then.

"Of course I'm not afraid!" she whispered, insulted. Did I think she was a baby, or what? The noise was awful, that was all. And Claudia wasn't there to annoy. She smiled.

Another crack, and simultaneous thunder. Her bony shoulders and little breasts shuddered under the cotton-knit shirt. "Wow. Daddy sleeps through everything." Actually, he'd woken as we'd left the room, murmured, and sighed himself back to sleep.

The meeting with Solow had ended at an impasse. Solow wanted to dump Greavy now. The old man was driving him crazy, walking around the office with a stapler in his hand, eavesdropping on Solow's consultations. The problem seemed like a hand grenade they were throwing back and forth; the boom could come at any time. "Daddy's so exhausted these days," I said.

She nodded. A far-off silent flash of lightning illuminated her thoughtful face like a cinematographer's floods. "But he's going to stay all right, isn't he?"

The room was cluttered with clothes, empty cans of Coke and Pepsi, a dismembered old radio, souvenirs from trips we'd taken, old riding hats, ancient magazines, piles of tapes and rolled-up posters, pictures of horses on every wall. A pair of stirrups, blue and red ribbons, all this an illustrated guide to the adolescent mind and its jumpy circuits. "Yes. Don't worry about that. Daddy's going to stay all right."

"I once saw Jennifer Torpin's father when he was drunk. Boy. He was coming down the stairs and I go, 'Jen, did your father hurt his legs?' and she goes, 'No, why?' and I go, 'He's, like, limping,' and right away I wanted to take it back, y'know? God, he couldn't walk, he was like completely wasted."

I'd only met the Torpins once or twice at open school nights. A pleasant, tweedy, standard -issue local couple.

"And the smell!" Ellery made a face, held her nose, looking like she looks when she is about to dive off the high board.

"Poor soul."

"Daddy was never like *that,* was he?"

"Daddy was never like that."

"So, what was he like?"

"Different. He'd become someone else."

"How?"

"As I've told you and told you. He'd get sort of—mean."

Ellery's eyes got big. Mommy had to watch her verbal step. A drunk is just a drunk, unless he's your father, as described by your mother.

"Tell me about the time with the mirror."

"Where did you hear that?"

"Claudia told me. Claudia remembers."

"She can't remember. She was a toddler."

"Maybe Daddy told her. He showed us the scars. On his arm."

It was right after we'd moved to this house. The painters had plastered the ceilings and painted the whole upstairs, and pictures were piled up against the walls in the hall, waiting to be hung. So were two full-length mirrors, which were due to be installed in our bathroom. Peter had been drinking heavily, had fallen asleep naked on top of the covers, and had woken, or half-woken, an hour or two later, to go to the bathroom. "I'm going to lift a leg," he'd said, shaking and waking me. Whenever he was drunk, his voice fell an octave, and sounded more oratorical than inebriated. He never slurred his words, but his breathing was raspy. It was as if he were addressing a group, instead of just one human being. Subtly maniacal is how he always seemed. He'd leaned very near to my ear and his breath had not been all that alcoholic. Vodka was his poison, although not inevitably. When we were young, Pimm's Cup was trendy and did it. In Japanese restaurants, he did very well with sake, and in Italian places, even lowly Spumante could do the trick.

I'd listened as he'd staggered out into the hall. I remember the smell of fresh paint to this day, and the sudden torrent of raging obscenities that shook the walls. Claudia had awoken, but was still in her crib. She'd cried a bit, but never saw anything. I'd jumped out of bed and run into the hall just in time to see Peter raise his fist and run like a gladiator at the naked intruder at the end of the hall, his own mirror image threatening him with its fist in the air. He'd smashed one of the two mirrors, slashing his arm in cuts of varying lengths and depths from wrist to elbow and one ugly cut right below the navel. The blood had spurted out of those gashes and the cut he'd made in his upper lip, the scar which his mustache now conceals.

I don't remember what gave me the courage to rip

the sheets off our bed, soak them in cold water, and make a tourniquet to wrap around his upper arm. Somehow, lessons taught in summer camp came back. He had been lowing like a farm animal, his teeth red from blood. I couldn't have taken him to the hospital, revealed the new doctor as a raging, sodden dipsomaniac. His career and our lives in Crandall had been at stake. I'd calmed Claudia down and sat up with Peter until morning and the steadying light of sobriety. With Claudia in the backseat, we'd driven to the hospital at six, and Peter, then totally his sober doctor self, had told his hospital colleagues he'd tripped over a ladder the builder had left in the hall onto a mirror leaning against a door. He'd joked about seeing himself in flight.

"And that's how Daddy got those scars on his arm and his lip and that's why he grew his mustache to cover it?"

The girls were such careful family archivists.

"How many stitches?"

To Ellery it was like a yarn from Grimm with a funny twist. Daddy the inebriated clown, the punishment many stitches. Lesson learned, sobriety followed. "I don't know how many stitches, dear. Lots."

"I can't imagine Daddy drunk. I can't."

*Don't ever try.* We never talked about the other time, the time in the snow.

"Never again. He promised."

"Daddy never breaks promises," she said, and after a few minutes, she asked me to hand her the stuffed monkey she sometimes sleeps with. The storm was still raging, and I began to worry about Claudia, somewhere in Ess's van at this very moment, possibly barreling along on a slick road. Mexican Night at the club would have ended by now and they'd be on their way home, or possibly pulled off the road somewhere having sex. For all I knew they'd done something stupid—even sensible teenagers were forever doing dangerous things—gone skinny-dipping in a thunderstorm, or fallen asleep in Ess's van.

And then I heard the front door open, heard her step on the stairs. Safe at home. Let the rain beat over our heads, and the lightning crack through the stars; we were all here now, under our sheltering slate roof. My sun and moon, my family, all soon to be tucked in behind the substantial walls of our two-story colonial. I thought about Annie. Blessed is what we surely were. Now I could sleep through anything.

"You fucking promised!"

"I fucking never promised!"

"You fucking did!"

It was Sunday morning the following week.

"Girls! Knock it off!" Peter called upstairs. He'd had three calls this morning—one from the hospital, two from a patient's wife who'd managed to get our home telephone number because she had a relative working at the Connecticut phone company. She wanted to know if her husband could eat sausages, have sex, and ride in a convertible if the top was down. Not the slightest bit of conscience about disturbing the doctor on a Sunday he wasn't on call.

"No peace," Peter said. Fortunately, Greavy was off this week, vacationing in Lake Louise. At least the office had been quiet. Solow had suggested Greavy take three weeks, but no such luck. He was due back Wednesday.

"I'm gonna tell!" Ellery yelled. A door opened, closed.

"Tell us what?" I stood in the doorway of Claudia's room, where I thought I discerned the smell of smoke. "I hope to God you're not smoking, Claudia."

"Of course not." Claudia lying is hard to read. Her face is inevitably immobile, not unlike Ess's.

Ellery was sitting cross-legged on Claudia's bed, glowering at her sister, who was sitting at the edge of the mattress, polishing her toenails.

"Nobody was smoking."

"What's the problem up here then?"

"She said she'd take me to Playland. She promised. Now she says I can't go."

"I said I'd take you *sometime,*" Claudia continued making deep pink brush strokes on her toenails, and her hair, still slightly damp from the shower, hung across her cheeks in pastalike tangles, hiding her expression. "I didn't promise *today.*"

"The fuck you didn't!"

"Ellery, I don't want to hear that word out of you every five minutes!"

"She said last week that Sunday Ess was taking her to Playland and that I could come along. And Claudia says 'fuck' more than I do."

"I said it was a possibility. Just a fucking possibility."

"See!"

I suppose there was a bit of my own history that played into the sympathy I felt for Ellery. My sister and I were only eighteen months apart, but I'd always stood very tall, much too tall for the boys my age, looked down from the heights at my dancing-school partners, friends' boyfriends, my sister's beaux. I had none until college. My sister was the one with the giggle, the winning graceful wisp of teenage femininity. She'd make her voice go high as she could, and her shoe size was three. They called me Your High Royalness.

"I'd take you myself, Ell, but I have to look over an estate on Round Hill Road today."

Her eyes filmed over. She wiped them with the back of her hand.

"Next week, we'll take you next week." Claudia stopped polishing to look at her sister. "Tonight, when we get back, maybe we'll play a game of SET, okay?" I discerned a touch of heart in her voice.

Downstairs, Ess had arrived. We heard Peter let him in.

Ellery sniffed a few times but didn't answer.

"I need a couple of more minutes till my nails dry. I gotta change my blouse, too. Ell, would you go down and keep Daddy away from Ess?" Claudia asked.

Ellery gave her the fisheye, but moved slowly off the bed. The American flag had peeled half off and the cast was beginning to look hangdog. "I'm always doing things for you. I'm a second-class citizen around here, an indented slave."

"Indentured. You mean indentured."

"Right. Isn't that what I said?" Her eyes narrowed at me.

"Wait a minute," I said. "What were you going to tell, Ellery? What don't we know that we should know?" Ellery threw a look at Claudia that spoke some sort of volumes.

"Not a thing. Nada. This isn't *NYPD Blue*! It's Crandall, Connecticut! Mom, why are you always looking for bad stuff?" Claudia walked past me and stomped downstairs.

"It's my job description, sweetheart," I called after her, but I don't think she heard me.

When Claudia and Ess had left, and Peter had gone downstairs to his gym, Ellery and I sat out on the patio watching Moxie sitting on the brick wall eyeing birds. Ellery must have been recently trying Claudia's eye makeup, because a trace of blue-green followed the lower line of her lashes. It echoed the aqua-blue of her eyes, and although I didn't say it, I thought it becoming. "I told Mrs. Bergin I wanted a boy kitten."

"Like Laszlo."

"Laszlo was like my baby. He'd curl up at the foot of

my bed every single night. I think he preferred me to Claudia."

And then, after a pause, and for no reason whatsoever, she asked, "Do you think Claudia is really in love with Ess?"

"I hope not."

"You think Ess is dangerous, Mommy?"

*"Dangerous?"*

"I mean daring. I think he's *daring*."

"Well, he did rescue that dog. That was daring, I guess."

"He's not afraid of anything. Like those guys at the Pizza Hut."

"What guys at the Pizza Hut?"

"Didn't Claudia tell you?"

"No."

Ellery bit her lip. "Maybe she didn't want I should say anything."

"What happened at the Pizza Hut, Ellery?"

There was an endless pause while Ellery nervously scratched a mosquito bite on her leg, weighing her responsibility to her sister to keep her mouth shut. "I don't think it's a big secret."

"You might as well go ahead. I'm listening."

"Well, me and Ess and Claudia were over at the Pizza Hut and we were just leaving and this bunch of guys in a silver car pull up and they start yelling at Claudia. They're going like, 'We want to sexually harass you, honeybuns,' and stuff like that and Ess, like, turns purple. I was so scared. Anyhow, he is so ballsy, he just turns right around and goes back into Pizza Hut and he grabs a bottle of Italian dressing from the salad bar and walks out with it and goes right over to the guys in the car and opens the gas whatchamacallit in the back and just pours the salad dressing in the gas tank. Boy! Claudia and I are like, 'Wow.' Now these guys are screaming at him, they couldn't, like, *believe* it, they didn't get what was happening at first, then they go wild, but by this time Ess is back in the van and he sticks his head out at them and says, 'And if you guys ever annoy my G.F. again, you're in for it, maybe next time it won't be salad dressing, it'll be a *lit match*!' And he takes off."

Ellery was thoughtful for a moment. So was I. It had once been so easy; supervising my daughters had meant keeping an eye out on the playground, in the backyard, in the basement playroom. It had meant keeping the bleach bottles out of reach and the Tylenol well capped. Fresh food, pure water, and a fever thermometer, tools of a mother's trade, no longer did the trick. Now, the hazards were out of reach, innumerable, and unimaginable. I was supposed to say something, but couldn't put my finger on what it was. I recoiled at the possibility of the next chapter in this story. Then Ellery said, "If he'd lived in another century, I bet he'd of been an outlaw."

"Yes, probably."

"I bet he could do anything. I bet he could get Claudia to run away with him and elope if he wanted to."

"Oh, God, I hope not!"

"Claudia says, whatever he wants, he just zeroes in on. And he always, always gets it. It's the same thing for Claudia. Exact same thing. She just snaps her fingers and *pffft* . . ." Ellery's voice trailed off, like she'd been singing a song and had forgotten the lyrics.

I didn't mention it to Peter. He was in the basement trying to beat tension on the treadmill today. "Do you suppose you could take Ellery to lunch at the club?" I asked him. "It's June, love is in the air, and she seems to feel she's running on empty."

He said he'd wanted to stay home and catch up on his reading, was behind three months with material Solow had given him to look over and he hadn't touched, couldn't get all the information he should be getting on the audiotape in the car, and so on. I reminded him that he'd taken Claudia to lunch alone two weeks ago, and that now Ellery needed a boost. "In that case," he said, "of course and absolutely," he would take her, if only for an hour, and if I really thought it was that important.

Darley called a half hour later. She'd just put in her Sunday call to the Ethel Carpenter Nursing Home. Should she proceed to Greece on the *Stella Solaris* or stay here and wait for Meggie's demise? It seemed imminent. I put Peter on and he comfortingly spoke the obvious. To sit in Rowayton and wait would be useless, and to travel again to the nursing home where her own sister wouldn't know her—well, she'd just been there a few months ago, hadn't she? We all seem to need to hear what we already know, but spoken by authorized people. That would be Peter, for all of us.

Annie and I were in the office together, digging into the yogurt of the day, blueberry, with our plastic spoons. "This is much better than the stuff I get at the mall," Annie remarked, which reminded her that her husband had reported seeing Claudia and Ellery there a few days ago. He thought Claudia was a knockout, Annie said, but stopped in midsentence when she saw my face. "Oh, Ellery is getting lovely, too." Annie is as tactful as a finishing-school headmistress, always. "They were at the Earring Corral and Ess was with them. They all seemed to be having a grand time." Annie was just crowding in conversation to get past the sensitive spot, but I imagined there was something else she knew and didn't want to tell me. Why else would she have gotten up and made a point of going to the window? She stood there looking out at nothing at all, her back to me.

"You know Ess, Annie?"

"No, I don't. I just heard about his saving that dog up in Vermont. I understand it made all the Vermont papers."

"Who did you hear that from?"

"Lila Vermiglia. She used to be in my bridge group before they moved away. Did you know her?"

"Slightly."

"Ess used to go with her daughter."

"Really?"

"Uh-huh. He was doing masonry work for the Vermigilias then."

"You know his family, Annie?"

"No. Aren't they from out of town?" Annie had returned from the window and sat in her chair, swiveling back and forth, nervously, I thought.

"Danbury."

"Well, I know people in Danbury. Do you want me to try to find out about his family?"

"Oh, no, Annie, this is not a spy saga. He seems like a nice enough boy. And Claudia is only sixteen. This is not serious! These young romances fall through as often as mortgages."

When I'd finished my yogurt I picked up my pocketbook and told Annie that I'd be heading home to prepare dinner, and as I got up to leave, something I suddenly remembered nudged me. "Lila's daughter—wasn't she very pretty, doing appearances on the TV shopping channel a few years ago?"

"Yes, that's the one. She has sort of—oh, Olympic Gold looks, you could say. Very muscular legs, too. She was a runner. Eight miles every day."

"But she must be twenty-two years old!"

"He was mad about her. Lila said they sat around their pool all summer." Annie was scraping the bottom of the yogurt styrofoam cup, not looking at me.

"And—?"

"Well, Ess threw the pool boy into the water once because he made a move on the girl. He got . . . well . . . really possessive."

"He must have had some crush on her!"

"I think it was mutual."

"Really?"

"Whatever he's got, he's certainly got lots of it!" Annie smiled and raised her spoon in a salute.

There was something incongruous about this story. I was scrutinizing Annie's face, which told me nothing. "But what would a twenty-two-year-old girl want with a teenage boy?" *Like Ess?* I didn't add.

"Oh, kids." She brushed the question off, crumpled the cup, and tossed it into the pail. "Anyway, aren't we both old enough to know that lust is stronger than reason?"

Peter was dozing in front of CNN when I walked in, and Ellery was up in her room, sitting in front of the mirror over her corner vanity table. It was a posture I had never seen. The vanity table was usually littered with CDs, homework papers, and potato chip wrappers, never used for vanity.

"How was lunch with Dad?" I asked, passing her open door on the way to my bedroom. "Did you eat a clam roll as usual?"

She considered the question very seriously, adjusting the sling at her neck where it had caught a strand of hair. "Like always." Pausing dramatically, she looked almost as if she intended to step to the podium to make an announcement. Instead, she slumped a bit, good elbow on the vanity table. "We talk about my arm and how it's healing. Then we talk about who I'm going to become in the future."

Strewn across her bed were the pictures we'd taken on Memorial Day. I'd picked up the photos Friday, but most had turned out strange. The flowers were close, trees far away, everybody looked touched-up.

Her mouth puckered and pulled in air. "Can't you see what these pictures say about me? Can't you see that I failed at the one and only thing I could do better than Claudia? Look at me in those snapshots! A little shadow, a little zero. A broken arm because I couldn't even get Fast Forward, one of the *easiest, slowest* animals in, like, all of the state of Connecticut, under control. No one has ever been thrown by Fast Forward in the history of the Red Riding Hood Stable. And there I am, a total nobody. A Jane Roe."

"Doe."

"I wouldn't have been surprised if I turned out in black-and-white next to Claudia. Just look at her hair. Her face! And the way she plays the harp!"

"Let's not forget, Ell. You could have stayed with *your* harp lessons. You might have been just as good."

"In your dreams! Mommy, you just don't *get* it!"

"Listen, Ellery. I had a size-nine shoe when I was twelve years old. My sister had a three. I think I have an idea."

"Well, Mommy, what's feet got to do with it? Daddy doesn't want me the way I am. No! He goes, 'As soon as your arm heals, we'll see if we can get you tennis lessons.' And then he's talking about getting me started on the violin, since I hated the harp and the piano! And then he's telling me he's going to send me to Paris to learn French without an accent. So, does he want a new and improved version or what?"

"He just wants the best for his daughters, Ellery." It was human after all, to let some fatherly pride, reflected glory, creep in. He'd pushed hard to become a Cornell Med School star grad, swam through hospital politics to get himself noticed at Crandall General. It looked like next year, maybe the year after, he'd be head of the department in a hospital second only to the big one in New Haven. It was in his nature to aim high, and then to soar.

"I'm not the best. That's the problem. Nowhere near."

"You're best enough for us, Ellery."

"I'm not fit to be 'the doctor's daughter.' " Ellery lowered her voice to a whisper reminiscent of throat infections. "I'm just the doctor's *other* daughter."

We were interrupted by the telephone, and I was glad to have an excuse to get away, to think about a sagacious, distress-alleviating, contradicting response.

It was Solow calling Peter.

Peter came upstairs to take the phone, and I watched his face, which went from thoughtful to tense to grim. Beneath his mustache, his mouth hardly moved, except to open wide enough to say, "Hmmm," "Mmmmm," and "Hmmm. All right."

I hardly was able to get it out of him after he'd hung up: Greavy had suggested aspirin to an elderly patient who was already taking Warfarin, which he himself had prescribed last year. Solow said he'd gone straight to the office, but the old doctor had stapled closed her folder with ten staples. Solow counted them. The patient was hemorrhaging, saved in the nick by her husband and a run to the emergency room. Solow said it was the patient's word against Greavy's, and if there were bets being taken, he would put money on the patient. Solow was pushing Peter not to put it off any longer; it had already gone too far.

Before he fell into a despondent silence, Peter asked me what I thought he could say to the old doctor, whose only son was out of another job somewhere in California, whose wife was a woman with rheumatoid arthritis who walked on two canes, and who had made up for whatever was deficient in his personal life by giving his soul to his medical practice. Peter did agree that Solow was right: Greavy was "losing his touch." The word "litigious" had come up many times in this conversation; easing out the old man had to be done, probably sooner than he'd thought.

"You'll approach him through the right door. You always do."

"The man was my guardian angel for so many years." We both were quiet for a moment. I remembered a time Greavy brought Peter home from a local bar when I called him for help. Someone had spotted him, disheveled and barefoot, starting a fight about a loud jukebox in a place called Wuzzy's. An anonymous phone call I later thought came from the kindhearted Wuzzy himself alerted me. If Greavy hadn't dragged Peter out of there, within twenty-four hours half the town might have heard about the episode. Peter must have been remembering it, too. I could still see him walking shoeless from Greavy's car to the front door in January, his coat buttoned wrong, his mouth bubbling with saliva. I remember Dr. Greavy coming into the house, saying, "This has got to be the last time, Lib," and putting both paternal arms around me, as soon as we'd gotten Peter to the couch and under a blanket. It had taken a while to calm me down. Now Peter pressed his forehead with the tips of four fingers and closed his eyes. "I'm going to come home with white hair, Lib."

"It may be much easier than you imagined. He's sensitive enough to know it's coming. He has to know he's failing."

Peter got a sardonic look, an expression that reminded me of Claudia in one of her moods. "It's not easy to foreclose on a man's life." He looked at a point over my left shoulder and blinked hard. I was suddenly aware of how deeply I was moved by his compassion, and wanted to say it, but it seemed incongruous and awkward. I had no response for him *or* Ellery. I stayed silent.

* * *

It was the following Wednesday that Sarah Jane stopped me in the driveway. On anyone else, brilliant birds cavorting through specimen shrubs all over a blouse-and-shorts set might seem overpowering. With Sarah Jane's red sandals and toenails painted to match, the package looked like a department-store window. She wanted to show me a picture she and Barry had bought for fourteen hundred dollars at an auction near Lenox. "Do you have a minute?"

Leading me into her dining room, Sarah Jane pointed to a large, dark oil leaning against the dining-room table, a pastoral, with cows, meadows, and dark sky, a plume of gray clouds, elaborately framed in gold leaf. "I fell in love with it! Look at the delicate colors, the way the light touches those trees, the way it would go with this old furniture wherever we moved, and, well, more than that, I could see it was a steal. It's early nineteenth-century, and the auctioneer assured us that he'd expected a bid of at least three thousand and was basically giving it away." She moved the painting to the light to give me a better look, pulled back the draperies so the sun could shine directly on the brush strokes. "What do you think?"

I kneeled down to examine the paint and to look at the back of the canvas. I saw immediately that there was no mistaking the period or the quality of the work.

"It's a lovely picture, and I don't blame you for grabbing it, but I'm afraid it's not what it seems." Disappointing clients and friends is an occupational hazard. Aside from losing good cash, they know they've been had, and feel dumb.

Sarah Jane's face and voice took a nosedive. Even the birds on her shorts and shirt seemed to swoop downward. "What? Are you saying it's not the real thing?"

"Well, Sarah Jane, I'm afraid your shoes may be older

than this antique. I know these reproductions, and they are coming in from Holland by the shipload, and of course, they look very attractive. . . ." I hated watching her face sag. "And so authentic. They could fool anyone."

"But he said—he *swore*—are you *sure*?"

"Yes. It's Dutch. It was painted last week or last month in the Netherlands and it's worth maybe seventy-five, a hundred dollars, although I don't think you could easily sell it even for that. There's not much of a market." I felt my own forehead crease. "I'm really sorry, Sarah Jane."

"Oh!" She sank into a dining-room chair and stared long and hard at the picture, as if by sheer hypnotic force she could get it to age a hundred years.

Finally, she put her palms flat down on the shorts where they half covered her thighs. "You could be wrong, couldn't you? After all, we bought this from a reputable auction house. The place has been there fifty years!"—a lead weight pause while she shifted in her chair and redirected her gaze from the picture to me—"I'm going to get a second opinion, Libby, if you don't mind."

The climate in the dining room darkened and clouded, like the sky in the picture leaning against the chair rail. Sarah Jane was mad at me, as if it were my fault she'd been taken. I wanted to get out of there fast, and told her the girls were waiting, that we were going to eat an early dinner. Actually, I wasn't even sure they were home, but it was the first thing that came to mind.

"Oh, the girls," Sarah Jane said, dismissively. Her eyes narrowed and her hands disappeared into the pockets of her shorts, which until now, had not looked as if they had pockets. "Did Claudia tell you I ran into her at the library the other day?" Sarah Jane's voice got a little buzz of a belligerent edge.

"No. When?" Not that Claudia would likely consider

worth mentioning meeting anyone over forty, an age group she considered uninteresting enough to be invisible.

"Oh, last week some time."

"She never told me. I suppose it slipped her mind."

Sarah Jane hesitated. She was clearly marinating what she was about to tell me. The message from me that an auctioneer had gulled her had ruined her day, and now she was mustering her forces—quid pro quo—to ruin mine.

"I think it was Thursday night. The library is open Thursday night, and I was doing some research on prehistoric footwear—you know, I like to keep my hand in." Her smile was ersatz, like the smile of some bellhop you've just undertipped.

"Thursday night—well, that's very possible," I said, and instead of bolting for the door, out of an understandable curiosity, I waited to hear the rest of it.

"And Claudia was checking out some French videos. I was very impressed." She wasn't really impressed, and we both knew it.

"Oh, she's taking French conversation this summer—"

Now Sarah Jane put a hand on my arm. "Lib. I don't know whether to—well, to mention this, but—" I watched her mouth, a puckered red plum, heard, "for your own good . . ."

When people say they want to tell you something for your own good, what they mean is they want to watch you squirm for *their* own good. "But if I were a mother—," she continued.

If she were a mother, she would be in a glass house and not throwing stones.

"What happened was when she opened her purse to find her library card—well, how can I say this?—when she was rummaging through her purse, *things* fell out."

"Things?"

"Her keys and a little bottle of hair spray, and you know, tissues, and, and, ah, well, some of the *things* fell on the floor and I bent down to help her pick them up and there was a . . . right next to my foot, a . . . a . . . condom." Sarah Jane, who always talked fast, was slowly savoring every word as if it were sprinkled with truffles.

"A condom?" I saw a flying insect nearby and suddenly wished it would land on her, somewhere where I could whack it.

"Yes, a condom."

"Really? You're sure?"

"I'm sure."

"Did you notice what brand?"

Sarah Jane blinked, looked as if she'd swallowed air. "What *brand*?"

"Yes. Some are safer than others."

"I tell you your teenage daughter is carrying a condom in her purse and you ask me what brand?"

"Right. Could you tell? Peter asked me the same question."

"Jesus, Libby, I can't believe this."

"What don't you believe?"

"Claudia is what, sixteen? And running around with that—that Rumpleforeskin with a van?"

"And Peter and I want her to be sure to have safe sex."

"Sixteen years old! And Peter is so prominent! A cardiologist! My God, it's certainly a new world."

"For a minute, I was afraid you were going to tell me she had drugs in her purse. That would get us very worried!"

Sarah Jane brightened. "She had those, too!"

"What?"

Her eyes lit with a *gotcha* look. "Well, not exactly *crack*, but very funny cigarettes, in a strange package."

As I left the Bergins' house, Sarah Jane actually called after me that she still hadn't gotten to the post office but that she'd return my stamps as soon as she did—maybe tomorrow or the next day.

When I got home, Peter was on the telephone. I could tell the call had nothing to do with Dr. Greavy. He looked relaxed, had kicked off his shoes, and was checking the next number on the list the answering service had accumulated for him.

I plunked down the bag of groceries I'd pulled out of the trunk of the car, didn't even head for the kitchen to put away the things that had to go into the refrigerator. Between calls, Peter told me the girls were down at the schoolyard watching a softball game, that Greavy was due back in the office tomorrow morning, and that we'd run out of tomato juice. Then, looking at my face, he said that a silence accompanied by a vertical crease between the eyes meant something was wrong.

Peter has lectured the girls on the hazards of nicotine, pot, alcohol, cocaine, glue, and hair spray. Over the years, he has drawn diagrams, brought home hospital anecdotes of the horrors of toxicity, and discussed case studies of stretcher cases he always calls "avoidable tragedies." He's done everything except put the girls through orthodox aversion therapy. It has to do with what he sees every day in Crandall General and St. Anthony's. It has to do with what he sees in Bridgeport. It comes from his own addiction. And it is because, disinterested in poetry, but still summoning his recollection of college lit courses, he still quotes Shelley, and has called Claudia—not Ellery—his "white radiance of eternity."

"Well, goddamn it, you know what, Lib? I don't believe it," Peter said, putting aside his telephone list. "I don't believe your Sarah Jane. I don't think Claudia's smoking anything, drinking anything, sniffing anything. And I don't think my daughter would lie."

The girls didn't come inside immediately. They stood in the middle of the front walk for a few minutes in the deepening dusk, playing with a neighbor's Labrador. From the living-room window, where I watched uneasily, I saw Claudia kneel down to tie Ellery's shoelace. It seemed a gesture so warm and sisterly—Ellery was now capable of tying her own shoelace, although with some difficulty—that everything inside me softened, including the conviction that Claudia was anything but a lovely, veracious angel-child.

"Could we have a word with you, Claudia?" Peter said almost as soon as the girls came in. They were heading for the refrigerator, and had greeted us with good cheer in the kitchen. Ellery was popping a few grapes into her mouth from the bunch I was about to rinse off in the sink.

"What'd I do?"

"What'd she do?"

"Come into the den, Claudia," Peter said, pretty lightly. "And have no fear. In the state of Connecticut you're innocent until proven guilty."

"Should I come into the den, too?"

"No, sweetie." I asked Ellery to finish putting groceries away, and please not to eat unwashed fruit.

"What'd she do? Is it about Ess?"

"No. Nothing to do with Ess." It struck me later that when I said that, Ellery looked relieved.

We put it to Claudia. Had she met Sarah Jane in the library? She had. Had she dropped her purse? Hesitation. Yes, she had.

And then, "Are you smoking pot?"

Claudia threw her pocketbook on the couch and pulled her ten fingers haughtily through her hair, chin up, very insulted. "I can't *believe* you would even think that!"

Peter and I exchanged looks. Under his mustache, his lips were taut and waxy, his face was getting patches of color. He shot up from his chair and took a sudden step toward the couch. Upstairs, in our telephone booth, the telephone rang, and Ellery ran up the stairs from her eavesdropping position in the kitchen to answer it. Without warning, Peter now made a lunge for the couch and grabbed Claudia's pocketbook off the cushion onto which she'd thrown it.

In retrospect, rushing home to rip Claudia's head off was overreacting, but it wasn't my idea to decapitate a child over sneaking an occasional joint. I had sneaked Pall Malls as early as fourteen, in an age when an early adolescent smoking nicotine spelled as much trouble as pot did today. No. It was the expressionless face-to-face lie of which she was capable. The relaxed muscles around her mouth, the unblinking opacity of her eyes—what had I done between the sandbox and last week to create such a facile liar?

"What are you *doing*, Daddy?"

It unsnapped and fell open when he pulled at the strap.

"Let's take a look, Claudia!"

She screamed, "It's an invasion of privacy! You can't!"

All the careful and diplomatic delivery I'd heard night after night discussing life and death with patients in extremis vanished instantly. "I'm your father. I can and I will!" Peter's eyes were glowing bright and hard. "There's nothing to hide here, is there? Hmmm? Is there?"

Claudia's face looked as if a roller covered with pink paint had just run over it. "Is this the gestapo? Or what?" she yelled.

Very soon, I was sorry I'd ever voiced a suspicion to Peter. Much later, I thought that telling my husband what Sarah Jane had said might have been the single biggest mistake of my life.

The contents tumbled out: hairbrush, hair spray, keys, wallet, condoms (Kimono Microthins), lip gloss, spray perfume, tissues, cigarette lighter, French cigarettes, and a folded newspaper clipping in a little plastic envelope. No marijuana. She was smoking Gauloises, not pot.

If she hadn't practically thrown herself on it, tried to grab it off the floor before we saw it, he might never have bothered to grab and unfold it, flatten it, taken it under the light to read. If her eyes hadn't looked like those of an animal caught in the beam of a flashlight when Peter picked it up, he wouldn't have snatched the plastic-covered wad of newspaper out of her hands, and insisted on seeing what the big-deal secret was all about and what was there left to hide, anyway? "Give it to me, Daddy! It's private property!" Claudia lunged forward, bumped her shin against the glass coffee table, and let out a howl, but Peter pulled the newspaper out of its pouch and her reach.

Could I have stopped his reading it? Should I have? In hindsight, probably.

"It's for you!" Ellery's voice called downstairs from the telephone booth. "Claud—it's Ess!"

"I can't talk now," Claudia called upstairs, standing on one foot and rubbing her shin, without taking her eyes off her father.

Peter was unfolding the newspaper clipping. I was reminded of old mystery-movie scenes, in which the camera does a close-up of the detective's hands as he pulls the clue out of the dead man's wallet and his fingers gingerly unfold the letter, the map, the fragile, crumbling receipt, to keep it from tearing. The scene takes seconds that seem like hours. Like this one. Then, as Claudia lunged at Peter once more to try to wrest it out of his hands, he held the paper at arm's length to read the headline without his glasses.

" 'Man wades into frozen pond and saves dog,' " he read aloud.

"Give it back to me, Daddy!" Claudia looked like a statue of a martyr on a pedestal in a park, palms upraised, the same stony, pleading look.

Peter ignored her. He took his reading glasses out of his shirt pocket and slipped them on with one hand while he held tight to the newsclip with the other. " 'Wells, Vermont. In an unusually daring rescue, Salvatore DiBuono, a native of Danbury, Connecticut, risked his life by wading into partially frozen North Cumberland pond to save the life of a three-year-old corgi, Humphrey Bogart, owned by Mr. and Mrs. George Duchamps, of Shelton, formerly of Middlebury. The twenty-two-year-old limousine driver—' " Peter stopped, squinted down at the paper for a very long moment, then tore off his glasses and glared at Claudia. The green of his irises seemed to leap out from behind his lashes.

Claudia opened her mouth and closed it. I heard Ellery's step somewhere upstairs; she must have been crouched at one of the heat registers, ear to the duct.

"Twenty-two years old! That kid is twenty-two?" The air around Peter seemed to shake. The floor creaked above. "What the hell do you think you're doing with a goddamn golden ager?"

Of course, we all knew what she was doing with Ess, but the question was, what was he doing with a sixteen-year-old girl? And, more to the point, what difference did it make whether he was eighteen and slightly immature, or twenty-two and very immature? To Peter, his white radiance to eternity involved with a senior citizen of twenty-two with no degree and many part-time jobs was scandalous, outrageous, and dangerous. His voice thundered, "Twenty-two years old!" as if he were yelling, "Fire!" In my heart, although he claimed to condone it, I felt it was his way of putting an end to Claudia's teenage sex life. In fact, the thought crossed my mind that he was pretty pleased to have found the weapon with which to dispose of Ess.

Claudia, defiant, stood speechless and immobilized. But where was the high wattage passion we anticipated? Where were the tantrums, the sobs, the protesting cries? Her hands gripped the sides of the shirttails she'd pulled out of her jeans a few minutes ago. After a moment of dead calm, "I don't believe this," in a voice that sounded as if it were coming from under water. "I am not hearing this." I sent an uneasy glance toward Peter. Claudia's park-statue control was not good news.

Peter must have sensed it, too. The navigator quickly changed course. He took a breath, seized the helm, turned into calmer waters. Drug addiction might have been easier. There were no rehabs for an addiction to Ess DiBuono. Peter handed Claudia the unfolded piece of newspaper and put a hand tenderly on her cheek. "I love you, Claud, please don't look at me like that, sweetie. You're sixteen years old! Although you won't forgive me for a while, sooner or later, you'll thank me." And then he told Claudia that her relationship with Ess was over, "history, as of now. He's never again to set foot in our house, or your life, as of this moment!" And if he ever caught her smoking anything again, she'd be grounded for a year.

Claudia needed only a blindfold to give her the look of a person about to be led in front of a firing squad. "I'll never forgive you. Never," she said, ripping his hand off her shoulder where it had slid down from her cheek, and she turned and walked out of the room with her chin held so high one could imagine an invisible basket of fruit balanced on her head.

* * *

She refused to speak or look at him the following day. He was late leaving for the hospital, stalling, perhaps. Looking at the clock, he sipped coffee in the kitchen, made phone calls from the den, and finally Claudia appeared, wished me good morning, asked Ellery if she'd seen her white cable-knit sweater, grabbed a banana from the bowl on the counter, and passed him without speaking. Then, as she was about to walk out the kitchen door, she turned to Peter and said, "You might as well get rid of it, because I'm never going to touch the harp again. And by the way, I'm going to love Ess until the day I die."

As soon as the door had slammed behind her, Peter put his mug of coffee in the sink, took his car keys out of his pocket, and gave me a kiss. "She'll be over it in two weeks," he said. "I'll make you a bet, Lib. Want to bet?"

The telephone rang at four the following morning. It is not unusual for Peter to be summoned at all hours in an emergency, and there are two bedroom telephones. One is on the night table next to my bed and one, with a mute button, is next to his. I usually screen the calls.

"You or me?" I murmured, at the first ring.

"You," Peter never opened his eyes.

"Mrs. Ehrlich?"

"Yes."

"Salvatore DiBuono here."

"Ess?"

"Right. I'm sorry to disturb you at this hour, Mrs. E."

Peter's eyes opened. My heart thumped.

"What is it?"

"Everything is okay. Don't worry. I'm not coming near Claudia. Don't get shook."

"It's not a good time to call for a chat, Ess."

"It took all this time to get up the courage, Mrs. E."

"And all those beers?" Our Achilles' heel; the accusation slipped out of me.

"I don't usually drink, Mrs. E. I'm standing here with my fifth glass of cranberry juice, but I admit they did put some kind of coffin varnish in it."

"Where are you calling from?" I was afraid he was somewhere near—around the corner or, worse, in front of the house.

"Wuzzy's."

*Wuzzy's.* There were at least eight taverns in Crandall. Why did it have to be Wuzzy's? Certainly Claudia had played a part in this; she must have told Ess about Peter, his former life, the long-ago drunken jukebox fight. Then again, no. The girls never talked about Peter's history. It was deeply buried family shame. Wuzzy's stayed open illegally till dawn, that's why Ess had gone there. Just hearing the name, Wuzzy's, was like being hit in the head by a stone.

"I was gonna wait till morning, but I've got to drive someone to the airport at six."

"I'm afraid you've wakened us both and I definitely don't want to talk now."

Out of the corner of my eye I saw Peter lift himself on one elbow to look at the clock on his night table.

"I just want to say one thing, Mrs. E."

"What is it?"

"I've been crying. All night. First time since I was eleven years old and caught my finger in the door of my father's Impala."

"Ess, I'm sorry, but it's four in the morning."

"What I wanted to say was you're a beautiful family. One beautiful perfect American family like in the movies. I realize I wasn't in love with just Claudia. I was in love with all of you guys. That's what I wanted to say, soon as I could stop crying."

"Good night, Ess."

"I just wanted you to know that."

"Thank you. Good night, Ess."

"You give my apologies to Dr. Ehrlich, will you?"

"I will. Good luck, Ess."

"What did he say?" Peter asked, after I'd hung up. He was sitting up in bed, had turned on his bedside lamp, and had just taken a sip of the water from the glass set next to the pictures of the girls, who smiled blandly into the room from their Victorian frames.

"He said he was in love with our whole family."

"And he had to tell us that at 4:12 A.M."

"I can't help feeling sorry for the boy. He's Romeo and we've taken away his Juliet."

"He'll get over it in two weeks, too, find someone closer to his own age and class, and then we'll all get to sleep really well."

"Mom! Have you looked outside?"

Ellery ran into our room at eight that morning while Peter was in the shower. "Did you see it? Did you?"

"See what?" I was only half-awake and wishing for another hour of sleep. Of peace.

"What Claudia did in the middle of the night?"

She was barefoot, still in her T-shirt nightie, toothpaste in the corner of her mouth. "Look!" She held back the curtain and pulled up the blind, while I squinted into the bright morning sunlight. Beyond the walls of our bedroom, Claudia's radio throbbed rock.

"Do you believe this? Is this for real?"

I bounded out of bed, but then took nervous and hesitating steps toward the window.

Down below, covering the hedges that huddled against the clapboard facade of our house, sprinkled over the evergreens guarding our front door, scattered across half our lawn, our new tulips and the chrysanthemum bushes we'd planted not three weeks ago, was white stuff. Paper? Ticker tape? Shredded newsprint?

"What is it?"

"It's all of Claudia's harp music. About eight books of it. She tore it into one million little bits. I think she worked on it all night long."

It took a moment to process, this chalky confetti covering our lawn, a dazzle of paper snow reflecting the sun. "Oh, good God."

"Isn't it wild?" Ellery watched my reaction. "On first glance, I thought it was winter again."

I hate snow. I hate the touch, the feel, the thought of it. Snow represents a memory I haven't the power to forget, a memory that encroaches on my dream and waking life, too. It is embalmed somewhere up in my head and revives, in all its chalkbone color, like now. Looking down, I felt as if a window had opened, and an arctic draft had indeed swept into the room, and into the dead center of my life.

Peter, who almost never got angry at the girls, was angry. Hair dripping, still damp in his terry-cloth robe, he stormed barefoot into Claudia's room, snapped off the radio, and told her that she was responsible for getting every scrap, every tiny bit of paper off the property. If any had blown next door or across the street, that was her responsibility as well. Until the confetti was off every leaf and every blade, she was going nowhere. Had she lost her mind? This act of thoughtless defiance was going to teach her a hard lesson. "We are all responsible for our own actions in the long run!"

"You have no heart! It'll take me a fucking year!"

"End of discussion!"

Later, he asked if I agreed with him. I told him I did, most certainly. And that I was in awe of his spontaneity. His judgment came bubbling up clear and pure as a freshly pickaxed geyser. In the split second of a decisive moment, he found exactly the right way to deal with adolescent storms. I did privately waver about cutting Claudia off from Ess, though. It seemed too abrupt, too harsh, guillotining a romance that was certainly destined to end on its own. I worried about rebellion. I worried about repercussions. On the other hand, putting an end to it seemed right; Ess was, after all, a man, Claudia, a baby. Perhaps I was an adolescent too long ago, when supervision, as Darley put it, worked. Now I stared out the window at the sky, paced the room, pushed my imagination to its limits and still had no answers about where it could go or, in this day and age, what the backlash might be.

After school, Claudia spent two sullen hours picking scraps of paper off the front lawn. Ellery helped without being asked. She collected paper pieces in the handy container of her sling and then dumped them in the plastic bag Claudia had brought from the garage. When Sarah Jane Bergin came over to ask what had caused the paper blizzard, I told her that having a cat was easier than having two teenage daughters. I didn't go into details. Sarah Jane, very pleasant again, tactfully asked no questions and never mentioned her painting. We did talk a few minutes about the possibility of getting one of Moxie's kittens for Ellery, and she also told me Trevor Eddy would begin to renovate the kitchen, an upstairs bathroom, and do a number of miscellaneous repairs next week. I cut her off, excused myself, and escaped into the house.

When Peter came home that same night, he had the tense and shaken look of a sole disaster survivor. I thought he was still focused on Claudia's paper blizzard, although, with some tiny scraps still clinging to high tree branches and a few paper bits visible in the unreachable center of the border hedges, the front yard was pristinely green again.

With all of it, I'd forgotten tonight was the night. Greavy had returned from vacation.

"He took it badly." Peter's voice was tremolo. "We took him by surprise, I guess. Asked him to step into Solow's office, offered him a Coke, and he thought we'd just asked him in to hear about his trip."

We were sitting on the terrace together; as soon as Claudia had come home, she'd gone directly to her room with a bag of nacho chips and a bunch of grapes, without more than a "hi" to me, and no words for Peter. She had the rosary around her neck, like a necklace over her T-shirt. Ellery had gone to talk to Sarah Jane about the new kittens. Peter and I were alone.

The very qualities of compassion and heart that make Peter an excellent physician, make him unsuited to be both a physician and a man at peace with the wheel of life. It took me all these years to see how easily he bruises. "So, how did it end?"

"We both, very gently, pointed out the recent events—the dozing off in his chair, the prescription error, the omission of correct record-keeping, errors on patients' charts, and I just could see that in the middle of this old, rock-hard face, there was such despair, I tell you, Lib, I couldn't stand to look at it. Solow took it in stride, but for me—it was hell."

As he spoke, it occurred to me that while the softie couldn't stand to see another's torment, I couldn't bear to look at his. "When he finally shuffled out, Greavy looked as if we'd already chosen his pallbearers and the wood grain of his casket."

"Next week he could have written a prescription that poisoned someone."

"I think what I can't stand to see is someone's light permanently extinguished. By me."

I was silent, thinking not of Greavy, but of Claudia.

So was he. "What was Claudia like today?" Peter said a minute or two later.

"You saw it. Today her light is also extinguished."

Peter rattled the ice in his glass. "Claudia will be bouncing in here with a new beau before Labor Day."

Such an old-fashioned word: How had we gone from *beau* to *stud* in one generation? "Pete, I hope you're right."

"Lib, it's a sure thing."

After he stopped drinking, our navigator had almost always been infallible. When it came to health and medication, investments, vacation venues, even friends, his choices were meticulous. I'd trusted his judgment in every department and had never been let down. Now, he ran the back of his finger across his mustache, looked up at the sky, and told me he thought it looked like rain. Sure enough, when we were halfway through making quiet love a few hours later, it began to pour.

# Chapter Four

Ellery and I were driving home from the orthopedist's about two weeks later when she asked me to drop her off at the junior-high schoolyard. She said the crowd that was stuck in Crandall ("the leftovers") hung out there watching summer softball games. Her new cast was smaller and less cumbersome, would be removed in two to three weeks. I noted that Albertson, Peter's colleague and former squash partner, spent much more energy describing his new Japanese rock garden than discussing Ellery's mending bones.

"Will she be able to get back on a horse by the end of this month?" Discussing Japanese gardeners made his eyes gleam; Ellery's fractures did not. Politely, he said he thought there should be no problems riding, but recommended physical therapy before she returned to a normal schedule of athletics.

"Perhaps she should think about giving up camp this summer," he said, with a hefty sigh. In any case, as soon as his rock garden was finished, he would be inviting us all over to see it.

I stole a glance at Ellery, expecting despair. I pictured the trunk in our basement, half filled with tin canteens, flashlight, flannel nighties, romance paperbacks, a sleeping bag and brand-new jodhpurs, yet she didn't turn a hair. Six weeks ago, when she'd broken her arm, she'd acted as if the universe had been decimated by an act of God in one lightning spill at the Red Riding Hood Stables. Horses were her life and breath, but that was then. Here was quintessential teenage resilience. Misery one moment, new earrings the next.

Even Claudia. Two nights ago, when Peter and I came home from the movies, as we drove into the garage, we thought we heard the plink of strings. As soon as we opened the kitchen door, all was silent. "She was playing the harp while we were out," Peter whispered. "We heard it. 'Ode to Joy,' Beethoven. Didn't we, Lib?" I wasn't sure, but he was beaming. I thought it was too early to expect Claudia to have recovered from Ess. She was still ice to us both, often stood looking out the window at nothing much, listening to loud, minor-key, heart-ripping country music up in her room. Smoking Marlboros or Gauloises behind the locked bathroom door, the French videos abandoned on the floor of her room. Sleeping with his gift bracelet on her arm, the rosary hanging on a hook over her desk, thanks to Marguerita, who had found it lying on the floor and taken the trouble to soak the beads in Liquid Joy. More than once, I'd seen Ess's dented black van pass our house. I'd watched it slow down, caught sight of the flash of Ess's black mirror sunglasses as it went by, once or twice heard the music blasting from the car radio, but I never told Peter.

Now I saw it again, parked at the schoolyard as I dropped Ellery off. "Isn't that Ess's van?" I asked her.

"He's here all the time," Ellery said. "I feel sorry for him. After all the graduations were over, he got laid off at the limo service. All he's doing these days is walking dogs for the vet and moping about Claudia. He bites his cuticles. And you know what, Mommy? He told me he quit drinking forever four years ago, but now every time I look at him I see he's got a can of Bud in his hand."

"I feel sorry for him, too, but look, he's too old to be pining for a sixteen-year-old girl."

"I told him he's going to ruin his life, drinking. 'You'll end up in the subbasement of nowhere,' is what I said."

This twelve-year-old sagacity must have come from substance-abuse school programs and television public-service documentaries, not from Ellery's own experience. I was in my fourth month with Ellery when Peter had his last drink, and she'd never seen her father except cold sober.

Her dreams and imaginings were an altogether different matter. "How did you get Daddy to stop, Mommy?" she wanted to know now.

"He stopped on his own," I said. On March 18th, 1988, the day of that season's worst snowstorm, I didn't say. I keep that memory under lock and key.

"Why? What made him?"

I didn't answer.

"Mommy?"

I wouldn't answer.

Darley was back. She called from Rowayton at eleven at night with the news that the airport limousine had broken down on I-95 and that Meggie had rallied at the Ethel Carpenter Nursing Home and was responding positively to Procardia XL. Peter had been right to prevent her canceling the trip, Peter was always right. This had been a memorable cruise, extraordinary. She's seen the most beautiful rainbow of her life, right over Delos, it was like a painting in the Metropolitan Museum. "Mykonos, it should have its own flag, it's unbelievable!" But for the moment, she was tired. Peter took the call on his side of the bed and I picked up the extension. He told her she did not sound as if she'd flown in from Athens and then been stuck in her seat on the highway for two hours. She sounded as if she'd "just replaced some batteries." She giggled, sounding like one of Claudia's friends. "Well, I met some nice people."

"Wait a minute—do I smell romance?" he asked.

She has a throaty smoker's giggle, although she quit cigarettes long ago.

"Hang up, Peter, darling. You go to sleep, like a good boy. Lib, are you there?"

The good boy replaced the receiver and turned his attention back to the play-offs on CNN.

"Well, Lib, I've met a judge." Ah, a judge. She elongated the vowel, sounding southern. A *federal* judge, it turned out, retired. Widowed twice. With homes in—she named a few American cities, Palm Beach being one, and Greenwich another. "And listen, Lib, he wears a chain across his necktie and parts his hair in the middle, but otherwise, a very handsome man."

"No doctors aboard?"

"None that played bridge."

"Leave it to you, Countess, you'll make him over to your specifications."

"He's right in my backyard," Darley continued. "We're going to the Westport Summer Theatre Saturday. We're seeing a new comedy. He used to play squash and hates politicians, just like you-know-who. Peter will just love him." Another hoarse laugh and then, "He's a year younger than I am and of course I lied off a few years. You won't tell, will you, darling?"

"Not a chance."

"Of course, no one is perfect, Lib, but more about that later. How are the girls? How is Ellery's arm? Tell me your news!"

* * *

I began seeing the white van with the green wrench logo in the Bergins' driveway—it had a newly broken brake light—was only slightly conscious of its being next door, and only once caught a glimpse of Trevor Eddy lifting something that looked like steel pipe out of the back of the van. He was wearing new squared-off sunglasses and his hair looked somewhat longer; otherwise, he was unchanged. Sooner or later, I'd just stroll past the hedges that separated our property from the Bergins' and exchange a few pleasant words with him, just to make it clear that there was nothing but good ashes left between us. I was so busy these days, driving Ellery here and there, shopping for our trip, getting the house in order, and trying to cook and freeze a few dinners for Marguerita just to make sure the girls didn't eat at fast-food places every night we were away, that there was hardly time even to glance across the hedge.

Until Sarah Jane Bergin telephoned me to tell me Moxie had given birth and Ellery and I were free to come over anytime and check out the litter. The return of postage stamps did not come up in the conversation. Ellery had already named the new kitten Dumpling without seeing which one of the five it would be, so it was, "Let's go, when can we go?" until she wore me down. I picked her up from school the very afternoon after the kittens came into the world and we went directly to the Bergins'.

Trevor Eddy's van was in the driveway, and so were two others that turned out to belong to members of his crew, one of whom was on a ladder leaning against the side of the house. Barry Bergin greeted us at the door. Sarah Jane had run to town to exchange switch plates and he was home early because he had a golf date and was just going up to change his clothes. He invited us in and led us straight to the kitchen, where a brown cardboard box stuffed with shredded newspaper held Moxie and company in a corner behind the pine hutch. Barry took Ellery's hand in a gesture I thought particularly warm, and led her to the cardboard nursery.

Like Sarah Jane, Barry had very curly hair (his was gray), a sharp nose, and fudge-syrup eyes. Unlike Sarah Jane, he looked middle-aged, was sinewy and hefty, with big, comic-strip size shoulders that seemed to bulge under his navy blue blazer, and sort of a permanent five o'clock shadow. I'd caught sight of him leaving for work in the morning and even then he looked as if he needed a shave. Peter called him "a nice guy with more jazz than most Wall Street types," and considered him "solid." It seemed to describe both the man and his body.

Ellery looked at the five mouselike, practically bald kittens, eyes pink and closed, and bodies squirming against each other, and dropped to her knees. "Oh, Mommy . . ." and went on, exclaiming over every tiny ear, bitsy paw, and teensy mouth in a stream of consciousness flow of veneration.

It was never easy to tell whether Barry was kidding; he always looked serious. "We meant to have Moxie spayed, but we kept putting it off, and now look. A big mistake. The ASPCA would be mad as hell."

Trevor Eddy appeared in the kitchen at about this point, arriving from upstairs at the door to the back staircase, and seeming to fill it completely. He also seemed to have to bend to step into the room, although the door was plenty high and wide enough for him. This was my own optical illusion, my having imagined him as sort of a Gulliver in a land of Lilliput, although he was hardly six feet tall and certainly not as wide as any door. His scalp was visible through the front of his hair and he was a bit heavier, but he had hardly changed. If he was surprised to see me, there was no hint. Just a smile that said everything in one silent stretch of lips over teeth. Sex, sex, sex. As he moved into the space between me and the refrigerator, the light in the room seemed to change into a dappled haze.

"You know Trevor Eddy, don't you?" Barry was doing introductions, while my mind wandered.

Trevor brought to mind every Marlon Brando, James Dean, Sean Penn hi-test part in every dark-lit movie. Attached to the back of his belt was a ring of a dozen or more keys that clanked whenever he took a step. I'd always wondered what locks those keys opened, and also remembered his diver's watch, with its big, expandable watchband circling a heavy-duty kind of don't-mess-with-me wrist.

"Of course. Trevor remodeled our upstairs. Built a wonderful phone booth and made us the first on this street with *two* bathroom skylights." There was the sizzle of eye contact now. Barry was saying something about northern light or southern light but I wasn't listening. I was remembering not the bathroom skylights, but the bedroom chaise.

"Oh, sure. I remember seeing it all right after Trevor finished it."

Now a bit of silence while Trevor continued the killer smile that had haunted my dreams for two years. "We have a problem with that damp back wall, Barry," he finally said, eyes off mine, calling Barry "Barry" instead of Mr. Bergin, letting the smile do a fade, and going on to detail the problems of rotting timber and crumbling masonry, and asking Barry if he could come up and take a look at what he'd uncovered in the back bedroom.

Barry threw me a covert look that said he wanted to be left out of rotting stucco and crumbling masonry, and I quickly gathered up my purse and told Ellery we'd have to be on our way.

Trevor took a step toward me. I had the mad thought he wanted to block my exit. "Aren't they something?"

he asked, chin pointing to the kitten box. He never looked at the newborns, but directed the question to me.

"They certainly are." All the banalities had a certain flavor and depth. I imagined the keys on his clinking chain were the keys to all the bedroom doors of the women he'd seduced. I tried to imagine him in real life, eating corn flakes with his wife, still alive, still not well, in some cozy small kitchen in Norwalk.

"It makes you want to pick them up and hold them, doesn't it?" he asked.

"Yes, mmm, yes."

"Or get into the box with the mama. Just lie down and get licked all over."

I laughed nervously and stole a quick look at Barry. These meaningful, loaded comments had slid right by him.

"What ever happened to Laszlo?" he asked now.

"You remember Laszlo?"

"One notched ear, four white paws."

It was like a code. He was telling me he hadn't forgotten our cat, therefore hadn't forgotten any of the rest of it, either. Here was a man who meant nothing whatsoever to me, but to this day, pushed his way aggressively, irritatingly, like the sun's afterimage on the eyelid, into my quotidian life.

Ellery, wearing her new gold studs (Claudia's gift) in her newly pierced-by-Daddy ears, the new Swatch Putti (Peter's gift) on her wrist, and dressed in the Lauren outfit (my gift), her hair apricot-shampooed and coconut-conditioned and fingernails gleaming in No More Blues Pink, stepped into the front seat of her father's car, and adjusted the seat belt across her decked-out, spiffed-up thirteen-year-old body in the passenger side of Peter's

Lexus. Birthday girl up front with Daddy is family tradition.

The new smaller cast slipped easily into and out of the short flowered Lauren sleeve, and this summer day all seemed smooth to him between the girls and me, and between the girls and Peter, whose spirits were higher this week than last. He seemed somewhat recovered from Greavy's actual departure from the office and his practice, which took place on the last day of June. There would be a retirement dinner at some later time, possibly not until everyone was back in town in September and Peter's reaction, comalike silences and heavy treadmill activity, now seemed behind him. Claudia and I sat in the back, Claudia all in white, but sparked up with the painted bead necklace Darley had brought her from some Caribbean port last year. The Countess would come by with her Greek gifts tomorrow, assuming the mechanic got her Seville's electrical system back in operation.

As Peter drove our car under the porte cochere, the parking attendant, dressed in a blazer with the club crest over his heart, greeted us politely, opening doors, and standing at attention as Peter stepped out of the car. "This is the third Lexus in a row," he said, shaking his head incredulously, as he slipped into the driver's seat. He had the neat, clipped, blond look of a British Isles palace guard, and seemed the type who could stand at attention with heels locked indefinitely.

"Is he the one?" Ellery whispered to Claudia.

"Will you please shut up? Someone will hear you," Claudia hissed as we stepped through the glass-and-wrought-iron doors into the club's lounge.

"The one who what?" I asked.

"Sshh." Claudia sashayed past me, past Ellery, preceding us all into the dining room, walking behind the maître d', totally oblivious of Miss Manners.

"He's in her French class. His name is Kevin Bevan. It rhymes. Is that dumb?"

I felt all eyes were on Claudia as usual, the maiden aglow in pristine white, hips swinging through the place like it was a runway and she was about to get a bunch of roses put in her arms. Stealing more thunder from the birthday girl. I wanted to promote Ellery, get a spotlight on her on the first day of her teenage life, something tangible, a real birthday ego boost she needed more than a watch or ear studs. Tonight, for once, it actually happened. Mary Frances O'Connell, ubiquitous presence in the club dining room, president of the ladies' auxiliary and wife of the club commodore, remarked that while Claudia looked as radiant as ever, Ellery had been entirely transformed since seen at the swimming pool last summer! She had already heard about the unfortunate riding accident, and although she adored horses and always had, betting on them, not getting on them, was her motto. Mary Frances's husband, who always looked to me like one of the posthumous oil-portraits that hung in the club's upstairs lounge, said that we had hit the jackpot. Two dynamite daughters. Did we want to trade them for his three sons? "He's only kidding," Mary Frances, swirling red wine in her glass, quickly said.

Ellery and Claudia were giggling together. It had to do with the busboy, who had poured water into our glasses a few minutes ago, and put the basket of rolls on the table. They were in total accord this time: He was adorable, except for the geeky haircut. Nobody would want to be seen with him until it grew out. Peter took a sip of his water and then put it down definitively. "Maybe we could talk about something more meaningful than busboys," he suggested.

*"Mon Dieu!* There he goes. He is always switching us

to the educational channel!'' I threw Claudia a grateful look, sending her my silent version of an Instant Message. If there were icicles hanging from her behavior toward her father yesterday or even an hour ago, she'd managed to melt them. It was often that way with my older daughter, whose moods, like the air currents during some changeable weather patterns, would alter unpredictably. ''If you don't like the weather, wait fifteen minutes,'' people say about the climate in some arctic regions; this was also true of Claudia. Her icicles had melted; I sent her telepathic thanks, but she was not looking my way. She was letting her eyes sweep the dining room. No other boys spotted, she turned her attention back to her father. ''So, what shall it be, Daddy? The Persian Gulf? Fossil beds? Safer reactor designs?''

''Well, girls, I can't help but want to try to elevate the subject matter. All these years I've waited for you to grow up so we could all be adult people together, discussing intelligent subjects—ideas versus busboys. How would it be if we talked about what's happening in Asia, or global warming, or, Claud—your French class? How's it going?''

''But you asked her that yesterday, remember, Daddy?'' I noted for the first time that Ellery had applied a bit of mascara to her upper and lower lashes. It added a glossy, spidery glimmer to her eyes, and made them seem bluer and lighter.

Claudia nodded energetically. ''Every day, practically. Daddy loves talking about French class. Loves it to pieces.''

Peter, unflapped, picked up the basket and offered me a roll, which I accepted.

''So, Claudia. What do you do in class?''

The girls nudged each other and simultaneously burst into whoops of hilarity. ''Speak French!'' And while Claudia bunched up her hair and squinted at the new arrivals, Ellery looked at me and shook her head and said the four words to describe Daddy were "im possible and hope less," which description Claudia absolutely thought was "per fect." More giggles.

When the waitress put Peter's club soda on the table, he called her Madonna. "You look exactly like her, doesn't she, Lib?"

"Come on!" the waitress said, pleased to bits.

"Only you're better looking!" Peter said. "Isn't she?"

"Absolutely." *Oh, for Christ's sake,* I thought.

The girls rolled their eyes. "In her dreams," they simultaneously said, as soon as she'd walked away, and covered their mouths so the laughter wouldn't be heard at the next table.

After the salad and entree, our Madonna-like waitress brought out a little cake with the thirteen candles and one for good luck I'd ordered on the telephone this morning, and we sang, joined by the diners at tables at all sides. Ellery cut the best piece, the one with the candy raspberry slices, praised the club baker to the skies, and as she lifted her fork to her lips, I heard someone say, "He's a prominent cardiologist. Wonderful family." I could practically feel myself expand and puff. Not perfect, but yes, "top-notch"! Peter and I had done it together, put in sixteen years of dedicated family work. I thought at that moment that getting it right was just a question of staying on top of things, keeping both eyes open, being patient. Peter was right and maybe his mother even had a point. One had to be strong, get rid of the Esses along the way. Be watchful every minute.

Kevin Bevan fetched our car, pretending not to eye Claudia. When she slipped into the backseat next to me, I saw her reorganize her face to hide the fluttery little smile she'd sent his way through the dim light of the electrified lantern that illuminated the porte cochere. As the car door closed and Peter hit the gas pedal, Claudia's head swiveled around to catch one more glimpse of him before we pulled out of sight.

As soon as we got past the stone portals at the club exit, Ellery turned to face her sister. "You think he's cute? You really think he's *cute*?"

"Sort of."

"Boy, I'm glad I don't have your taste in my mouth, Claud. I don't know how you can go from Ess to him. I really don't."

*"Chacun à son goût,"* Claudia said, as Peter looked up into the rearview mirror to catch my eyes.

"See? French," he said and he turned up the car radio to 104.3 ("Ssshhh, girls, let's listen to this!") and Tchaikovsky's Quartet in D drowned them both out.

Marguerita has moods. She cleans when I'm at home and watches television when I'm not and cries at the drop of a hat, not to speak of the drop of a dish. Her English has hardly improved in the three years she's been with us, and she still gets pronouns mixed ("my brother, she very sick"), but otherwise, we communicate pretty well. I don't like to see Marguerita cry, although her reasons are often unclear. It is usually a broken heart, although once it was because someone broke into the room she rents in Bridgeport and stole her television set.

Putting her in charge of Claudia and Ellery when we are in Europe is not a great risk. Marguerita is twenty-nine years old and has been on her own since she was sixteen. I feel she is qualified for two weeks of light governing, or at least, making sure the doors are locked, the oven is off, and there are not the kind of parties held to which police have to be summoned. She is capable of those rudimentary overseeing skills, and calling 911, the doctor, or a neighbor, in the event of a crisis.

So I prepared lists, numbers, frozen foods, and wrote out directions, pinning Darley's number, Annie's, the Bergins', the fire and police telephone numbers over the kitchen and bedroom extensions, and I put money into envelopes marked FOOD, ALLOWANCES, and MISCELLANEOUS, and in the office I duplicated our itinerary, adding telephone numbers in red Magic Marker.

"I'll call your house every day. Don't worry." Annie Wickes and I were walking through a house in which a tag sale was in progress. We do this often, and sometimes uncover treasures, like the genuine layered Belter chair and an eighteenth-century cellarette we found in March. As Peter once said, while his life is about saving lives between breakfast and dinner, I deal for the most part with ghosts. Who owned, bought, polished, used these bedsteps, that fire screen? What faces appeared in that cheval glass almost two hundred years ago? Who was born or died in that mission bedstead, or made love in it last week?

We examined some Tiffany lamp replicas with outrageous price tags, and went upstairs to check out the bedrooms. The master bedroom was all built-ins and modern, with one interesting nineteenth-century weathervane standing on a dresser, marked NOT FOR SALE. Annie meandered into another bedroom.

What I spotted a few minutes later was a painted-over Canterbury music rack, which was standing in the corner of a child's room and overflowing with toys. I examined the front, the sides, took off the toys and tipped it over to see the underside. 1790. I looked at the price tag. They were giving it away.

I ran my fingers along the open back shelf. In our computer back in the office we had a listing of at least twelve people who would be interested in this piece. Serendipity exhilarates; the prospect swept me into euphoria.

Annie wandered into the room. "Anything good?" She stood in the path of a beam of light coming through the glass panel window, and she looked celestial. It was as if she'd been brought into this room from some other sphere to touch my find with heavenly luck.

"They painted it *pink*." I told her it was certainly two hundred years old, and definitely looked like the real thing.

She walked up to the music rack to take a closer look. Annie tends to be skeptical enough always to pull me down to earth. "Are you sure it's not a repro?" Sometimes she makes me feel as if I'm back in school, justifying a perfectly justifiable answer on exam day.

I picked it up, turned it over again. "Seventeen ninety, I'm pretty sure," I said firmly, and walked it over to the window to see it in better light. She was right behind me.

"Yes, look here—" I began, pointing to the manufacturer's name, barely visible, but clearly definable, and pulled back the translucent ecru curtain to shed even more light on the lettering.

While she rummaged in her purse to pull out what turned out to be a magnifying glass, I tried not to be impatient. Simultaneously, I glanced from her pocketbook to the music stand and then, quite accidentally, out the window and into the street.

I quickly set the music stand down. "Oh, good lord," I said, and strained toward the window for a better view.

Annie had pulled out the magnifying glass and assumed I was talking about the piece of furniture. "What's wrong with it?"

"Look down there!"

"What? At the woman walking two poodles?"

"No! Across the street! Over there, under the tree. That's Ess's van!"

"Really?" Annie let out a quiet laugh that sounded more like the whir of an electric fan. "I thought it was part of this sale—one of the antiques!"

"It's not funny. He's probably followed me here, Annie."

"He has?"

"I'm sure of it."

"But why?"

"I don't know, but Peter's forbidden Claudia to see him. Last week, he called us in the middle of the night. . . . He sounded so—desperate. Scary, when I think about it. Maybe—it could be—he might have it in for us." *God knows what's going on in his head.*

"Well, shall we call the police then, or what?"

"I can't have him arrested for simply parking his van on the street, though, can I? How can I even prove he's following me? Annie, do you think I'm being paranoid?"

"Why don't we just go down and ask him what he's doing here? It's broad daylight and there are zillions of people around. He doesn't—he doesn't have a gun or anything, does he?"

"Oh, no! Not that I know of, anyway."

"So, what's the risk?"

"I don't know."

"I'll go with you. We'll just act—friendly. I mean, what's the worst thing that could happen?"

"You're right. What can happen?"

A woman with Heidi braids wrapped around her head was trying to maneuver a large etched mirror through the front door, and Annie and I had to wait while she cleared the jamb and managed the front steps. Annie knew her—from the Holy Rosary Society, it turned out—and offered to give her a hand.

"No, not necessary, I have a helper," she said, and she pointed across the street, at Ess's van. "Salvatore! Over here!" she called, in an operatic soprano. "Did you get the lamps in?" and then, her voice trilled into an alto filled with pure joy, "I've had a field day here, a field day!"

There was Ess, an open denim vest over shirtless chest, innocently opening the back of his van and trying to push a drum table through its doors.

"I'll be right with you, Mrs. L," he called to the woman with the mirror, and then spotted me, did a modified double take, and sprinted across the street to take the burden from Mrs. L's arms.

"Howyadoin', Mrs. E?" he asked. Below the sunglasses was his usual no-emotion expression, this time with the most subtle hint of a smile caught before it could get away. As he lifted the glass, it caught the sun and I got a glimpse of my reflection: lipstick talked off, shiny forehead and cheeks, checked blouse knotted above khaki skirt; then, almost simultaneously, as he lifted it, I looked past the mirror and spotted the new Byzantine cross emblazoning the tight skin of his bicep. Block letters formed the design on the crosspiece of the ink blue cross—the size of a newborn's foot—in the space between his shoulder and elbow. I imagined hours spent in some boardwalk tattoo parlor, pictured him sitting nonchalantly in a chair while the needle was stitching his skin. I must have blinked a few times to rid myself of the glare of the sun in the mirror, and on second sight noted that the cross was also embellished with tattooed barbed wire snaking around its transverse and encircling its base like ivy. There was drab red lettering on the crosspiece I couldn't immediately read, and then, shading my eyes by putting my hand over my eyebrows and squinting hard, I could.

Ess caught me staring.

"Modern art," he said, and, lifting the mirror high in his arms, shuffled down the walk, then stopped, turned, and asked me to give my best to the doctor and the girls and wished me a nice day.

"You're perspiring like crazy," Annie said, as I watched him go.

"Till death us do part," I mumbled. "He had that tattooed on his arm!"

As if I were handicapped, she turned me around and led me back into the house by my elbow. "He's a kid. He's harmless," she said. "For all we know, he could have been thinking about his truck."

"Not a chance, Annie. He was talking about Claudia—and us," I said.

By the time we got upstairs, the pink music stand was in the arms of a young man. "I can't believe they're asking forty dollars for this!" he was saying. His wife said, "Maybe we can get them down to thirty." Her voice was low register, as if she didn't want anyone to hear, and possibly outbid her. "I'll have such fun refinishing it."

"It's just as well they're taking it," Annie said to me under her breath. "I didn't feel good about stealing the thing."

*"Stealing?"*

"Well, we know what it's worth, after all."

"Don't be such a saint, Annie. It doesn't pay to wind up in the middle of a birdbath."

"I'm a Catholic. It's like being in an elastic harness that only stretches so far. It's a safety thing, see?"

"Lucky you," I said.

I didn't mention my encounter with Ess or his tattoo to Peter. When he came home I made him a cocktail of cranberry and grapefruit juice with a squirt of tonic, and poured myself a plain tonic over lots of ice. I'd pretty much given up the Tom Collinses I used to love, hardly drank wine with dinner, and if I yearned for an icy beer now and then, I'd manage with a Diet Coke instead. A small sacrifice; I was always aware of what Peter himself had given up over the years for the sake of our own family and partnership. He'd quit not only wine, beer, sake, martinis, and gin and tonics. Over the years he'd given up so much more. Flying lessons, for one. I'd watched him climb into the baby plane, which looked like something made out of folded paper, as it lifted off the ground and came this close to tangling with telephone wires. I carried on until he promised us all never again.

He quit squash because he dislocated his shoulder once, and once was hit in his protective eyeglasses, which flew off his face and left his eyelid slightly bruised. "It's no sport for a surgeon with a family to support," Peter said, and the squash rackets went to the resale shop. He put an end to skiing because the girls and I didn't take well to the bitter weather on the Vermont slopes and one or the other of us invariably caught the flu or twisted a frozen muscle. He stopped sailing; it took time, hours he preferred spending at the club watching the girls learn to swim, at the stable watching them on the backs of horses, or even at the ballet recitals we'd sat through year after year before they both gave up dancing. If he felt he'd made sacrifices, given up half his life, he never said it.

The Monday after the tag sale, there was a message for me from Maribel Greavy. She wanted me to come by to give her ideas on pricing some pieces she didn't want to take to the new place, pieces she'd inherited or collected over the years. Her voice sounded like a mountain echo. "I heard Dr. Greavy gave someone a prescription for antihistamines instead of nitroglycerine recently,'' Annie said to me, after I'd hung up. ''Is that true?'' I told Annie it was an outrageous distortion and hoped she'd set people straight if she had the opportunity. The Greavys were retiring to Hilton Head and he was tired, not dangerous.

''I'm sick! I'm so sick!'' Claudia was standing in the doorway to our room at three in the morning. I shot up and so did Peter.

''I think . . . I'm . . . going . . . to . . . I think I'm going to barf,'' she said.

Peter snapped on the light. He sat right up, blinking his eyes, reached for his glasses. Claudia was standing in the doorway, looking like an apparition in a white summer nightie, one hand wrapped around her neck, the other curled around the door frame. I jumped up and let her lean on me while I led her quickly into our bathroom.

''Oh, God, oh, God, oh, God.'' She was shaking, and her face was covered with sweat. A moment later, Peter, knotting the belt of his seersucker bathrobe, was behind us while she sank to her knees and gagged over the open toilet.

''What'd you eat, sweetie?'' Peter asked Claudia, who couldn't answer. She'd started to heave over the bowl. ''What'd she eat?'' he asked me. I was holding her forehead, turning my own head away and trying not to get queasy myself.

''We all had the same thing for dinner. Broiled shrimp. That wouldn't make her sick. I used fresh garlic. The salad was made with romaine and tomatoes Annie brought to the office from her garden yesterday. That's all. Brown rice. And that sourdough bread from the French bakery. How could that make her sick? She's been at home all night, watching a rented video with

Ellery. If we're all right, how could any of that make her sick?"

"Maybe it was something she ate earlier, at lunch."

"Possibly. Or a bug. Or those purple plums. Too many of those. Couldn't that be it, Pete?"

"Well, maybe."

"She could have had one bad shrimp, that's possible."

"Hmmm. Right."

"Claudia, sweetie, are you all right?" She'd stopped vomiting but was still hanging over the open bowl of the john.

Peter was stroking her back, murmuring, "It's okay, Claud. Get it all up."

She was sick two more times, and finally, I walked her back to her bed, turned down the air conditioner—she said she was freezing—and pulled up the extra summer blanket that was folded at the foot.

"Mommy, I never felt so sick in my life," she said, eyes at half-mast. Peter had brought up Coke and ice in a glass and she was taking sips. I told him I'd sit with her a while, to go back to bed. When he'd left, Claudia said, "I thought I was definitely checking out. I'm still spinning. No, wait, the room is spinning. No, wait, the bed—but don't tell Daddy. He gets totally hyper."

"Well, you'll be okay now, sweetie. I'll wait here till you fall asleep. I bet it was too many purple plums. Did you eat any?"

"Just two."

"Maybe you ought to skip French tomorrow?"

"Oh, I don't think so. No, I'll be all right by then, not to worry." She sighed, and I remembered Kevin Bevan was in her class and she'd recover in time for French, no doubt about it. Peter had been right. Ess already seemed as dim a memory as last year's fireworks. By the amber glow of the glass teddy bear night-light, I watched her eyes flutter open once before they closed tight, and her eyelashes cast their centipede shadows on her sunburned cheeks, and I caught myself smiling. Relief was distinctly a distilled form of pleasure. She was exhausted, but fine again.

Peter was not in bed. I found him in the kitchen, the refrigerator door open, half of its contents spread on the kitchen table.

"Pete, what are you doing, for heaven's sake?" Some appliance, possibly the fluorescent tubing over the stove or the automatic ice-maker, purred electrically. The clock, a marginally reliable electrified 1897 schoolhouse artifact, said 4:10.

"Some of this stuff is moldy, Lib," he said.

I stood barefoot, hardly aware of the stone tiles, cold as winter pavement, under my feet.

"You're going to clean out the refrigerator now?"

"Well, I couldn't sleep anyway. I was curious to see what could have made the poor kid so damn sick. Doesn't Marguerita ever clean out the refrigerator?"

I started to answer but he cut me off.

"I mean, some of this must have been back here, God knows how long." Peter was pulling out jars of pickle relish, pimento, and a covered dish of hard-boiled eggs. "How long have those eggs been here?" he asked.

"I just boiled them this morning. I was going to make egg salad. Actually, at 10:03 this morning."

"Salmonella is typically carried by eggs, Lib."

"Peter, you're taking a severe tone with me. You're acting as if Claudia's being sick was my fault."

"Lib, please, dear, don't get defensive. I'm just checking this stuff out. A lot of it should have been thrown out long ago. Marguerita doesn't sound very competent."

"Ah, that's what it's about."

"What? What what's about?"

"Marguerita."

"I don't like to see my daughter sick as a dog. I see people I don't even care about suffering day in day out and I don't even deal well with that. If my daughter has salmonella—"

"*My* daughter?"

"Okay, *our* daughter."

"Peter, let's go to bed."

"I couldn't sleep now on a bet. I might as well finish this job."

"Pete, I'll help you, and tomorrow, Marguerita can scrub the whole inside of the refrigerator. Anyway, I don't think Claudia had a serious attack of salmonella, if she had it at all. She's fast asleep and wants to go to class tomorrow. Obviously she's not all that sick."

"It's a good thing this happened while we were still here," Peter said.

"Well, that's true."

"Yes! When I think about it . . . what if we were already gone?"

"Marguerita could have handled it."

"I wonder."

"Pete, I think you're building a case against Marguerita."

Peter stopped holding a jar of ketchup to the light to look at me. "Why would I do that?"

"It's about going away, I think. Leaving the girls. You never like leaving them. And now you're saying we're putting them in the care of a woman who doesn't know enough to clean mold out of the refrigerator. An incompetent, in other words."

Peter set down the ketchup and wiped the palm of his hand across his mustache, as if he'd been the sick one. "Okay, sweetie. Teenagers are not easy to leave. This is a new and tough world. I see them wheeled in on stretchers day after day. Car wrecks, drugs, alcohol, botched abortions, suicides. All sorts of accidents—remember that thunderstorm a few weeks ago? A kid in Stamford thought it would be fun to swim in his grandparents' flooded basement. He touched a wire and—bingo—electrocuted. Fourteen years old. In Hartford a kid was trying to walk a high wire between two buildings. One misstep, *pffft*. Born in '87, dead in '01. One minute they're fine, the next minute—well, I don't want to think about it now, Lib. You know how unexpectedly—hmm—unexpected they can be." He picked up a jar of pimento and put it down again. "I admit it. I don't like to leave the girls alone for two weeks. And I'm not sure that kid still isn't trouble."

"Ess."

"Right."

"Are you saying you want to cancel the trip?"

I read the answer in the slump of his shoulders, the reappearance of the little electricity in his upper lip. It came, it went. "We'll go," he said, and he twisted up his hands at the wrists, as if he were carrying a tray of drinks, "but that kid gives me the creeps. I don't know, Lib. I just don't trust him."

"At some point, we have to let go," I said, remembering the fresh red tattoo. "Some things we can't hang on to forever."

"I see it always comes down to the same thing in the final frame. It's not antiques or sex or golf, Lib, no. Those things all pass. It's *family*. Blood. It's all that matters, ultimately."

Lucas Greavy's housekeeper answered the door, keeping one hand on the collar of an old beige German shepherd who looked more likely to roll over and fall asleep than to attack unwelcome visitors, but then the housekeeper seemed to be acting out some immemorial custom, leading me to the living room, pointing to an olive velvet wingback chair and telling me "the Mrs." would be "soon coming, please."

We'd been to the Greavys' years ago, for a dinner party honoring a colleague; I remembered the convex eagle mirror over the fireplace, the festive Madeira lace tablecloth on an endless length of Gothic revival dining-room table, gleaming wineglasses in deep jewel colors under a bright chandelier. The table was bare now except for a bowl filled with a dried arrangement of tired flowers, and the living room furniture had been slipcovered in a yellowing crewel-design fabric. Everything was muted, hushed, and reminiscent of some other, finer time.

The minute stretched into five, and Mrs. Greavy, arms surrounded by the aluminum cuffs of her twin canes, appeared in the arched stucco door in a long, flowered dress with a starchy white collar, gray hair held back with a velvet band, a grown-old Alice in Wonderland smelling of fresh floral cologne.

There seemed to be no way to help her move easily from the threshold of the living room across the carpet and into the one strangely mismatched white, nail-studded leather chair opposite mine. She managed it finally, and placed the canes against each of the arms of the chair. I noticed for the first time that her face was blown out and up on each side, as if she'd stuck cotton balls into each cheek.

"I'm up to my kazoo in steroids." Seated, it was her opening sentence, the prologue. "Which is why I look like this."

I protested as sincerely as I could, telling her not much change was noticeable, when in fact, I remembered another face entirely. I'd always thought of Maribel Greavy as being very nicely designed, with noble and delicate features, like those in the framed silhouette pictures women of my mother's generation hung in hallways. Her hair had lost its volume and luster, frizzed around her headband as if she'd just come in from the rain. When she wasn't talking, the corners of her mouth drooped, reminding me of someone about to deliver a eulogy.

"Inez is going to take you around, Libby. I hope you don't mind my not coming along. Every step"—she moved her hand through the air as if she were greeting a ghost—"it's probably a good idea to leave this house and move to a one-level place, which is what we have down in Hilton Head. Although Lib, I don't know what I'm going to do with all that sunlight. What am I going to do with all that vitamin D?" She let out a laugh that was part cough, part sob.

Having been there once for four days six years before with Peter at a medical convention, I pumped it up, about the easy life, leisure, and the new friends they'd be meeting, piling up cliché after cliché. "They say the restaurants are absolutely marvelous."

She shook her head. "We don't go to restaurants, dear." Her face took a nosedive. She meant, *we don't go anywhere anymore. We are the capsizing pair, being swept along life's final undertow, with you helping to give the final push.*

"Libby, my dear, we built this house. We are the cobwebs and creaks here. And you know what? Lucas has stopped sleeping. That's what." She turned her head away toward the dog, who had collapsed at her feet, head between his paws, eyes up at me, and I looked at her sitting erect in that out-of-place white leather chair and ran right out of knowing what to say.

I had my clipboard under my arm as the housekeeper preceded me up the stairs. She led me first through the bedrooms and then to an upstairs study, then excused herself, leaving me to examine the pieces Maribel Greavy had instructed her to show me. I made notes and jotted next to each item its probable worth, found an interesting but not too valuable Maryland pierced-tin pie safe with a turn-button lock, and a colonial secretary that might have been worth more if someone hadn't "wedded" a bookcase to its top. In the upstairs hall was a Pennsylvania blanket chest decorated with unicorns, men on horseback, and floral designs. That piece, I was certain, was worth a fortune.

I was finishing up in the master bedroom when my eye fell on the family photographs on the Federal chest of drawers which had been placed between two elaborately swagged windows. I glanced at the Greavys' wedding picture, framed in mother-of-pearl and ebony, a barely recognizable young pair formally posed, the pallid bride, with thin lipsticked lips showing the remnants of a smile, the groom, already losing hair, somber. This wedding picture might have been taken the year I was born. There were other family photos scattered around this large one, small satellites in eclectic picture frames. My eye fell on one I'd never seen, or seen and forgotten, of the four of us, taken at a hospital charity event by a professional photographer. I examined the thin and wishy-washy me in that taffeta dress I'd thought elegant then. Dr. Greavy had asked me to dance; his wife was already afflicted, and encouraging us, "Go ahead, take a spin, you two," and now I remembered something Greavy had said to me as we did our five-minute foxtrot on the dance floor. It was a year or two after he'd brought Peter home from Wuzzy's.

"You two have conquered unhappiness," he'd said to me as we did our spins and dips, "but don't forget, what a victory may bring, a misstep can take away."

I quickly put the picture back. What had followed that winter, perhaps a month or six weeks later, was the snowstorm, that sinister day that almost decimated our family. So, the fragility of Peter's temperance was always with me, and it was at odd moments and unexpectedly, that my thoughts cut free and flew back there, to that afternoon in March. I had a mission cut out for me—to keep my husband's precincts and climate tranquil, his soul at peace. The possibility of a misstep was never far from my consciousness, but I wanted Prague. And it never occurred to me that leaving the girls for two short weeks could constitute any kind of risk.

# Chapter Five

Arm in arm, Peter and I walked down Wenceslas Square. Still somewhat groggy from jet lag and airplane wine, we were hanging on to each other, a pair of young-again lovebirds soaking in the scene: natives, tourists, gypsies, all wearing the same running shoes and jeans, shops selling glass with window after window displaying vases, dishes, pitchers, bowls, cups, and figurines, push-carts loaded with vegetables and fruits, street vendors peddling souvenirs, outdoor cafés as lively as those in Paris, clerks in kiosks slathering mustard on Czech dogs—in the shadow of majestic Gothic spires and curving turrets, in a city eloquent with architecture and spectral with history, we were kids again. How liberating it felt to walk this exotic street with its mixture of scaffolding and scrollwork, ladders and lintels, next to a man who was now neither a doctor nor a father, but just at this moment, exclusively my husband. Here we were, strolling along something with the unpronounceable name of Václavské Náměstí, thrown into another age; Peter relaxed and Crandall, Connecticut, was left far behind.

We found a small restaurant that first evening, a cozy inn-type of place near the Charles Bridge. The dark-wood-and-stone floor quaintness might have been imported directly from Elizabethan England. The food offered was fried Wiener schnitzel and roast everything else—pork, goose, duck, all with sauce or gravy, none of these intended for the guardians of cholesterol, but these two weeks, we would do as the Czechs did.

"Aren't you going to try some of the beer?" Peter asked me.

"No, I don't think so."

"I don't mind, Lib."

"I don't want any, really."

"You sure?"

"I'm sure." I was able to be high drinking only Mattoni mineral water, just like Carvalhelhos last year in Portugal, Kasvjet the year before in Scandinavia. It was a tiny miracle, to find unfunny things funny, to find attractive a person one has looked at every day for over twenty years, who is beginning to get the shadow of an extra chin, whose lower teeth—I just noticed for the first time—seemed to be moving slightly apart.

I touched the back of my husband's hair and smoothed it down where it leaned against his collar. Was it my perception or something here, in the air? Coddled by time, to me he looked mature but unchanged, frozen forever into his patrician handsomeness. He saw me looking at him, smiled, and a minute later, said, "Lib, you eat a sexy dumpling." Sex seemed so much more on our minds when we were halfway across the world from our own plumbing, our own telephone, the girls.

For dessert, the waiter suggested a Malakoff bombe, the chocolate specialty of the house.

Peter ordered two.

"Wait—," I said. "Is there any—I mean, is it made, by any chance, with alcohol?"

The waiter tilted his head and pursed his lips apologetically. He didn't understand. "M'dam?"

"Liqueur? Any liqueur in the bombe?"

I felt Peter's eyes on me.

"No, no liqueur," the waiter assured me. He shook his head and his hands like a minstrel singer.

"You're sure?"

"Libby." Peter put his hand on my arm.

"I'm sure, *paní.* A little coffee, fresh cream. But if you feel not good, I could ask the chef, to make for sure."

"Don't bother," Peter said, and then, after a silence, "Sometimes, we go too far, Libby. Too far. Don't we?"

When he said, "we," we both knew he meant me. Peter never mentions the boozy past, euphemizes the weekly meetings—"going to be with the friends of Bill W."—or doesn't mention them at all. If I inadvertently brush that spot on his inner arm, those old, faded and almost invisible scars, he pulls away as if the cut were fresh and still painful to the touch. And he never wears short-sleeved shirts, even in August, when the thermometer hits one hundred. So I knew better than to cross the line and act the watchdog, but couldn't stop myself. It was my own psychological, inadvertent twitch.

But soon we were amicably sharing the bombe, a silky chocolate milk pudding that tasted to me like the god of pastry had whipped it up himself. I decided the dessert was sensual. To me, tonight, everything was. My hand slid over Peter's on the table.

But by the time we got back to the hotel, we were both drowsy, and fell into almost immediate jet-lagged sleep. From which I awoke at 4:30, charged with sexual energy.

I got out of bed and went to the bathroom, and when I came back, Peter was in my bed, eyes closed, waiting for me. On vacation, we simultaneously wanted it. And sex far away from home seemed hungrier, needier and more uninhibited, complete with thrashing and vigor and the luxury of noisy moans—just what the doctor's wife ordered: a rousing erotic revival. After all those years of practice, we knew where to touch and where to kiss, when to hesitate. This is what I'd—we'd—needed. I felt I had Peter back. The honeyed and hot way it used to be. Peter stroked my hair. How long since Peter had stroked my hair? He sighed at the meltdown. It was so mindless and nice, the letting go. We'd been at sex for more than twenty years, fine-tuned it, and when it was good, it was still—after all this time—fervid and lovely.

For me, now would come the best part. He'd tell me what was in his heart. I'd tell him what was in mine. There never seemed to be a moment at home.

"Honey, I'm all worn out. We'll talk tomorrow."

"Tomorrow." I was disappointed.

"G'night."

"This is as good a time as any to tell you that I love you, Peter."

"Still?"

"Still."

"Ditto, sweetheart."

Peter rubbed my feet later, turned on the radio, had coffee sent up to the room, told me that he himself was feeling better than he had in months. He said he owed it all to me, I'd forced him to "move off that dime" and really cut free from Crandall for a couple of weeks. Solow could manage and so would the girls. As soon as we got back he was going to take one of the new 3-D photos and replace the old one of me he was still carrying in his wallet.

The next afternoon, on the banks of the Vltava River, in the shadow of the Charles Bridge, we were watching swans. It was after a beerless lunch of goulash at a restaurant famous for its dark beer, and we had already walked across the bridge, where Peter had photographed the Baroque saints' statues, soaring gulls, riverboats, in 3-D. Now he was aiming at these swans, with the idea of fitting one serenely floating bird on the surface of the river and another fluttering above it into the same frame with the bridge as a background. A few shots and then he turned and aimed it at me. "Move a little to the right, sweetie. Now, 'cheese.' Wait, lift your chin a bit. There we go—got it!"

"We have three shots left." He looked over my shoulder. "Let's get you over there, next to that guy in the ridiculous hat selling postcards, okay?" He took forever to position, to focus, to snap.

I smiled the broadest of smiles.

"A perfect subject, a perfect composition," Peter said.

*You are my life,* I thought, and tried not to look impatient.

We were in Peter's bed. At his request, I'd done a slow striptease to the radio music, a violin quartet playing Janacek, using the bedspread from my bed. I felt twenty again, lusty and free. The window was open; in the street below, an argument was beginning. Maybe a traffic altercation. Over the radio music, the escalating voices of two men were raised in verbal combat. It was a strange accompaniment to lovemaking, but we went over the top smoothly, as if the men below had turned into a twenty-piece orchestra playing love songs. Finally, the screaming and shouting subsided, a motor revved up, and a peaceful *Midsummer Night's Dream* oozed out of the radio.

"I wonder what they were fighting about." I sighed.

Peter said, "I bet they were brothers. It had the hysterical, maniacal, and frenetic sound of a sibling war."

"The girls are on your mind."

"Not for the last twenty minutes, sweetie."

After he filled a glass of water and put it on his night table, Peter got into bed and closed his eyes.

"Peter, last time you said we were going to talk."

He opened his eyes. "Okay, sweetie. You start."

"Well. When you put it like that, dear, I'm not sure I know what to say."

"Okay. We'll talk tomorrow, then."

"No, wait a minute. I think I want to say that sometimes I think I have it too good."

"Well, we do. We both do. No question about it."

"When we met, well, I thought, how would I ever make my own mark in his shadow? How would I carry my weight in a relationship where the man—you—has all this prestige and power and . . . and *gloss*? I thought I'd have to work too hard all my life to measure up. It would be a day in, day out effort, like a job that would take all my waking hours, to transform myself into someone, into a fourteen-karat somebody out of this garden-variety person, me."

Peter was pulling on his pajamas, putting his arm into the sleeve—even in the dim glow of the pink-shaded bedside lamp I caught sight of the zig and zag of the old scars, now white and slightly reminiscent of a comic-book lightning bolt—and he sighed. Peter hates these sorts of conversations, knows I know he hates them. "This is a hoary subject, sweetie. We've gone over it before, like a million times."

"No, really, Pete, you were seeing someone named Susannah La Fleur or something—and she was painting murals for museums and spoke four languages . . . so why me?" I don't know why I needed a replay of this reassurance, but every so often, I did.

"What the hell, Lib, your kind of girl was my style, down-to-earth, functional, long-wearing and"—he gave me a smile—"in mint condition? Look—I saw it the other way around. What was a nice girl like you doing with a . . . a swilling, unhappy boozehound like Dr. Ehrlich's son?"

"But you weren't—in the early days. It started sort of slowly." True, but not true. I'd closed my eyes to three drinks before dinner and eight beers in a row at parties. I'd looked the other way when he paid the package store bills and the empty bottles filled our garbage pails, ignored ten o'clock dried-out dinners that had waited in the oven for the end of the cocktail hour. The endless refills seemed to come out of some disappointment I couldn't get a handle on. I wanted him to assure me I'd seen it wrong: I'd become the treasure, the love of his life that had turned him around and brought sober happiness into his soul.

"Haven't we gone over this too often? I didn't want to be my father's son. I wanted to be Lucas Greavy. Just like him. As for Susannah, her name was LaBonfleur; she made it up, changed it from Sue Lantz, or maybe Lintz, and yes, I was crazy, wildly, madly infatuated with her. I thought we were soul mates, shot through the heart with Shakespeare, Browning, and Proust, besotted with each other's, as they say. But you know, infatuation is easy. It's love that's hard."

Trevor Eddy zipped into my thoughts and quickly out again.

"She found another mural painter in Barcelona or someplace and I never heard from Susannah again. All I remember about her was she had red hair and a beauty mark over one eyebrow."

"And then I came along."

"Yes. And Libby, from the first minute I saw you, I knew you'd be sure to get the floors stenciled right."

I tried to force a smile but it was no go. "I came along and for a long time, we both tried to make me into a perfect person. Remember you sent me to some fancy hairstylist in Greenwich? And you suggested I take a course in making hors d'oeuvres? You went shopping with me and bought me books about current affairs. . . ."

"Okay. I was an insufferable striver, even then. But look how great you turned out!"

"Sometimes, Peter, I still feel as if you'd like an enhanced version of me."

"Libby, let's go to sleep. This is déjà vu. I love you now, I loved you then, but sometimes—"

"—sometimes?"

"I feel you're the one who tries too hard."

"To please you? It's only because, because it's such a stretch—I can't seem to shine brightly enough, and . . ."

"And?" Peter's head turned toward me, his half-closed eyes challenged me. I was going to say that Ellery wasn't shining brightly enough for him, either. That it was obvious, his sin of omission, the kingdom-of-heaven expression when he looked at Claudia, the dutiful you-too pleasantries extended toward Ellery.

"And, and—I can see you're tired. So, good night, Pete."

"There you go. Too solicitous. Libby, don't try so hard not to ruffle my feathers. You don't want to upset me. You see me as walking on a rope, no, not a rope, a *hair,* without a net underneath, all set to topple off."

"No, no—!" But, yes.

"Lib, let's quit while we're ahead. We're a good team. And speaking of stenciled floors, shouldn't we call home? See if everything is all right?"

"But we just left!"

"I want to make sure Ess is out of the picture."

"Oh, Pete, you know your word is the law. Besides, she already had her eye on that boy at the club before we left. I guarantee Ess is out of the picture."

"Those are really beautiful words, Lib. 'Out of the picture.' A phrase to go to sleep to, a lullaby!"

"I'm glad I cheered you up." I felt mildly let down.

Peter was here with me, but not quite. Not fully, never with his whole heart. Were the girls, Lucas Greavy, and every waitress not more important, not the real focuses of his attention?

"Okay. We'll call home tomorrow. Remind me."

"Okay, Peter." We both knew I wouldn't have to remind him.

Over the next few days we examined the stained glass windows in St. Vitus's Cathedral and went to the Kotva department store where I bought a butter dish made of cut glass and flowered cotton skirts for the girls. We bought more souvenirs on the street—crystal beads for Darley, perfume flacons for the girls, and a brooch made out of a semiprecious stone for Annie. We wrote postcards and ate dinner in a restaurant at the top of a television tower that overlooked the city.

Peter missed no photo opportunities, snapped everything from the equestrian statue of St. Wenceslas to street-cleaning trucks spraying water on pavement. He photographed the outside of the city museum where we examined paleontological fossils and old musical instruments, captured on film the street musicians and St. Jacob's Church, where we went to an organ concert.

We called home. We got Marguerita first. It took forever to get her to get Claudia on the line.

Peter was holding the telephone, and relayed parts of the conversation to me. "She's in the shower." He covered the receiver. "When *isn't* she in the shower?"

"When Ellery is."

"How is French going, honey? Ah, wonderful. We're seeing everything. Leaving no tern unstoned. The city is wonderful. We're getting totally castled out. Yes, thanks, sweetie, we are! We're having a great time.

"Three inches? You're kidding. Is the basement flooded? You're sure? But just in case, you have the plumber's number, right?

"Where's Ellery? Okay, tell her we miss you guys a lot, right? Don't forget, sweetheart! I love you!

"You want to talk to Mommy?" He handed the receiver to me.

"Hi, sweetheart? Everything all right? Claudia?"

Claudia sounded funny.

"Where's Ellery?"

She said Ellery had to take the kitten to the vet's for shots.

"The kitten's moved in!"

It had joined the household yesterday. Claudia said it was the cutest kitten in the United States of America and loved eating peanut butter. "Wait till you see it. You'll die."

"How did Ellery get to the vet's?" I asked.

Ess drove Ellery over. *Ess?* Ess!

*"Je lui ne vent pas, Maman."*

"What?"

"I hardly ever see him, Mommy. It was just a favor he did Ellery." I wanted to hear in great detail how come Ess and why Ess but didn't want Peter to hear me ask. I let it go.

"How's Ellery's arm doing?" is what Peter wanted to know.

"Fine. Out of the sling. She starts physical therapy tomorrow."

"You all well?"

Yes, everybody.

"You're sure?" She wanted to know about the gypsies. The Bergins told her they'd seen lots of gypsies. "I'll tell you everything when we get home. Is everything else all right?" I asked.

A mother has that intrinsic extrasensory circuitry. It spans oceans, traveling with or without telephone signals. I'm not a gypsy, but something wasn't all right; I could feel it.

It was the day before we were to depart for Karlovy Vary. After buying ice cream at a nearby kiosk, we were sitting on stone mushroom stools in front of the National Theater, watching a juggler. He was balancing a knife, a flaming torch, and what looked like an American bowling ball, chattering all the while. Peter, having finished his cone, was just getting up closer to the juggler for yet another "great shot" when we heard, "Dr. Ehrlich! Is it really Doc Ehrlich? In Prague? Good God! I don't believe it!"

"Oh, for heaven's sake! Leonard Mayer!"

Peter's patient, someone I'd never met, and his wife, a plump face with a Band-Aid across one cheek I recognized faintly as a Crandall local, came rushing over, leaving their tour group a few feet away. Peter introduced me to Len, and Leonard introduced us to Nita, and we shook hands, went through the predictable exclamations of delight and disbelief, exchanged information about hotels and airlines, remarked on the probabilities of this kind of unheard-of coincidence, noted that of course we never, ever would run into each other in Crandall, that in fact, if we hadn't stopped to watch this juggler, who was now furiously spinning a plate on a stick, we would never have been sitting in this square at all, and would have missed each other altogether.

"And what a coincidence, in view of the fact that we were just discussing you on the plane coming over yesterday," Leonard Mayer said somberly, and his wife, looking suddenly even more sorrowful, nodded.

"Oh, were you? Something good, I hope?" Peter said brightly. I sensed something sinister as I looked at the Mayers, who had exchanged glances and turned awkwardly silent. I looked for a place to dump the last bit of my ice-cream cone, which had suddenly lost all its flavor.

"Wasn't—wasn't Lucas Greavy in your medical group?" Leonard asked. I felt as if a cold hand had landed on my shoulder. Leonard was a tall and angular sort of man, a bit reminiscent of those old billboard Uncle Sam posters, although he was clean-shaven. He looked ready to give advice or to administer punishment.

"Yes, sure." Peter's twitch came and went so fast the Mayers might have missed it. "Until recently. He retired."

The Mayers looked at each other.

"Is it possible"—Leonard looked from Peter to me, to Nita and back to Peter—"Is it possible you didn't hear what *happened*?"

"We've been here a week," I began. I realized the Mayers had flown over yesterday and that since our departure from Crandall, something unspeakable had occurred. I automatically put my hand on Peter's arm. He was still holding the camera with both hands, and now reminded me of his mother, the clutching way she held the handles of her pocketbook.

"Oh, my." Nita moved closer to Leonard as her eyebrows inched toward each other. "I suppose you were, hmmm, very close." She struck me as having a voice that sounded much younger than her age. A little puppy of a voice.

"My God, Dr. Ehrlich. Peter. If I'd known you didn't know, I wouldn't have under any circumstances—" Leonard Mayer looked so distraught I wanted to step forward, put my arm around his shoulder, and comfort him.

Peter's voice sounded as if it were coming from a ventriloquist. "What about Lucas? I talked to him a couple of days before—"

The Mayers' faces blurred into embarrassed anguish.

"He did away with himself. It was—when was it, Nita? The Sunday before we left?"

"I think so." Nita hooked her arm into her husband's and bit the inside of her lip the way I always did when I was in grade school. Leonard cleared his throat, nodded.

"He did away with himself, and his wife—they both—they found them right away because their housekeeper came back early from a weekend in New York City, although I understand she wasn't supposed to come back till Monday morning by train—someone gave her a lift or something—I think she got there while he was still breathing—Jesus, Doct—I mean, Peter, I shouldn't have said a word, oh, shit, it was in the paper but I heard all the details from Doc Feiffer when I took Nita to have that thing taken off her cheek—Dr. Greavy left a note to his son, that's all. She was lying in bed, he was sitting in a chair holding her hand, God, this is your vacation, and they prob'ly didn't call you because they didn't want to ruin your trip and here I opened my big mouth—"

"We didn't know," Nita said. "We're so sorry, we're ever so—"

"Opened my big mouth and prob'ly ruined your holiday."

Peter walked back a step and sat down on one of the stone toadstools. I watched closely. Now his face was inert, seemingly mesmerized by the juggler, who was throwing a jumble of knives and scissors into the air. Peter's hands rested on the leather camera case held against his chest. In my mind's eye I saw Mrs. Greavy on her twin canes, her face a gray death mask above a white lace collar. I saw the chair, it must have been the reproduction Massachusetts lolling chair with the upholstery threadbare where Dr. Greavy's head had worn away the velour. Although I couldn't remember the carpet or the exact color of the walls, I saw the entire bedroom, the mirror over the dresser, the framed photographs, the high post bedstead and chest of drawers with its looking glass. I saw it with a remarkable clarity. I even remembered what I'd forgotten, that the chest of drawers had inserts of Japanese tile. It was as if I were back in the room with my clipboard, taking it all in, then realized the ice cream was dripping all over my fingers. I looked for somewhere to throw it.

Finally, the Mayers, offering further condolences, apologies, and expressions of hope that we would get together for dinner some time back in Connecticut, moved away, his arm around her shoulder, to rejoin their tour guide, who had moved farther off toward the National Theater with the rest of the group.

Peter and I were alone.

I found a tissue in my purse and wrapped the remaining bits of dripping cone in it. The sun was reflected in the glass facade of the National Theatre and shining right in my eyes. With my hand still sticky from the ice cream, I reached into my bag for my sunglasses.

"He was more a father than my father, Libby."

"I know."

"It's the end of the world," my husband said.

That night, Peter talked about flying home. If he'd insisted, I would have gone along, although there was absolutely nothing to be gained by aborting our vacation. Even the funeral must already be over. We called home again, got Marguerita, who told us that Claudia was at the library, and Ellery was outside with the "keedie," everything was fine except the "keedie" kept tearing up the upholstery of the living-room couch, nothing would stop the little paws from scratching! As we were talking, I heard a man's voice in the background.

"Who's there, Marguerita?" I asked.

"Ess. She carrying the groce-rees. Just for favor,

because of the laundry blitch and the blidda for the keedie and the soda. She drove Ellery and me, a nice boy." *Blidda* turned out to mean kitty litter. *Blitch* was bleach.

"Who's at our house?" Peter asked, stopping in his tracks. He'd been pacing, window to bed, bed to window.

I hesitated. "Ess."

"What?"

"He's being very helpful, Peter. Just seems to want to stay a friend of the family."

Peter's mouth seemed to disappear into his mustache. "I think you're being naive, Lib. Put Claudia on."

"The girls aren't there."

"What do you mean, not there? Where are they?"

It turned out that now that Ellery had been decreed by the physical therapist ready to ride her bike, Ess and his van had been summoned to help get it to the shop. The front tire was misaligned, or something like that. And since they were going to get the bike fixed, they'd stop off for the kitty litter, the soda, and some special brand of bleach Marguerita needed to get the grass stains off Ellery's white shorts. And when they were bringing all these items into the house, the kitten got out, which is where Ellery was, running after Dumpling. Claudia was at the beach.

I told Peter it seemed in Ess's nature to want to be a sort of helper, a hero, like when he'd saved Humphrey Bogart in Vermont. I tried to paint a portrait of the young man as more than a devious bum.

"We should be flying home on the next plane."

I know I looked punished when he said it. We had Karlsbad ahead of us, another week of liberation from kitty litter, broken bikes, and teenage detonations. And I wanted to keep the Atlantic between us and a double suicide as long as possible. I wanted to stay here, being carefree lovers our one more allotted week.

Peter suddenly saw the city of Prague as jail.

"Libby, I'm jumpy."

"Peter, please."

"Lib—"

*"Please."*

"Since it means so much to you."

I told Marguerita to tell the girls we already knew about Dr. Greavy and they were not to worry about their father. He was upset, but he was doing fine, just fine.

Peter got through to Solow in his office immediately. They talked for ten minutes. Patients of Dr. Greavy were calling from all corners of the earth, but the new woman at the switchboard was handling it. Solow himself had gone to meet the Greavys' son's plane, and some other relatives arrived from California. The memorial service had been held at the Presbyterian Church and lasted for an hour and three quarters despite faulty air-conditioning, since so many people took turns at the lectern, praising both Dr. Greavy and his wife. It was wall-to-wall flowers, a state senator had come, and the actress, Peter had forgotten her name, who'd played opposite Harrison Ford in that action movie, he'd forgotten the name of that, too. *Canonizing* was the word Peter told me Jack Solow had used to describe the eulogies.

When Peter got back, he and Solow and Greavy's son would talk about establishing some kind of scholarship in Lucas Greavy's name. The real-estate people were already swarming over the property, but for the moment the son seemed wary about selling the house's contents.

I heard Peter tell Solow that we'd met the Mayers, who'd told us the news. And I heard him say he was having a wonderful, a really terrific vacation.

Peter had rented a manual-shift Skoda—cute and maneuverable, he called it, although the radio wasn't working. I thought it sounded definitely like a Peter thing, renting a car I couldn't drive, but no point in getting into a silly argument about something that didn't mean much.

We began the trip under a sky the color of pale denim, but when we were about halfway there, clouds gathered and a thin rain began. As the rain got heavier, Peter's silences grew longer. "Why aren't we talking?" I asked. I'd tried making conversation, but there was only give, no take.

"Visibility isn't that great and I'm just busy following the directions," Peter answered.

"It's not just the rain. It's Lucas."

"I'm trying to figure out some alternative means we could have used to ease him out more gently."

"Peter. Please. Don't carry the Greavys' coffin on your back."

"It's easy to say, but I keep thinking."

"You had no more to do with what happened than you have in controlling the rain."

"If he'd had something solid in his life, even one little thing, other than work."

"That's it. One needs more to look forward to than a next page that's blank."

Some people go into their declining years with hearts wallpapered in cheerful AT&T stocks. Some take jazz piano lessons or tour the Galapagos Islands. My mother and Rudy cook, tidy up, and watch the Weather Channel. On the other hand, I did note that the older people got, the more they seemed like satellites circling the sun of sons and daughters, and especially grandchildren.

Peter said Greavy had never talked about his child except once, when he said that raising him he'd felt like Sisyphus. "Kicked out of schools, withdrawn, belligerent, rebellious." Peter had heard from people who knew the boy. "And they were exemplary parents, as far as one could see. God, it makes you think."

Peter could hardly be heard over the noise of the windshield wipers.

The car had stalled once or twice, seemed to struggle on inclines. I tensed a bit; a sign ahead read POZOR VLAK. There was a railroad crossing ahead—on an incline—and I don't like driving across tracks in any vehicle, especially in the rain, which had, in fact, gotten even heavier. There were safety gates, which might or might not work. No train was approaching from either direction and we drove uneventfully up and down the little hill, across the tracks. Peter worked the stick shift masterfully, but fell into another heavy silence.

"I think we ought to play a word game." I was watching the windshield wipers, feeling mesmerized.

"I don't want to play word games, Lib, do you mind?"

"Well, I only thought it would be a distraction, sweetheart!"

"Are we never allowed to be quiet?"

"Well, of course, Pete. Let's be quiet, if you prefer."

"Let's," my husband said.

And for forty minutes, until we pulled into the parking lot of the Pupp Hotel, there was only the sound of the windshield wipers—*swsssssshhhhhh-swsssh*—and we were very, very quiet.

Peter was not convinced of the medicinal powers of the waters that spurted out of spigots in the spa, but we took our china cups to the faucets anyway. The place was all glass, soaring ceilings—it looked like a contemporary art gallery, a corridor better suited to stone sculpture than columns spouting bubbling and steamy potion. The stuff tasted like warm tonic water as we pulled it in through the china straw that was the integral part of these quaint little drinking vessels, sold a few paces from the fountains and as souvenirs up and down the Karlovy Vary main street.

Peter handed me his cup. "Hold this a minute, Libby, I want to get a picture." People strolled here and there, sipping and chatting, sitting, pushing strollers, or being rolled in wheelchairs, getting refills.

Peter wanted me to pose now, raise the cup to the spigot and face the camera. "Now look this way, Lib." Out of the corner of my eye I saw three women. Could they be gypsies or just harmless tourists? I kept my eye on my things, which I'd put carefully at my feet. Carrying satchels, the women, two young, one middle-aged, and all coated with cosmetics, their hair the color of raw liver, were nowhere near me. They'd moved off. I smiled at the camera. "Get a little closer in, sweetie." I stepped forward. "Chin up a little, honey," and I put up my chin. "Are you ready?" I was ready. He was down to the last shot in yet another roll of film. I posed cooperatively, raised chin and cup, smiled into the lens.

"That does it," he said, and just as he was removing the roll of film from his camera, we became aware of a commotion a few feet away, not far from the entry doors. A dark-haired woman in a wheelchair seemed to have taken ill, was slumped forward and gasping for breath. Although I couldn't see her face at the moment, I remembered noticing her earlier, and thinking that she seemed young, that she might in fact have come from a great distance with the hope that these waters would help her. I also remember looking into the face of the young man who was pushing her, his dark eyes expressionless, in my imagination hiding self-sacrifice, maybe resentment for what the deities had dished out in his life. A larger crowd was gathering. I caught sight of the invalid's waving arms in the sleeves of her sweater, a purple windmill in the air, people offering her a cup of mineral water, her husband kneeling at her side.

"I suppose I ought to go over there." He hates to involve himself in emergencies because of the threat of legal action, but with Peter, old-fashioned moral responsibility wins hands down. In three strides, he'd reached the periphery of the circle surrounding the wheelchair. "I'm a doctor." The jostling crowd immediately parted for him. I'd seen this happen once or twice before, each time felt tremendously elevated—my husband!—and not a little proud.

But a moment later, he had reappeared, his eyebrows raised. "They didn't want a doctor."

"What do you mean, they didn't want a doctor?"

"The husband put up his hand like a traffic cop and wouldn't let me near her."

"How strange, how very strange," I said.

"I guess it's my foreignness," he said. "I think they were gypsies. Probably superstitious." He gave me a quick smile. "Or maybe it was my bow tie."

"You think they'll let her die because you don't speak Czech?"

"Oh, I think she'll be all right. Her color didn't look bad. Her eyes looked perfectly clear, as far as I could see."

We looked at the crowd slowly dispersing; the wheelchair was moving out of the spa. I caught sight of purple sleeves, the young husband's oppressed back as he pushed his wife through the glass doors. My first thought was that it might have been a riding accident. Was Peter thinking the same thing? He put a hand on my shoulder, assured me she'd seemed okay, and looked at his watch.

"At this point, I guess I've had enough of the spa, how about you? Are you hungry?"

We headed for a small place we'd passed on the corner near our hotel.

We had a longer than usual lunch because the waiter talked us into a dessert of apricot fruit dumplings, specialty of the house, the town, and of the Czech Republic. We had to wait for a new batch that arrived, plump and steaming, covered with melted butter and cinnamon sugar. It was when we were heading out of the restaurant that Peter looked across the street and decided he wanted a picture of me seated on a bench at the bus stop, so we headed over the little bridge that spanned the stream dividing the main street. We were about halfway across when Peter stopped dead in his tracks.

"So, you have it?"

"Have what?"

"The camera."

"The camera? No."

"No? Didn't I hand it to you to hold for me in the spa?"

"You had it, Peter, when you dashed off to help that woman in the wheelchair."

"Are you sure?"

"You had it hanging around your neck."

We stopped and looked at each other.

"Goddamn it to hell! It's gone!"

"Where is it?"

"Stolen!"

"Stolen? How could they have pulled it off your neck without your feeling it?"

"They must have cut the strap!"

"Cut the strap?"

"Of course!"

"You didn't notice?"

"I didn't feel a thing."

"Professionals!"

"She was no more sick than you are."

I was shocked. "You really think?" I saw again the purple sleeves, the young man with the dead eyes.

"I'm lucky I carry my wallet in my inside pocket."

"Imagine! Using a wheelchair to fool the quarry."

"To fool the fools! I'm an idiot! Nothing wrong with the woman! Not a goddamn thing!"

"Good heavens. In little Karslbad."

* * *

The concierge already knew about it. The police were investigating. Three other guests of the hotel had reported missing jewelry and money. The same gang of gypsies had hit Marienbad three weeks ago, had disappeared in a truck that some said was gray, others said was blue. One lady said they took her passport and diamond watch; the hotel had to call a doctor, she was so upset, had difficulty breathing. She thought that a gypsy snatching something meant more than it actually did. It was an old superstition, about gypsies stealing your soul. It was considered very bad luck in some quarters. The concierge smiled at us, understood that we were much too sophisticated to buy into meaningless items of folklore. We were lucky that it was only the camera they got. Sometimes, he said, eyes rolling, they grabbed children right out of their mothers' arms.

"It's only a camera," Peter said.

"It's only a camera," I repeated.

We were walking through an art gallery filled with contemporary art, and every time I stopped to admire a painting or a piece of sculpture, Peter said it was derivative, obscure, lacking in depth, pop, or postage-stamp art. Under his mustache, his lips were a firm hyphen.

I suggested we go for coffee.

Peter said the coffee here seemed too intense. One needed to add cream, sugar, and Pepto-Bismol.

Ice cream, then? He didn't feel like it after all that lunch. A mineral water? Cup of tea? Peter said he didn't want any of those things. He didn't know what exactly he felt like eating, drinking, or doing.

"Shall we go take a nap?" I asked. He stopped in front of a huge oil of what looked like golf tees sticking out of a porcupine. "A fungus, or what? I *am* tired," he said.

"A nap will be fine with me," I said.

"You're always accommodating, ever agreeable." When Peter said it, the words sounded less like a compliment than something he was reading from a printed page.

We were headed back to Prague in the Skoda, driving through a small town, which seemed a duplicate of villages we'd passed through last year in Portugal, and the year before in Scandinavia, all huddled stone buildings no higher than a story and a half, twisting streets, a stray dog, flowers on a windowsill: a beige and gray village against a blue sky, all of it looking as if it had been put together four hundred years ago by one stucco purveyor.

"I bet you could stay longer, couldn't you?" He meant, *You could but I couldn't.*

I could stay another month, easily.

"I miss the kids," Peter said. "At least the gypsies didn't steal all our exposed film. We'll have a few things to show them, won't we?"

*But what will they have to show us?* is what passed through my mind. I thought of gypsies, curses, and omens. I imagined Claudia had sneaked in a party. She did it every time we went away.

"All I hope is that no more bones got broken." *Or hearts,* I thought.

Mostly, the car behaved well. Once it stalled at a red light, and once on a hill in the town of Krsk. Peter got it started immediately. Masterfully. "If all fails you can drive cabs in the Czech Republic." I was trying to get up a conversation, but Peter was quiet.

Ahead, the same railroad crossing—or was it another one?—loomed. Again, and this time in bright sunshine, I grew wary. Had I seen too many car chase movies? Had anyone sitting in a rented car ever in this century actually been cut in half by a train? These things existed in fiction, not in life, not here. But the car was chugging along, showing signs of breathing disorders. Speed up, is what I wanted him to do. Slow down, is what he seemed to be doing. The car was limping up that little hill, passing the black-and-white railroad barriers, the sun was bright in the sky, and there was no train in sight.

But my hands turned clammy in my lap. "Peter?"

"What?"

He was slowing down. No, the car was slowing down. The car with a malevolent mind of its own, chugged, gasped, died just as we rolled onto the tracks, stuck on the rails, somehow.

I screamed "Peter!" as he was twisting the shift, his foot stomping the clutch. Each second was five minutes long. My eyes were burning, my heart hammering. And now, a rush in my ears. "I hear the train!" My hand was on the door handle, in panic. I was ready to bolt.

His face was as wet as if I'd interrupted his morning shower. His lip twitched. I watched his hand maneuver the stick with the knob, he swallowed, the engine sputtered. It was a nightmare that lasted seventy seconds, which is the time it took Peter to get it started again and what it took to get us moving out of the path of a train that I'd imagined and which was nowhere in sight. We lurched forward. I could breathe.

We were safe.

"God, oh, God," I said, and Peter's eyes left the road to throw a look at me.

The car purred down the tracks away from the incline, and suddenly, after we'd gone about a quarter of a mile, Peter twisted the steering wheel with a dramatic flourish and pulled to the side of the road. While behind him and all around us cows grazed in tranquil pastures, something churned behind his eyes.

"It's always there with you, isn't it?" When he turned to me his eyes were blazing, his cheeks so red it looked as if he'd been slapped.

I looked out the windshield down the road, to try to figure out what had made Peter stop here, of all places. A two-lane paved road, a barn, some hills in the distance, and two men fixing a truck parked half on the road and half on the adjacent field. Nothing.

"It's written all over your face."

"What?"

"You're glad I'm sober."

It hadn't even crossed my mind. I'd been thinking we were soon to be dead meat, is what I'd been thinking.

"You're glad I wasn't drunk, because if I'd been drunk, we'd have been mashed by the train you conjured up out of your imagination."

"You're dead wrong. I never gave your being sober a thought."

Peter pronounced his words slowly, as if English was his second language. "It's always just under the surface. You reveal it in a thousand little ways."

"What's under the surface?" The piercing green of his and Claudia's eyes startled me into speechlessness.

"The psychological chicken soup you're cooking up for me. The hand-holding, anesthetizing! Always agreeable, conciliatory."

I certainly was now. I remembered a Czech word we'd seen at the railroad crossing: *pozor*. Watch out.

"Peter, what's really the matter?"

"This country is the beer capital of the world, Libby."

"What?"

"I said, the best beer in the world is made here."

"So?"

"And in all this time, you didn't have one bottle, one glass, one taste!"

"Well, why would I?"

"Why wouldn't you?" Peter's teeth showed for a minute and I was reminded of Laszlo's bared little row of fangs whenever I tried to brush his fur. Peter's bottom ones were definitely moving farther apart. "We went into Ufleku, and you drank mineral water—"

"I don't like beer."

"—in the most famous beer hall in the world."

"I used to like beer in college, but I grew out of it." Was this true? It didn't matter; I'd trained myself not to like to drink anymore. That's what was important. I began to elaborate. "What's more important to me, is—," but he cut me off.

"Admit it, Libby. You live in the grip of clammy terror that I'm going to take that first drink. Drive us all in front of an oncoming train."

"I'm not!"

"Goddamn it, be honest. You're always trying to cushion the world for me. You're afraid that if I get upset enough, worried enough, depressed enough, or just irritated enough, I'll fall off the wagon. If I miss one meeting, you get frantic. You still think it's possible that after all these years I'd do it."

"No."

"That I'd turn into a roaring, mindless, lawless drunk."

"Oh, Peter, no."

"You won't take a sip of anything near me, lest it tempt me. You won't get into an argument, or express any displeasure—Jesus, I know how annoyed you get when I take photographs. You think it doesn't show? You were thrilled when my camera was stolen. Ecstatic!"

"Pete, I didn't want your camera stolen."

"You cringed every time I took a picture. Don't you think I could see it?"

"Sometimes you take too long to focus, that's true."

"How do you think I feel being with someone who is forever monitoring me, waiting for, and anticipating my relapse!"

"I didn't know how you felt about my not drinking, Pete."

"It's not only that, it's everything. Don't you ever want to begin trusting me? Didn't I take an oath, swear to you on that day—"

Ordinarily I don't get PMS, but I was beginning to feel touchy and on the rack. "Let's not talk about that now."

"Didn't I make a promise, on that day, and have I ever gone back on my word?"

"No, of course not."

"Haven't I stayed dry as the Sahara? Thirteen years ago I said, 'Never again,' and I meant, 'Never again.' Why can't you believe me with your whole heart, instead of just with one small gear in your head?"

I fumbled in my pocketbook for the little plastic bottle of Advil I always carry. Right now, with this body and mind pressure, I couldn't think. I was a trembling blank.

"No matter what, Libby! Even if the sky should fall, even if Lucas Greavy"—he choked up a bit—"is dead, I'll never touch a drop again! I won't—please look at me, Lib, do you have to rummage in your pocketbook *now*?—just look at me. It's a promise and I'm making it again to you and the girls. I'm not going to take a drink again. My days as a wino are over! I am not going to turn into—" He didn't have to say, "my father." We both knew who he didn't want to turn into.

"But you"—Peter was holding the steering wheel as if it might disconnect from its column—"have to let up! Since that day—ever since that day thirteen years ago, have I ever even once let you down?"

Every marriage has its bad memories, and despite not being resurrected in words or print, they live in the house and go along on every vacation, like an extra piece of luggage. I've felt the weight of ours at odd times, although in good times not at all, but whenever there's a bout of flak, an unrelated marital skirmish, the snow blizzard gets dredged up, that riveting documentary that changed our lives. I've hated snow since the day of that storm thirteen years ago, dramatized it in my memory into something whiter and icier, enlarged it into something deeper and more dire, stigmatized and diabolized it. In my head, snow forebodes. When it snows in Crandall, Connecticut, I stay inside and try not to think of that day in March. I try not to think at all.

I was three months pregnant, and aside from little spells of sleepiness, a never-ceasing desire for salted and spicy foods, and a very rare bout of nausea, I felt marvelous. That day, Peter had made his hospital rounds early, before the heaviest accumulations, and later, because most of Crandall's roads were impassable, he canceled office hours. I was due at a fund-raising meeting of Planned Parenthood and at eight, my evening class of either crewel or decoupage—I was learning what were considered womanly skills in those days—but everything, including nursery school, was canceled. It was a bit of a holiday, and I remember thinking I hadn't prepared for the contingency of snow by stocking up on cocoa or hot-chocolate mix; I would have to make it from scratch by melting a bar of chocolate in a double boiler and adding it to milk. Who could live through a snowstorm without a fire in the fireplace and hot chocolate in a mug? I remember standing over the stove after lunch, stirring chocolate and heating milk, and looking through the cupboards for marshmallows.

It was quite a storm, blowing up in a dramatic way, hurling icy flakes against the windows and decreasing visibility to nil. It was the sort of storm during which drifts pile up against doors and there are electrical failures. It turned dark in the middle of the day in sort of a wintry twilight, and although the electricity stayed on, no traffic moved outside. We were a cozy trio, the stereo playing, Laszlo curled up on some couch or chair, muffins from a mix waiting to be pulled out of the oven, the mugs of hot chocolate on the coffee table.

Claudia was intoxicated with the view from every window, and desperate to go out for two reasons: to get into the heaps of snow, body and soul, and also because the new Christmas snowsuit, a gift from her grandmother in Florida, had finally been exchanged for one that fit. This one was snazzy and white, with a white fake-furry hood and a kiddie version of a designer label shaped like a gold emblem over the heart. It had pink stripes on the sleeves and along the sides of its leggings—the toddler version of skiwear. All in all, it was impractical, but Claudia was our first child and her grandmother's first grandchild, and aesthetics won out over utility. She couldn't wait to get it on.

"As soon as the snow stops," we told her, and, to give us a respite, we promised "after your nap."

Claudia had pretty much given up sleeping during the day, but could be persuaded to lie down quietly for an hour or so, especially with a bribe. Sometimes she actually fell asleep, sometimes she just turned picture-book pages, talked to dolls, sang to herself. This afternoon her hiatus gave me a chance to rest, and, as it turned out, for Peter to drink.

Of course, I'd noticed that while Claudia and I were

sitting together on the living-room couch in front of the fire with the mugs of hot chocolate, Peter had settled himself in the wing chair, with his choice of a winter-storm drink, the hot toddy. Followed by refills.

Alcohol in his glass always split me into two halves that locked horns. I wanted to stop him, and I didn't. Sometimes he only drank a few, just enough to get into a harmless, good-fellow mood, and sometimes he drank enough to throw him into a stupor, turn him into a belligerent crackpot, and of course, there were stages in between. At times, if I tried to stop him, he'd spin off into philosophical lunacy (*"Mole ruit sua!* I'm a great physician! I protract dying! I make it more expensive!") or turn dangerous, like the time he shattered the mirror in the hall. Another time, at a colleague's barbecue, he unzipped his pants behind a hedge, just out of the glare of the Chinese lanterns strung around the patio, and relieved himself. Auspiciously, the hired guitar player was getting all the center-stage attention, and no one but me noticed that while the guitarist was playing "Red Roses for a Blue Lady," Peter was irrigating the rhododendrons.

On the day of the snowstorm, the stop-him half won. "Aren't you on call this afternoon?" I asked.

"I'm not on call until eight tonight. *Gebraucht der Zeit!* Let's make love! On the Au-boo-sson!"

When he drank, my libido got annihilated.

I crept upstairs to the bedroom, to the Ruth Rendell mystery that was waiting for me on the night table. A half hour later, hearing Claudia softly, peacefully, trustingly talking to herself in her room, I was the one who fell asleep.

I woke up thinking muffins. Their smell had perfumed the house and my mouth was watering as I pushed my feet into slippers. Thinking of food as I groggily began moving through the bedroom, I glanced outside, noted the snow had stopped, and that the sun was turning treetops and roofs into glistening Dream Whip. No sounds were coming from Claudia's room, and downstairs, everything was quiet.

"Peter?" I looked into the living room. The fire had burned down, Laszlo was curled up on one of the shelves of the bookcase, and Peter was nowhere to be seen. Music was coming from the stereo, and the room had turned cool, as if the heat had been turned down, or a window left open. "Peter?" My eye fell to the coffee table and my heart began to pump. There stood a rum bottle, empty. "Peter!"

"Hey, you're up!"

I spun around. He was heading toward the couch, empty glass in one hand, a new bottle and the bottle opener—a penguin-shaped stainless-steel tool that was part of a fancy wedding present bar set—in the other. "I was taking a leak," he said. He was barefoot, glassy-eyed, smashed. His eyes were ringed in red and he had that deranged look that terrified me. "Have a nice nap?"

"Where's Claudia?"

"Ah, that's the question!" He wove his way to the couch, hurled himself into a sitting position and began ferociously pulling the foil off the neck of the bottle. The thing about Peter was that no matter how drunk he became, whether he could remain perfectly erect or his knees gave way and he had to be pulled off the floor, he always seemed to keep his power of normal speech. Like his father, who in his most abysmally drunken moments, was capable of faultlessly quoting Alexander Pope in an unslurred theatrical voice.

"Is she asleep?"

"She was. Had a nice nappie."

"Where is she?"

"Outside."

"What do you mean, outside?"

"She wanted to play in the snow, so I put on her snowsuit, and"—he made a gesture that swooped through the air like an aerobic exercise—"out she went."

I went running to the coat closet. "You let her go outside—into the street—alone?"

"There's no traffic. No cars. Nothing moving. What could happen?"

He was totally logical and totally drunk. "What could happen?" he asked again. "She likes snow."

How many times have the next few minutes replayed themselves in my imagination? That is the thing about living through an episode black with the texture of tragedy: Even though it has a duration of only two or three minutes, it never happens only once. It adheres to the brain circuits in its entirety forever, and replays itself tenaciously at unexpected moments. Again and again, the frantic terror of the moment, in all its full-bodied reality, crowds back into the mind's eye, pops up in the middle of a conversation, bulldozes through some unrelated memory, bursts into the mind mornings or midnights, during sleep or coming out of it, like a swimmer forever coming up for air. It is always there.

The thing was, Claudia, in her white snowsuit, the fuzzy white hood around her head and covering her chin, turned invisible in the snow. My first thought when I saw her rubber boots standing in the hall—Peter hadn't bothered with those, hadn't been *capable,* more likely, to get them over her sneakers—my first thought was that her feet would be soaked and freezing. I was more angry than worried. But when I pulled on my own rubber boots and opened the front door I took heart—

she'd left tracks. I relaxed a bit, thinking I'd find her pretty quickly. The sun was out and the snow was reflecting the glare, he was right, there was no traffic after all, and I remember buttoning my jacket as I ran, squinting, thinking I should have grabbed my sunglasses.

At that time, Claudia had a playmate who lived around the corner, and although she was not quite three, I had a hunch she might go in that direction. Sure enough, the footprints seemed to head that way although the snow, falling in clumps from trees and roofs now, began to obliterate most of them. I remember calling to a neighbor who was out shoveling his walk, "Have you seen Claudia?" getting in return a shrug, a shake of the head. The trees, with their sleeves of frost, dripped wet ice pellets as I made my way to the corner, and every so often, what was left of the wind lifted a cloud of icy snow and blew it around my head. Although I was bareheaded and without gloves, I began to perspire.

Before I even got to the corner, I heard it, but the implication of the grinding hum did not penetrate. I didn't associate it with danger, until I made the corner turn and saw it lumbering in my direction, straight ahead. Right ahead with its sinister drone, coming down the street, not ten feet from me. And practically on top of Claudia.

I freeze in an emergency. Fear pours into me like paralyzing novocaine, I become inert, a piece of lifeless plastic with burning, bulging eyes. Claudia was about to be, within the next two breaths, scooped up by the jaws of the town's mastodonic snow-removal machinery. The truck, as wide as the street, as tall as a tree, was bearing down on her, with its droning, bulldozing, heartless black claw. She was in its direct path, meandering unawares in the winter wonderland of the street, unseen by the driver high in his cab.

My throat locked and a rush of blood filled my head. I couldn't let out a sound or move a muscle. I just stood there immobilized, ready to watch my daughter be lifted by the streetwide knife cutting through the drifts, hurled into the air with the snow and into the chomp of the machine's gears. He didn't see her, he couldn't see her, if I screamed until I snapped a vocal cord, the driver would never hear me over the thundering sound of the truck as the snow flew left and right, the roar filled the air. I stopped breathing.

Then, out of nowhere, a dark angel appeared. Dropping his shovel, a black boy hired to clear a walk or a driveway, someone I'd never seen before and have never seen since, burst into our lives, to hurl his body in front of the truck, tackling Claudia out of the way of death's plow. He let out a yell, rolled into the snow and away with her as she, startled into shrieking hysteria, was dragged to the opposite side of the street out of harm's way. When the driver of the cab, finally seeing the figures through his second-story windshield, stopped the truck, I came to life. I crossed the street, and while Claudia clung to my knees, hiccuping with sobs, I swayed, gagged, and finally, hanging onto the trunk of a tree, felt below hot drops of blood oozing out of me.

When I tried to find the boy later, to give him folding money, more thanks, a new bicycle, whatever would please him, I couldn't find him anywhere. He's in my dreams to this day. And of course, in my nightmares.

When we got back, Peter greeted us at the door.

"D'ja have fun in the snow, sweetie?" he asked, hanging onto the doorjamb, a red-eyed, slobbering clown. "D'ja make snow angels?"

Dr. Irvine would never commit to citing this event as the reason for my excessive cramping, spotting, and general malaise during the rest of my pregnancy. He took the fifth during the two false alarms and premature delivery, but I never recovered from this not-quite-happy ending. The subject of Claudia's brush with death is something I don't talk about and certainly never to Peter. It was the next day that he went to the basement, pulled out a few old cartons, filled them with the bottles in our liquor cabinet, and put the cartons in the trunk of his car. They disappeared and I never asked what he did with them. He almost had one relapse at his sister's wedding a month later, but when I saw the drink in his hand, I started to cry, and in the car going home, he promised me AA, Antabuse, the pledge, swore never again, and as far as I know, was abstinent from that time on.

We haven't had so much as a can of beer at home since—my house rules, as rigid as no playing with matches, no loaded guns.

Right after that, Peter bought me a Cartier watch with a black face and little dots of gold for numbers, but a year later I lost it, left it in a bathroom of a restaurant where I'd put it on the sink while I was washing my hands. I suppose, deep inside, I always wanted to lose it.

Now, as soon as we arrived back in Prague, Peter's tone became more gentle, more solicitous, more apologetic. He said he was sorry he'd stormed at me at the railroad crossing, I shouldn't take his outburst too seriously, Lucas Greavy's death had really upset him. "Loosened my moorings" is how he put it. And as we waited for Flight Number OK600, Czechoslovak Air, to take us back to Kennedy Airport, he dragged me into the duty-free shop and tried to buy me a Chopard with a gold face and little diamonds that spun around in a circle in the rim when you tilted it. I talked him out of it and picked out a silk scarf instead. It was floral, mostly red, white, and blue, the colors of the Czech Republic, and of the United States of America. I was now happy to be heading back there, looking forward to seeing my girls. The air had changed; our vacation had run its course.

# Chapter Six

"We're home!"

The girls came running down the stairs, Ellery, her hair in molecular curlers, carrying Dumpling, Claudia behind her, waving her just-manicured fingernails, wearing sort of a sack thing I'd never seen and with a new silver-and-turquoise ring—no more gold bracelet—on the middle finger of her right hand, behind her. There is something festive about walking into the house after an absence that seems so much longer than it actually was. Everything is the same but refreshingly amended. There are the children with cheeks that look leaner and two weeks older, a new hairdo, infatuation, or absurd jumper—Claudia had borrowed this omelette-colored disaster from a new friend in her French class because it looked really "biff." "Biff?" In two weeks there are even vocabulary innovations. And piles of mail, messages, bits of news: Dumpling learned how to use the kitty litter but scratched up the legs of the couch in the den, Marguerita got a letter that made her cry all day Saturday, the physical therapist said that Ellery's arm would be strong enough for weight lifting by October, there was a three-inch rain and little puddle in our basement, everyone was evacuated from the cineplex when a fire broke out in the popcorn machine, Darley was bitten by a wasp in Savannah and had to go to the doctor's.

More than anything, I saw a change in Ellery. Something subtle, like a weight gain of three or four pounds, and less subtle, like a borrowed T-shirt that showed her breasts—now proudly, it seemed. And one of Claudia's conch belts, showing off the waist and curve of hips underneath. Also, shiny lips. Was that lip gloss?

Peter seemed tired, dragging the suitcases upstairs, but revived and happier with the girls hard on his heels, ready to bubble over with more revelations, ready to pounce on the souvenirs waiting for them in his two-suiter. Claudia loved the skirts I'd bought and therefore Ellery also did, they both wanted to hear about the gypsies, but not much about the food, and certainly nothing about the history, politics, or architecture of Prague. The phone rang in the girls' phone booth and Claudia ran to answer it. The minute she was out of the room, Ellery inadvertently spilled the beans. I asked about the turquoise ring—it wasn't from Ess? Absolutely not, Ellery said, very adamant. I couldn't get my eyes off her shiny lips. And her teeth looked phosphorescent. Was she using tooth whitener?

Claudia was "having it bad" for Kevin Bevan. He gave her the silver ring she was wearing, but hadn't really found it in the street, he'd bought it for someone named Leigh, dropped her the minute Claudia appeared on the scene. Claudia felt bad about stealing him from Leigh, but was definitely getting "hooked on" Kevin, got up at six o'clock at least twice when we were away to go to the gym and watch him pump iron. "It's more than I want to know," Peter told Ellery, but later, when we were in bed and about to fall asleep, he reminded me that I'd been nervous about his giving the coup de grâce to Ess. "You were worried, Lib, but where are the dire consequences? A new beau. Dear consequences! Getting Ess out of Claudia's life was the smartest thing we ever did," he said.

*"We?"*

"Okay. I ever did."

But the very next morning, I saw Ess's van. It was passing our house, and when it approached, it slowed down. It had a new dent in the left front fender, and a yellow sign in the window: NO TV, but Ess was wearing the same mirror sunglasses, the same braid grown even longer. I saw the van from the bedroom window, saw it slow to a crawl, caught sight of Ess's face, which turned toward our house as it passed. Turned longingly, is how I interpreted his neck craning and head swiveling. Claudia was at school and Ellery was asleep, Marguerita was just leaving. She'd told me the girls were "good, very good" but it seemed to me, as she took the crystal perfume bottle I'd brought her and the cash I put into an envelope, that her teeth were smiling, but not her heart, and no question about it, short of the girls torching the house, she wasn't capable of turning informer. She did tell me she'd gotten a letter telling her her old sweetheart had gotten married. "She was a good man but sometimes a bad man." Five minutes after she left, Ess drove by again.

Ellery had seemingly given up on the Niagara puzzle. Every so often, Claudia or I might sit at the table and poke around the remaining pieces, but the lowest quarter, the foam, seemed too uniformly white and difficult. "Oh, not to worry, I'll get the pieces in place," Ellery said, when Peter asked about it. "By the time the Countess comes again, it'll be finished, glued down, and framed." The Countess, busy in sizzling love in Connecticut, called often but did not appear. She and the judge were planning to visit Meggie, who in her decline had reached some sort of plateau between living and dying. The Countess said Meggie had all her faculties except her appetite, and her hearing was going. The Countess also said she'd gotten the judge to stop wearing a chain across his necktie, but that he was still parting his hair down the middle.

In the meantime, Ellery was bicycling to the club every day, Rollerblading in the schoolyard, and baby-sitting for a new family with twin girls—Peter didn't much like the idea but gave in when she pleaded, saying they were "just like dollies that have those strings in back"—and sometimes going to the library of her own accord the evenings it was open, just to "hang out and look at the magazines." She seemed vague and dreamy these days, was giving her perm extra help by curling her hair to look like twisted telephone cords ("never cutting it again as long as I live"), and had taken down the pictures of horses in her room. She'd replaced them with rock stars and photographs of Dumpling, who was really an impeccable orange-and-white kitten, aside from furniture-scratching and occasional loud meowing. He had a bland, baby face, purred on demand, played with balled-up socks ("fourteen-karat adorable!") and didn't bite when we tickled his nose. Laszlo had had an aggressive streak, but Dumpling showed signs of what the girls called dumplingness.

Claudia was playing her harp every so often without being asked ("Traumerie" with her eyes half-closed last night), and every week, both girls went to the local nursing home, to read to the patients, or to run their errands, bringing flowers they'd cut from our garden. Around the house, Claudia was singing French songs and reciting lines from Hugo and Stendhal. We had landed on sort of a golden peak of halcyon peace. Peter, swept up in a backlog of work, still found time to make a dinner date with Josh Greavy, and began interviewing doctors to take his father's place in the Crandall Medical Group. Tuesday nights when he went to his AA meeting in Greenwich were the nights I called my mother; I usually got a rundown on her week's menus, reports on weather, the price of leeks, and many, many questions about the girls.

"You fucking had to tell them? Why the fuck did you have to tell them, *Mademoiselle Bouche Grande*?"

The music was shaking the walls, but the door to Claudia's room was open and I heard every word very clearly in the kitchen.

"You fucking couldn't keep your mouth shut for once?"

"Mom maneuvered it out of me, I couldn't help it! She goes, 'Is that ring from Ess? I go, 'No way,' she goes, 'Who gave it to her?' so what am I gonna say, 'Brad Pitt'?"

I was thinking that this was not exactly the way it happened, but recited my mantra, *Let it go, let it go.*

"How would you like it if I blabbed about your private affairs? How would you? *Tu donne moi un mal à la tête!*"

"Claudia, you know you're gonna have to get a tonsil transplant if you keep talking like a French hand puppet?"

"Why don't you just shut your *bouche,* okay, Ellery? Just *fermez* it!"

Claudia became slightly more subdued. "This morning, Mommy goes, 'Do we know the Bevans?' " When she was imitating me, her voice went up like Celine Dion's. " 'Where do they live? Is he a bodybuilder?' And she gets that look, like, 'What kind of family is this? Are they good enough for us great Ehrlichs?' "

I wanted to storm upstairs and cry foul. Is this how

the girls saw reasonable parental concern and interest? As motherly malpractice?

"Well, so Mom and Dad are minisnobs, so what else is new? They mean well, don't forget."

"Listen, Ellery. You just stop shooting off your mouth or I'm going to return the favor. And if you touch any of my sweatshirts, bras, or bikinis again, you're dead meat!"

"Dead meat, dead meat! I bet you can't say that in French!"

"You wannna bet? *Viand morte, viand morte!*"

Five minutes later, they were downstairs together in the kitchen, laughing like the best of friends, watching Dumpling try to capture a Baggie. I was still steaming, but held back. Peter was due home within twenty minutes and he needs household harmony. I kept my voice modulated, asked them to set the table, fill the iced-tea pitcher, and told them to please keep their hands out of the chicken salad until it came to the table, or I would kill them.

It was Thursday of the following week. Peter came in as I was putting our 3-D Czech photographs into an album I'd bought just for the purpose. I hated the way I looked in most of them, with hair blowing, or my eyes looking as if I were having trouble reading an eye chart, and no matter how I turned, ten pounds heavier than in my full-length mirror upstairs. Peter had taken quite a liking to the snapshots, and intended to have a few enlarged. He particularly liked the one of me sharing space with the Charles Bridge and two swans. "I look like someone is stepping on my toes," I protested.

"It's very real life," he said.

"Too real," I said.

Peter had taken Josh Greavy to the club for dinner, although I'd offered to invite him to our house. Peter wanted time alone with Josh, to give him an opportunity to redeem himself. He felt he and the young man wouldn't be able to have a heart-to-heart with Claudia and Ellery here, and even my presence at the club might make the atmosphere "too convivial."

"Where are the girls?" was the first question he asked as he stepped over the threshold when he came home after his early dinner. It was a wet-hot evening and his summer suit was crushed. His bow tie, a bluish one, hung limp at his neck like a pair of deflated balloons.

Claudia was out with Kevin, and after Ellery and I had warmed up some leftover chili and eaten in front of the television set watching a special report she wanted to see about people who communicate with ghosts via fax machines, she'd gone off to the library.

"How is she getting back?" The jovial TV weatherman had predicted rain right through the weekend.

"Mrs. Honecker."

"Which one is Mrs. Honecker?"

"She's the young one with the beauty mark over her lip, the one that has kind of a Streisand nose—?"

Peter, who makes an appearance at the library only at the annual famous authors fund-raising event and wouldn't know one librarian from another, always asks me that. And he likes details. "She just got married. Remember, Ellery showed us her picture in the paper?"

Peter didn't remember. He went upstairs to close the window he thought might be open in the bedroom. It looked like it might begin to pour at any minute.

"Take your rain poncho," I'd told Ellery as she was getting ready to go. She was lacing up her sneakers, and it was still looking bright, not a cloud in the sky.

"Oh, Mommy, it's not going to rain." Ellery had stopped to look at herself in the hall mirror and while I'd watched, she'd smoothed her eyebrows, and pulled her fingers through her hair, in a perfect imitation of her older sister. "Anyhow, I like walking in the rain. It reminds me of how I used to love to run barefoot under the sprinkler when I was a child."

"When you were a child? So very long ago?"

"Oh, Mommy, don't get sentimental!"

"Aren't you going to tell me about your dinner with Josh Greavy?" I asked Peter now.

He had settled himself on the den sofa with the remote control, shoes off, feet up. Peter's eyes were at half-mast. "His occupation is fortune hunting. He's traveled from Alaska to Nicaragua to Staten Island, or wherever there are what he called 'natural resources,' for example, religious artifacts, fortunes hidden in the walls of old churches or, in one case, a gold mine in which there was actually, and for real, gold. Or so he said. He would take jobs here and there to tide him over, and said he thinks the big hit is right around the corner, in La Paz, where they're digging for a Portuguese icon. As soon as the estate is cleared up here, he's heading there. No interest at all in a scholarship fund in his father's name. No interest in anything to do with his father. And he's so arrogant."

"It sounds like the big hit happened right here when his parents died."

"Lib, that's what I was thinking all through dinner. But it was hard for me to look at this boy—although he's not really a boy, he's close to forty. His eyes, his teeth—he's his father all over again. He sounds just exactly like Lucas when he laughs, and the way he tilts his head when he talks—all through dinner I kept seeing Lucas."

I thought of Peter's father—his son much like him on the surface, but thank God, really nothing at all like the old man.

"And he's been all over the globe but wouldn't go to the cemetery. Allergies. I couldn't believe my ears."

"Maybe he's asthmatic?"

"Just afraid to sneeze. More likely, didn't want to be bothered.

"It's not that the boy is a bad seed. No criminal activity, it's nothing like that. It's only that he's sort of a mutant. He says he'll never marry, wants no children. Would rather go to the Adirondacks to look for lodes of granite, or to Key West, or Guadalajara, *unencumbered.* His word. He used it every five minutes. I'll tell you, I got tired of hearing 'unencumbered' because I kept thinking, well, he certainly got what he wanted. He's all alone in this world. His father, his mother—you'd think he'd be in a catatonic state. But no. The boy is missing something. Call it a soul, maybe. So you see"—Peter clicked the remote control at the TV but didn't really look at the screen—"Lucas, well, poor man, I suppose one way of looking at his death is not considering it as self-inflicted. Maybe it was a slow murder. If we can't find the comfort of hope, or a future in our children, we become, oh, I don't know what we become, Libby. Broken machines, I guess."

Ellery came in just as the first drops fell. She said she was totally exhausted and couldn't wait to fall into bed, although she'd take a shower first. "How many does that make today?" Peter asked. "Are we into the double digits?"

"Oh, Daddy!"

"Did Mrs. Honecker drive you right to the door?" I asked. "I didn't even hear the car."

"She dropped me at the corner. I told her to."

"Ellery, I don't like you walking alone at night."

"Mommy! Two doors—I mean, *two* little doors? And

it's not even 'do you know where your children are?' time—it's like five after *nine*?"

"Ell, we'll come and pick you up next time. End of discussion. Now, you come and sit with your old man a few minutes? Tell us what you read at the library. And massage my neck. I really need it."

But Ellery had found Dumpling under the lap desk in the corner and was busy smooching him, had to have a snack, had to get her yucky, sweaty clothes off, was so, so tired.

"Tomorrow, Daddy, okay? I'll massage your neck tomorrow night."

"Promise?"

"Promise."

The following afternoon, a Friday, while the rain poured against the windows and the girls were in the kitchen baking raisin cookies to take to a birthday party at the nursing home, there was a tap on the glass of the back door.

Trevor Eddy, wearing a khaki rain jacket with a hood that threw his features into sinister shadow, stood framed by the door of our mud room, his cheeks wet with either rain or perspiration, I couldn't tell which. Ellery had let him in, and he was stamping his wet shoes on the small mat in the mud room, smiling at me, asking "for a small favor." The distance between my feet and the mud room seemed to stretch as I moved across the floor, trying to imagine why he would be here, pulling off his hood, unbuttoning his jacket, in our house, now. Jacket open, hood off, he stood in my kitchen.

"I smell cinnamon!" he said, talking loud over the CD player, which Claudia had perched nearby on the kitchen counter. It was the most ordinary of remarks, the kitchen did reek of it, but I reacted as if he'd taken a hand wet with rain, and put it at the back of my neck.

Words rushed out of me one after another like an auctioneer holding a gavel. "Would you like to taste a cookie? These are with raisins. Do you like raisins? I mean, the girls are baking, they go to the nursing home and bring, umm, something, for a celebration, today someone turns one hundred—Ellery, could you turn down the music, dear? Thanks."

"One hundred two!" Claudia reached out a plate overflowing with cookies the girls had just a moment ago deemed too brown, held it toward Trevor.

He took one. "Looks like I stopped in at just the right time." He smiled all over the place—at Claudia, at me, at Ellery. Seemed slightly embarrassed. I thought he was thinking he'd probably stopped in at exactly not the right time. I imagined he'd hoped to find me alone. On the other hand, the idea was ridiculous. He'd been at work next door on and off most of the summer and had never come by before. "Mrs. Ehrlich. I just wondered if I could use your telephone?"

Mrs. Ehrlich, he called me. It was because the girls were here, but never mind, it reminded me he was four years younger and made me feel like I'd turned from a celadon bud into a yellow leaf in the three years since he'd worked here. He'd called me Libby then.

"We're moving some jacks and one of the crew cut a phone wire by mistake, then another guy took off with my cell phone."

"Go right ahead." I pointed to the kitchen wall telephone. Cool, casual, so, so polite; he could have been anyone, the mailman, a stranger off the street.

"I've got to get through to the electrician. He was due here at eleven and he's holding up the works."

I left the kitchen while he dialed, sneaking off to examine myself in the hall mirror. "Hey, Lou, we got the plaster waiting in the bucket, so where are you?" God, how pale I looked without blush. "Come on, Lou, it's going on three o'clock!" And lipstick. If I ran into the bedroom and put on a bit of lipstick, combed my hair, how would it look? Obvious, is how it would look. "If your van broke down, I'll send one of my crew down to pick you up, c'mon, let's get on with it, Louie." I pinched my cheeks to get a little color in them, fluffed up my hair à la Claudia. Then I thought it inexcusable for me, the yellow leaf, to be primping for Trevor Eddy, and stepped away. He was suddenly in the hall, standing there, looking at me and guessing I must have been looking at myself. "The best things about you don't show in a mirror."

I know I turned red. Simultaneously, the music in the kitchen returned to full blast.

"Girls, please!" I called. "Not so loud!"

"The girls are beautiful," he said.

"Thank you."

"I saw Salvatore DiBuono hanging around—"

"You know Ess?"

"He worked for me a couple of summers ago."

"I had no idea."

"He's not a bad kid, but a bit of a wild sheikh, if you know what I mean. I'd keep my eye on him if I were you."

I thought, *Look who's talking.*

"Peter's forbidden Claudia to see him."

"Probably a smart move. Not that he's that bad a kid. He's not into drugs, like a lot of them."

"No, not a bad kid."

"A bit of a fire-eater, that's all."

Now Trevor took a step toward me. The girls' voices got louder over the music, involved in an argument about whether or not to lower the oven temperature. Trevor's voice dropped an octave. "You know that four-leaf clover you gave me three years ago?"

"Yes."

"I still have it. I'll always have it." The way he spoke, the way his eyes and teeth and hands and shoulders looked, threw me off balance. Some men are good at golf, and some are good at business or bridge or playing the harmonica. Trevor was good at women. The old feelings were knocking around in me.

There was his usual Trevor aura of wood shavings and polyurethane, but mostly I imagined the scent of gasoline. It was my senses gone amok, throwing me back into the rear seat of the jalopies in which as a teenager I'd make out with the boy who was my passion of the moment. That's when the mere mention of the name of the object of my affection made my whole body cook, and here was the feeling back, just at the sight of Trevor Eddy. I imagined myself doing it with him, the "it" a confusing mix of sex and love, scrunched up against those worn old-car leather cushions, fighting him off, then going totally wild and giving in. I saw us crushed together in the erotic confines of that backseat, the motor running. I saw us sweating in the tropics on a four-poster under mosquito netting. I pictured us together in meadows and forests, coupling on beaches, wrapped around each other in front of roaring fires or lying side by side on moss near a waterfall. Call it chemistry or heat or infatuation, I now think it was just my trying to get back into sync with life.

"And the four-leaf clover brought you luck?" I asked him.

"Not yet, not yet," he said, and he opened his palms as if he were holding a package, and seared me with a look. "Do you think we could go somewhere private and talk sometime?"

"I'm sorry."

"Just talk?"

"I can't do that. I'm sorry."

As we passed through the kitchen on the way out, he asked the girls about Dumpling. It was sort of a mechanically polite query. "Is she all right after her big adventure?"

"It's a he," Claudia said, and I saw the girls exchange glances. Ellery's eyes slid in my direction and slid away fast.

"I forgot, a he," Trevor said.

"What big adventure?" I felt a tingle.

"Oh, he got lost for a little while one night," Claudia said, and began singing with the radio.

Trevor's eyes darted from Claudia to Ellery, but not to me.

"Lost?"

"*Pas de* sweat, Mommy. We found him, safe and sound."

"Where did you find him?"

"In the Dubersteins' garage. Should we turn the oven temperature down to three hundred? The cookies are getting too brown, *Maman*!"

She was changing the subject, but Trevor Eddy had turned at the door to thank me for letting him use the phone and I was distracted.

"Another cookie, Trevor?" Claudia asked.

"Thanks. One for the road," he said, taking one. He never took his eyes off mine.

"What about you, Mommy? Want to try one?"

"I'm not having any," I said, very pointedly, looking at Trevor. "But thanks anyway, girls."

I was still trying to get Trevor out of my mind when I stepped out of the shower the next morning. The doorbell rang and I waited a minute to see if Ellery would answer it. Claudia was asleep, Peter doing his hospital rounds. "Ellery? Are you going to get it?" No answer. "Ellery? Where are you?" I'd heard her playing with Dumpling in the hall not fifteen minutes ago. I threw on a terry cloth robe, wrapped my head in a towel, and ran downstairs.

"Hi, Mrs. E."

His black van was at the curb, this time with a ladder fixed to the top, and he stood in the doorway looking slicked down, his hair either wetted or greased into a shiny flat helmet, tied back by a red rubber band. The same blue-mirror sunglasses, and not a smidgen nervous.

"Ess."

"G'morning, Mrs. E. How are you this morning?" His mother had had eight babies, so how much time could she give each little one, how many little loving hugs, pats, and kisses, compliments, pep talks? Where had all his self-esteem come from?

He was holding out a brown paper sack. "For you and the girls. With my compliments."

I hesitated. I don't like unexpected things, and this was an unexpected thing. Something ghoulish could be in that bag, something severed, or explosive.

"Just some tomatoes from the DiBuono garden, Mrs. E. We had a decent crop, for once."

No, he was just friendly puppy Ess, keeping on our good side. But why?

"That's really nice of you, Ess."

"I thought they might come in handy for your salad. No pesticides. And there's some arugula in there, too. The dressing you're going to have to supply, sorry about that. We only grow tomatoes, radishes, arugula. I don't know why my father refuses to plant oil and vinegar. Maybe the soil is better for burying Caesar—"

When I was fifteen I had an Ess in my life. I must have repressed his memory until this minute. Like Ess, he was incorrigible, a jack of no trades, but for charisma, no one came close. Like Ess, he was seductive, funny, wrong to love, impossible to hate.

Ess asked about Peter, the cat, Darley's health, and then, "So, I thought I'd stop by with these. Just saying hello."

"I'd ask you in, but—" I could think of twenty reasons

for not asking him in, Peter hitting the roof being the first.

"Oh, that's all right. I gotta go to work. I'm a little late already."

"Oh, you got a new job?"

"When the sun shines. I'm painting houses. The Picasso of clapboard and the Renoir of brick. Shutters my specialty."

"Well, that's nice."

"I'm going back to school come winter."

"Well, that's nice, too." I guessed that's why he'd come, to let us know he'd reformed and wasn't going to be doing odd jobs forever.

"So, I'll be seeing you, Mrs. E."

School or no, I hoped never, but took the tomatoes and thanked him politely.

When he turned to leave, I read the back of his T-shirt: WINGS IN SHOP FOR 1000 MILE CHECKUP. I also had a glimpse of the tattoo—still there. It would be there till death did us part.

Ellery was in the kitchen, eating a mango. "Where were you a minute ago?" I asked. "I had to run downstairs soaking wet in my bare feet to answer the door."

"In the basement."

"Doing what?"

"I was changing the kitty litter. You're always asking me to change the kitty litter."

"Of your own accord! Am I dreaming?"

"There's always a first time, Mommy."

I pulled out the lettuce and six thin-skinned, gorgeous tomatoes. A bunch of deep green arugula. "Ess is not all bad," I said. Ellery offered to wash the tomatoes without being asked. There was always a first time for that, too. "I definitely must be dreaming."

"I was in a tomato-washing mood, Mommy."

She'd brought the CD player into the kitchen, à la Claudia, and I practically had to yell over it. "So, are you also in the mood to tell me what was Dumpling's big adventure?"

Ellery wouldn't look at me. She was wearing not only lip gloss but a bit of mascara, too. "He got lost for a couple of hours, when you were away, that's all. We found him. Now everything's biff."

I was looking for my car keys the following morning when there was an urgent tap on the glass of the kitchen door. Sarah Jane was in brilliant blue-and-white dots. White on blue, blue on white, canvas blue shoes with white buttons, with painted toenails peeping out, and a long white sort of vest thing. These were clothes seen in magazines, not in shops, and certainly not on people in Crandall, especially when the temperature was hovering near ninety-five degrees.

"I hate to bother you, Libby, but could you spare a roll of paper towels? We're in a mess at my house, they're finally painting the upstairs baths, some of my suntan lotion got spilled, I just went to get another roll of paper towels out of the cupboard, and you know me"—giggle-giggle—"there wasn't any." Her tone reminded me of Ellery's Jennifers.

She stepped into the kitchen on the waft of her scent, some esoteric cologne I would never have worn before midnight, sailed comfortably in like she was part of the family, and walked over to the utility closet, sort of waiting for me to open it and hand over a roll of paper towels out of my personal cache. My mind hopscotched over all her other sins, searching for the right words with which to begin telling her very kindly I wasn't going to lend her so much as a rubber band after I helped her out this time, until she'd returned the forty or fifty things she'd borrowed over the years. I'd made up my mind. It had finally come to the line in the sand.

"No, wait a minute, Lib. It's not just paper towels I

need. Would you believe I've run out of coffee?" How does anyone run out of coffee? "And I want to make some for Trevor's crew. I always make a pot and leave it in the kitchen for the guys."

"The guys." I echoed. I don't care what the Bible says. This is one neighbor I could no way love.

"All I keep doing is going to the supemarket and buying radishes. Radishes! I swear, I bought three sacks of radishes this week alone."

"Radishes."

"It's because—I, because, Libby, I can't believe I'm telling you this. Why am I telling you this? I should be telling a therapist, where in fact, I'm going in twenty minutes. I have an appointment at eleven. Oh, what the hell, Lib, Barry and I, we're having problems. Sex? I swear he'd rather wash his car. It's not exactly that he doesn't care about me, it's like, he used up all his serious love on his first family. His ex-wife, his girls, they took off the cream. Now here we are, remodeling the house top to bottom and he says he's decided not to move after all this renovation. He wants to stay right here, just the two of us. The idea of spending the rest of my life with a family man whose whole focus is on a family, of which I'm not really a part—well, what am I doing here? Oh, God, I can't think! I keep forgetting to buy things, or get home and find radishes in my grocery bags."

I opened the utility closet to get a roll of paper towels. "You know something else? Last year, when Barry and I were in Prague, some gypsies tried to steal my purse. They had a knife and were ready to cut the shoulder strap. We were coming out of a shop and a few of them appeared out of nowhere."

"You heard about Peter's camera. They cut the strap. Same exact thing."

She cut me off again. "And suddenly I realized, here I am, almost forty years old, and what would I have if they'd killed poor Barry? No career, no kids, just a fancy five-bedroom house in Crandall, Connecticut, and one hundred twelve pairs of shoes? Anyway, it got me thinking about how much of my life I've already spent on a man who puts me last." She slumped into a chair and her white vest fell open to reveal a blue-dotted lining. I saw a life dedicated to sartorial coordination as a substitute for something she really wanted: a brood. Or at least, an Ellery and Claudia of her own. Against my will, my hand reached out to touch her shoulder in sympathy.

"What's brought this to a head"—she lowered her voice and, when she spoke, sounded like a recording made at another time—"is Trevor Eddy."

"Trevor Eddy?"

"I'm ashamed. Ashamed to tell you this. Please, don't tell Peter. You won't tell Peter?"

"Tell him what?"

"I'm very, very attracted to Trevor."

"To Trevor *Eddy*?"

"I think about him all the time. He's the sort of man who should come with a warning label."

I pulled my hand away. "The pinking shears," I said.

"What?"

"You borrowed my pinking shears. Do you suppose I could have them back, Sarah Jane?"

"The pinking shears? When did I borrow them?" The blue and white dots seemed to jump as she fidgeted in her chair. "I'm telling you I'm in a dangerous, crazy attraction, and you're talking pinking shears?"

"I need them."

"You need the pinking shears—now?"

"No, actually, I don't need them. But I think you should return them. And the stamps, and the world atlas, all the eggs, and the jar of mustard and—I'll give you a list."

"What's wrong, Lib? Oh, why did I bother to ask you that? I know what's wrong! You don't approve, is what's wrong. You think I shouldn't be thinking of having an affair."

"It's none of my business."

"Well, I can see it in your eyes, but look, this is not the most unusual circumstance these days, is it? It's common as carpenter ants. We have problems. They're bigger than a fall off a horse and a fractured arm. They're *serious* problems. Barry's younger daughter doesn't speak to me because she says I stole him from her mother, Barry's mother keeps calling me by his first wife's name, his older daughter is sweet as pie to my face but tells everyone I'm killing her father, spending all his money. So, Barry and I wanted to buy another house to make a fresh start—before we got married he said okay to more children—but forget it. Everything's changed. You might not understand an extramarital attraction, but it's like a drug high without the drug. See, an affair is like breaking out of the pain of your life."

There was a pause, during which we both stared at the floor.

"Right into the frying pan," I said.

"You just happen to be very happily married. You just happen to have it all. You just happen, if you don't mind my saying it, Lib, to be a tiny, itsy bit smug. The perfect doctor's perfect wife, the perfect daughters' perfect mommy, and so on. We aren't all that lucky, you see."

I sort of waved my arm, trying to think of a kind way to tell her to get off it, but Sarah Jane cut me off.

"I shouldn't have said that."

I handed her a roll of paper towels. "Well, I'm not sure," I said, and she apologized, thanked me for the towels, and said she'd look for the pinking shears tonight.

* * *

It was Monday at eight. Peter was on call and the phone had not stopped ringing this entire weekend. He was at the hospital this morning, so I took the newspaper up to bed with coffee and a croissant, closed the door, and prepared for an hour of solitude and peace.

"Oh, my God! I don't believe this!" Footsteps, doors banging open, the crash of the toilet lid; I'd just started reading about the heroic efforts of the Red Cross to save the starving in Somalia, and I wanted the girls to please, please leave me in peace for a whole sixty minutes, long enough to also let me check out the human interest stories, the Wall Street reports, the political news—but no. Last night, Claudia had invited six friends for a barbecue in honor of Kevin's leaving for Wesleyan, and sixty more had appeared at eleven. Or, at least, it had seemed like sixty. It's the way adolescent social life works in Crandall. Invitations are irrelevant. The teenage grapevine is relevant. Their racket had shaken the trees. Peter, Dumpling, and I had sat trapped in the bedroom, trying to shut out the noise.

Ellery had gone out. Despite Peter's resistance, she had jumped heavily into baby-sitting for the Riley twins, promising never to accept a job that would keep her out later than eleven. Eleven had stretched to 11:30 and lately, to midnight. Last night it had been ten after, but fortunately, Peter's attention had been focused on keeping down the party noise in our yard, watching out for pot and cocaine, and monitoring the couples who kept disappearing behind trees. Claudia's father-detection radar had kept her and Kevin conspicuously visible on the patio. Still, we hadn't gotten much sleep.

Forget making up for last night with a bit of quiet time this morning. Claudia's voice rang out, ricocheting through the rooms. "What's wrong with you, Ellery? Mommy! Mommy!"

I dropped the newspaper and ran out to the hall.

"She's barfed all over the bathroom floor!"

"Ellery! What's wrong? Sweetheart, what?"

She was standing over the toilet now, retching and shaking. "Poor Ellery! Not you, too!" I felt her forehead. Cool. "Honey, what did you eat?"

She stopped gagging and stood glassy-eyed, shaking her head. "Yuck."

"What did you eat last night when you were baby-sitting?"

"Cheez Doodles and chocolate-chip ice cream."

"That wouldn't make you sick, sweetheart. What else?"

"I'm better. I'm okay."

"You girls are probably eating junk somewhere without realizing it."

"I drank root beer, too."

"Root beer. Not beer?"

"Root beer, Mommy."

"You're sure?"

"I'm sure!"

"Maybe same bug Claudia had a few weeks ago."

"I'm all better now, anyway, Mommy."

"Are you sure?"

"Much better."

"You look pale. Why not lie down for a while?"

She went back to bed and I sat with her for half an hour, relieved to see the color come back into her cheeks. As she sipped Coke and became more animated, the life seemed to flow into her and she talked about a movie she'd seen, about getting a CD album, about bungee jumping, what kind of car she'd drive when she turned seventeen, and then she said, "You know, Mommy, ever since I was a child"—I did not let her see me smile at this—"I've always felt very old. Isn't that funny? I mean, I feel like I'm much older than Claudia. Claudia behaves, umm, so immature, sometimes."

"In what way?"

"Like these ditsy friends of hers. And she's always looking into the store windows in the mall, just to see herself. And when she's with Kevin and he's driving, she'll go, 'Floor it, Kev.' Like that."

I made a quick note to tell Claudia she was never, ever to say that to someone behind a wheel again.

"And even with Ess—" She stopped. Beans she hadn't meant to spill.

"What about Ess?"

"She used to tell him, like, he wasn't allowed to talk sports or she'd walk right away from him, no matter where they were. And then she goes, 'I'd like my photo back, if you don't mind.' I mean, he bought her so many presents it's, like, ridiculous, and she's got to have her picture back? Is she for real?"

"So he gave it back to her?"

"Of course. He doesn't care diddly for Claudia anymore."

"Why did he bring over the tomatoes, then?"

"He loves our family, is all."

"How do you know?"

"I just know. See what I mean? I just know things about people. He's a good person. And, I feel things better than most kids my age. Maybe I've lived before."

"As a senior citizen?"

"Oh, Mommy, I'm serious. Don't you think age is irrevelant?"

"Irrelevant, dear."

"Irrelevant. Don't you think some people are just born older than they are?"

"Maybe, dear. Maybe. Are you feeling better?"

"Much. I'm hungry. Would you make me some toast and jelly?" Her smile was back. It always turned on a switch in me. I told her I loved her and went scurrying to the kitchen to put on the kettle and plug in the toaster.

By the time Peter came home, Ellery had eaten breakfast, changed her clothes, and run off on her Rollerblades and I'd cleaned up the upstairs bathroom. I never told him Ellery had been sick; I didn't want him going back into the refrigerator and cleaning it out again, and anyway, she was fine now, so I didn't see any reason. It would be likely to ruin his day, and for sure, mine.

Before he put his car keys away, before he took off his shoes, checked with his service, or lowered himself into a chair, it was always, "Where are the girls?" Peter's query was as automatic as a dial tone. But today it was preceded by, "Who left this sack at the back door?" And he handed me a brown paper bag filled with twelve ears of corn. There was no note.

"The kid makes me nervous," Peter said.

"I think he's basically harmless." I really wasn't sure now. "But I'll call Ess tomorrow and thank him and tell him please not to leave any more produce, all right?"

"Nothing is that easy. You know the world is full of—of tabloid stories." Peter, looking somehow newly round-shouldered, shook his head. "Where are the girls now?"

"Ellery's going to the schoolyard. Rollerblading. Claudia is at a clambake."

"I suppose she's sleeping with this one, now."

"Oh, Pete, let's not get into that today."

"Goddamn it, first a bum and now this Kevin. And this kid definitely has a shifty look. Like he's wholesome on the outside, but not so wholesome all the way through. Ess never knew when to shut up and this one never talks at all."

"Oh, Peter, he's only seventeen."

"And probably doesn't know a thing about condoms."

"Maybe they're holding off."

"And maybe next year taxes will go down."

"I'll try to talk to her."

"You know how far we get trying to talk to Claudia."

"At least he drives his father's car and it's got double-sided air bags. That's something."

"That is something."

"Pete, are you very tired? We ought to get out of the house. You dwell on the girls so much when we're home. Especially Claudia."

"It's the HIV thing. I see it every day. And hepatitis. Late abortions. STDs. If I could put her in a chastity belt—"

"But you said sex was healthy."

"It is. Statistically. And for other people's daughters."

"Pete, there's an auction in Ridgefield. I thought we could drive up after lunch."

"Lib, I'm on call."

"I know, dear, but you've got a beeper. And Ridgefield is only thirty, thirty-five minutes away—"

"I've got Simon Yancey in the hospital. He's in a severely bad way, and there's Mrs. Constantino. They had to resuscitate her at four this morning. I'd better stick around. You go."

"Oh, no, Pete. It's not that important. I'd rather stay home with you." I could never keep up with Peter's list of ailing hearts.

"Maybe when the girls come home we can all go out for pizza. You won't have to cook."

I remembered Ellery's upset stomach. "Or maybe I'll

just grill some hamburgers. I don't mind. And don't forget, we've got lots of corn."

Ellery was sick to her stomach again. She didn't actually vomit, but ran to the bathroom and stood gagging over the toilet just as Trevor Eddy's van was pulling into the driveway next door and Peter's car was pulling out of ours. I ran downstairs to try to stop him, but by the time I got to the door, Peter had turned the corner. I went to the telephone to call his car phone to get him back, but remembered Mr. Yancey and Mrs. Constantino—or was it Mrs. Yancey and Mr. Constantino?—and put down the receiver. I could always reach him later. He hates to be late for his morning hospital rounds. These very sick people need him more than a daughter with an upset stomach.

"What did you eat, Ellery?"

"The same thing everyone else ate. Those hamburgers you made and the corn on the cob Ess brought, and the salad, and I didn't even have the grizpacho, 'cause you told me not to eat it."

"Gazpacho. What about later? Did you eat anything later in the evening? Or drink anything?"

"Just a few nachos. And a scoop of Heath bar ice cream, is all. I didn't drink anything, Mommy."

"Maybe it was the ice cream. Lactose intolerance, possibly. We better tell Daddy this time and have him take a look at you."

"I'm feeling better, Mommy."

"I think you ought to stay home today."

"Really, I'm okay. I've got some books I've got to take back to the library."

"I'll take them back for you. You're to stay in."

"Oh, Mommy—"

"In. You're staying. In."

* * *

The August edition of *Southern Connecticut Life* had a picture of Paul Newman and Joanne Woodward on the cover. "When the Newmans entertain, they prefer small dinners for six or eight, and a cocktail hour that never exceeds forty-five minutes," was the tone of this family profile. The emphasis was on the Newmans' dedication to charity, fast cars, their garden in Westport, spaghetti sauce, and being out of the limelight. Airbrushed prose written by the same reporter who had interviewed us for *Southern Connecticut Life.* The photographs were flattering and bland. A good sign.

I took the magazine and two others to the front desk to check out. To show Peter. I piled Ellery's books on the desk, found my library card, and waited for the librarian.

"Is Mrs. Honecker in today?" I asked the young man who took my card and pushed it into what looked like the mouth of an ATM. A tiny sci-fi spark ignited when he pulled it out.

"No, I'm afraid she's not. Did you want to speak to someone else?" The young man had a particularly clipped, English way of pronouncing vowels. *Not* was *nut,* he elongated the *her* and reminded me of every teacher of English I'd ever had.

"Oh, no, it's nothing special. As long as I was here, I wanted to thank her for driving my daughter home from the library the last few weeks."

"Oh, wull, she's in Maine. She should be beck"—he turned to a woman who was putting books back on a shelf right behind him—"Barbara, when is Muriel due beck?"

The woman turned and said, "Not until after Labor Day. Can I help with something?"

"Oh, no, nothing important. I'll thank her when she gets back."

The Barbara woman stepped forward. "Did I hear you say you wanted to thank her for driving your daughter home?"

"Yes, actually. She's been so nice to go out of her way."

The Barbara librarian looked thoughtful for a moment. Then she produced a serviceable smile. "You may have Mrs. Honecker mixed up with one of our other librarians?"

I told her I didn't think so, but why did she assume?

"Mrs. Honecker took the summer off. She's honeymooning in Maine for two months. In fact, we just got a card from her today. From Bar Harbor. They've already had frost up there, would you believe it?"

I pounded up the stairs and, behind the closed door of her room, I confronted Ellery as soon as I got home. I turned the music off with a snap.

"I walked home," she said.

"Alone?" I was breathless. This was the child who never lied.

"Yes." She was lying.

"Why? You know we don't allow you to go anywhere at night alone!"

"It's okay, Mommy. This is a safe town. Everybody else—" *Everybody else*—it's the déjà heard lyric of an old familiar song, a fighting phrase.

"Not everybody else lies!"

"I don't lie!"

"You lied about Mrs. Honecker!"

"I didn't want to be babied! I didn't want to be picked up by my mommy or daddy like a kid in nursery school!"

"You'd rather be dragged off into some bush and mugged—or worse?"

"You can pick me up next time, but, Mommy, please"—her eyes pleaded with me for a few seething minutes—"don't tell Daddy. You know how upset he gets."

At dinner, Ellery scarfed down four pieces of chicken, two ears of corn and a tomato from Ess's contributions, and two kaiser rolls. Peter wouldn't let her drink milk, eat ice cream, or leave the house. We would all be home tonight—"Let's call it Family Night like the Mormons do"—and we might try our hands at finally finishing that Niagara Falls puzzle that was gathering dust in the living room. Mrs. Constantino had died peacefully, and the attending nurse reported she'd passed on with her fingers curled around the hands of two of her grandchildren. She would have been ninety-six on her next birthday, and this seemed the gentlest of endings for a good and long life. It was the way, Peter remarked, he'd like to leave this earth. But not yet. He smiled broadly at Claudia, not until we'd heard more from *"la fille belle"* about her progress in French.

Whereupon Claudia slammed down her fork and ran upstairs to answer the ringing telephone.

"I really hate it when that phone constantly interrupts life," he said.

"I bet if I jumped up and interrupted dinner like that I wouldn't get away with it." Ellery wiped her hands on a napkin. "If Claudia does it, well, it's like, so what."

Peter ignores what he wants to ignore. "Did you put butter on that corn? I don't want you putting butter on the corn, sweetheart."

"I'm feeling fine. Absolutely fine. In fact, I don't see why I can't go to the library." Ellery looked at me and I glared back.

"We're all staying home together tonight." Peter took

the buttered ear off her plate and replaced it with an unbuttered one. "We can watch the shooting stars. Heaven's light show."

Not an hour later, Mrs. Riley stopped by. She was dropping off Ellery's denim jacket, left at her house three weeks ago. She said she'd tried to call, but the girls' phone was "forever busy. I was a teenager once, so I know what that's all about," she said, looking not much older than that now.

I thanked her for the jacket and asked if she wanted to come in. "I wish I could but the twins are in the car," she said, and bounced off down the walk. When she was at the curb, about to open the car door, she turned to wave good-bye and called out, "Tell Ellery the girls miss her! Now that they're over their ear infections, I'll be calling her again!"

We stayed home that night, but not together. Peter and I sat on the patio and watched heaven's light show. The girls stayed upstairs, playing video games, talking on the phone, fighting, coming downstairs for a refill on sodas or nachos or to look at the *TV Guide.* The stereo blared ("Turn it down!") and later, the TV blared ("It's too loud!"), and at eleven, while we watched the news, Claudia appeared in the den in denim shorts and a shirt tied to expose a stripe of perfect suntanned midriff. She licked her lips and untangled her hair with her fingers and then bunched it into tangles again. Every three minutes she pulled back the curtain and looked out the window.

"You're not going out *now*?"

"Now, Daddy, please. We always go through this."

"It's after eleven, sweetie."

"Mommy, have I explained to your husband the doctor how Kevin works late and how all the kids go out late and have I told him *une mille* times that I can nap during the day at the beach, and anyway Friday is the last day of summer school and I'll have what's left of the summer to catch up on my z's?"

I heard the telephone ring at twenty to twelve, and later, after Peter had fallen asleep, the sounds of Claudia pounding down the stairs. I fell asleep trying to remember whether I'd mixed things up. Hadn't Ellery gone to baby-sit at the Rileys' just last Saturday night?

I woke up at quarter to four, but not from a bad dream about snow. I was as bright alert as noon, without the slightest chance of falling back to sleep. It was like that sci-fi spark at the library, an electric discharge, a *ping* in my head. Ellery had definitely stated that she was going to the Rileys' Saturday night, but please not to call her there; the telephone sometimes woke one of the babies. *Pozor:* A train was about to barrel through our lives, full blast.

I waited until Peter left.

Chemically revved up, I waited in bed, aware of the adrenaline pump doing its job.

As soon as I heard his car pull out of the driveway, I barreled into Ellery's room. It was empty. I found her in the bathroom, leaning over the toilet. She was breathing deeply and her face was clammy, as if she'd just been pulled out of a river.

"Ellery."

She didn't look at me.

"Ellery!"

Slowly, she turned her head and her eyes caught mine. They were the color of cut limes, watery, transparent.

"This isn't the same stomach virus Claudia had, is it?"

No answer.

"No purple plums! No lactose intolerance!

"Speak to me!"

No answer.

I leaned my head against the door frame. It seemed made of rough iron, not painted wood.

"Oh, God, Ellery, oh, God! Tell me I'm wrong!"

# Chapter Seven

Peter came lumbering into the coffee shop, his eyes jumping left and right over the people sitting in booths until he found me. He slid into the seat opposite mine and my first thought was that he looked as crisp at the end of the day as he had when he'd walked out of the house this morning. This was not the first time I'd noted that the drama of life and death did not leave a visible mark on him.

"So? Why have we called this meeting?" Peter's mouth curled up under his mustache. I'd called him at noon to set this coffee-shop rendezvous at four. It seemed best to be away from the house and the girls when I broke the news, in a setting that dictated self-control. It seemed best to have him in a neutral place with hot coffee in his hand, anchored in a booth, rather than at home, where he might—might what? I couldn't guess.

The waitress had arrived to take our order. RITA was the name printed on her name-tag brooch.

"Hello, Rita," Peter said, making a point of squinting

at the name. "Lib, are you having anything more than coffee?"

"No. Just coffee, please."

Rita had plucked out her eyebrows and penciled in new ones. "Leaded or unleaded?"

"Well, Rita. Two leaded, I guess." He broadened his smile. "If you made it yourself."

*Please, Peter,* I thought, *not now.*

"Rita, I swear, you look just like Audrey Hepburn. I bet everybody tells you that. Doesn't she, Lib?"

*Peter, please, please shut up.* "I think we ought to order, Peter."

"Okay. The boss says to order. Coffee, if you made it yourself, and a very small piece of that blueberry pie I saw going by on the way to another table."

Rita scribbled on her pad and asked if Peter would like some ice cream on top of his pie. "I try never to touch it. The most dangerous food in the refrigerator, did you know that, ladies?"

Rita hadn't known that, and told us no one ever said she looked like Audrey Hepburn, but people often mistook her for Julia Roberts. When she smiled she had a dimple on one side of her face but not the other. It was so deep it looked like someone had gouged it out with the same pencil that had drawn her eyebrows.

"She doesn't look like anyone," I said under my breath, as soon as she'd left.

"Oh, it makes them feel good, y'know, sweetie. And what does it cost?"

"My nerves. It gets on my nerves."

"What's the matter, sweetie? What's wrong?"

"I'm sorry, Pete, but I have something terrible, horrible . . . I have something to tell you that I don't know how to tell you."

Peter's fingers, absently playing with the packets of sweetener on the table, froze in motion.

"Ellery is pregnant."

The pull of his lip away from his teeth. "Ellery is—?"

I nodded. "Yes, yes. You heard right. Pregnant."

His face fell forward as if an ax had fallen on the back of his neck, then snapped back. He shook his head. "Say it again."

"Ellery is pregnant."

"No."

"It's so."

"Libby, you can't be sitting here telling me that my twelve-year-old baby is pregnant."

"She's thirteen. And she is. Yes. Is in a family way. As they say."

I was suddenly so angry, so full of fury, I wanted to hurl everything in sight—the sugar substitute, the salt and pepper shakers, the napkin dispenser, and all the while, I didn't know why. Maybe because Peter called her "my baby," when she was "our baby," or maybe because he always had to kid with waitresses like some high-school junior, or maybe just because there was no one else here to be angry at except God.

"You know this for sure?" His face said he was doubting me, and now I felt I could throw the table at him, I was so furious. As if I'd call him and pull him out of his office while sick people sat in connected leatherette chairs waiting their turn to see the Almighty Doctor if it weren't so. As if I'd say such a thing unless I knew absolutely for dead certain. As if I'd ask him to meet me in a diner in the middle of his day just to tell him her period was late.

"I ran out this morning and bought one of those doohingy pregnancy tests and the stain turned blue as a forget-me-not and anyway, I *knew* it. It all added up. I could see it in her face. I *felt it.* I sensed it. I'm her *mother.*" I think I felt a tear gather in one eye as I said this. "Anyway, I ran out later, got another brand. It registered a plus. A little plus sign."

"And who—" He swallowed the next few words, got

them down as if they were chewed beef, but I assumed he was asking whose sperm had been shot into Ellery's love canal. *Love canal* was a phrase I'd read in some pornographic book when I was probably Ellery's age. How awful and how strange that it was making an unexpected revival now.

"Ess."

Chin to hairline, Peter's face stretched into an expression so strange one would have sworn the sun was melting it. *"Ess DiBuono?"*

I nodded. The tear ran out of my eye and I picked up a napkin to wipe it away.

"I don't believe it." Peter swallowed. And then he said it again. "No, I don't. Not possible."

Rita put the pie in front of him. "Who gets the decaf?" she asked, holding a cup over the table. It was a mistake, someone in the next booth. Peter didn't look at her, and she seemed confused. I could see why; he was Mr. Party-Time one minute, and embalmed the next. Now there was some business about exchanging the coffee, she tried kidding a bit, and he never even looked at her. He never picked up the fork, either. Just looked at the pie as if it had been left on the table by former diners. When the waitress had replaced the coffee and moved off, he said, "I feel as if water is rushing over my head. I think I'm drowning."

And he put his head in both his hands and covered his face.

The anger seeped out of me. "Peter."

I looked furtively left and right to see if anyone was watching. He was still The Doctor in a town where gossip was the principal form of recreation. I caught sight of a familiar face or two; this coffee shop had not been a good idea. Peter's hands finally slid down from his face and he pulled a handkerchief out of his inside pocket. He wiped his eyes, wadded it up, and stuck it back into his pocket. His eyes looked small and red, like a laboratory bunny's. I reached over and held his wrist very tight, felt the soft hairs under my fingertips. "Peter, please."

"Don't, Libby."

I pulled my hand off his wrist as if I'd cracked it.

"What?" he asked, looking blank.

"What what?"

"What did we do?" I thought he meant, *to deserve this?* but it's not what he meant. He was asking what we'd done wrong, what parenting flaws, oversights, carelessness, neglect, or abuse had created a child who would become pregnant at age thirteen. How had we created a barely teen girl who would succumb to the sexual allure of a twenty-two-year-old ne'er-do-well? Where had we gone awry? Pregnancy at thirteen was against all statistical odds. It happened in ghettos in the Bronx, in equatorial Africa, or in institutions where mentally handicapped nubile girls were raped in broom closets. It happened in other, dark, poor, frightening places where there were drugs and roaches, fire escapes and rats, unemployment, absent fathers, crack-addicted mothers. It was an inner-city, other-place, faraway-from-us modern catastrophe, children getting pregnant at an age where in our generation they were playing hopscotch. It couldn't, hadn't, didn't happen in a place like Crandall, Connecticut. And it never happened to people like us.

Rita stopped by to offer us a refill. "Anything wrong with the pie?" Peter couldn't answer. I had to answer for him. "No. Just changed his mind."

When Ellery had fallen off her horse and fractured her arm, Peter had comforted me. I had fallen against him physically and spiritually; his strength had seemed immortal. Now our roles had reversed; I was Atlas and he was the world. As we walked out of the coffee shop together, I felt the man walking next to me had aged a decade, had stooped, grown gray, tired, and defeated in the spin of the last twenty minutes. He walked me to my car, leaned on my arm as if we were walking uphill, and felt as if he'd added lead weight with each step.

"When you called, I thought you were going to tell me you found a sixteenth-century icon at a garage sale, or something. That's what I thought."

"Peter, what do we do?" I asked.

"All I can think of is killing him. Just seeing him on the ground with his eyes rolled up, dead as a deer on a fender, that's all that seems to come to mind."

Claudia, with Dumpling rubbing against her legs, was opening a can of cat food when I walked into the kitchen. Kevin Bevan, with a half-empty glass of milk in one hand and a brownie in the other, stood politely to greet me when I walked in. Claudia's head spun in my direction. "Did you tell Daddy?"

She saw my face. "It's all right. Kevin would never tell."

Kevin swallowed the remainder of his mouthful of brownie and shook his head to confirm that he'd never utter a word. He raised his hand into the air as if he were taking an oath to keep our secret, but I knew life and Claudia didn't. Kevin wouldn't tell until next month, or next year. Until he'd had two Bloody Marys or someone brought up the subject of Dr. Ehrlich. Or some other junior-high miss, some local subteen, got pregnant. Long after Claudia had moved on to the next boy, or the one after that, he'd talk. "Keep this quiet," he'd begin, and it would pour out of him like lemonade from a pitcher. He'd raise his right hand again, but this time to swear it was true: Dr. Ehrlich's *younger* daughter. The Doctor's little just-out-of-diapers kid got herself knocked up by some loser from the wrong side of the tracks, some kid whose parents didn't even belong to a country club.

My sad and devastated little girl. This morning, she'd pushed herself into the corner of her bed, telescoped herself knees-up into the white pillows with the fancy eyelet ruffles, crushed her body into them as if they could swallow her. All the prettiness I'd seen in her, the emerging honeyed blossom, the rosy ingenuousness, was gone. The looks I'd wished on her, bestowed on her through a mother's eyes, were my illusion. She was not a beautiful girl; she was not a peachy, scrumptious doe, not a lush debutante-to-be. Not brilliant or witty, either. She was intense and angular. Her nose pointed too sharply, her eyes were too close together. As she'd held her little brown monkey, one of the stuffed animals that still sat in a row on a shelf above her bed, I'd seen her as she was, and been inundated with an overwhelming rush of love.

She'd alternated sobs with hiccups. I'd alternated tears and anger. He hadn't raped her. Hadn't used force. She kept insisting. So, it was consensual. Ellery having sex. No possible image came to mind. The guileless child who'd fallen off her horse—how many weeks ago?—a mother-to-be? It seemed as far-fetched as going over the Falls in a barrel. "How could you?" "How did it happen?" My voice had ricocheted against the walls of the room. In my passion, I think I tore a picture of some coyote-eyed rock star off the wall and threw it in the trash, for no reason at all.

Ess had saved Dumpling, while we were away. Well, not exactly saved, but helped find. Dumpling had disappeared one night. Gone out the back door and vanished. Marguerita, Claudia, and Ellery had searched the neighborhood. Called the neighbors. They'd needed a car to drive them up and down the streets to continue the search; Ess had been at the schoolyard, and not by coincidence; he was always there, always available.

Ellery had gone with him. They'd checked the trees. Sometimes kittens climbed telephone poles or lofty oaks and then couldn't get down. Garage roofs, too. Ess had climbed one, thinking he saw Dumpling hiding behind a branch. It was the Dubersteins' garage, Ellery said, and the slate had been very slippery; he'd almost slid off. Nearly broke his ankle. And he'd been wrong. Dumpling had disappeared like a night fog. Not a sign of him anywhere. Ellery had been afraid he'd fallen into a well, but hadn't known of any wells nearby. They'd driven and driven, it seemed like half the night. Ellery hadn't wanted to give up the search, and Ess had been willing to keep going indefinitely. Claudia, having been forbidden to fraternize with Ess, had stayed behind with Marguerita, so Ellery and Ess alone had scoured the neighborhood, driven up and down the streets calling Dumpling's name. Ess had had an idea that Dumpling might have meandered too far and gotten lost. Did cats follow scents like dogs? No one knew for sure. He'd driven down to the schoolyard and it had been night-lit for softball—no sign of Dumpling there—and he'd asked a few of the kids if they'd seen a cat with an orange face and one white paw. One of the kids, a boy on a bike, had said he'd seen one like that down on the beach. "And we really believed him," Ellery sobbed. Then, taking deep breaths, she pulled herself together. She'd been afraid the kitten might have drowned. Ess had comforted her. And then, walking along the shore, she'd fallen down, just tripped on something in the dark; she'd been so tired, so cold and tired, worn out, it had been so late, and he'd picked her up to carry her back to the van. But then, halfway there, he'd stopped to rest.

Ellery covered her eyes with her hands and I watched her fingers wipe tears out of them, watched her lower lip tremble the way it had when she'd wet her pants when she was two years old.

"That's when."

"On the beach?"

She nodded. "Behind a boat. A cataraman."

"Catamaran."

"Catamaran."

This is what swallowing Drano must feel like. "And that was the only time?"

She didn't answer.

I heard my voice lose control. "Were there other times?"

Silence.

"How many other times?" My head was an echo chamber for the boom of my voice.

"Mommy, I don't want to talk about it!"

"You have to talk about it! You're pregnant. You goddamn well have to talk about it!"

"I can't, I can't, I can't!"

"Your father—"

Her face contorted into a mask of pain.

"—will kill Ess." At this moment, I actually hoped he would.

"Only three other times. Once at the Rileys'. Twice when I said I was going to the library. But he used condoms those times, Mommy!"

Ellery turned her head into one of her frilly, starchy white pillows and I just sat there and watched, as her little-girl's body heaved with sobs.

I wanted to reach out and put my arms around those skinny shoulders and hold her in my lap the way I used to, in the rocking chair that was still standing six feet away from us. I wanted to give comfort, give the loving maternal warmth that used to be teamed with a breast or baby bottle, and that profound center-of-the-universe feeling of peace, but something stopped me cold. I think it was a straitjacket of anger—certainly at Ess, and, yes, at Ellery, who despite innocence, youth, and immaturity, certainly knew better—but it was more. I felt a rage at the world that was raining bilgewater down on us out of a sky that, in Crandall, Connecticut, despite clouds and occasional thunder, had always seemed predictably, traditionally, and reliably blue.

"Where's Ellery now?" I'd come back from telling Peter and felt my mouth go taut as a snap bean when I spoke. Claudia had picked up a brownie, chipping off crumbs, all she would allow herself to eat.

"Up in her room. She's all right, Mommy."

"She's not all right. She'll never be all right." I was taking it out on everyone, and so be it.

"What's going to happen?"

"Your father will have to come home and tell us, because I don't know. I just don't know."

"You told him! What'd he say?"

"He didn't believe me. Well, at first he didn't believe me."

"I did warn her, Mommy. I told her, like, a million times, to be careful with Ess. She had, like, a thing for him. Right from the beginning. Even when I was going with him. It was, like, unreal!"

"Wait a minute! *Waitaminute!* You knew, right from the beginning, that your little sister was infatuated with him? You knew all along that Ellery, who is very, very vulnerable, as you know, was an easy mark for Ess?"

"Easy mark? I didn't think of her as an easy mark! I mean, Mommy, how could I predict what was going to go down here? She's a baby!"

"That's it! A baby! And you should know what it is when you're very young and you think you're in love with someone! Why didn't you just come to Daddy and me and send up some red flags? You're supposed to be the mature sister here!"

"Were you away, or *what*? And 'mature sister'? You

never think of me as mature and we both know it! Besides, I'm no psychic! I don't read tea leaves, do I, Mommy? How could I possibly guess she'd do what she did!"

"Your silence, Claudia, your *insensitivity* to the circumstances, the *danger*—you should have sensed something, given us a hint!"

I was pacing now, actually wringing my hands, not thinking, hardly hearing myself as I sounded to Claudia. She jumped up and pushed her fingers through her hair, pulling up the skin of her temples with it.

"You're blaming me, aren't you, Mommy? Now what happened is my fault, isn't it? My God, Mommy! I never had sex when I was that young! How could I guess she would?" Claudia dropped her hands to her sides and her lower lip started to tremble. I had so often over the course of her life seen the beginnings of little-girl meltdown that my reaction was automatic. I did what I always do when one of the girls is in extremis. I threw my arms around her and fought off my own responsive emotion. "Not your fault, Claudia. Not your fault, dear! I'm tottering. I'm just overwhelmed. I'm sorry, darling. So sorry!"

Much later, after I'd taken two Advil, a cool shower, and a strong cup of coffee, I asked Claudia where they'd finally found Dumpling.

"They never really found him. He'd been locked inside the Dubersteins' garage when the automatic doors closed at night and Mr. Duberstein discovered him when he opened the garage doors the next day. It was a lucky thing Dumpling was on top of the car instead of under it, too."

My mouth was dry. "A lucky thing," I said.

* * *

Sometime after Kevin had left and just before Peter came home, the telephone rang. When I picked it up, it was Darley, telling me that she'd just gotten a call from the Ethel Carpenter Nursing Home. Meggie had died this morning. I think I put together a few words of condolence and, for all I know, I may even have sounded normal. I told her I'd tell Peter as soon as he got home.

And I did tell Peter, but I don't think he heard me. He walked into the kitchen and asked me whether Ellery was up in her room. He seemed to have recovered his strength, and his purpose.

"Sleeping," I said.

"I've been on the telephone with Carmen for the last half hour."

Carmen Brenner is our lawyer. It would never have occurred to me to go for legal help. "Carmen? Why?"

"About getting the police involved."

"Police involved!"

"Statutory rape. The boy is twenty-two years old. Ellery is thirteen. I want to see him in jail."

I did, too, with all my heart and soul. Jail, or worse. "But Peter, that's going to make the papers. That's going to be a big, public mess. And anyway, the sex was consensual."

Peter's mouth twisted as if he'd bit into something hard. "There's no such thing when a girl is thirteen!"

"But she says—"

"Forget what she says! I call it rape!"

"You can call it rape, but she calls it love."

"That's what she said? Love?"

"No. Not that actual word. You just have to look at her to see it."

"For Christ's sake. She's thirteen years old, Libby."

"If you're old enough to get pregnant, I guess you're old enough to fall in love."

"It's laughable. He's the scum of the earth."

"And she thinks he's some kind of god."

"I called Ted Irvine, too."

Ted Irvine is Peter's colleague at Crandall General, and my OB-GYN man. His partner, Dr. Mattis, delivered Claudia, and after Dr. Mattis gave up delivering babies, citing escalating malpractice insurance costs, Ted Irvine took over obstetrics and delivered Ellery. I'd always liked his partner better; Ted always seemed hurried and brusque. "And what did he say?"

"He can have her in and out in half an hour. She'll be back to school in two, three days. Phys. ed. in a week. He can do it in his office or in the hospital, whichever we prefer. His office is really high-tech. You've seen it."

"School starts day after Labor Day. That's a week from tomorrow."

"He'll squeeze her in. No problem, he said. He thinks I saved his wife's mother when she went into heart failure after her hysterectomy, but with me or without me, she would have recovered. I've told him a half dozen times, but he still thinks he owes me."

As always, Peter is the doctor-czar, and I suppose I was relieved. I tried to play the same game I used to play when I was a child sitting in the dentist's chair: It will be over soon, it will be over by the time the little hand on the big clock has moved to the next number. Now I told myself that it would be over when the September page of the calendar in the kitchen, the pictorial calendar I'd bought last year in Portugal, had turned to October, like those pages tearing off calendars in old movies. It would be just a sordid, despicable memory. Gone, like the September page with the aerial view of Cascais, flown on the winds of time.

Ted Irvine, assisted by one of those two nurses in his

office—hopefully not the very obese one, she might be too sluggish—everything taken care of by our reliable navigator. Smoothed over, arranged, pushed into history. Rebounded, he was Atlas again, with all of us in the big, fat world on his back.

Peter went upstairs to talk to Ellery. I paced the kitchen, sat on the kitchen stool, scraped carrots, looked out the window. I searched through the cupboards for Pepto-Bismol—my stomach was churning—hadn't I put some down here in the kitchen? Claudia was watching Oprah, and it crossed my mind that we had become likely Oprah guests: a fifties family, nicely verbal and well groomed, with a turn-of-the-century scenario of upscale lives gone trailer park. The Pepto-Bismol was missing, where had I put it? And suddenly, there was the pounding of feet on the stairs, a cry from Ellery, and I turned away from the cupboard just as she burst into the kitchen. She came tearing in barefoot, stood facing me at the sink, wearing her sister's T-shirt, Ess's rosary clutched against her chest with both hands.

I couldn't understand what she was saying. Tears running like rain down her cheeks, dripping from her chin.

"He doesn't get it, Mommy, he doesn't get it!"

"What, what, what?"

"Me and Ess." She looked bathetic, standing there in that striped shirt, her hair flattened on one side, hanging on to the rosary for dear life, reminding me of the way she used to hold leather reins when she was learning to ride and still afraid of slipping out of the saddle.

She clutched the beads as if the horse were about to leap off a cliff: "It wasn't Ess's fault."

The hell it wasn't. "Well, sweetheart, I know that's how you see it right now—"

"He wants to put Ess in jail! Ess didn't do anything wrong!"

"You're thirteen years old! He's a full-grown man!"

"I told you, I feel much, much older. I'm nothing like kids my age. Nothing!"

"Yes, I know, Ellery. But the fact is, you've only lived thirteen years. Ess has been on this earth much longer. He's an adult *by law,* he's allowed to vote, to drive, to drink, and has to be held accountable for all his actions." I amazed myself. I was staying so cool. Pedantic and stable, right through a death-dealing cyclone.

"But you hold me responsible for my actions, too!"

"Returning overdue library books, yes. Cleaning up your room, yes. But sexually—"

"He wouldn't've, though, if I didn't say it was okay!"

I felt as if I'd swallowed a fist. "Even if you'd begged and pleaded, it wouldn't have been okay!"

"Daddy wants to get the police on him!" Ellery looked now like those photos of abused children one sees in the newspaper: hollow-eyed, sad, and scarred for life. No one would believe we'd never laid a hand on this child. Nobody would believe she'd grown up in an intact, cohesive, dinner-at-six, bills-paid-on-time, carpet-covered, lawn-mowed, spring-cleaned American home, surrounded by a loving all-American family. "Just for having sex with me when I wanted him to!"

"He took advantage of you."

"He did not!"

I heard Peter on the stairs.

"You'll see things differently again at sixteen, and at twenty, and at twenty-six. It's a biological fact—your body and your judgment will keep changing and changing and changing!"

"I told you, Mommy, didn't I tell you? You think of me as just some ditsy thirteen-year-old kid, but I'm more mature than anyone else my age. I think like a grown-up." She pronounced mature "match-her," and added, "and I'll never go along with it—that it's right to punish Ess for something that wasn't his fault!"

Peter stepped into the kitchen. He had a handkerchief in his hand and wiped his forehead with it. I had the feeling that he'd just a minute ago used it to wipe his eyes. "I just spoke to Ted," he said to me, ignoring Ellery. "We have an appointment day after tomorrow. He's got to determine first of all that there definitely is a pregnancy, and then he'll take it from there."

Ellery's eyes grew large and dark. "Daddy, what?"

Peter's eyes fell on Ellery as if she'd just materialized in front of the sink. "What the hell is she doing with that rosary in her hand?" he asked, as if she were an inanimate object.

I shrugged. Concern about a rosary while Ellery's thirteen-year-old body was gestating seemed very much beside the point.

"Daddy, what do you mean, 'take it from there'? What are they going to do to me?"

"It won't hurt, honey, I promise."

"What won't hurt?"

"They suck the cells out with this instrument, sort of a vacuum cleaner, but you'll be half-asleep and you won't feel a thing."

"Daddy!"

"Ellery, all it takes is, like, ten minutes." I took a step forward, wanting to touch her, but she pulled back, hugging the rosary closer to her chest. Now I could see why it provoked Peter; the gesture got to me, too. "What is it with that rosary? Will you stop holding that thing like you're some kind of granite icon, for God's sake?"

In answer, she put it up to her lips, defensively. For a wild moment, I thought she was going to kiss it.

Peter's face flamed red. "Ellery, for Christ's sake!" And then, "Does that lowlife know? Does that creep know what he's done to you?"

"He's not a creep!" Ellery's tears rolled from her eyes like eyedrops. "He knows," she sobbed. "He's sorry. He's so sorry!"

Peter was trying to control himself, but the twitch

came, again and again. "Look, sweetheart, please, calm down. We're here. Sweetie, listen, sweetie. Ellery? Please, honey, now stop crying. I said, stop crying! No one's going to hurt you. Your mother and I discussed this, and we're going to see you through it. Day after tomorrow, all three of us are going to Dr. Irvine's, he'll take care of you right there in his office, it'll be one-two-three, and a week later, you'll be in school. That's it. End of discussion." He mopped his forehead with the handkerchief he'd balled up in his hand again.

Ellery had backed up against the sink and there was the rosary, still tight in her hands. She looked at Peter, and then at me. I was nodding in agreement. "It'll be over in no time. It's a very simple thing, darling. Honestly. Not as bad as the dentist's. And certainly nothing like having a full-term baby."

She was staring at me, saying nothing.

"No one has to know," I added.

She shook her head then. Her eyes seemed to sink deeper into her face. "I don't want an abortion, Mommy. I don't."

"Of course you do."

I misunderstood. I thought she meant she was afraid, that it would mean pain or unknown danger, and I kept trying to explain that "you'll just sort of doze," that Dr. Irvine was a fine doctor, that he'd done this minor operation hundreds of times. It went on and on.

"But, Mommy."

"Really, it's nothing. Dr. Irvine does abortions routinely."

"But I want to have the baby."

I told myself not to scream, not to run out of the room and slam the door.

"Oh, honey! Of course you don't mean it. You're just a baby yourself!"

"Don't be ridiculous, Ellery. Don't talk crazy nonsense." I noticed perspiration staining Peter's shirt in a vertical stripe, adjacent to its buttons, left and right.

"Ess doesn't believe in abortion. He doesn't want me to have one!"

Now Peter's face went into a deeper, more furious red. He let out a sound halfway between a bark and a car horn. "Ess doesn't want you to have an abortion!"

Ellery seemed to get smaller. She shook her head.

I heard a movement in the den. Oprah had concluded; Claudia was listening.

"Well, I'm your father, and I'm damn well telling you you're going to have an abortion!"

"It's the best way, honey, the best way. The only way—!" I stopped breathing.

"I don't want to, I don't want to, I don't want to!"

Peter stepped forward. He spoke to me as if Ellery wasn't there. "I never did it before in my life, Libby, but now I want to take my hand and just slap her face, smack some sense into her thirteen-year-old head!"

"Daddy!"

"Don't Daddy me!"

"Maybe some counseling, a family counselor—" I sounded like Oprah.

Peter cut in. "You're getting an abortion, Ellery, and you're getting it this week!"

"No, Daddy, no!"

Peter, whose complexion had gone to the color of borscht, lunged for Ellery. He tore the rosary out of her hands and hurled it across the kitchen. It hit the front of a cupboard, got momentarily caught on its handle, then slid to land in a crystal puddle on the floor.

"I'm your father," he said. "And you're going to do what I say. And I say you're getting an abortion, did you hear me?"

A moment later, he threw his arms around Ellery and stood clutching her as if she were a pillar in a hurricane, while she sobbed her heart out on his shoulder.

* * *

The telephone rang at midnight. Peter was asleep, his mouth slightly open, his expression calm, everything exactly as always except that both his pillows had fallen—or been thrown—to the floor, and his head lay turned to mine on the mattress, reminding me of a baby in a crib. I was used to midnight calls, but this time I sat up, charged and apprehensive. I picked up the receiver. It was Darley.

Peter hadn't called her. To Darley it was simple: Her sister had died this morning and her son had not found time to dial her number to speak a few words of support or condolence. I only heard his side of the conversation, which was punctuated with hesitations, evasions, and apologies. He is not a good liar, not even a good concealer. He told her he'd been called into emergency surgery. An automobile accident on one of the back roads. His voice crackled perceptibly when he lied. Said he'd gotten home so late he was afraid he'd wake her and intended to call her first thing in the morning. It wasn't clear whether she was buying this.

"Tell her we'll be up to see her tomorrow," I whispered.

"We'll drive up to take you to dinner tomorrow, Darley." There was a hesitation, and occasionally I heard her voice, not specific words, emanating from the receiver in Peter's hand. "Darling, I can't. You know I would fly down with you, but I have four patients scheduled for surgery, one of them critical, one of them already postponed twice. And I have one hanging by a thread in ICU." There was another pause, and then, "No, I don't think Libby can either, Countess. Darling, you know she would, but she has to . . ." His face turned to me, in the darkened bedroom I could still make out his chin up, eyes going from the ceiling and then turning to mine, his look of pleading. "She has a commitment to vet an entire estate going up for auction on the weekend."

He wanted to hand me the telephone, but I shook my head; I had an appointment to check the authenticity of four pieces a Crandall psychiatrist had bought at auction, and had promised to look over a pewter chandelier owned by the Crandall Garden Club. Those two assignments might take an hour and a half, altogether.

"The damn thing is my sister's up in that cabin in Canada for the summer and she's impossible to reach," Peter said into the darkness when he'd hung up. He sounded like a voice coming out of a speaker. "But if she can't get hold of her, my mother's going to ask the judge to go down to Virginia with her."

"Maybe we should have just come clean, told her about Ellery. It's terrible for your mother to think we're just abandoning her now."

Peter had retrieved his pillows and was pushing them against the headboard. "I hope you're not serious." He positioned his head flat into their center and pulled the covers up to his chin.

"I believe in truth, Pete."

He made a loud sniffing sound, as if he were inhaling perfume. "It won't always set you free, Lib. Sometimes it'll just cut what's left of your oxygen off."

I'd been awake since the awful scene in the kitchen. I'd taken tea and Pepto-Bismol and my stomach had finally settled down, but I couldn't sleep. I'd lain here next to my husband, staring at the dark shapes in the bedroom, the valet holding Peter's clothes, my familiar Chippendale dresser, the draperies I'd finally gotten to close properly neatly pleated, swagged, tied back, the very things that used to give me fathomless comfort, and now I might have been sleeping in some impersonal motel room at the side of an upstate highway.

"Peter. What's going to happen if Ellery refuses to have an abortion?"

"She can't refuse to have an abortion." Peter's eyes were closed, and so was his tone. "She's thirteen years old."

"Are you sure?"

His head did not move on the pillow; I was reminded of every corpse I'd ever seen in an open casket. "I'm sure, Libby, goddamn sure."

"Claudia, where is she?" Peter had checked Ellery's room—empty—called her name three times from the top of the stairs, and was now confronting Claudia, who was sitting at the kitchen table cutting a banana into a bowl of muesli. I had finally dozed off, but not until dawn had begun to turn the bedroom gray and lavender, and now, groggy, half-awake, I'd followed Peter downstairs. It was just after seven. I'd thrown on my terry cloth robe but hadn't even brushed my teeth, and my mouth felt as if I'd just eaten cotton.

"Ess picked her up early this morning and they took off."

"What! Where to?" Peter was fully dressed, dashing off to surgery. I wouldn't have wanted to be the patient on the table this morning, although in all those years no sponge had ever been left inside a chest, no valve inserted upside down. Peter had always managed to separate technology from emotional turmoil.

"Peter, what should we do?"

"I think I'm going to call the cops," he said, and headed for the kitchen telephone.

"Oh, Daddy, she's safe! He's not going to kidnap her!"

"Where did they go? Did you see her leave?"

"She called him, like, at five. He said he'd pick her up before going to work so they could talk. They're prob'ly just having breakfast at McDonald's or something."

"Work? Since when does that insect work?"

"He's started working for his father. See? He's settling down. It's a real job."

"His father? What does his father do?"

"Tombstones. He's in the monument business."

Peter rolled his eyes. "Jesus."

Claudia dimpled. "Well, somebody's got to do it."

"Let's not call the police yet." I was going to the coffeemaker, hurrying to get the Yuban in there; it would calm us down, distract Peter, wake me up.

"I'm going to call the hospital and tell them I've been delayed. Then"—he looked up at the clock over the refrigerator—"I'm going to give him one hour. One hour to get her back to this house. And then, I call the police."

I made coffee and tried to make conversation. Claudia was going to spend Kevin's last day at home with him, had gone upstairs to dress, and Peter and I sat listlessly together at the kitchen table. When I heard the thwack of the newspaper against the front door, I ran out to get it, glad for the diversion. Busy, busy. Keep moving. I straightened the doormat, brushed a moth off the screen door, looked up and down the empty street. Peter wasn't interested in reading anything, not now, for God's sake, he said, so I unfolded the paper in front of me and tried to focus on the headlines, but mostly I was listening for the sound of a van in the gravel of our driveway, or the ring of the telephone. I heard other noises—a power mower outside, the occasional hum of an appliance somewhere under this roof. Cars. A motorcycle. Children. Birds, birds, birds. I'd never realized our neighborhood was practically an aviary.

When Dumpling ambled into the kitchen I found a

fish-shaped catnip toy in the cupboard and put it on the floor in front of him. Peter and I watched indifferently while the kitten pushed the mouse along the baseboards with alternating paws. Nothing seemed bright or amusing; no warmth, light, or kitten play could penetrate this gloom.

I thought about taking a drink. Peter was right. A little scotch, a vodka on ice, a Pilsner glass full of beer, ice cold, would go down well right now. One little sip, then another. The edges of anxiety would soften, like ice cubes losing their sharp edges in a glass. If I kept liquor in the house, I might really be tempted for once. Instead, I poured a third or fourth cup of coffee, and pictured pouring coffee for the police, their cars lining the curb, the flashing red lights, the men in uniform swarming. I was certain Ellery was safe, but there would be a polite and sensitive detective, doing his duty, asking endless, probing, and intimate questions. I could see the headlines in tomorrow's local newspaper: PROMINENT DOC'S DAUGHTER SUBJECT OF POLICE SEARCH.

Peter stood up now, not for the first time, and paced to the window. He looked at his watch or the kitchen clock every few minutes and wiped his forehead with his handkerchief intermittently, although the air-conditioning was on and the house was cool.

Suddenly, he turned around and began walking out of the kitchen.

"Where are you going?" I was so jumpy, my voice seemed piercing even to my own ears.

He spun around, his eyebrows high, his lips puckered. I recognized the expression—anger under wraps.

"To take a pee."

"Oh."

"Where did you *think* I was going?"

"I didn't think, Peter."

"I know where. To the liquor store. That's exactly where you thought I was headed."

"That's ridiculous. It never even occurred to me!"

"Always trying to protect the prominent doctor from the furry beast!"

Inflamed and hurt, I was about to stammer out a defense, but at that moment, the telephone rang, and we both jumped. I was nearer; I grabbed the receiver.

"Mommy."

"Ellery! Where are you?"

"At Jennifer's."

"Which Jennifer? What are you doing there?"

"Jennifer Hellman's. I didn't feel like coming home right now. Ess dropped me off here."

"Daddy and I have been waiting for you for over an hour. Daddy has to leave; they're waiting for him at the hospital!"

"I can't talk now, Mommy. Mrs. Hellman needs to use the phone. I just wanted to tell you where I was so you wouldn't worry."

"I'll come and get you."

"Ess is coming over to talk to Daddy and you tonight. I'll come back with him."

"Are you feeling all right, Ellery?"

"I was just a little sick, but I'm okay now. Mrs. Hellman gave me some arrowroot cookies."

"She knows!"

"No, no! I told her I had an upset stomach. Just Jenny knows."

"Oh, my God. Just Jenny." Just the neighborhood, the school, the world.

Peter stepped into the kitchen right after I hung up. "Ess is coming over tonight to talk to us," I told him, still stung.

"I wish I could get my hands on a gun," he murmured.

"What are you saying?" I said.

And without hesitation, and with a fierce look at me, Peter growled, "I said a gun, not a fifth, Libby."

* * *

After he'd left, the telephone rang again. It was Annie. "You're in *Southern Connecticut Life*, page forty-six! Gorgeous! The October issue. I think it's out early! And listen to the headline: 'Distinguished Doctor's Family Is Bigger Than Life.' Don't you love it? I happened to look at it at the dentist's last night. My goodness, what a spread they gave you. And you know who looks absolutely the most stunning in the family photograph? You do! Although you all look, absolutely—"

I, who almost never cry, choked up and couldn't speak.

"What? What's wrong?"

"Nothing."

"Come on!"

"Just—a little family business."

"What? Is anyone sick?"

"Listen, Annie. Something unthinkable."

"What? I'm listening."

I wasn't going to tell anyone. "Ellery is pregnant." I had to tell Annie.

A long pause, then, "I don't believe it."

I was swallowing air. "I don't, either."

"Who? By whom? Do you know?"

"Ess DiBuono."

"No."

"You heard right."

"I'm coming right over."

"No, no, Annie. Please."

"What can I do?"

"Just cancel my appointments. I guess for the rest of the week. That's all you can do."

She said she'd reschedule the appointment I had with the historian of the Crandall Garden Club and the luncheon in honor of the retiring docent of the Stratford Historical Museum. And to call her day or night if I needed her. I went up to the bedroom, turned down the air-conditioning, took a bath, and wrapped myself in my terry robe. I pulled some family photographs out of the Federal blanket chest in the upstairs hall, spread them out on the bed, and searched through them, picture by picture. What might I have done that summer in Cape Cod when she was three, the Disney trip when she was four, or right here in this snapshot, at age five, exactly eight years ago, on her first day of school? She was all in yellow that day, with yellow grosgrain bows I'd found to clip onto her patent leather shoes, a daffodil of a little girl, with a flower-pure heart and the innocence of Laszlo, whom she didn't want to leave at home and was hugging in the photograph.

Marguerita had returned from her vacation, and for once we reversed mood roles. I stayed in my room, verging on tears behind the closed door, and she vacuumed and dusted downstairs, humming MTV hits. She assumed I wasn't feeling well and brought me a sandwich soppy with mayonnaise, a glass of cranberry juice, and yogurt, acting solicitous, and motherly.

Peter called twice during the day to ask if Ellery had showed up at home and suggesting I call her at the Hellmans. "She belongs at home," he said a few times. I thought of it as closing the barn door after the horses left, but didn't say it. On the other hand, I never made the call to the Hellmans, and it wasn't until Ellery walked in with Ess that she reappeared.

Marguerita had left for the day when Ess's van arrived in the driveway. I heard the tires on the gravel and ran to the bedroom window, watched as Ess emerged from his side of the car, came around to Ellery's side to open her door for her. He helped her out, sort of hoisting her down and escorting her to the front door, holding her elbow, as if she were already in her ninth month.

I descended the stairs; it all seemed so proper. Ordinarily the girls came in through the kitchen door, but Ellery must have decided the occasion called for formality. She and Ess had arrived earlier than I expected, Peter wasn't home yet, and I opened the door as if they were invited guests come for a party.

"Good evening, Mrs. Ehrlich." Ess was filled as always with the self-confidence I associate with weatherproof-siding sales, and I could see immediately that he'd just showered, possibly even reshaved. His braid was slicked back and damp, his shirt, a collarless, black, no-message T-shirt, was tucked into poplin pants. I noticed the gold hoop in his nose was gone and the odor of aftershave clogging the air around him, a scent I would have called *Clout.* All nerves, I backed away, led them into the den, and instinctively circumvented the living room. Ess would look even more ridiculous in the atmosphere of needlepoint rugs and silk upholstery. As for the kitchen, it smacked of homeyness and family living, our own private club. I didn't want him here, a part of the Ehrlich inner circle.

"Is Daddy home?" Ellery's first question.

"Not yet."

They sat together on the sofa, side by side, Ellery stiff as one of the stuffed animals on her bed, Ess quite at ease, tapping a sneakered foot now and then, and I offered cookies, sodas, iced tea. Ellery kicked off her sandals and shook her head. "No, thank you, Mommy."

Ess declined by saying, "No, thank you very much, Mrs. Ehrlich. I'm not thirsty."

"Where's Claudia?" Ellery wanted to know.

"It's Kevin's last night. They went to New York City, to the Hard Rock Cafe."

"Oh, that's right. She was all bummed out about his leaving, but by next week, just wait."

There was an awkward silence; my head grappled for a hook on which to hang a conversation.

"Daddy was doing two bypass procedures today," I offered.

"Uh-huh."

Another silence. Ess's eyes were roving the room.

"Did you eat lunch?" I asked Ellery.

"I had an egg salad sandwich and a shake."

"That's good."

I had never seen Ess so subdued. His eyes searched the den as if he'd never been here before. He began to take an interest in the art on the wall, pointed to a small painting with two splayed fingers. "Is the dog in the picture up there a water spaniel? Or what?"

"I think it's a King Charles spaniel." I turned to scrutinize the picture we'd hung over the Wooten desk fourteen years ago.

"My cousin had a dog just like that. My cousin in Philly. His name was Jonah. Boy, a smart animal. Could've learned to read if they'd of sent him to school." The smile froze.

Another silence.

"I bet this room could be in *House Beautiful,*" Ess continued.

"It was once used in a television commercial. So was the telephone booth. So was the kitchen."

"Yeah. So Ellery said. That's cool. Maybe I even seen it. Saw it, I mean."

"They played it for a year."

"You're all in a magazine this month. Ellery showed me it. 'Bigger than life,' it said."

"Right."

"A beautiful family, like I always said."

Another silence, another spurt of forced conversation, and so it went, until almost forty minutes later, when Peter walked in.

* * *

Ess shot up as soon as he stepped into the room. "Good evening, Dr. Ehrlich," he said.

A whisper-light "hi, Daddy."

Peter's mouth barely opened when he spoke. "Ellery, get me a glass of cold water, will you? With lots of ice." She jumped up, slid back into the sandals she'd kicked off earlier, and ran to the kitchen. Then, "Sit down, Ess." Peter went to the window and pulled closed the draperies, as if there was the possibility of voyeurs peering at us through the glass, as if the whole neighborhood was lining up for a peek into our catastrophe. I expected Peter to sit in the wing chair facing the couch, but instead, he pulled one of the balloonback chairs from next to the card table to face the sofa, and sat on it, his back straight as the andirons on the left of the fireplace. He cleared his throat. "You're in trouble, Ess," he said, and crossed his legs.

"Sir?"

"I said, you're in trouble, and I meant, *serious trouble,* with me, for starters. And maybe with the law, although that's yet to be determined."

Ess looked uncomfortable for the very first time. He was sitting with his legs slightly apart, his hands between them, and began rubbing the insides of his wrists nervously together.

"You've taken advantage of my daughter. My thirteen-year-old daughter—" Peter's voice broke here, and he looked past Ess, past the couch, past the walls, the calm, determined opening gone, fighting off tears. I jumped up and stood behind his chair, put my hands on his shoulders, and held tight. "And made this little girl—this little girl pregnant."

Ellery reappeared with the glass of water and handed it to Peter, then took her place back on the couch, now even closer to Ess.

"Believe me, Dr. E, believe me," Ess began. He looked at the floor as if he'd spotted something crawling there.

"I've been, been real upset, real upset. You better believe I'm not sleeping much these nights, Dr. Ehrlich, I'm up, pacing, you wouldn't want to know how this has gotten to me, gotten into my head. It's like, like all I think, think about day and night, night and day. Now, I know saying I'm sorry isn't gonna cut it with you, Dr. E, but it's all I can say, is I am sorry. I am sorry big-time."

"Well, now, that's a very nice thing that you're apologetic, Ess, that you're sitting there nice and comfortable on my couch telling me how sorry you are, but in the meantime you've just corrupted, no, *ruined,* my daughter"—his voice got a bitter edge—*"big-time.* My younger daughter, who was innocent, a baby, a child, until you came along and got your dirty—"

"Daddy!"

"Until you got your . . . hands on her!" Peter was leaning over in his chair so far I saw the danger that he might tip forward and land on the coffee table. I tried to pull him back. "How could you, how the hell dared you, you"—he grappled for a noun—"perverted devil—"

*"Daddy!"*

"I don't blame your dad for being mad, no, I can't blame the doctor, Ell, he's got a right, I see where he's coming from, but Dr. E, I just want to say—"

"I don't give a diddly-squat what the hell you have to say!" Peter's eyes were slits. His breath was coming in hisses, and if he'd had a weapon at hand, I felt he would have used it. In thirteen sober years, I couldn't remember ever seeing such fury written on his face.

"I told you, Daddy, it wasn't Ess's fault!" Ellery's voice sounded like a squealing brake. "I asked him to kiss me. I did! And then, it just, just, oh, it just"—she covered her eyes with her knuckles and began shaking with sobs—*"happened."* Ess put a hand on her shoulder.

It was too much for Peter. He stood up abruptly; the

chair rocked. He caught it before it fell. "It happened," he mimicked.

"I'm willing—" Ess began.

"Quiet!" Peter barked. "Ellery. You're going to have an abortion day after tomorrow. Dr. Irvine is making time for this very quickly, as a favor to me."

She'd wiped her eyes one last time with the knuckles of both hands. I went to my purse, which was lying on an end table, opened it, found a Kleenex packet, and pulled out a tissue. I handed it to Ellery.

She took it and wiped her eyes. "Ess and I decided"—she swallowed hard—"I'm not going to have an abortion." She put her hand on Ess's knee and his fingers immediately covered it.

Peter's lip pulled, showing his whole row of upper teeth. "Two P.M., Eastern Standard Time, day after tomorrow. End of discussion."

"Sir, if I may say something."

"No, you may not say a thing."

"Peter. Maybe we should." I made a motion to let Ess speak.

"What could he have to say, Libby? What could he have to say that I'd want to hear?"

"I don't believe abortion is right, Dr. Ehrlich."

"You don't believe abortion is right? And I don't believe ravishing thirteen-year-old girls is right!"

"Daddy, I told you! It wasn't like that!"

Ess was smoothing back his smooth hair, still poised. Amazing. "Sir, I think abortion is murder."

"Don't use the word *murder* to me." Peter pointed his finger into Ess's face. "And I don't give a tinker's fart what you think!"

"I believe Ellery has the right to decide the fate of our unborn child." An orator in a T-shirt. Unbelievable the way he oozed *sangfroid*.

" 'Our unborn child'! You are going to make me throw up, you—" Peter took a threatening step forward, but held off. "She's a child. A child has no rights—not in this house!"

"I'm afraid, Ess, there's not a choice here." I sounded to myself rational, unhysterical, both feet on the ground. "Ellery is very young, she's got about ten more years of school ahead of her, about ten more years of maturity to grow into before she can think about having children." There was no hand-wringing; I amazed myself, sounding like a school principal explaining to children why they have to leave a building quickly during a fire.

Ess and Ellery sat quietly, heard me out when I spelled out the very, very obvious: that a girl Ellery's age wasn't equipped to raise a child; that to make her carry a baby to full term might be hazardous to her physical health and would definitely blemish her psychologically; that as long as abortion was legal in the state of Connecticut, we would avail ourselves of the best available doctor; and an abortion was definitely, absolutely, and without a doubt, nonnegotiable.

Ellery, trembling, looking as if she'd just been out in a storm, her hand now clutching Ess's, said, "I'm not going to do it, Mommy. I'm not going to. Ess says I don't have to if I don't want to."

"Ess says—?" Peter's eyes were like burning holes in his head. "*Ess says!* I say, you are going to get rid of that pregnancy in forty-eight hours, whether you want one or not!"

Upstairs, in the girls' telephone booth, the phone began ringing. No one made a move to answer it.

"But, honey, what are you, what do you"—I had to swallow away the taste of panic in my mouth—"intend to do with a baby? A baby that's going to be born in eight months—let me see—in April. What then?"

Ellery had never, in all her thirteen years, been defiant. Was this my child speaking, or some ventriloquist's dummy? "We're going to get married. And we're going to raise the baby together."

Peter let out a yelp.

"Oh, Ellery!" I clasped my hands together. "Raise the baby!"

They nodded together like a pair of marionettes, clutching hands. Huddling.

"This is not a cat, Ellery!" I cried. "This is not Dumpling!"

"And you're not getting married! That is the most ridiculous, the most far-fetched, brainsick thing I've ever heard!" Peter's voice was booming now. Despite the closed windows, the Bergins might hear. Or anyone else, passing on the street.

"My mom and dad will help." Now Ess had turned into the school principal, advising us of the facts in a composed and tuitional way. "My mom loves babies."

I jumped up from my chair. "What are you saying? My daughter is a baby!"

"My parents will take care of Ellery, too."

Now I wanted to throw some object at him. For one mad moment, my eyes actually roamed the room. *Stay calm, stay calm.* "You've told your parents! They know?"

"I told them yesterday."

"You told them yesterday. And what did they say?"

"To tell it like it is, they weren't thrilled, Mrs. Ehrlich."

"Weren't thrilled," Peter's voice echoed. He'd closed his eyes and was rubbing them with two index fingers.

"My dad was not pleased. He went ballistic, actually."

"And your mother?"

"Mom didn't say much. She doesn't talk a lot. She's sort of like Ellery. She just cries."

Peter and I looked at each other.

Then, through some enormous exertion, Peter, the navigator, gained control of his emotions, settled into some worn-down level of calm, and told Ess to go home and tell his parents that we'd be paying them a visit tomorrow night.

I went to sleep with the help of two Excedrin PMs and a glass of hot milk, but Peter got a call at quarter to twelve, talked patiently and encouragingly to a woman whose husband, Peter's patient, had just been brought into the emergency room by the VAC with a gastric problem he'd imagined was a coronary. As soon as he'd put the phone back on the hook it rang again; another patient was experiencing breathing difficulty. As I listened to his verbal soothing, the calming, holy-water sound of his voice, I almost thought I'd dreamed the Hotspur scene I'd seen three hours ago. As soon as Ess had left, Peter had shouted at Ellery, sent her off to her room, told her he would not put up with bratty defiance and that as soon as this was all over, he was going to ground her indefinitely. He would not permit her to wreck her life, although she was certainly getting a head start in that direction. Worst of all, he was totally devastated by what she'd done. Crushed. Profoundly disappointed. Let down by her. He'd stormed into the kitchen and slammed a cupboard door, slapped the counter with his open palm. "I'm not letting those girls . . . fall into a black hole!" he'd shouted at me, and then I got dry-mouthed and shaky, because in the next breath, he mentioned Lucas Greavy's son, and said it was times like these he could really understand. He knew now how the old man could be driven to do what he did.

Now, the old, rock-solid calm Peter was lying next to me. "I can't sleep, Lib. What did we do? What caused this?"

"I've been asking myself," I said.

"Was there a fork in the road we didn't take?"

"I don't know."

"Maybe we really had nothing to do with it. Maybe it's like a meteor falling in a random way."

"She's never done a thing wrong, that child. Obedient."

"Yes. Sweet. And cooperative."

"Agreeable. Submissive."

"With him, too. Submissive." Peter was seething again, quietly this time.

"So yielding, always."

"We're all tempted. Why do some have the strength to win the battle over temptation and others are just, just *vanquished* by it?"

I looked across the darkened room and made out the outline of the settee where I'd let Trevor Eddy make love to me. I didn't answer.

Suddenly Peter's voice pounced. "Goddamn it, I knew we shouldn't have gone to Europe!"

"Are you saying—"

"I didn't particularly think it was a good idea to leave the girls, do you remember?"

"My fault?"

"I didn't say that, Libby."

"You implied."

"As you remember, I really didn't think Marguerita was up to being in charge."

Mea culpa. I looked at the settee and it was all I could do not to tell Peter everything. Shoot him down right now. Get even.

"And maybe you think I was responsible for Ellery's falling off the horse, too. Like your mother."

"Libby, let's not bring my *mother* into this."

It was all I could do not to turn on the light, point to the settee, and tell him all about it. Instead, I got out of bed and told him I was going downstairs for another glass of milk. I detoured into Ellery's room. I thought

I'd just sit in the rocker in the dark and watch her sleep, maybe wait here for Claudia to come home. She had called to tell us she and Kevin had missed the 10:40 train and would be taking the 11:40. She'd be home any minute, then. I'd just rock a bit and listen for the wheels of Kevin's car.

But Ellery was not asleep. "Mommy?" She sat up and peered at me in the dim glow of the night-light. She was holding her stuffed monkey, had her arms wrapped around its tired little body.

"I'm here."

"What time is it?"

"After midnight."

"Mommy?"

"Yes?"

"I really, really love Ess."

"Oh, Ellery."

"I know he's really too old for me and all that, and he really liked Claudia first, but he loves me now, he really does."

"At the moment, I'm sure."

"Why do you say that? Why do you say, 'at the moment'? It's so cyntical!"

"Cynical, you mean cynical, dear."

"Cynical. Don't you believe Ess and I could keep loving each other forever? Like you and Daddy?"

"There's an old Persian proverb: 'Trust in God, but tie your camel.' "

"I'm glad I'm not cynical. Ess will stay with me. He swore on the Bible."

"Ellery, go to sleep, dear, it's late."

"Like Dad promised and never broke his promise."

"It's a different thing."

"I won't go through with it. I can't get rid of this baby. It's his and mine, and I can't."

"Listen, Ell. I don't think there's much choice."

"Ess says there is. He's given the baby a nickname. Scooter."

"Let's talk tomorrow."

"I love it. Scooter is alive, already alive. Just waiting to be born. I just know he's going to be adorable."

I saw myself in a flashback, suddenly. I saw myself standing next to Darley at the display window of Stork Time, looking at the mannequins in tent dresses. We'd just had lunch together and were walking through the mall. I remembered the moment very clearly, looking at the plate-glass window and wondering whether I should go inside with Darley and try on some maternity clothes or wait until I could go alone. And I felt a little knock. Right below the navel. A movement of a two-inch limb, maybe a foot, or an elbow. The thing I was going to cover with a maternity dress was alive. It was the first time I'd felt it, and now, during this playback, I heard myself say, "I remember," and it was almost as if something had kicked me again, softened me deep inside. "I know how you feel, sweetheart, I do."

When I got back to bed, Peter was asleep. I lay awake, listening to the sounds of the house, heard Claudia come in, climb the stairs, close her door. I looked around at our bedroom, and it no longer seemed safe, it was no longer a haven. When I finally fell asleep, I dreamed about gypsies, dreamed they came into the house and tried to steal everything we had. It was snowing; it snows in all my bad dreams. I don't remember how the dream ended, but I remember Peter saying that it wasn't their fault they were thieves. It was society, he said, that had corrupted them.

# Chapter Eight

Bathing-suit season was almost over. Claudia was eating a slice at a little white table in the food court at the mall, and I was sitting opposite, sipping 7UP out of a paper container. I'd taken her to buy a new fall jacket and already she'd talked me into two new pairs of jeans, a hand-knitted sweater imported from Uruguay, new boots, and a rain jacket. She didn't, after all, expect me to see her dress "like a dork" in her senior year?

What had always been fun—the annual trek for refreshing the school wardrobe—seemed like Herculean labor. I had dragged my feet from shop to shop, sank into any available chair and waited, trying not to show my impatience, while Claudia waltzed out of dressing rooms to show me how things made her look fat.

All I saw all around me were other people's thirteen-year-olds trying on school clothes, carefree, not pregnant, wholesome girls.

"You look so sad, Mommy. Don't be so quiet. It's going to work out all right." The cheese hung in a string from the pie to her chin.

"You think so."

*"Oui. Je pense."*

"I don't know. You really think Ellery will come around?"

"I talked to her again last night."

"What did she say?"

"She said I was still in love with Ess, that I was jealous of her. I told her to go take a wheat-grass enema. I told her she was dreaming."

"Why would she say that? She knows you like Kevin!"

"She's in her own Idaho, Mom! She thinks Ess is like some kind of Brad Pitt, I mean, *really*! Ess is great in his way, but come on—!"

"So, you said she's going to think about it?"

"God, if I hear the word *abortion* one more time I'm going to be the one barfing over the john. Last night, she goes, 'Scooter is going to love me whether I'm beautiful or ugly, smart or dumb, whether I play the harp or not, forever.' She's calling this fetus Scooter, I mean, do you believe it? So I go, 'You're going to change diapers while all your friends are having fun, hanging out, Rollerblading, like that?' And she looks at me and goes, 'I'm more grown-up than you are,' and I go, 'We'll see the next time I'm going to Playland and you're home warming bottles for Scooter'."

"So, what did she say?"

"Like, maybe it sunk in. But, *je ne sais pas,* 'cause Ess has some kind of hold on her like, umm, he's the knife thrower and she's his assistant. Like she's learned when not to move, y'know?"

"I know."

"Mommy."

"What?"

"Are you and Daddy all right? I mean, you never fight, but at dinner, were you fighting, or what? He sat there, never said a word. He looked so mad. Just the way he chewed his meat and all."

"We disagreed about going to the DiBuonos'. He wanted to just get into the car and go. Ring their bell, just like that. But Ess said they were having a family birthday celebration last night. One of his brothers. I said how could we barge in? So Daddy said he didn't believe Ess anyway, and the hell with their family dinners, but I talked him into waiting until tonight."

"*Mon dieu.* I'm glad I don't have to be there. Whew."

I watched Claudia bite into her second slice of pizza. She was wearing Kevin's denim jacket, the silver-and-turquoise ring, and around her neck, a silk cord with a crystal dangling from it. The going-away present. "Mommy. Does the Countess know?"

"No."

"Are you going to tell her?"

"No."

"She'd freak, wouldn't she? Yeah, I know she would."

I picked up a napkin and pressed it into my watering right eye.

"Do you want some of this, Mommy? I can't finish it. Here, you didn't eat anything. Take some." Claudia, watching me nervously, pushed the half-eaten slice of pizza in my direction, then wiped her hands carefully with her napkin.

"I'm okay," I said, and for a minute, she scrutinized me. Then she thanked me profusely for the beautiful clothes, said she couldn't believe she'd be back in the salt mines next week, and when we got up to leave, she pushed her fingers into her hair, said at least this year she'd be driving like everyone else, then pulled it up and out, so it would look bigger, fuller, and more glamorous.

As we were walking out of the house to get into the car to go to the DiBuonos', the telephone rang.

When I picked it up, Darley's voice startled me. She

sounded so flat and distant, she seemed to be speaking into a defective instrument.

"Thank God the judge was with me. I couldn't have gone through it without him."

"I wish we could have come down with you, but it was impossible, what with Peter, and the girls . . ." I trailed off, and there was this little silence, while my voice dried out.

Finally, Darley went on, each word lead. "So, Meggie was all decked out. I don't know who decided on an open casket, I guess maybe my nephews. Remember that Ultrasuede outfit I sent her? The rose one I used to wear in the seventies? It had that scalloped collar and those gold buttons? Well, they dressed her in that—I had no idea she still had it, poor baby—and they matched her lipstick, Libby, they matched her lipstick, *exactly,* to the color, the color of the suit—" Darley's voice broke. "You know, you know, I kept looking into her funny dead face, I mean funny strange, not funny ha-ha, and all I could think about was how sad a life she lived, with that deadbeat husband of hers, that man who drove her to two breakdowns, and those big-shot sons who ignored her until the funeral, then got up, you should have heard them eulogizing her like poet laureates, praising their mom from the pulpit. When she was alive, where were they? Selling Chinese herbs to movie stars in Los Angeles, never a thought about their mother tied into a wheelchair eight hours a day. I'm saying it's not right, it's just not right!"

I heard Peter's car running its motor in the driveway; Ellery—hair pulled back severely in barrettes, wearing a flowered blouse over jeans and resisting to the last minute—was already a prisoner in the backseat. They were waiting for me to finish feeding Dumpling, getting on my lipstick, changing my shoes.

"You're going out?"

"Yes."

"You said Peter's waiting in the car."

"I'm afraid so, Darley."

Another pause. "I kept looking at Meggie's face thinking she'd had a hard and sad life. Remember when I was sending them money every month, for years and years? I kept looking down at Meggie's face, it was like a shriveled mask under a rainbow of makeup, and I kept thinking, 'You're the one they expected the most from.' Isn't life *unpredictable*?"

"It is, Darley, it is."

"Peter will call me when he gets home?"

"Yes, definitely, Darley. You hang in, now, dear."

It took forty minutes to drive to the DiBuonos'. It should have taken only thirty, but although Ess's directions were explicit enough, Peter made a mistake at Exit 6, turning right instead of left, and by the time we pulled up in front of their house, he was even more morose than he'd been when I'd finally gotten Darley off the telephone and climbed into the car. He was interested in a synopsis of his mother's comments about her sister's funeral, but for the moment, not very. The road directions, the traffic, and stoplights were everything. In a corner of the backseat, Ellery sat hunched, pallid, and silent, taking small bites out of the dry crackers I'd put into a Baggie, while in the passenger seat, I agonized about what this meeting could possibly gain.

Peter said that Ted Irvine had backed down. Wouldn't perform an abortion on an unwilling subject under any circumstances. Didn't know of any physician worth a damn who would; the probability of a lawsuit was too great. The issues of ethics, the moral questions, were problems he didn't want to deal with. Of course, if at any time Ellery were to change her mind, he could be counted upon. Until the sixteenth week, anyway. He personally did not like to perform abortions after the first trimester.

This morning, stepping out of the shower, standing naked in the bathroom, Peter had opened the door and called out to me. "We've run out of mouthwash!"

"Pete, wait a minute, I think there's some right under the sink, still in a plastic bag. Down there, behind the rolls of toilet paper."

"What the hell is it doing back there?"

"Peter, you're screaming—"

"I can't find it!"

"It'll all be behind us tomorrow, Pete."

" 'Behind us tomorrow'? Let's face it, if we don't get these people to see the light, it's never going to be over!"

"Peter, please, lower your voice."

"I found the mouthwash. What the hell kind of brand is this?"

I let it go. "I think we should start by trying to act agreeable with these people. And reasonable, okay? That's how we'll get through this."

"Listen, it's like floods and air crashes. Hey, people get through those, right?"

I didn't answer, and no answer always makes my husband furious.

"Stick to Odol or Listerine, and never buy this cheesy brand again, okay, Libby?" he said.

It was a green-painted three-story frame house that was higher than wide, on a street of other frame houses, set near the street and adjacent to the DiBuonos' place of business. We came upon that first, a one-story brick building behind a cyclone fence, festooned with Styrofoam crosses and cones, each adorned with artificial bouquets in magenta, yellow, white, blue. Hanging from the brick were several signs: ROCK OF AGES, AUTHORIZED

DEALER, MEMBER OF BURRE GUILD, DANBURY MEMORIALS. Standing guard at the double glass doors were assorted white stone statues of Jesus, and what looked like miscellaneous saints and nuns. To the side was a garden of gravestones in polished granite of assorted colors, and as Peter parked the car at the curb adjacent to the fence, my eye caught legends—IN GOD'S CARE, DAD, GRANDMOTHER—and carved profiles of Mary, the infant Jesus, and lilies, in bas-relief.

"I'm not getting out of the car," Ellery said, as soon as Peter turned off the ignition.

Peter swiveled in his seat to glare at her. "Yes, you are."

"I told you I didn't want to come," she said. Her voice was little-girl small.

"Ellery, we're not going to have a scene now."

"I told you, Daddy, I told you I didn't want to come!"

"Ellery, honey, I think you ought to come inside and meet Ess's folks."

"Mommy, didn't I say I didn't want to come?"

"Yes, you said it, but sweetheart, here we are. They're waiting for us."

"They're waiting for *you*!"

Peter cut her off. "We didn't want to come, either, Ellery!" He ran his hand back and forth across the leather of the seat behind my head. "I sure as hell have a lot of things I'd rather be doing!"

Ellery threw her head forward. "I'm so nauseous! I'll throw up!" I sat in the front seat, watching a dog up the street pee against a tree, not knowing what to do. "Does she really have to go inside?" I asked Peter.

"I think she should hear what goes on. Yes, I do."

"Ellery, come on, pull yourself together, dear." I found a packet of tissues in the glove compartment and passed it into the backseat. "Take deep breaths.

"Peter, let's let her sit in the car until she feels better. Then, we can come out here and bring her in."

Peter hesitated. With a theatrical sigh, he opened the car door and stepped out onto the sidewalk. Above us, a ceiling of power lines seemed to stretch like a canopy from the telephone poles on the street to the roof of the house. "I can't believe this place," Peter said under his breath.

The steps to the scalloped front door were steep. I counted them, an unconscious habit I'd had most of my life: fourteen from the sidewalk. At the seventh, a plateau, a yard on each side of the steps, a riot of chrysanthemums, gladiolus, hydrangeas. One rose stuck out like a raised hand, a last red memento of summer. Over the door, the house number was written in cursive wrought iron: TWO FORTY-SIX. A little wood-engraved sign was fixed to a space above the mailbox: THE DIBUONO'S. Peter muttered, "Jesus," and rang the bell.

Ess opened the door almost immediately and my first reaction was, *Is this Ess?* The ponytail was gone; the haircut was military short, and he was in a checked sports coat under which the spread collar of an open-necked shirt—navy blue—showed.

"Hi, Dr. E, Mrs. E." He looked over our shoulders for Ellery for the second before Peter said, "She's waiting in the car," and then stepped aside so we could move into the small hall.

My first impression about the interior of the DiBuonos' house was cooking smells and wood. Everything seemed coated with maple-color vertical planks: the entry hall, the living room, and beyond that, the small dining room. Gold carpet, interrupted here and there with Oriental-style scatter rugs, stretched as far as the eye could see, except in the kitchen straight ahead, in the doorway of which both DiBuonos now appeared. For a moment Mrs. DiBuono stood, her husband behind her, like a couple posed by a photographer for a family still. Inside I glimpsed two teenaged boys in football jerseys sitting at the kitchen table.

I expected a Mediterranean-looking couple, and Mr. DiBuono did not disappoint me. He was swarthy, bulky, a head of magnificent, theatrical, graying hair, with a beginning-to-bulge stomach, one long brow that serviced both chocolate-syrup eyes, and a pair of fleshy arms hanging from elbow-length plaid sleeves. His mouth and elegant row of teeth were Ess's, exactly. Mrs. DiBuono was the surprise; she was taller than her husband, slender, with Marilyn Monroe hair and weimaraner blue eyes behind enormous, sparkly eyeglass frames from which pearl beaded ropes looped. She must have waved pom-poms, strutted, and twirled batons twenty-five years ago. Now a surgical collar bunched a second chin up over her cotton overblouse, spattered with gold swirls and glitter.

"We're the DiBuonos." Mr. DiBuono stepped forward and held out his hand to Peter. "Vito. And this is Marjorie."

"Libby Ehrlich," I said.

"Peter Ehrlich." Peter shook hands with Vito. It was quick as an eyeblink, like the obligatory winner-loser handshake after a sporting match. He led us into the paneled living room and we took seats awkwardly, Peter and I side by side on a floral couch, Marjorie facing us on a hardback carved wooden chair.

"My wife was in a little accident," Vito began. "Slipped and fell during a dance class she was teaching, broke her collarbone." Vito looked at Peter. "Luckily we got a good orthopedic man up here, Indian fellow, Patel. Do you know him?" Peter said he didn't. "Must have been very painful," I said to Marjorie, being civil, being nice, and she said, "It's the sleeping that's hard. You wouldn't believe." Her blue eyes rolled behind her glasses.

"So now I got the kitchen detail, mostly." Vito offered

wine or beer, which we declined. "Coffee, then? We got a pot of decaf waiting."

"No, thank you," Peter said immediately.

Ess had taken the piano stool, intended to service an upright in the corner. This room smelled of pine-forest air freshener, and was decorated mainly with dishes. Rows and rows were hung on the paneled walls behind couches and chairs and between windows. Marjorie was clearly a collector of pictorial plates, and they had overflowed the dining room and filled the living room as well—scenes of cities, World's Fairs, pontiffs and presidents, kittens and puppies, ballerinas, Christmas trees and waterfalls. The hall was exempt, and was hung instead with family photographs—mostly weddings and portraits in mortarboards.

"So, we got a little problem," Vito began, picking up a glass bowl of mixed nuts from the coffee table and leaning over to offer it to us.

I put up my hand like a traffic policeman. "No, thank you."

Peter looked sternly at Vito and cleared his throat. "We have a *big* problem." He was sitting on the edge of the couch, knees apart, hands folded between them.

"Yes, yes, of course. It was just a manner of speech, don't get me wrong. A big problem is what we got. It's big trouble, no doubt about it."

"Right." Peter's laser glance went to Ess, whose face was implacable, but who swiveled slightly on his stool, left to right, right to left.

"Marjorie and I stayed up half the night, you gotta know. Shed a few tears. We dittn't take it lightly—no. So, you shouttn't think we tossed it off. Salvatore and I had a man-to-man, dittn't we, son? He's gotta think over a few things. He's gotta think over what it means to be a man, act like a man."

"Right," Peter said.

"What he did, pardon the expression, Marjorie and

I think is disgusting. Goes against all our teaching. All his Catholic schooling, all we ever taught our kids. Right from the time they were little." He threw an angry look at Ess. "Right, Salvatore?"

"Our daughter is thirteen years old," Peter said.

"Yeah. I know. And I got two daughters, Doctor, so don't think I'm not sensitive to your situation. I got one married, one in school to be a physical therapist, both wonderful girls—"

"It's *our* situation," Peter corrected firmly, "yours and ours. Anyway, you can imagine how my wife and I feel, Mr. DiBuono. Vito. You have a good idea what we're going through. She's in the car outside"—as if it were motorized, Peter's head jerked in the general direction of the front door—"and she is out there, sitting in the car, feeling sick. Scared. And she's going into her second month. We feel there's no time to lose."

Mrs. DiBuono was sitting mummy-rigid, head unmoving, back up against the straight back of the chair. Behind her glasses, her blue eyes shot back and forth between Peter and Vito.

"No time to lose, for . . . ?" Mr. DiBuono's eyes narrowed. He knew the answer.

"For getting an abortion. We intend to get Ellery an abortion as soon as possible."

Mr. DiBuono shot a look at his wife. "We understand how you're feeling, Marjorie and me, we do. But as I know Ess told you, we, our family, we're very solid on this, real firm about taking a human life, see, we don't think it's right."

"We don't think it's right," Marjorie echoed. Her hands played with the rings on her fingers and I noticed her fingernails for the first time: artificial or real? They had the color and gloss of candy apples, as if they'd had a final coat a few minutes ago.

"It's easy for you to say." Peter was holding back temper and I touched his sleeve, proud of the way he was handling this so far. "We don't love abortion, either, but look at Ellery's age, look at the situation."

Ess cleared his throat. "Ellery doesn't want one," he said. It was the first time I'd seen him looking uncomfortable, eyes going from his mother to his father, back to us.

"That's why we're here, Ess," Peter said.

"We want you—" I began, but Vito cut me off.

"My wife is the one, my wife is the one who is very strong on this. It goes against us. It goes real deep, y'see. It's wrong. She's got a sister, a nun in the Dominican order—"

"Vito, this has nothing to do with my sister. Abortion is taking a life. Taking a life is wrong." The light glanced off Marjorie's glasses momentarily, giving her a gleaming, extraterrestrial look.

Peter licked his lips, ran his finger across his mustache. "What's wrong, Mr. and Mrs. DiBuono, is that your son has impregnated our child. Our little daughter. Isn't that taking a life? My daughter's life? I think it is!"

"Yes, yes, we know how you feel, Doctor. And don't think we haven't told Salvatore a few things!"

Ess nodded in response to this. "I'll show you some bruises," he said, but no one smiled. He put his toes on the floor, to stop swiveling. Simultaneously, there was a commotion in the kitchen, a door slammed, then, the sound of a radio, footsteps up above.

"We raised a houseful," Vito took a cue. "It's not easy, I know it's not easy, but you don't just get rid of a baby because it's inconvenient, Doctor."

"Inconvenient? This is not inconvenience! It's *tragedy*! How would you expect my thirteen-year-old daughter to raise a *baby*?"

"My wife and I discussed this, Doctor. Now, see, it's very hard for us, because my wife is a working girl, teaches ballroom dancing three afternoons, two nights a week, y'know, and I have a business that's, like, twelve hours a day, but we're thinking if Salvatore and your daughter got your permission to marry, why, we could put them up here, on the third floor. I still got four at home, but the boys could double up, no problem, they're never home anyway, and I'd put in a little more insulation, a kitchenette up there for them, it wouttn't take me and the boys long, and for now, they could live here with us and we'd all pitch in."

I suppressed a knee-jerk shriek. I saw Ellery pregnant out to here, sitting in this room or climbing the narrow stairs to the attic, and thought, *This is so ghastly, it's almost funny.*

Peter's cheeks were gathering blood. "That's out of the question."

"Well, the other possibility, then, we were talking about this half the night, y'got to understand, this is nothing we dittn't look at real close, the other possibility is we give this baby to some couple who would love it and give it the kind of home we'd want for our first grandchild."

The horror of the phrase *our first grandchild* punched into my head like a boxing glove. Their grandchild? Any minute my usually disciplined eyes would begin watering, I'd become a gushing waterfall splashing out my heart on the DiBuonos' couch. "We don't want our child to go through a full term pregnancy," I managed.

When Ess spoke, it sounded like oratory: "This couple, I painted their house this summer? They were neat guys, and they'd been trying to have a kid for seven years. Seven years! Ellery said she thought someone like that would take Scooter and raise it, do a great job. Or, she said, even the Bergins. Your neighbors. They would love a baby. That way she could be nearby, and she wouldn't lose her baby altogether. And I could be there, too. Every day. It would be great for the kid. And I know you and Dr. E would be right in town, um, in an emergency. Hey, it would be good for everybody, the best of all worlds."

"That's totally unheard of and ridiculous." Peter, getting redder, was extraordinarily steady, stayed his course without flying apart, as I felt I might, at any minute. "This crack-brained idea is something a thirteen-year-old child would conjure up, you can't be serious, it's totally puerile. . . ."

"It's totally what?" Vito was opening a pack of cigarettes. "Do you mind?" he asked us.

I did. It was hard enough breathing as it was. I said, no, to go ahead. Then I said, "A *childish* and *simplistic* idea."

"But it seems like an idea that would make everybody happy. This couple would like a baby, I mean, she's a lawyer and he's—what?—some bigshot at CBS, kept offering me baseball tickets. Ellery could bop right back into school and life could go on." Ess swiveled, self-confidence back.

I wanted to jump up, let out a scream—maybe take some of the hanging plates and smash them against the standing ashtray into which Vito was now placing a burned match. "Ess, Ellery listens to you. That's why we came here, to ask you to help us get Ellery to see it our way. Not to come up with some lunatic-fringe, cuckoo, way-out scheme."

Marjorie was shaking her head back and forth very slightly, very slowly, chin up, so as not to cause herself further neck pain. "It's wrong. Wrong . . ."

Vito held up his cigarette with his thumb and index finger. "Mrs. Ehrlich—Libby—Salvatore is our son, and no son of ours is ever going to try to convince anyone to commit a murder."

Peter's upper lip was going full speed ahead. "I'm afraid, Vito, that we're going to have to make an exception here. Scraping away a few cells in a ten-minute procedure is not murder. You're just spouting pro-life propaganda, that's all it is."

"We don't see eye to eye, Doctor. Marj and I, we want to be reasonable, stay cordial, but you're putting us in a bad situation here. Real bad. There's a baby growing here that's our blood and deserves life, just like you do, like everyone here in this room does!" Vito took an angry puff of his cigarette and let the smoke out through his mouth and nose simultaneously.

Peter suddenly reached over and took my hand. It was completely unexpected, a gesture of either solidarity, fear, or some effort to show the strength of our team. "Libby and I didn't come here to war with you, Vito. Maybe you ought to see Ellery, see how fragile, how young, how sweet a child she is—" Peter's voice broke. He seemed meek and fragile himself, and I was afraid he might break down, actually let go and cry.

Ess, nervous, jumped up from the piano stool. "I'll go get her. I'll bring her in," he said.

As soon as the door closed behind Ess, Peter let go of my hand. He sat straight up, back almost but not quite touching the sofa cushions behind him, crossed his arms over his chest; the tone of his voice changed. It seemed charged and forceful, the inner Peter, the man inside the doctor, speaking with a raised fist in his voice.

"Since Ess stepped out, this is my opportunity to tell you, Mr. and Mrs. DiBuono, that the age of consent in the state of Connecticut is sixteen. My daughter is three years short of the age of consent, and your son . . . your son is guilty of statutory rape. In this state"—he took a sigh so deep it was as if he'd been asked to inhale for a medical exam—"in this state, the probable prison sentence for a crime of this sort is seven years. Seven years, Vito."

Vito's chin went up and his mouth curled over his teeth, which I now realized were so white and well aligned, they were possibly laminated. There was a silence that seemed to go on and on. Marjorie's eyes were on Peter, her fingers nervously turning her wedding and diamond engagement rings. I saw her hands shaking.

"Only if you bring charges, Doctor," Vito finally said.

"Not if you're reasonable. Not if you let Ess off the hook. I don't think for a minute he wants to be responsible for a wife and a child at his age! He doesn't even have a job!"

"He has a job as of Wednesday. At my place. He's never been very interested in the family business but, see, he's come around. We need him, anyways. We're going to open a new showroom in Norwalk, need a man there. People dying in Norwalk, too." A little smile came and went. The cloud of smoke around Vito's head was making me want to cough. I waved the smoke away from my face and Vito became immediately solicitous. "I'm sorry, Libby, I'll put it right out," he said, and jammed the cigarette into the ashtray. "I've quit six times, that's the God's honest truth."

"There's a prison in Danbury, isn't there?" I was startled. The near-tears had given way to a new hard edge that was totally out of character for Peter.

Vito's eyes narrowed. "Doc. You're not going to pull that, are you? You're not going to threaten us? You're a father, aren't you? How could you talk prison to another father? I got eight kids, all good kids, nobody in serious trouble until this, we're decent people! You're a big doctor, you got a bit more education, a bit more money, you think you can come into my home here, and push us around, threaten us in our own living room?"

"I'm not pushing you around, I'm trying to save my daughter!" Peter covered his mouth with his hand, probably trying to control his twitch. Perspiration ran in stripes from his eyebrows to his chin.

"And we have our principles, we live by our principles,

and I'm telling you, Doctor—Marjorie, I'm standing by you one hundred percent on this—that you can call the cops this minute, this second, get 'em to put handcuffs on Salvatore, and it's not goin' to change our minds one degree. It's not a hard choice for us, I'm saying we're not budging one inch! Abortion is killing! Abortion is murder! You want to lock up my kid—"

A sound came from Marjorie, who had taken a tissue from her pocket and was pushing it into her eye under one of the lenses of her glasses.

"You want to lock up Salvatore, that'll be on your conscience, Doctor, that'll be between you and the Boss"—Vito, perspiring, too, his voice sounding like a series of gasps, pointed at the ceiling—"because as I understand it, your daughter, your little girl, she may be young, she may be a doctor's daughter, but she came on to my son pretty strong, and Salvatore is just like any other hot-blooded Italian-American kid—"

Peter shot up, practically knocking over the glass dish filled with nuts and a bowl of marble eggs next to it on the coffee table.

"Why, you—you bastard! Watch what you say about my daughter!" I felt the couch shaking under me, the floor rock, and I looked at Marjorie, blowing her nose, unashamedly crying now, and I thought she must be just about my age, might easily have been a schoolmate of mine, was a mother and wife like me, and I couldn't figure it. How did we come to such disparate, such polarized points of view? Where in her thought-process did her logic short-circuit? She was willing to ruin all our lives for the sake of dogma, to stick us all to her pernicious Right to Life flypaper. Of all the choices in the world, Ellery had coupled with the son of this martyr of Danbury; it was sad and bizarre, horrible luck.

"Listen, Vito, I haven't been in a punching match with anyone since third grade," Peter said, more calmly now, "and I don't intend to start a fight now. But one more word about my daughter, and I start hitting. And, one way or the other, I do intend to get justice here, Vito. I intend to get justice."

Vito's face grew dark. He pointed two splayed fingers at Peter the way Ess had pointed to the King Charles spaniel on our den wall. "You doctors! You all think you're effing big shots. Every last one. Saving lives every day, huh? But down deep, you got no regard at all for human life. You got zilch," he muttered, and his one eyebrow V'd over his eyes.

Peter turned to me. "We're not getting anywhere. C'mon. Let's go."

"What about Ellery?" I asked.

"Obviously Ess isn't having any luck getting her in here, either, and now there's no point anyway. C'mon, Libby." I looked for my pocketbook, steadied my feet on the gold carpet. "Let's go, Libby," he repeated, when I took more than a half second to pick my handbag off the floor and get up out of the sofa.

At the door, he turned. "Vito, I'll give you twenty-four hours to get Ess to come around. After that, get a good lawyer. You're going to need one, my friend."

It had gotten dark outside, but the illuminated signs from Vito's place of business cast a fluorescent glow that made the tombstones, crosses, and flowers look eerily festive. Ess and Ellery were standing together, leaning against the cyclone fence, and Ess's arm was encircling Ellery's shoulder. Not far above them, the black letters spelling DANBURY MEMORIALS were emblazoned on a lighted white glass rectangle, and on every side behind them, statues hovered like small dark sentinels.

Descending to the sidewalk, step by step, I kept my eye on my daughter and Ess, squeezing together as if we were about to blindfold and shoot them. I was reminded of flickering old movies about refugees—young lovers about to be torn apart by war, parted under a sky filled with bombers and shrapnel. I was reminded of myself, the old tremors of adolescence, the soul-tearing feelings of love and pain and destiny. I remembered the intensity of passion, I remembered lust, I remembered Trevor Eddy's breath and smell and skin. Were those the only times I'd ever really believed in God? It all came back and I was Ellery now, in cataclysmic, weak-kneed, elysian love.

She and Ess were looking at each other, oblivious to us. I saw Ess pull a strand of Ellery's hair out of her eyes, saw him lean over and kiss the side of her forehead. That intimacy hurt—goddamn it, not Ess!—but the tenderness touched something primitive in me. Something melted and gave way.

As we got to the bottom step of the DiBuonos' property, Peter's beeper sounded and my private spell was broken.

"C'mon, Ellery, get in the car!" he ordered, and obediently, silently, she left the embrace of Salvatore DiBuono and climbed into the backseat.

"Your boyfriend's parents are a bunch of assholes," the navigator said, and he reached for his cell phone to call his office. There was no response from me and none from Ellery, but most of the way home, my daughter wept silently, heartbreakingly in the backseat.

When Peter got home from his emergency call, it was two in the morning. He was surprised to see me still up, hunched over copies of *Southern Connecticut Life* at the kitchen table. We had not made the cover—Kathie Lee and family were smiling from *their* front door—but we had four pages. I was clipping the article and pictures for my mother, Darley, my sister. I couldn't sleep anyway. Looking at the photos—most of them flattering—reading and rereading the photo captions: *From left to right in the Ehrlich living room: Mrs. Ehrlich, Dr. Ehrlich, Ellery,*

*Claudia. Mrs. Ehrlich attributes her love for antiques to nostalgia for the America of a mellower time. Ellery's tumble from a horse this spring will not deter her from continuing her favorite sport. Dr. Ehrlich attending to a patient at the Bridgeport Hospital clinic.* I felt I should add, *FYI: Sham* on the top of every page.

"After the day we had, I thought you'd be out like a light." Peter's eyes looked as if they'd sunken more deeply into their sockets just since this morning.

"I slept for an hour. That may be it for the night."

"A forty-eight-year-old, two-hundred-eighty-pound CPA. Cardiac arrest at the wheel of his car on I-95. For a minute there, for a minute, I lost all my concentration. I was thinking Ellery, Ellery, Ellery. It was like—it's hard to explain, but I asked one of the VAC guys to get me some Amoxycillin. Jesus. It would have been the end. The end for that man. He was wearing a Medic Alert bracelet—allergic to penicillin—I broke out in a cold sweat. Just in time, I snapped out of it; I corrected myself. Well, there was this horrible moment where I came this close to killing this poor slob. Then, I sort of came to and it was okay. Not that it was easy, getting through all that fat, but I think we got him patched up, more than you can say for the Mercedes."

I remembered Vito's words about saving lives. A hero. "You're lucky. You're a hero. The best distraction."

"It's not really much of a distraction. I've been thinking."

"What, Pete?"

"If Ted Irvine won't do it, there are quite a few competent men up in Bridgeport who'll take care of Ellery."

"Without her consent?"

"Without her consent."

"How competent? How competent are these men in Bridgeport?"

"I'm going to get some names tomorrow."

"In the hospital? In Bridgeport Hospital?"

"No. Not at the hospital, no. At a private clinic."

"What kind of clinic?"

"I said, a private clinic." He averted his eyes.

"An abortion clinic."

"Yes."

"A factory."

No answer.

"You wouldn't do that, Pete."

"I would."

"No, Peter, please."

"Look, sweetie, I'm going to look into it tomorrow. I mean today. Today is tomorrow, isn't it?"

It was the Saturday before Labor Day. "Today is tomorrow," I said.

At four o'clock, Annie appeared at the front door with a cellophane-wrapped basket. She said I'd been one of the three winners of the raffle at the Stratford Historical Museum luncheon, and she'd stopped by to drop it off. "When they called out your name, I was so happy! Winning a prize just when you need a lift. And yours was the best! Midge Donovan got a basket filled with perfumed soaps and all Marilyn Glass got was two tickets to the cineplex. Your basket is filled with all sorts of goodies—pâté de foie gras, black caviar, cookies, a million different cheeses, Swiss chocolate candies, champagne—"

"Wait, Annie, let me get the champagne out of here; we don't drink. You take it home."

"I know Pete doesn't, but you—?"

"I don't have it in the house."

"I thought you'd *need* a lift. You sure?"

"You take it home."

"You sure?"

"Sure."

"We don't have a lot to celebrate, either, Libby."

"New Year's. Maybe by that time Bud will have a better job and come home again. You'll need it New Year's."

"How is it going here?" Annie lowered her voice as I pulled the bottle out of the cellophane wrap and handed it to her.

"As you'd expect."

"That poor kid. How is Peter taking it?"

"Not well. Of course."

"What's going to happen?"

"Ellery will get an abortion, although Ess is against it. We met with his family and they tried to—" I couldn't finish.

Annie touched my arm. "Ellery wants an abortion?"

"She thinks she's in love with Ess. Believe it or not, she doesn't want one."

"But then, Libby, you can't very well force her into it?"

"She's thirteen years old. The day she fell off the horse was the day of her first period."

"She doesn't want an abortion, she shouldn't have one."

"If it were your child, you'd insist—"

"If it were my child, I'd *never* push her. Do you have any idea what the risks are?"

"I don't think I want to hear them, Annie."

"But you should! If the cervix is dilated too rapidly by someone incompetent, it can damage her tubes permanently. Or there can be a major infection, or a doctor can perforate her uterus or there can be excessive bleeding, she can go into shock. She could die!"

"Annie, having a baby is a greater risk. Why are you trying to frighten the hell out of me!"

Her tired face became animated. "Because, because I don't believe abortion is right!"

I remembered the remark she'd made about honesty when I'd discovered the eighteenth-century music rack. "We don't think alike," I said, rather coolly.

"It seems we don't. I can't imagine forcing a person to give up having her baby. And making the decision not to let a life that's already started live!"

"If you had a daughter—"

"Well, I don't have a daughter. And I don't have a son, either, do I? And so it's particularly galling to have you take a life when some people—some people—would have done pretty much everything they could to keep their"—her eyes filled up—"their child. And the world is still full of people who would *die* to take Ellery's baby and give it a wonderful life."

"Annie. I can't talk about this now. I can't!"

"I just hope you change your mind!" Her vehemence dumbfounded me. I felt there was something intrinsically very holy in Annie I'd never really looked at before, and her super virtue made me feel profane and decidedly unholy.

"It's a family matter." I pulled myself up. "Annie, I'm sorry, but it's basically our business."

"It's basically God's business!"

She turned and walked down the front three steps, then stopped and turned. "And I'm sorry I brought that basket to you," she said. "It was me who won it, Libby, not you."

"I don't understand. I don't understand!" Darley's voice on the telephone was little-girl pleading. Peter still hadn't been in touch. Hadn't so much as returned her midnight call to speak a word to her in all this time, let alone paid a condolence call! And the girls! Not a peep from either of them. If it weren't for the judge, where would she be? It was automatic the way I tried to smooth it over, cough up some decent excuses. I told her about last night's highway emergency call, about school beginning, Kevin Bevan's leaving, but she wasn't listening.

"For heaven's sakes, Libby! How do you think I feel?" She hesitated, and having absorbed not a word of what I'd said, she plunged ahead. "Not even a card from the girls! You know, Libby, Peter was always so compassionate, so thoughtful, a considerate person, a kind and loving son, before—I mean, what has happened to him? He was never like this!"

Never like this—*before me*! It's what she meant. I, Libby, had happened to her thoughtful, considerate and compassionate son. Another breaking down of the quality control of civilized behavior here, due to my inertia or incompetence or whatever assortment of shortcomings she had listed under my name in her mental directory.

I have spent my life restraining impulses. To tell. To rage. To hurl objects across rooms. To confront. Even in crisis I am a background person, quiet, not distracting, born to stand behind someone more in focus. Like in one of the photos taken with Peter's three-dimensional camera. A pretty hedge, a placid lake. Ever the handy prop, the doctor's wife. And so I said, "I'll have him get to you today. He'll call you later. And I'm sorry, really sorry. I know how you must feel."

Ellery stood over the toilet an hour later, retching. I had never been this sick during pregnancy, so it had to be fear and stress, her tender age. I sponged off her forehead and gave her ice to chew, and when the worst of it was over, I sat in the rocker in her room while she faced me from the edge of her bed, holding Dumpling on her lap, scratching his head, looking even more hollow-eyed and pathetic than last night, at the DiBuonos'. Not like my daughter at all—not my little girl anymore.

Again last night, I'd spent what seemed like one half hour asleep and the rest wide awake, thinking.

In my mind's eye I saw Ellery over and over, standing under the fluorescent light of the Danbury Monuments sign with Ess at her side. Somewhere near dawn there was a sudden correction in my vision. It was like the windshield of my car on a steamy night. Limited visibility until I pushed the defrost button and then—one, two, three—the glass beyond the dashboard clarified, and my view of the road turned crystal clear.

Now I looked around her room, returning the gaze of stuffed animals, the little brown monkey with bead eyes, rock stars with airbrushed faces.

"It should be your decision," I said.

Ellery blinked. Her hand stopped stroking the cat in her lap.

"If you want to—to—to"—I had to swallow, take a deep breath, stop my mouth from stammering—"go through with this and have this baby, Ell, no one should coerce you, no one should pressure you, or . . . *force* you to get rid of it." Until this time, my interest in abortion protests, marches, and politics were sideline. I had heard the strident rhetoric on both sides, aligned myself philosophically with the pro-choice contingent, but then again, we were the family of the most prominent physician in Crandall, wholesome as our press in *Southern Connecticut Life,* so what did it all have to do with us?

Now it had to do with us. And now I was voting pro-choice. "Your decision," I repeated. "And remember, we'll—I'll stand by you. No matter what."

"Mommy!" Wide-eyed, she looked just like the nine-year-old Ellery in an old photograph my mother used to carry in a plastic folder in her purse.

"No matter what anyone else says, Ellery."

"But Daddy!"

"We both know what would be best for you, dear. Get rid of it, go on with school, put it all behind you. That's what Daddy wants. Me, too. Oh, me, too! But—" I think I'd never felt as close to breaking down as at that moment, just folding up, sinking to the carpet and begging her to make what seemed the only right decision, pleading with her to get it done and get it over with. "In the final frame, it is only up to you."

I heard Peter come in. He'd done his morning hospital rounds; there would be no office hours this weekend. I heard the refrigerator open and close, the scrape of a chair in the kitchen; he must have poured a glass of orange juice, found one of the bran muffins I'd left on the counter for him.

I went to the top of the stairs and tried to be normal. "Peter, hi, dear? Did you find those muffins I left out on the counter? There's some apple jelly in the fridge."

"Yeah, thanks, sweetie. Where is Ellery?"

"Up here."

"What is she doing?"

"Not feeling great."

"Did we hear from the DiBuonos?"

"No."

Silence.

"I don't think we'll hear from them. And Peter, there's no way we can call the police. They know it, too."

Then, "Where's Claudia?"

"Asleep. Still asleep. Peter—"

"Yes?"

"Did you find time to call your mother?"

"Oh, Jesus, thanks for reminding me."

I fell asleep at noon and slept a seamless sleep until five. No dreams, no snow. When I awoke, Peter was standing at the foot of the bed. He was holding a glass of orange juice in his hand and my first thought was that he was still sipping from the same glass of juice, that it was still morning.

"We have to talk," he said, and his voice was ominous.

He was in his sweats, perspiring, must have just come up from working out in the basement. He had a towel around his neck. In my drowsiness a non sequitur popped into my head: *He's still so good-looking.* It seemed a strange time for erotic stirrings.

"Let me just wake up a little." I needed five minutes, the way I always do in the morning.

He wasn't going to wait any five minutes. "What did you say to Ellery?"

The erotic feelings evaporated. "Peter, what time is it?"

"It's a few minutes after five."

"I'm still a little groggy. I hardly slept last night, the night before—"

"What did you say to Ellery?"

"Why? What did she say I said?"

"You told her it was her choice? You gave her permission to go ahead, just like that, make a life's decision, this baby, this *tot,* this immature *little girl,* told her to go right ahead, have Ess DiBuono's child? Libby, have you lost your mind?"

"I told her I didn't want—we didn't want that, but Pete, listen, you can't, you can't force Ellery, you can't force *anyone*—listen, there are no answers, no answers, but in the final analysis, how can we *compel, coerce* anyone to terminate a—to do such a thing?"

"What are you talking about? We're talking about a kid who's been on this earth thirteen years! This is her *life*!"

"Exactly! *Hers.*"

"Libby, this—this Ess DiBuono—you want our little, little—girl, to, to"—Peter pulled the towel off his neck and wiped his face—"to be stuck, be stuck for life with the offspring of, of—" His voice broke, and he sank onto the Baltimore settee and glared at me.

"No, of course not, God, no."

"Then, then?"

"Ess may be irritating, may be, I don't know, weak-chinned or inadequate—and he's probably temporary, I mean, this can't last—but she's made the choice. Her destiny. Her decision."

"Libby. Wake up! Wake up! We're not talking philosophy here. We're talking about our daughter, who just started menstruating—when was it? Four months ago! This is not some pygmy in Africa, some third-world crack baby in Bridgeport, Connecticut! This is my—*our* child! What if she was going to take her own life, would that be her decision, too?"

"It's different, it's different! You've never been pregnant. You've never been a mother."

"Libby, oh, for Christ's sake! I've never been a fireman, either, but I know what smoke smells like!"

"What if you force her and something goes wrong? It could, it could!" Annie's itemized list of disasters fizzed and buzzed in my head.

"No, nothing will go wrong. It's a very simple procedure."

"Things go wrong all the time, you know they do, Peter."

"And things go wrong in the delivery room. More likely, in fact, at thirteen!"

"But then, she will have decided her own fate. And it won't be on our conscience."

"Goddamn it! I can't believe that you could take this position! Your own daughter."

"Exactly. Last night, when I watched Ess and Ellery together, something in me waved a white flag. I just collapsed. Now, I feel free. It's her decision. That's it. I feel unburdened. And maybe, Peter, if we let up on the pressure, she'll come around. If we let up trying to push her, then, then, who knows? She's a confused teenager. She might just change her mind."

"That's a risk we can't take! There's not that much time."

"It's the only way! There's no other choice."

"She's under that creep's spell. And that family . . ." Peter shook his head. "My God! Can't you see it? That's why I want him locked up!"

"No, God, Peter, no. Think about it."

"I've thought about it. Behind bars!"

Ellery and Ess. The passion that spins the world. "She's got his baby in her stomach. You can't put him in jail!"

Peter's twitch seemed like some malevolent punctuation mark. "You've lost your reason, Libby."

"I think I've found it. It's my daughter's life. She gets to live it. End of discussion!" I yelled.

Peter took the towel, snapped it in the air as if he were swatting a hornet, and suddenly threw it to the floor. Then, he spun to face me. "We've been married how long, Libby? Twenty years?"

"Twenty-one."

The lip quiver—and how I'd come to hate it—appeared and disappeared. "And you know? It's the first time I've ever felt like hitting you."

*And it's the first time in that mountainous pileup of years that I've ever stood up to you,* I thought.

At eight that night, Peter and I sat together in the den at opposite ends of the couch, hardly speaking, eyes on the television set. Ellery, eyes swollen from crying, chin resting on the back of her hands, sat hunched and silent over the Niagara Falls puzzle on the card table. Claudia was upstairs in her room, showing her new clothes to three girlfriends, who had stopped by an hour ago. Every so often, the sounds of music or a squeal of laughter filtered down into the den.

A Labor Day weekend barbecue, complete with boisterous guests and a banjo player, was in progress at the Bergins'. We'd been invited, but declined, using Aunt

Meggie's death as an excuse, although Peter was now unwilling to make the condolence call we'd said we had to make. He'd put Darley off, still certain the DiBuonos would call. Rather than go to jail, Ess would appear and beg and plead for Ellery to go ahead, go through with it, get the abortion. Peter sat unnaturally still, seeming to be wrapped in his clothes instead of wearing them, a stiff mummy waiting, alert to every ring of the telephone and the sound of every passing car.

When we heard a knock at the back door, I saw his eyes dart in the direction of the kitchen. "I'll go," we both said simultaneously. I was all nerves, too. I don't recover easily from confrontations; they dry me up, sometimes for days. Peter went—we were both still expecting Ess—but a moment later it was Sarah Jane Bergin who was standing in the doorway of the den. "Thank goodness you're still here." She sighed. *She's come to borrow something again,* my first killer thought. She was all smiles, head to toe in pale orange, the unripe mango color in all this season's mail-order catalogs, and her shoes, white sandals with heels shaped like lucite ice cream cones. "Ellery! How's the puzzle going? You're looking a bit sad. Feeling bad about your aunt?"

Ellery mumbled a courteous greeting and Sarah Jane threw me a quizzical look I pretended to ignore.

The mustache often hid nuances of expression, and only I would have perceived the tightness around Peter's mouth as he offered to get Sarah Jane the ice for which she'd come. The friendly neighbor-doctor's voice came up cordial as ever. "Sounds like a lively party over there."

"I was afraid you'd already left!" she breathed, eyes sparkling, lipstick fresh and glossed. She was holding her drink—probably vodka and tonic, likely not her first. "Barry's grilling lamb and couldn't leave the coals. He said he'd save you some English trifle. He made it himself."

"Peter can't eat trifle," I said without thinking, and I felt Peter's eyes zing toward me.

"Why not?" she asked, just as automatically. Out of the corner of my eye I saw Ellery's quizzical face turn in my direction, too.

"It doesn't like him." Peter, going off to the kitchen, added, "The eccentric, non-trifle-eating doctor."

"Well, I'll bring some just for you, then, Lib. And the girls. It's wonderful, if I do say so." She winked. "Lotsa cream, lotsa rum." Thanks to the vodka, she didn't notice the crackle of tension. "Claudia out with one of her millions of boyfriends?"

"She's upstairs with her girlfriends."

The girls' telephone rang before I'd finished the sentence, and a moment later, Claudia's voice rang out. "Ellery, for you!" and Ellery shot up, shaking a few puzzle pieces to the floor. "Excuse me," she said, ever well brought up and polite, as she flew past Sarah Jane to get to the stairs.

"I gather by the speed of the response, there's a boyfriend already?" Sarah Jane looked as if she was about to raise a toast, as soon as Ellery had left the room.

"Well, you could say."

"Goodness, they're starting young these days!" She had picked up the puzzle pieces and busied herself trying to fit them into the puzzle. "Well, she's getting to be quite a looker, too. You know, I try not to be envious, but your girls and your family life are about as idyllic as anybody's I know. In fact, two people at our party read the article about you in *Southern Connecticut Life*—one of them was terribly disappointed you weren't going to be at our house tonight. They thought they'd get to meet the 'bigger-than-life Ehrlichs'!"

Then, she lowered her voice. "Listen, keep this under your hat. You remember our last conversation?"

"About the pastoral painting?"

"No, I took that to the resale shop. I mean, about Trevor."

"What about Trevor?"

"I told you I was attracted to him. Didn't I tell you?"

"You did."

"I think it's reciprocated. I really do. Sometimes I catch him looking at me a certain way."

I knew the way and was silent.

"I've been thinking. He's a gorgeous thing. He's smart. He's even got lineage. He's a gorgeous, smart sperm bank, is what I'm saying."

"Sarah Jane."

"Don't look at me like that. I'm just going to—"

"I know. Get him to donate a little fertilization. I think that's carrying borrowing too far."

"I think it would solve all my problems. What could be wrong?"

As soon as she'd left with the two plastic bags of ice Peter had gotten out of the freezer for her, I told Peter I intended never to lend anything to Sarah Jane again.

"I'm not sure I like the new you, Lib."

"Peter, I'm not sure that I care whether you're not sure you like the new me."

Peter's eyebrows went up. "Libby. Not PMS again? You know it never existed before talk shows. I'm too old to appreciate it."

"It's not about PMS, Peter. It's about my right to have an opinion."

"Libby, let's have peace. I won't lend her any more ice. Is that better?"

"You know it's not about ice."

"Libby, can I please watch the news? We'll talk about it tomorrow, okay?"

"It can't wait until tomorrow. It's about Ellery. You've got to leave her alone."

"That's out of the question."

"Out of the question? You're only a doctor, Peter, not Zeus. There's no malpractice insurance for deities!"

Peter sank into the sofa and picked up the remote control, aiming it at the television screen. "I'm tired," he said, as if he were here alone, as if I weren't in the room at all.

"What did Ess say?" I asked Ellery as soon as she came back downstairs. Peter had gone to bed to read, he'd said clearly. To get away from me.

"I told him what you said, Mommy, that you felt it was my decision."

"I suppose Daddy's threat didn't change his mind?"

"Well, he's scared. But no. He says one day in heaven, there'll be this judge. And we'll have done it right. And we'll be rewarded."

"But you don't believe that?"

"Ess believes it."

"But you? I don't know how you could have grown up in this house and even listen, let alone believe one word of that fundamentalist craziness."

"Well, I don't know if I believe it or not, Mommy."

"It's total nonsense."

"I don't know. The DiBuonos believe it, and all the Catholics in the world believe it. Ess took me to Mass once when you were away and I loved it. What if they're right?"

"Then the earth is flat and there's life on Mars."

"And Jennifer believes it, too!"

"You told Jennifer? Which Jennifer?"

"Jennifer Hellman, I told you. Jennifer Torpin, too. And Jennifer Torpin's mother overheard us talking. Just those three. I can really, really trust them, Mommy."

"Oh, Ellery!"

"They're my best friends!"

It would be all over town in a week.

"What's wrong, Libby?" It was my mother, the next morning, calling from Florida. Darley had called her to find out if something was wrong at our house. Our absence was finally making her suspicious. "Is something happening?"

"No, nothing."

"Why didn't you tell me Darley's sister died? You know I would have sent her a card."

"I was going to tell you."

"When?"

"Today."

"You sound funny. I'm your mother. I can tell. What is it?"

"Everything's fine. How's Rudy?"

"He was making a fiftieth anniversary cake for the couple who run the bridge group I was telling you about last week, and it caved in the minute he took it out of the oven. He had to do the whole thing over again. She has Parkinson's."

"That's nice."

"Parkinson's is nice?"

"No, the cake, the cake is nice."

"I'm your mother; tell me, Libby. What's going on up there?"

# Chapter Nine

It was ten in the morning on Labor Day. The navigator had summoned us into the kitchen for what he called a family meeting, prior to leaving to go to his mother's. We sat at the kitchen table in the glow of the September sun that sparkled through the unshaded windows. Dumpling lay curled on his cushion near the back door in a patch of light and around us, appliances gleamed—granite counters, the tile floor, the basket of fruit, the Portuguese calendar—everything slick and bright. Peter was in a cord jacket, the girls in summer dresses; it was a tableau fit to be captured by a camera, the camera stolen by a gypsy who might now have discovered its curse: To photograph things in three dimensions, to examine things too closely, precipitates calamity.

Peter and I had our coffee cups and the girls were drinking Snapple. The new doctor who had replaced Dr. Greavy, Theresa Wu, was on call today, and our instructions were that no telephone calls were to interrupt this meeting. Peter said today would be the beginning of a new priority: parents and children interacting on a weekly basis. If he could attend regular meetings of the "friends of Bill W.", certainly he could afford to give one afternoon or evening to family solidarity. And improvement. Felt guilty, in fact, for having waited so long to create this regular assembly.

I reminded him he'd not at all neglected the girls, that we'd had family occasions consistently, that he'd given up flying, squash, and skiing for us, but he cut me off. "This is a *meeting,*" he said. "A little conference. Everyone gets to speak his mind. Her mind, I should say. I think it's way overdue. You know they do it all the time, the Latter Day Saints in Salt Lake. It's a wonderful idea."

The girls exchanged glances. Claudia asked how long did he think the meeting was to last, and how soon we could get going to the Countess's, since she'd promised to go fishing with "Stephanie's brother" later this afternoon.

"Not today, I just told you, it's Family Day," Peter said.

"But I promised!" Claudia wailed.

"End of discussion." Peter put his palms flat down on the table and glowered at no one in particular.

Claudia folded her arms over the flowered front of her dress. "See? Dad was born under the Sign of Never Give It Up. I get punished because my sister gets knocked up. Is that fair?"

"Don't say 'knocked up,' please. I hate that term." I took a sip of coffee and thought I'd made it too strong. Peter liked it that way, but I didn't.

"You're not being punished and nothing is fair." Peter looked into his mug as if he were reading tea leaves. "Every day I see people who get really mangled by life. When they say that life isn't fair, it has more weight. Death is fair. Everyone gets a turn. So, drop it."

Claudia rolled her eyes. "Now we're going to have philosophy! Look at the sun out there. It's gorgeous!

And day after tomorrow, it's back to the salt mines. I can't believe this!"

"Claudia," I warned.

"Well, I can't help it. Listen, Ellery, just tell him you want an abortion and we'll all be on our way. Stephanie's brother was going to give me a driving lesson, too."

Peter's look reminded me of Vito DiBuono's. It had thunder behind the eyes. "Enough, Claudia."

"Okay, okay. So let's begin." Claudia picked up a spoon and clinked her Snapple bottle. "I hereby call the meeting to order."

"Ellery. Listen, dear," I began. Upstairs, the telephone began to ring. The girls, fidgety, looked at each other. "I just want to say, well, dear, this is a decision you have to make, and *without* Ess. In this situation, you're the soldier and he's the civilian. Even if we gave permission to marry—"

"Never," Peter interrupted.

"Peter, please."

"Forget marry."

"Anyway, I don't think he's going to be with you even for the next five years, let alone fifty. A child is a lifetime responsibility. How do you think you're going to support a baby? Or are you really planning to give it up after you have it? Could you actually live with the idea that out there somewhere was your own flesh and blood, living its life without you?"

Peter stared into his mug without speaking. The telephone kept ringing. Claudia said, "Oh, *merde*! Didn't you turn the machine on, Ell?" and Ellery shrugged.

I was calm and rational. This is how the psychotherapists talked and this is the way we must all speak. No explosions or fireworks, no booming voice or pointed fingers. Pacifically. Therapeutically. "You're not thinking ahead. If you keep it, what about school?"

"I hate school. I'll get a job."

"You never hated school before."

"I did. I could never do as well as Claudia. Never."

"Yes you could." Claudia's eyes were on her fingernails. "Of course you could. It's all in your head. You're basically smart. Very smart. You just need to concentrate. I said I'd help you with your math, didn't I?"

The telephone stopped ringing.

"What kind of work would you be equipped to do as a junior-high dropout?" Peter was keeping his composure, although I recognized the beginning of combat fatigue.

"I could baby-sit other kids while I was taking care of Scooter."

"Scooter! Now, sweetheart, for Christ's sake, will you stop anthropomorphizing a bunch of featureless cells!"

"What?"

"He means, calling the baby Scooter."

"But we're going to call him that even if it's a girl."

Claudia threw her head back and stared at the ceiling. "*Mon Dieu!* We're never going to get out of here!" Then she turned in her chair. "Listen, Ellery, have you really lost it? I swear, you're putting us all on! I thought you were, like, kidding when you said you were actually going to go through with this. *Je me sens déprimé!* Do you realize how fat you're gonna get? Did you ever see Mrs. Thompson down at the club? We're talking a major blimp, I don't know how she got in and out of her locker! She could have given birth to a Volvo she was that big. You want to blow up like that?"

"That's not the issue," I put in, and Peter's foot kicked mine under the table.

Ellery looked uneasy for only a split second. "See? See how immature? You're always thinking how you're going to look in a bathing suit. Is that all you're ever going to care about? Anyways, the stomach is only temporary, and in fact I happened to see Mrs. Thompson playing tennis last week and she got thin again."

"Okay. You go ahead. You're determined you're

going to wreck your life. Get fat, get stretch marks, change diapers, live on beans, go right ahead. You're going to be a walking varicose vein by the time you're twenty."

"Wait a minute, Claudia. It's not only mine. It's half Ess's. And he wants it. And he loves me. He really does. He's going to buy me a ring. With a ruby. My birthstone. He showed it to me in a catalog."

Peter looked at me and shook his head. "You see what we're dealing with? This is who you're going to allow to make an intelligent decision? To raise a child?"

I leaned over and put my hand on Ellery's arm. It seemed especially frail to me, a piece of suede pulled over a curtain rod. "Do you really want to go over there and live with the DiBuonos, dear?"

She shook her head.

"You're not going to live *here*," Peter immediately said. "Not a pregnant Lolita in my house!"

"Peter—"

"End of discussion!"

"Not the end of discussion!" My voice shot through the kitchen like the clang of the dinner bell I'd stopped using five years ago. "She's our child. No matter what!"

"I'll go to a home for unwed mothers." Ellery's chin sank into her chest. Her eyes closed and I saw the wet under her eyelashes.

"My God, when I hear this sort of dialogue, I feel I'm in some bad movie-of-the-week!"

"Is that what you really want to do, Ellery?"

No answer. Upstairs, the phone began ringing again. Simultaneously ours began on the extension right in the kitchen; it seemed to be turned to very loud.

"It's not happening in our house, is it?" Peter's voice rose above the rings. "Libby, is this a scenario you've ever envisioned in your life? Is this"—he pointed to Ellery, whose cheeks were all shiny and wet now—"really my flesh-and-blood daughter?"

"Peter! Don't ever say that!"

"I'll say what I want to say!"

I felt heat rising up my neck, right into my hair. "There you have it! Claudia said it about Ellery, but it's me, too. The knife thrower and the one who stands perfectly still. I've spent a whole lifetime never daring to move an inch!"

Peter's eyes bulged dramatically. "I'm a *knife thrower*?" The girls, shocked into silence, sat speechless.

"Mommy, Daddy, please—" Ellery cried.

Claudia said, "I don't believe this."

"It's my daughter you're talking to! And you're aborting more than a fetus! You're aborting her spirit, her soul, maybe the only possibility she'll have for motherhood. *What right have you?*"

"Libby, have you lost your—"

"It's her life! Her three-dimensional life!"

"—mind?" Peter twitched. It seemed more than his lip now. It seemed his nose, too.

"She gets to choose!"

"Goddamn it, she's in eighth grade and she gets to choose? I'm tired! Just bloody tired. A lifetime of sacrifice and where's the payoff? A fresh-mouthed sixteen-year-old and a gestating teenybopper!" He took a breath that sounded as if a sneeze were coming, or a sob.

"I hate that word, *teenybopper*!"

"And a hostile wife! Is that the load I've worked my, my *balls* off for all my life?"

I heard a gasp. Was it Claudia? Ellery? I could feel perspiration gathering under my hair. "Is that how you see these children? Is that how you see us? A *load*?"

Peter shot up from his chair. "A heartache. That's a better word. Fitting for a cardiologist! And that's what sobriety got me!" He picked up the chair with both hands and slammed it back down. Dumpling let out a frightened hiss and shot up.

Ellery stifled a sob, pushed back her chair, jumped

up, and flew to the refrigerator. She'd kicked off her shoes and run barefoot. Her eyes were wet and red, her skin pale. This is how she'd looked when she was four or five and burning with fever, the nights I'd sponged her back with alcohol and given her baby aspirin and ginger ale—the same clammy, sallow, frightened face. Damp wisps of hair around the hairline. This is how she'd looked when I'd known I had to call the doctor.

Now she tore open the refrigerator and pulled out the bowl of trifle Sarah Jane had delivered last night. It was in a china bowl painted with green leaves and red cherries, covered with Saran Wrap. "What are you doing with that?" I thought she was after something else in the refrigerator, that the trifle had gotten in her way. A moment later, when she walked across the kitchen floor with it, I was afraid she meant to hurl it across the room. *"What are you doing?"* How would I replace the bowl if she broke it? "Ellery!"

Instead, she ran over to the garbage pail in sort of a frenetic dance step, stepped on the pedal that opened it, grabbed a tablespoon out of the sink. "What the hell is she doing?" Peter asked no one in particular. She ripped off the plastic and scooped the trifle out of the bowl and into the pail. As if it were radioactive, toxic. The cream got all over her palms and wrists, spattered her forearms and her dress. A few dollops landed on the floor and we watched, mesmerized, as Dumpling ambled over to take a look.

Now Claudia unexpectedly threw her arms down on the table and began to sob. "What is it? What's going on?" I asked. Peter took a step toward her, then stopped. The telephone upstairs began to ring again. When Claudia lifted her head, her face was streaked with mascaraed tears. Her features looking like a melting wax-museum replica of Peter's. "Claudia, *what*?" I jumped up, confused.

"Daddy! We can't all be so fucking perfect! It's too

hard!'' Then, she cried out to her sister, "You didn't have to do that, Ell! He wouldn't have touched it!'' Under the careful tan, a delicate version of Peter's eyes and chin. The expression his and his father's. Then I saw it for the first time: Claudia's upper lip pulling away from her teeth. I almost missed it; it came and went that fast—the almost imperceptible pull of her upper lip, the glimpse of tooth—her father's too-familiar involuntary twitch.

Peter was standing, legs apart, at the back door, holding his car keys in his hands. Jiggling them in his fingers. He'd already started the car, moved it out of the garage, Windexed the windshield, checked the tires, while he waited for the girls to get ready, waited for me to cut some roses from the garden to bring to his mother. Under the cord jacket, he had on an old pair of chinos and the Italian shirt out of which the barbecue stains had never quite come out. Now the shirt was striped with perspiration as well, and stuck to his chest as if glued down. "Let's go, let's go!'' he kept saying. I was reminded of a camp counselor herding campers onto a bus. At any moment he might put a whistle in his mouth and blow.

Ellery had changed into one of Claudia's newish sundresses. Compassion had motivated her sister to offer something she'd only had on "once for three hours and twenty minutes.'' Ellery, when not weeping, was silent and wan above the blue stripes and white collar, her face as vacant as that of a missing child on a milk carton. She clutched her hands in her lap in the backseat of the car and leaned her forehead against the glass of the side window.

"We're going to have to cheer up before we get to the Countess's,'' Peter said, as we pulled out of the driveway. I managed a wave at Barry Bergin, holding a hose in his driveway, but was unable to eke out a smile.

"He's going to wear the paint off that car," Claudia said, but got no response. The prospect of an hour spent at Darley Vine's, pretending we were as depicted in our profile in *Southern Connecticut Life*, was sinister. Peter had slipped on sunglasses and become silent and inscrutable. The girls had fallen into drugged-like compliance in the backseat. The roses wrapped in plastic in my lap, I sat staring out of the windshield at the endless Connecticut road signs, wishing we were on our way back.

Claudia, who had recovered from her outburst almost instantly, daubed her eyes with cold water and reapplied clear mascara ("Are my eyes all red and grungy now?") and asked her father to turn on the radio.

"Not now." Behind his sunglasses, his fixed chin, his tight-lipped mouth, Peter was a new, ominous figure, going over the speed limit, blowing his horn impatiently, changing lanes.

"Daddy!" Claudia cried out when he took a corner so sharply that the wheels hit the curb, jostled us all.

"I thought you were in a hurry. Weren't you in a hurry?"

"Peter." I put a restraining hand on his sleeve. Under it, I imagined his arm as a steel girder bolted to the steering wheel. "She's not in that much of a hurry."

"Libby. Since when, since when do you tell me how to drive?"

Darley's condominium was in a cluster of five natural-colored, wood, Colonial-style frame town houses with blue-gray shutters. Hers was the end unit, which had a deck overlooking a man-made pond, on which imported ducks floated and around which Canadian geese sometimes gathered. Until today, the baby animal population—ducklings, goslings, the occasional cygnet—were of intense interest to Ellery. Ordinarily she bounded out of the car and headed for the little zoo, cooing over one or another floating or waddling creature. Now when we stepped out of the car, her head was bowed and didn't even turn in the direction of the water.

We had just missed the judge. Darley opened the door and embraced us one after another, and told us he had just left for the golf course. He had a two o'clock tee-off time or would have stayed. He was anxious to meet us. "His niece lives on Westview Road in Crandall" and "of course" knew of our family. Who in our town hadn't heard of us? "My, what pretty dresses!" Darley said, of the girls. Her own was a turquoise at-home outfit busy with Mexican embroidery, and high heels, backless. She was so relieved to see us all, said she was really getting worried—"frantic," she said, as she hurried to put the roses I'd brought from the yard into a vase. "She seems to have recovered," I whispered to Peter, who had spotted *Southern Connecticut Life* prominently displayed on the coffee table.

Darley appeared with the flowers in a vase a minute later. Then, eyes on Ellery, she stopped in her tracks. "Is something wrong?"

"A little carsick. Ellery is a bit under the weather. Nothing serious."

"I could see it, right away." Darley gave me sort of a wink. "Sweetheart, I'll make you some chamomile tea. I used to drink it every month at that time. It always helped. Would you like it with milk?"

We sat in the dinette, which looked out over the pond. Ellery ate a little tuna salad and some cookies, managed to look interested when Darley showed her a photograph of Peter at the Grand Canyon with his father. She'd just uncovered some old albums at Meggie's.

"God, look at Peter there. The image of Claudia. And there's a little Meggie around the mouth, do you see it?" Darley wept a bit, then laughed a moment later. I spotted a new ring cuddled between some familiar ones when she took a tissue to her eyes. "She was a bossy girl, that Meggie. And always trying to beat me at everything. Once, we each got a kite—"

Peter interrupted, "And she tried to tangle yours so hers would fly higher."

"We only have one set of memories, dear. Thank goodness your girls aren't nearly as competitive as we were."

Peter and Darley went upstairs to look over some documents Meggie had kept in a strongbox, and a few other mementos Darley had put in the bedroom she'd converted into a library. In winter she sat up there in front of the TV, with a glass of port or a cup of herbal tea, surrounded by Civil War uniform accessories framed and hung behind no-glare glass, antique firearms, and sepia photos of Abraham Lincoln, and watched old movies. The judge, she said, also loved the old black-and-whites. It was lucky, just providential she'd found him, was in fact considering giving up her trip around the South African Cape to stay here this fall. He was going to take her down to Crandall to meet his niece in a few weeks and on that occasion, would bring him to our house. She knew we'd like him, "though he's still parting his hair smack in the middle, like Jiggs. Remember Maggie and Jiggs?"

Darley, voluble and bustling, didn't note the dark rings under Ellery's eyes, didn't respond to Claudia's reaching over to lift her father's sleeve to look at his watch every ten minutes. With her perfectly manicured fingernails, her bejeweled hands, she dished out the tuna salad, the tomatoes, the sliced eggs, poured Bloody Marys for her and Virgin Marys for the rest of us, buttered bread, scooped out ice cream, talked and talked—

"When am I ever going to get a chance to teach these girls bridge?"—until it was, mercifully, finally time to leave.

And then, she insisted on taking me into the kitchen and pushing into plastic Baggies some of the overflow cookies neighbors had baked, to take home, showing me the fresh oregano the judge had brought over last night—"So thoughtful, such a dear!"—and telling me she was sorry her sister had died before she could be shown the "precious" article about us in "that wonderful magazine." It had brought tears to her eyes. Peter was standing in the doorway and overheard her, and she suddenly said, "Petie, that little tweak of yours is really getting out of hand! You must be working too hard! I'll bet you didn't do it once when you were in Czechoslovakia, or whatever they call it now." Peter turned away without answering, and a few minutes later we were all in the car. "We pulled it off; the Countess is clueless," Claudia remarked as we pulled away from Lakeside Estates and were heading south, sealed together in yet another charged silence.

Without warning, Peter turned off the highway at Exit 4 twenty minutes later.

"Where are we going, Daddy?" Claudia pitched forward in the backseat. "Where is he taking us?"

No answer from Peter. His face was immobilized below his sunglasses. I was reminded of the road from Karlovy Vary to Prague. I remembered the masklike set of his features at the railroad crossing, duplicated here and now. "Where is he *going*?"

"I don't know. Peter, where are we headed?"

Unfair, totally unfair of him to blame me for trying to help him beat the need to drink. Cruel to make me the *bête noir* for doing what any good wife of a recovering alcoholic would do: staying dry. I wanted the best for him, and loved him heart and soul. Didn't I?

"Where are you taking us, Peter?"

No answer.

"Peter?"

"You'll soon see."

"I don't believe this." Claudia *tsk*ed, sighed, and flung herself back against the seat cushion.

"Claudia, be quiet. And put your seat belt on."

"Mommy, Stephanie's brother is not going to wait all night—"

Peter's voice boomed as if it were being amplified. We all jumped. "Do you ever, Claudia, give a thought to anything but *boys*?"

"Okay, okay, oh-kay!" Claudia crossed her arms across her chest. "Okay, okay."

We drove along the Boston Post Road and now were in Greenwich. Last time I'd been here was almost a year ago, to buy a dress at Razook's for a St. Anthony's charity gala. I remembered driving down this very stretch, carefree then, feeling great and looking good, the frothy suburban matron, on top of the world. It struck me now, as I saw my very first autumn gold leaf fall from a green maple a few feet away, that I would never feel that lighthearted again.

"You're not going to tell us where we're going?"

"We're almost there."

He found Old Church Road and turned off to the right. Had I ever been on this road before? I didn't think so. Ellery sat, eyes closed, not sleeping but pretending to, hunched into the corner of the backseat. Every so often I turned, saw her position unchanged, knees up, in not quite, but almost, the fetal position.

"I should have brought my Walkman. I don't know how I could forget to bring my Walkman."

"Claudia, shh."

"Why won't he tell us where we're going?"

"Claudia!"

"At least, Daddy, could you *at least*, put on some decent music?"

Peter snapped on the radio to 104.3. Liszt burst into the car.

"I said decent."

Peter's dark glasses looked up at the rearview mirror. "Claudia, watch that fresh talk!"

We were driving through picture-pretty neighborhoods, surrounded on every side by ancient trees, front lawns rolling back against the sort of houses interchangeable with those in Crandall: colonials that seem constructed from dollhouse kits, Cape Cods with kitschy weather vanes and wishing wells, fieldstone-front ranches adjoined by three-car garages, wooded, hidden lanes leading to hideaways one could only imagine. Mindlessly, I read the names on roadside mailboxes, and now we passed a striped tent, pitched back from the road under towering trees for someone's wedding, coming-out party, one happy occasion or other. I imagined the festivities, the music, bartenders in black and white, a family celebrating together. I pictured dancing couples and wholesome bridesmaids, apple-cheeked and virginal. Oh, to be any one of them, anyone else right now!

When Peter pulled into the road between the iron gates of the Putnam Cemetery, I thought at first he was taking us to visit his father's grave. Yet Peter's father was buried farther up, at some cemetery in Old Greenwich, wasn't he? I wasn't sure. This place did not look familiar. Of course, we'd not visited Claude Ehrlich's grave even once since he'd been buried, and if Darley had paid her respects recently, I'd never heard about it. I tried to think back to his funeral, in the early years of our marriage. All I could remember was the overcast sky and Peter's stony, inebriated face, holding the umbrella he'd brought in case of rain, and Darley's diamond earrings and black, very high heels puncturing the dirt path to the grave site, as she held on to her son's arm.

Peter pulled the car to a stop in front of a little stone

building, which turned out to be the cemetery office. He jumped out, leaving the motor running.

"Where is he going?" Ellery came to life.

"What are we doing here? Is Daddy all right?" Claudia wanted to know. "I've never seen him like this."

"Why are we in a cemetery?"

"I don't believe this!"

The navigator had gotten a small map and was following his itinerary. We drove along a cement road through the graveyard, which looked much like an arboretum, a nature conservatory. The gravestones seemed an afterthought upstaged by the trees: hemlocks, pines, white poplar, horse chestnuts, weeping willows, one dramatically large Japanese maple glowing orange as fire, and dozens of species I couldn't identify. The effect was stunningly, brilliantly green, the color palette ranging from chartreuse to verdigris to deep olive, the grassy knolls shaded or bright, the headstones in every size, but without the ornament or flourish of the DiBuonos' monuments. The mausoleums were somber, Greek-columned, dignified. Here and there were parked cars while people strolled, moving between the trees and stones, some sparked with small bouquets of flowers.

We drove past the tombs and monuments, circled the largest mausoleum, a Doric-columned building reminding me of Mount Olympus. Peter slowed down, and we finally came to a stop.

"Around here somewhere," he said, and told the girls to get out of the car. Then, sunglasses in place, his mouth barely visible under his mustache, he asked if I wanted to come along, too.

"Why are we here? Where are we going?"

"The Greavys are buried here. It's down there, this side of the mausoleum somewhere." He waved his arm in the direction of a bunch of headstones under some white poplars.

The girls had become subdued.

"But, Pete, why?"

"To pay our respects. That's all. To pay our last respects."

"But the girls, I mean, they knew him, but after all, it's not as if they were *close* to either Lucas or his wife."

"Doesn't matter. He and I were close. I'm their father."

"Peter, I don't understand the purpose."

"Because I want them to!" His voice boomed again. A couple nearby turned to stare.

"Daddy!" Behind us, Claudia pushed her hair up in embarrassment.

I lowered my voice. "Peter, does it have to be now? This may be a traumatic thing for Ellery. Is it really absolutely necessary to put her through this? I mean, at this time? What is the point?" The girls were lagging behind, leaning on the fender of the car and whispering to each other.

"Are you coming?" he said to me as if I'd said absolutely nothing, as if we were on our way to a six-o'clock movie. Now I saw that he had something in the right breast pocket of his cord jacket, something making it buckle out, a protuberance like the bulge of a weapon. I was reminded of plainclothes police, holsters, guns, smuggled sawed-off shotguns, but it couldn't be a gun. Peter hates them and wouldn't own one.

"What's that in your pocket?"

"Follow me," the navigator said, and led the way, checking the names on headstones left and right as he went.

He stopped in front of a polished marble stone that reminded me of a bed's double headboard. It was simply marked, GREAVY. I'd never seen a stone without a date, without a Christian name. A piece of camelback marble wider than high, polished to a dusky pink luster, offering no information except the surname chiseled into its surface in large block letters, this headstone might have been put in place yesterday or five hundred years ago. It seemed like the final word in understatement.

"Unpretentious." I stood staring at the stone.

"He was." Legs apart, hands in his pockets, and eyes behind dark glasses, Peter stood looking down at the stone from one side of the grave while the girls and I clustered together at the other, wary. Claudia, on my left, began scratching her upper arm. Mosquito bite or nerves, I couldn't tell. Ellery was a wispy, unmoving shape next to me.

"I just wanted you to see the final resting place of the man who was my closest friend," Peter said. Or intoned. He might have been delivering a eulogy to a group of four hundred from a lectern. "Though sometimes *friend* is a word that falls short of describing someone who was the embodiment of sweetness and excellence. And compassion. There's hardly time to describe his mercy." Peter took a breath and looked beyond us to some invisible audience between two trees. "I remember one night not long ago, after a full day of work, he took a detour. Stopped in to talk to the ancient widow of a Hungarian man who'd died on the operating table a few days before. Just stopped by to see if she was all right. Well, he spent the entire night with that lady, who was half-deaf and afraid to be alone. Spent the entire night with a Hungarian-English dictionary and that old woman.

"Now, that's just one small example of the man's charity. I can't even go into the times he pulled me up, comforted me, saved and championed me." Peter stopped, seemed finally to take us into account. "What I've become—your mother knows this better than anyone—I owe to this dear friend. He wasn't a perfect doctor, no. He made mistakes. But he had a noble nature I've spent half my life trying to emulate. He wasn't capable of malevolence, selfishness, or greed. He was in every way what I wanted to be: the good Joe. No, the *best* Joe."

Claudia, scratching her arm, murmured, *"Chevalier sans peur et sans reproche."*

"What does that mean?" Peter, in a slightly suspicious voice, took off his sunglasses and squinted at her.

"A knight without fear and without reproach." She tried to conceal the little pleased-with-herself smile that crept across her lips when he smiled.

"That's nice," he said. "Yes, sweetie, very nice."

We were silent for a moment.

"And so, we've come here to say good-bye?" I asked. I was relieved. It turned out not to have been such a bad idea, after all.

"Exactly," Peter answered.

I tried to think of something appropriate to add. "Well, farewell, good friends, then."

"Yes. Farewell. Rest in peace. God bless." He took off his sunglasses, folded them into his pocket, and lowered his voice. "That's half of it."

Ellery moved closer to me. I felt her sleeve brush my arm.

"The other half is to discuss his death."

I watched Peter's face uneasily.

"To understand why he did what he did."

"I don't think the girls really need to understand why he did what he did, Peter. He was depressed is why."

"Libby. I have the floor." Twitch.

A woman on a cane passed and we waited until she was out of earshot.

"We know he died by his own hand. He was always methodical. It was carefully planned. Sitting square-shouldered in his bedroom next to his wife."

"Gross," Claudia said.

"But it wasn't exactly the injection of calcium chloride that killed him, no. That's like saying shoes teach you to dance. Shoes don't do it. Your head and heart and feet and the music, the *music* does it."

"Daddy, please, not so loud." Claudia was looking left and right; two women in dark dresses had noted Peter. Might be eavesdropping. They were at a nearby monument, glancing our way. Might even recognize him.

Peter ignored Claudia. He seemed oblivious to onlookers or our surroundings. "He died from a lack of fresh air. Life just took away his oxygen, little by little."

"We should have brought flowers," Ellery remarked.

"Yes, we should have," Claudia said. "Maybe we could come back some other time with flowers. It's getting very late, Daddy."

"His work was so important to him, and that deteriorated. And his wife—you remember her, Libby"—I nodded yes, that I certainly remembered her—"his wife, sadly, with that rheumatoid arthritis . . ." Peter looked up over our heads at a bird that was flying above us, but didn't really seem to see it. "Poor lady. Anyway, it was everything all at once falling apart for him, but if you ask me, the greatest disappointment, the greatest disaster, the worst misfortune, was his son."

It was warm here in the cemetery. Despite these shade trees, humid and suffocating.

"We are the victims of our children, aren't we?" he asked, but it was rhetorical.

I yearned for a breeze.

"His son, that strange and callous gink, that excuse for a human being, who didn't even come to the cemetery—Lib, do you see any ragweed here? Any ragweed whatsoever?"

I said I didn't. The girls turned their heads this way

and that and Claudia agreed there didn't seem to be a "shred" anywhere or she herself would be sneezing; no, there was no poison oak or any grasses that might cause wheezing, asthma, or clogged sinuses.

"And so, I can't help drawing a parallel here, Ellery."

"Peter, no."

"I can't help looking at you, Ellery, and thinking that you are cutting off my fresh air—" His voice grew louder.

"Peter! Waitaminute!"

Nothing prepared me for what happened next. How could it? The substantial, solid doctor-father, our personal deity, our unerring navigator, went crazily off course, and suddenly turned horn-mad.

He reached into his breast pocket, the bulging one, and pulled out a fifth of Johnnie Walker Red, three quarters full. For a moment I was baffled; where had it come from? Then I understood; he'd taken it from his mother's liquor supply. She kept her booze in a cabinet in the library upstairs.

Ellery gasped and Claudia cried out. Peter lifted the bottle into the air while the two ladies in their dark dresses turned again to witness the drama at the Greavy stone.

"You promised," I said under my breath. "You never break your word." The earth here in this part of the cemetery was moving. I could feel it under my feet, rocking.

"Yes, Daddy, you did!" the girls cried, two shrill birds, almost one voice. Ellery had grabbed my arm and Claudia stopped scratching but was clutching her elbow, squeezing the life out of it.

"I'm not drinking it, am I? No! I'm just *holding* it, raising it in my steady hand, waving it, to make a point!" he boomed.

"Peter, for Christ's sake! What the hell are you doing?"

"And the point is, I made a promise and I kept it! All these years! For the good of our lives and our family. For what, I ask you. For what? It's up to you to show me! I want a promise from you, Ellery. Also, for the good of our lives and our family! I want you to promise that you'll have Dr. Irvine—you'll have that nice, responsible doctor gently, sweetly, *painlessly,* sweep out, vacuum out, cut out a few cells, a few little microscopic cells! And save your fucking young life!

"Because—because if you don't, Ellery, if you keep cutting off my fresh air, my oxygen, I can't, I can't swear that I won't be led, won't be led to do something almost as surely self-destructive—"

"Peter, for Christ's sake!"

"—as was done by the man, my dearest dead friend, who is lying under this mound of grassy earth between us! You, *only you,* my little girl, can save me!"

The adrenaline surged. I practically leaped across a six-foot length of grassy space between us, under which the Greavys lay side by side, resting in peace in their coffins, and lunged for him. I heard the girls' gasps as I struggled to get the bottle out of Peter's hand, heard the cries as if they were behind glass. But he is stronger and taller and, holding me off, he raised the little bottle high, where I couldn't reach. His eyes were blazing, his face was wet and sinister. Over my head, as I pressed futilely against him, he unscrewed the cap and waved the bottle even higher, like a victor's bloody flag. Claudia was verging on hysteria. "No, Daddy, no!" While I pushed my hands on the wet, stained front of his shirt, he held the bottle at arm's length, then dramatically upended it. While the women in the dark dresses watched in frozen shock, and from the height of the star he always puts on top of our Christmas tree, Peter let the scotch pour, let it irrigate a grassy spot next to his leather loafer in a stream the color of ditch water.

* * *

Lying in bed that night, I watched him put his half-full glass of water on the night table next to his bed, watched his half-closed eyes following the CNN sports report as he lay next to me, the remote control on his chest. I looked around the room, trying to find comfort in the familiar configuration of settee, valet, highboy, and dresser. I'd picked out the honey wall color, the soft rug, I was the one who'd hung the pictures, and chosen the fabric for the draperies. What had seemed snug and intimate in this bedroom suffocated now. Where I'd felt cloistered, I felt enmeshed.

"It was the only way. She'll come around, you'll see," Peter had said when he'd climbed into bed.

Both girls had simmered in tense silence all the way home, and I hadn't spoken a word to him since the scene at the cemetery. Ellery had wept once, when we'd pulled up in front of the house and I'd told her I loved her. Had skipped dinner, and gone to the telephone, ostensibly to relay the news to Ess.

"You're going to be mad at me the rest of your life, Libby?" Now Peter turned to me while I stared straight ahead. "You're never going to speak a word to me again?"

His hand moved under the covers; my body felt hard as a Putnam Cemetery headstone.

"Not tonight? Is that what you're telling me? Or not ever?" Peter always called me "resilient," quick to "recover emotional balance." His hand moved under my nightgown and settled on my thigh.

I climbed out of bed, put on my slippers, and walked methodically around it to his night table, picked up the glass of water on his night table, and raised it over his head.

He looked up and smiled. Thought I was kidding. "Okay, okay. No sex."

I tipped the glass and let the water fall on his face in a nice, steady stream.

"What the hell do you think," he sputtered, his voice escalating into a howl, "you're doing?!"

I put the empty glass back on the table next to him, looked down at his sopping, dripping face. "I had to do it," I said. "To cool off."

When I walked downstairs the following morning, Ellery was at the foot of the stairs waiting for us. She was too sick to her stomach to discuss her decision, and I was certain that she would never in her life again feel whole enough to talk to us about it. While I sat in the den, pretending to read the newspaper, I heard Peter on the telephone making the arrangements. While I sat with my knees up and my too-strong cup of morning coffee in front of me, I heard the dauntless timbre of his voice as he asked about anesthetic and recovery time, and then, in a preposterous twist, heard him genially asking if Dr. Irvine recommended taking the girls to Kenya next year. Dr. Irvine, an annual visitor to Africa, was apparently somewhat of a local authority on photographic safaris. Peter concluded the conversation with "We'll think about a safari, then." Back in his own comfortable doctor's Garden of Eden, the apple, serpent, and eclipsed sun already pushed into the past.

I offered to take Ellery to Dr. Irvine's for the initial examination. The doctor had given some minuscule flyspeck of hope that two commercial testing products and morning sickness might still be red herrings, and a blood test was indicated. The hope of a mistake was vanquished by Dr. Irvine's pelvic exam, which revealed a "softened uterus," a definitive sign of a pregnancy he would say was probably in its fifth week. Nevertheless, the blood sample would confirm within twenty-four hours. He spoke comfortingly to us in the small office next to his examining room, Ellery a sphinx at my side. Everywhere on the grey-sueded walls were photos of wild animals he'd snapped in the bush himself. I saw Ellery's eyes skip from the wildebeests to the elephants to the half-submerged hippo and come to rest on the lioness and her young to the right of his desk. I reached over and took her hand, which felt small and inanimate in mine. It was late Wednesday and the doctor's schedule was full. He would fit us in Monday at nine; she was not to eat anything after midnight the night before. "You'll be just fine," he said, soothing, and told us to stop at the desk on the way out to get an instruction sheet from the receptionist.

As she got into the car, Ellery told me she'd thought it over and decided she wanted Ess with her. And only Ess.

On Saturday morning, Vito DiBuono called on the girls' telephone. Claudia took the call. Peter refused to speak to him. He called again six o'clock Saturday night. "Tell him I have nothing to say," Peter said.

It was a weekend of silences that seemed to hang in every room. We became like guests trapped in a resort hotel during a storm—fidgety, morose, maneuvering around each other in a polite dance of avoidance. It was "Have you seen the second part of the newspaper?" "I'm going out to turn on the sprinkler," and "Who was that on the telephone?" The telephone, in fact, never stopped ringing; even though Peter was not on call, it seemed as if everyone we knew had chosen this weekend to discover our *Southern Connecticut Life* profile, and to dial us up to offer congratulations. I cut off every conversation, saying someone was at the door. Or something on the stove was boiling over. When Ellery wasn't cloistered in her room, she appeared in the kitchen with her scared-rabbit face, and even Claudia soaked in the moribund ambience; she offered Ellery a manicure, a game of SET, a lesson in algebra. All were declined.

The squeak of the NordicTrack coming through the walls from the basement seemed amplified and intolerably annoying.

"Are we expecting anyone?" Peter asked me on Sunday night, when the doorbell rang. Pencil in hand, I was sitting alone in the kitchen, killing this already dead time, trying to concentrate on the Sunday crossword, which I hadn't done in three years. At any moment I knew my mother would call, with her rat-a-tat-tat of questions, and I would have to evade and duck her exhaustive radar. And now, the doorbell. "Expecting no one," I said. Peter and I had barely spoken since the water incident. He would never forgive it; we both knew that. Just seeing his face in the kitchen doorway now, the back-at-the-wheel face, the doctor-knows-best face, revved me up. His expression no longer reminded me of Claudia's. I saw him as the spitting image of his father.

The girls were both upstairs, and if they aren't around, it's always my job to answer the door. I'm the lookout in case some random kook patient has tracked down our address and wants to have an audience with the doctor. It happened only once in twenty years, but still. Now I pulled the curtain away from the glass panel at the side of the door and felt my hand press hard on the knob with the first jolt: the DiBuonos. No. Just Vito. "Peter," I called automatically as I unlatched the door. He'd brought someone—not Ess—with him.

Behind Vito, the second jolt: a man in a black jacket, white reversed collar. A priest. He'd brought a priest.

In a flash, Peter was behind me. "Good evening, Doctor, Mrs. Ehrlich. Hope we're not disturbing you. We'd like to talk to you for just a few minutes," Vito was saying. He had dressed up to come here. A suit and tie, dark and funereal. I'd already opened the door, and they were getting ready to step inside.

Peter jumped right in. "I'm sorry, Vito. We have nothing to say." It came out a bark. He had taken the doorknob out of my hand, literally pushed my fingers out of the way. Now he was slowly propelling the door closed.

"Doctor, we just need five minutes. I think we deserve five minutes." The priest was youngish, with an eager-to-please look. Very Dublin-Kilkenny. We'd done Ireland five, six years ago. Everywhere, just exactly this same fresh face.

Vito's voice was raspy, as if he'd spent the afternoon at the stadium, cheering the home team. "I brought Father DeLeo, he'd like to say just a few words."

DeLeo? I was wrong; not Irish. Maybe his mother was Irish. I probably would have let him in, but Peter had the door and the floor. "This is really an imposition."

"Five minutes," Vito pressed.

"Dr. Ehrlich." The priest's voice was surprisingly high-pitched. "If I may. We've met several times at St. Anthony's. I gave last rites to your patient, Mrs. Constantino, just two weeks ago. You may remember?"

Peter didn't remember. "Sorry."

"When the DiBuonos asked me to come, I hesitated, but, Doctor, this is not a frivolous errand."

"Your presence here is out of order." Peter's face and voice grew dark.

"Doctor, you are an ethical person, a man who is dedicated to the preservation, the continuation of life, who has to give a second thought, some *reflection* on what you're about to mandate—"

"You'll have to excuse me, Father." Peter had succeeded in almost closing the door.

"The termination of a human life!"

"The termination of this visit!"

"My wife is in bed, been crying off and on all weekend, now on top of her neck, she got herself a migraine, a sick headache that started when Salvatore come in with the news!"

"You have a moral imperative, sir!" The high-pitched voice floated in, just before the door closed, seeming to bounce off the walls in the hall, and was followed by Vito's glottal blown fuse. "Okay, Dr. Big, you want to slam the door in our faces, you think you can slam the door on us? You think this is the last of this? I dittn't come down all a way from Danbury to get a door slammed in my face. Well, I got news for you, Dr. Muckety-Muck! This isn't the last of it—you gonna hear from me!"

It was quarter to seven the following morning, twenty-three hours later, by my calculations. "Oh, my *God*! What the fuck is going *on*?!" Claudia's scream woke me. A moment later she came flying into the bedroom, dressed for school, red-faced, hair damp, one shoe on, the other in her hand. For the second time, the twitch. "Look out the window! Look out the fucking *window*!"

Peter leaped out of bed and got there before I did. He pulled aside the curtain and together we stared down at the front lawn. Where just a few months ago we were horrified to see a paper blizzard of shredded music, now we stood side by side, paralyzed. "Who are they?" I whispered.

"I don't know," Peter said, in a squashed croak.

A white van stood in the street, blocking our driveway. Out of it had come the six or eight men and women who had now taken positions on our lawn and the sidewalk in front of our house. One carried a placard that read, GOD IS WATCHING. Another carried a painted, wooden cross. They appeared simply to be passing observers, like people gathered to watch a man leap from a roof, and looked more like city dwellers than like the staid residents of Crandall, Connecticut.

"I think they're the Lambs of Christ," Claudia whispered. "At our house! Oh, my God, oh, my God! I just saw them on TV!"

Ellery had stumbled out of her room and stood barefoot behind us, staring out wordlessly. I could hear her deep breathing, a technique Dr. Irvine had suggested to diminish nausea.

An old station wagon pulled up behind the van and then, a faded red Jeep. More people appeared, young and old, assorted types, like movie extras. "What are they *doing*?" Claudia was bouncing from one foot to the other, trying to put on her shoe without leaving the window. "What do they *want*?"

I saw a baseball cap, a black face, denim, a heavy woman in lace-up shoes. And in the hand of one young man, a black, wooden-bead rosary. I turned, trying to read Ellery's face, a frightened blank. Now, a man was pulling a folding chair out of the back of the van, and setting it up on the front walk, facing our house.

"I'm going to call the police," Peter said.

I tried to hold him back, but he pulled away and headed for the telephone. "It'll be all over the newspapers, Peter!"

They were helping a pregnant woman out of the station wagon. She looked as if she might be in her seventh or eighth month, moving down the walk to the chair, hoisting herself gracefully into it, crossing her feet at the ankles, clasping her hands over her balloon of a stomach, settling in. A round face and round glasses, an experimental haircut, frizzed-up bangs, the sides and back of her head shaved. She was in a madras tentlike jumper over a T-shirt, older than Ellery, but not that much. Certainly she couldn't be twenty.

A placard appeared in her hand, hand-lettered unevenly: ALONE AND POOR, BUT MY BABY WILL LIVE. Someone handed her a plastic cup, poured something into it from a thermos.

Ellery burst into tears and fell weeping on our bed. I ran over to comfort her—she was shuddering as if she'd just been pulled out of icy rapids.

Outside, the group mobilized, gathered into a cluster at the edge of the property. A hum arose, grew louder.

"What are they saying?" I ran back and forth between Ellery and the window, afraid to open it more than a crack, but straining to distinguish what sounded like some kind of responsive reading. "Can you understand what they're *saying*?"

Claudia said, "Hail Marys. That's what they do. They say Hail Marys. Usually at abortion clinics. Oh, God, why us? And I'm gonna have to walk by them. How am I going to walk by them?"

"The hell with the newspapers. I'm going to call the cops, get them off the property." Peter reached for the telephone, which began to ring before he could pick it up. It was my mother.

"Get her off," he said to me, covering the receiver.

"We were at a progressive dinner last night, which is why I didn't call. Rudy made pineapple chicken curry and everyone—what's the matter, Libby?"

"Nothing!"

"You're not sounding right."

"Everything's fine!"

"You sound—"

"Something is boiling over on the stove!" I said, my voice a strangled squeak.

* * *

"I don't want to walk out of the house. I really don't. And if I don't leave now, I'm fucking going to be late for school!"

"It's all my fault!" Ellery was sitting up, shoulders up to her jaw, her face a pale and streaky watercolor portrait.

"Shut up, it's not your fault! Daddy, don't you have something to give Ellery to make her not so hysterical? Like a sedative, or something?"

"I'm scared. I'm so scared!" Ellery sat up, shaking.

By the time Peter called the police, there must have been a dozen people out there altogether, not counting the neighbors, which included the Bergins. I saw Barry and Sarah Jane together at the edge of the driveway, looking up at our house, zeroing right in on the bedroom window, although they couldn't see us hiding behind the draperies. I imagined that thanks to the DiBuonos, we might be hiding one way or another for years to come. I imagined Sarah Jane thinking that it wasn't such a bad idea, being childless. And I was certain every neighbor—and they stood in clusters at the curb, in driveways, on their porches—thought it was Claudia who'd brought the shame down on our family.

Little Ellery pregnant was as far-fetched as cracking open an egg and finding three blue yolks.

Peter decided Claudia was not to take the risk of walking out the front door now, but was to wait for him to drive her to school, see her safely into the building himself. He'd have to figure out a way to get even with Vito for siccing these crazies on us later. In the meantime, Ellery was to get dressed. It was getting late, and although he'd given in, finally allowed her to choose

Ess to take her to the doctor's instead of one of us, he would not want Dr. Irvine to be kept waiting. Not even for five minutes.

So I helped Ellery, wobbly-kneed and red-eyed, back to her room, while the police came, lining the street with their cars, bringing with them a trailing motorcade of rubbernecking drivers, kids on bikes, an oil truck and assorted commercial vehicles, and two men wearing safety helmets, on motorbikes. Witnesses. As Dr. Ehrlich, still in bathrobe and slippers, stood on his front step, talking to the police. Little by little, their red lights whirling on top of their parked cars, what looked like most of the Crandall force bustled about our street and lawn in crisp navy blue shirts and pants, guns safely holstered and untouched on their hips, with their dark glasses resting on their noses, scattering the Lambs of Christ peacefully and amicably. But not before I'd seen someone—perhaps just a civilian and not even a member of the press—snap photographs of the police, the Lambs, the street, and our house.

Which is how it came about that Ess, appearing toward the end of the dispersal, came not only to be included in the photographer's collection, but also to get a police escort to Dr. Irvine's. He moved his van to the back of our driveway, and I delivered a trembling Ellery to him out the back door. "Remember, I love you," I said to her, as she clung to his arm.

"It'll be fine, sweetie," Peter said, and he tried to lean over and kiss her, but it was too late; she'd moved away, out of his reach. "She'll be fine," Peter said again, to no one in particular. "You'll see. We all will."

Forty-eight hours later, Darley called from Rowayton, sounding as if someone had hands around her neck and was squeezing hard. "Libby. This is so hard for me to say, dear. Such an impossible thing even to bring up."

"What, dear? Is something wrong?"

"The judge, the judge just called me. He heard something about our family from his niece. I told him it was outrageous. For him even to suggest—well, it made me good and angry, I don't mind telling you. I'm afraid I lost my temper. The nerve, even to ask such a question, to imply that such a thing was possible. That Claudia, that sweet child, that Claudia could—"

"No. Wrong, Darley, dead wrong."

"You see! Who could have started such a vicious rumor?! People are awful, to my way of thinking."

"Well, I wouldn't upset you for the world, Darley, no. Certainly not now. But I have to give it to you straight. I mean, I don't know how we're going to clear it up with the world at large, but you're the girls' grandmother. You have to hear the truth. Darley, it wasn't Claudia who got pregnant. No. It was Ellery."

"What?"

"It was Ellery who had the abortion. Ellery. Not Claudia."

Her horror-film gasp sounded electronically amplified.

"I'm sorry you had to hear it from the judge."

"His sister read it in the, in the—" Darley's voice broke. Then, "Something like, something like—oh, God, Libby!—'The Lambs of Christ were clustered around the home of a prominent cardiologist late yesterday'—"

"I know."

A guttural, disbelieving cry from my mother-in-law.

"Listen, Darley. It's all over. She got the abortion. She's in bed resting. She goes back to school Monday. She's fine now. That's it."

"Oh, dear heaven!"

"I'm sorry, but that's it."

"Libby, excuse me, but, but, I'm sick."

"Listen, Darley. This has been a horrible few days. Horrible. You just lost Meggie, well, we thought we'd spare you."

"It was that Italian boy with his hair in a tail. The one who chews ice cubes."

"Right. Ess."

"Libby. I don't understand it. I just don't."

"We had a hard time understanding it, too, Darley."

"I mean, that you *allowed* that boy anywhere near the girls. That you didn't have him *arrested,* and that you didn't seem to be concerned when Claudia was seeing someone of that, that *caliber.*"

I put both hands around the telephone receiver and tried to choke it to death.

"I think we ought not to discuss this anymore, Darley."

"That you were so *unconcerned,* I mean, that's what I've always said. These girls need a little more, what? Control. And, supervision. Haven't I always said—"

"Something on the stove. Is boiling over," I said, and I put down the receiver and went upstairs to talk to Peter.

On my way into the bedroom, I stopped at Ellery's door. She was in bed, eating lemon sherbet out of a glass dish. "How are you feeling, honey?" I asked.

"Better," she said. She was looking right at me, answering the question, but where was she? Certainly not here.

"Cramping?"

"Very little." Those sad eyes, like the cheap acrylic paintings sold at street fairs. She held out her arm as if it were someone else's. "Did you see it? Did you see what Daddy gave me?"

"A watch. He bought you another watch."

"A gold Movado. It's got a ruby for twelve o'clock. My birthstone." It was as if I could see right through her aquamarine eyes to a discoloration behind them, a dark stain.

She looked down at her wrist. "Isn't it cool?" she said.

Peter was lying in bed, the remote control on his chest, the half glass of water on the night table next to his bed.

"I have to tell you something, Peter," I said.

"Libby, just wait two minutes, okay? I want to hear the scores here and I'll be right with you."

I waited the two minutes. Waited while the commercials for Metro-North Railroad, Minute Maid orange juice, Mitsubishis scrolled past us on the screen. Waited for visuals of football scrimmages, followed by the scores, waited until Peter put the remote control on mute and turned to me.

"What I want to tell you, Peter, is that I had sex with Trevor Eddy three years ago."

Peter's face, the face propped up on the pillow next to mine, reminded me of those death masks, plaster half-heads that hang forever dead on foyer walls. It was a clay face, immobilized by the near death of shock. "The—carpenter?"

"The contractor."

His eyes reminded me of the opaque buttons sewn into Ellery's monkey's face. "A joke?"

"Not a joke."

"Why would you tell me that now, Libby?"

*To get even, to hurt you.* "Because Claudia got it right. Only you are perfect, Peter. The rest of us, well, now and then we just fall off horses. And it's not like you can control it, or prescribe for it, or threaten us with suicide. We're people. Not just the doctor's top-notch family. Just a family. Not bigger than life. Just trying to get through it."

Peter leaped out of bed. His eyes glowed now, like a reflection of fire. I was reminded of the days when the smell of alcohol was everywhere, when empty bottles filled the kitchen trash, and when cataclysmic moments like this were routine. He was wearing pajama bottoms, light blue, creased, I'd bought them for him, chosen them carefully, the best pima, remembered now the irrelevant details of the purchase, made on a day I was coming down with a cold. Sore throat, headache that day, but I took the time, made the choice with great attention. That was not so long ago. On the day I bought those pajamas, didn't I care? Didn't I love him absolutely?

Peter's chest was bare and I could see the way deep breaths were making it rise and fall. What if he had a heart attack right now, and I'd caused it? How would I react? I had loved him absolutely, that was a fact. And now? *Now?*

"Sit down, Peter, please sit down!" I thought he might fall over; he looked unsteady, losing his balance, ready to topple.

"Oh, my God." Peter had crossed his wrists over his chest and his words were coming in spurts, as if he'd just run ten miles. "I feel the way I did when I was eight, pretending to shave, and cut my finger with my father's razor and saw the blood gushing out all over the sink. I thought I'd die. That's how I feel, Libby. That's how you make me feel, like the blood is rushing out of me. Oh, my God. The *carpenter!*"

He steadied himself in the doorway to the bathroom, holding on to the jamb as if he were on a ship's deck on the high seas. For a minute he stood there like that, eyes blazing. Then, the twitch. "The girls—do they know?"

"It was just once, Peter."

"I didn't ask for numbers, I didn't request an itemized list! I don't want to know where it was or how it was. I asked if the girls knew. Do they *know*?"

"No."

"Don't tell them. Promise me you'll never, never tell them."

Where did it go, that absolute and powerful love? When did it dissipate? "I won't tell them, Peter. You know I wouldn't," I said and watched as he moved backward into the bathroom, his eyes burning into me until he'd closed the door carefully and firmly between us.

The next day, when he took his jacket off the valet in the bedroom, pulled out his overnight case, and began to throw his underwear, his socks, and his shirts into it, I was thrown back. It swam in front of my eyes, the railroad crossing ahead, a big sign that warned of danger, and the possibility of an oncoming calamity.

# Chapter Ten

I was in the living room brushing Dumpling when Trevor Eddy pulled into the driveway. I had taken measurements, made a few sketches, and called him six weeks after Peter moved out, asking him to come by and give me an estimate on building a home office in the basement.

Since Annie and I had dissolved our partnership, I thought I'd save on rent and move my business operations into the house. Peter's gym equipment was still there, but as soon as he found a decent apartment and got out of the place he was temporarily subletting in Bridgeport, he said he'd send a man with a van to move it all out. I saw the space as all high-tech and twenty-first century, with a Victorian sitting area and a few good primitives on the walls.

At first, I'd decided to sell the house, move to a town house in Westport or Ridgefield. With Ellery away, and Claudia off to college next year—Peter and I were taking turns driving her to look at campuses weekends—why did I need this house? I'd looked at town houses, walked through their freshly painted rooms, examined the unexplored territory of empty closets, marble Jacuzzis. When it came to putting down a deposit, I couldn't do it. It turned out I still needed the buffer zone of my stenciled floors, shiny kitchen, purple clematis, the familiar explored territory of the museum of our family life.

Was my calling Trevor Eddy for an estimate to enclose water pipes and put a half bath in the basement also an excuse to see him again? I looked into the mirror before answering the door and asked my face for an answer to that one. He had long since finished working for the Bergins, and I'd not given him much thought until last week, when I pulled up behind his van at the drive-in ATM of the bank on the Post Road. He didn't see me, but that night I dreamed about him, although when I woke up, all I could remember was his throwing something to me from a ladder. His keys, I think, but I'm not sure, because when I went to pick them up, they disintegrated in my hands. Lately, dreaming had become a problem; I was having so many bad ones. I was waking at all hours, plodding through the empty rooms and listening to the sound of a silent house, a sound I'd never let myself hear before. My stomach was acting up, too. Without traveling anywhere, I seemed to be suffering a malaise, as if I'd eaten the wrong foods.

On the very day I called Trevor, Sarah Jane came by to return my pinking shears. She stood on my doorstep, top to toe in grayish beige and the trademark conspicuous shoes—these covered with suede buttons—and said she'd found the scissors in the back of the closet in the room she and Barry were going to turn into a nursery. "The baby is due the very last day of June," she said, and added that except for the heartburn, she'd been feeling better than she'd ever felt in her life. "And

Barry?" I asked. She hesitated. "He'll come around. You'll see," she said. The sun seemed to be shining right into her eyes, and she suddenly sneezed twice in a row. Were those tears of joy, or an allergy? It was hard to tell. Also, she hated to ask, but did I have any antacid in the house? She'd just run out. I suppose we were two leopards who would never change our spots. I hesitated, but found some for her. "Libby, you're a peach," she said, and gave me a hug. "I'm so sorry about what's happened to your family. Of all the people in Crandall, I never imagined . . ." She spoke very fast and I didn't catch the rest. It had something to do with the fickleness, the unpredictability of life's circumstances, like her making love with a syringe. She'd had herself artificially inseminated.

Trevor Eddy said he'd be by Friday evening at six, and here it was, Friday evening at six. I'd just dropped Claudia off at Peter's office from where they'd be heading to Bowdoin ("A reach, but we'll give it a shot. After all, she's *got* it, and if they've got a harp anywhere on campus, she's in."). I'd just finished a Pepto-Bismol tablet and put on fresh lipstick when the doorbell rang.

The thing I always noticed first about Trevor was his hair, which was a color a bit deeper than that of a golden retriever, the sort of glossy mane that "moves." Now, it had not only thinned a bit on top, but looked a little too long, a little overripe for a haircut, damp because it was raining. I'd been wrong about his not aging, though; as he stepped into the front hall, I saw in the deep gold glints the beginning of silver, and above the pale eyebrows, two horizontal lines, deeply drawn. Were these new or had I never noticed them before? Even Trevor was visibly growing older, and, it struck me now, more serious. The odd thing was that I could see in his ripe and solemn expression the face he must have had as a young boy, and for an instant I imagined myself his mother, stroking his hair and his cheek, as if he'd just been punched by a bully or scraped his knee.

I had not given much thought to Trevor Eddy since Peter's departure, but subconsciously, he must have been crouched and waiting up there in my head, a memory I might have been embellishing constantly. Which is why my hands seemed to take too long when I took his windbreaker and hung it in the front closet, and probably why my voice turned thick when I explained I'd called him for "a small job," and that since I'd decided to limit my expenses, I'd need a clear estimate, wanted to see if built-in shelves were cost-effective, and so on. It was as if I'd left my body in the front hall, stepped aside, and was listening to my voice go on and on, a radio someone forgot to turn off.

Trevor just stood there smiling at me, not saying a word, letting me go on and on without a response, on hold for the real whatever was going to happen to happen.

"I'll show you the basement," I finally said, and he tramped down the steps after me. There was the Nordic-Track under the fluorescent tubing light, the foam pad Peter used for push-ups, and a treadmill he'd long since unplugged and stopped using. A white towel I'd forgotten to throw in the wash was still draped across its bar and a discarded mirror leaned against a cinder-block wall across the floor, reflecting our legs and feet. I kept seeing the movement out of the corner of my eye. His chinos, my jeans. Dancing back and forth. His loafers, my retro clogs. "Peter is going to get this stuff out of here sometime in the next few weeks. We're living separately at the moment." Saying that felt to my ears like an invitation to stop everything and lie down on the exercise mat together.

"Since?" Trevor's eyebrows went up; I felt the tingle of blood in my cheeks.

"It happened one-two-three." It wasn't exactly true. After all, the erosion had been gradual, a spiky graph taking its downward course to the bottom line. Peter had come back that first time, reappeared the following evening, unpacked the socks, shirts, shaving stuff, without saying a word. Hung his jacket on the valet, as always. But in the days that followed, little by little, we'd taken to glowering at each other. It had gotten so I couldn't stand the way he held his fork, cleared his throat. The twitch and the unfashionable bow ties—how could I have lived with them so long?—the way he was with his patients on the telephone—condescending was how I heard it now—everything put my teeth on edge. I was sharp and edgy. He'd lapsed into silences, given curt replies to ordinary questions. We'd fought about trivial things. "Take your umbrella," I'd said one morning, "it's pouring."

"It's not pouring. It's simply raining," he'd said.

"Okay, then, *raining.*"

"Why do you always back down?" he'd lashed out, wanting a war.

Finally Peter had made arrangements to move out permanently. As we'd stood in the front hall next to his packed suitcases trying to find summing-up things to say, I'd heard Marguerita weeping in the kitchen. This time, the tears had been for us. I'd held on to Peter's lapels and felt as if someone were holding a feather pillow over my face and cutting off the air, but finally, it had been me who'd opened the door and lifted one of his cases onto the front step. It was as if I'd been trying to hold on to a jacket, a shirt, a pair of pants. There was a doctor in the house, and not much of a man in the doctor.

* * *

"I heard about Ellery." In this light, the lines in Trevor's forehead faded.

"From whom?" Why I asked this, I don't know. The town knew, the world knew. Annie, in our last (strained) conversation, said she'd overheard people discussing us in the yogurt shop, the alternative post office and the Korean grocers'. She'd looked me right in the eye as she told me she would no longer be comfortable sharing a business, an office, a friendship. I'd told her she was breaking my heart. She'd been my friend for so long; she was an angel. Why such a stubborn one? "Couldn't we talk it over, Annie? 'Every path has its puddle.' "

"Maybe some day, but not now," she'd said. I guessed she was a saint, but maybe a slightly too saintly one.

Trevor had slipped the piece of paper with the list of measurements I'd made into the pocket of his plaid shirt. "I don't remember where I heard it."

"Sarah Jane, probably."

He took a step toward me. "It doesn't matter, does it?"

I took a step back, almost bumped into the summer folding chairs stacked against the far wall. "Listen, Trevor. I have to know what I have to know. Did you sleep with her?"

He took my hand and lifted my palm against his cheek. I had forgotten the deep-sea diver's watch, still here, still circling his bulky and well-constructed wrist. "Never." I thought he might be lying.

"I happen to know it was on her agenda."

"I happen to know it wasn't on mine."

His skin seemed impossibly smooth. Had he shaved

again before coming here? "*You* were always the agenda."

I moved my hand over his chin, his ear, to the slick back of his head, where his hair was damp, glossy fur. For a moment I felt a reprise of maternal tenderness. He was the little boy I was comforting. *Come close, I'll make it all right again.* Still, I didn't know whether to believe him.

"Only you," he said. "I've thought about you for so long."

I led the way upstairs. The two flights that felt like five now. The light was on in the hall, throwing just enough murky glow into the bedroom to create shadowy onlookers out of the valet, the cushions on the Baltimore settee, the highboy, the basket full of magazines. "I'll race you," he said, and unbuttoned his shirt, unbuckled his belt, got out of his chinos. I unzipped my jeans, stepped out of them, pulled off my new terra-cotta sweater, the color Sarah Jane called "Santa Fe suntan." I should have worn a lacier bra, unhooked this cotton plain-Jane one fast. His ring of a thousand keys jangled, hitting the carpet. I had no more conscience about this room or this bed, felt the soft rug under my bare feet, the feather quilt under my knees as I climbed onto it. Everything soft, everything ready. It all seemed to be waiting for us.

"It's always been Libby," he said, and when he said my name, it had resonance and lyricism. It had sparkle. He was next to me, not touching me, just up on one elbow looking into my face, his skin so pale in the dim light coming in from the hall, like the color of those blond leather couches in the waiting room of Peter's office. "You smell of peppermint, I love it." My antacid, an aphrodisiac? My stomach was settling nicely. "I'm trying to process this memory," he said. It sounded good. "When I relive it, I'll remember every small detail." Very good. Lust kicked in. "Did you know your eyes are a little more than one eye apart? Your left eyebrow is a smidgen higher than your right, did you know that? And look at this! One slightly crooked tooth! God, I love your imperfections!" He took his finger and ran it from my hairline down the center of my forehead, traced my nose, lips, chin. There he stopped, to look at my body. I needed to relax and wished I'd thought to turn on music. Or had that one glass of wine. All I seemed to hear was an occasional car in the street and the tension of my own breathing. My thoughts zeroing in on *what's he going to do next?* Until I suddenly heard Peter's voice as if he were in the room. Navigating.

"Do you have a condom?" I asked Trevor. He swung off the bed with the agility of a gymnast and without hesitation found one somewhere in a pocket in the puddle of his chinos. The segue was graceful and took only a moment. I thought of *The Rite of Spring* and *Swan Lake.* Had he come prepared, or was he always ready? I heard Peter's voice rise again in my head. Inquiring about the brand.

It's so easy to be infatuated. One steps right into an enhanced world. Each kiss and touch is a direct circuit to the soul. One's breasts seem to grow smoother and whiter under erotic scrutiny, one's thighs quiver with tension. The infatuation leads to desire and desire has its own gravity; my eyes automatically yearned to close, my legs to fall apart. He smelled faintly of the outside and I imagined wind, highways, and smoke curling from campfires in mountain forests; I saw satin cushions in tents lit with candles. I breathed in this vague perfume and let the spinning red circles of lust whirl and twist until they got me.

I gasped, I guess. I tore at Trevor's shoulder and spoke his name and thrashed in my bed. The thermal burst inside, my little screams and then a big one, and that unseen shaft of light, heat, and spasm inside. I wasn't anyone's wife. Or mother. I wasn't a daughter, or daughter-in-law. I'd stepped out of myself and felt, for a few minutes, a woman struck by lightning and kissed by the gods. Trevor shuddered and let out a cry that seemed to shake the lampshades, the curtains, the walls.

He did the right things: held me, and while he was still inside me spoke my name and told me he'd loved me since the very first moment—or something like that. It sounded as glorious as poetry, as valid as twelve steps. I let it sink in, wrapped myself around his words.

"Look," he said. "Look at our thumbs. They're exactly the same. The way they curve, almost like a *C*." He held our fingers side by side. "It's no coincidence."

"It's not?"

"Look how similar the thumbnails."

I looked at thumbnails.

And then, "You know, it's funny. I had the feeling when I first met you that it was charted. I think everything is planned. We were meant to be here tonight, an inevitability."

But I didn't think so, no. It was unordered circumstance is how I saw it. "I guess I believe in randomness, Trevor."

"Nothing is random. When a leaf falls, a car stops short, a tornado hits, it's all a plan."

"A plan? Preordained, you mean?"

"Pre—what?"

"You think we're born with a fixed itinerary?"

"Yes. And everything that's happened—my building that telephone booth up here three years ago, the Bergins calling me to redo the upstairs, it's all just a series of stops leading to a final destination."

"You mean death?"

"The first death."

"The first—?"

"Well, there'll be many others. Each life is followed by another life, and in between there's a rest. That's death."

I wished we could talk of love instead of philosophy, but he continued: "I went to a channeler. Up in Waterbury. He took me back through former lives. Fascinating. I once was a painter's helper during the Renaissance, and before that, a water carrier for Hannibal in the Punic Wars. Would you believe it?"

"Well, Trevor, it's a stretch."

". . . and helped Michelangelo paint frescoes in the Sistine Chapel. I was a courtier to Russia's last czar. In one life I was buried by the eruption of the volcano Mount Pelée. In 1902. I have it all written down. That's only a few of the many lives I've lived, before this one. Before you."

I wished we hadn't gotten into this. Three years ago, when we'd talked every day, we spoke of more solid things, personal subjects. I remembered the conversation about the Korean War, in which Trevor's father had been killed. Touching, the way he'd opened his wallet, pulled out his driver's license, his credit cards, to find and show me his father's photograph, which he carried with him to this day. Beautiful, the way his eyes had grown moist as I remarked on the resemblance between them. And he talked about me then. Listened to frivolous anecdotes about auctions I'd attended, my antique finds, my girls, my prosaic daily life. My opinions on parrots and cartoonists! He was captivated by mundane childhood reminiscences, my one personal set of memories. Then, he'd never touched on the subject of Hannibal and ceiling frescoes.

"When did you get interested in past lives?"

"About a year ago. My wife, Dee, she got me into it. She thinks she's going to die soon, see, and it's gotten her interested in what's next. There is a next, you know. She's reading a lot. Mostly Indian writers. She's gotten me hooked on it, too. I'll take you up to Waterbury to the channeler, if you'd like."

I watched him leave an hour later. He was going back into his own, strangely foreign life to write up an estimate. I would be staying in my familiar one, to wait for it. Watched his back, the keys on his hip, as he moved down the front walk, that lovely, longish hair overlapping the collar of his windbreaker, and I thought: Infatuation is too easy and love is too hard. I didn't want to go to Waterbury. And I didn't want to see Trevor Eddy again.

On Ellery's first day back at school after the abortion, a group of girls had circled her in the bathroom. They'd wanted to know everything. She was the star attraction, a celebrity with a sordid, exciting, lascivious story to tell. They'd wanted to know if she'd been shaved and whether she'd been awake enough to see the baby when they took it out of her. Did it have hands and feet, was it a boy or a girl, was there any hair on its head? They'd wanted to know if an abortion hurt and if she bled and if sex hurt and if she was going to do it with Ess again.

But a day or two later, the same girls had begun to distance themselves, and soon it became obvious that Ellery was a curiosity being set apart, that she had been tainted in a way that made her no longer one of them. Two of her Jennifers were now forbidden to invite her to their homes. A third girl, Amy, gave a birthday party for most of the class and excluded Ellery. The boys began calling out words to her she'd never heard them use before. There were jeers in the halls and schoolyard and she found a note in her desk calling her *Numero Uno Crandall School District Slut.*

And one day, she came home from school nearly in hysteria.

"They put something horrible in my locker!" she cried. She pounded upstairs to throw herself on her bed.

I forced her to show me what she didn't want to show me. It was a doll, beheaded, and spattered with red paint. A note was pinned to the doll. *Your a baby killer,* it said.

Ellery sat in the house day after day after school, growing more listless and hollow-eyed. Sat with Dumpling on her lap looking out the window or at the TV screen. Ate whatever was put in front of her, glassy-eyed. She seemed to be here but not here at all. One day, she got up from the dinner table, went into the den, and dismantled the Niagara Falls jigsaw puzzle. "I knew I could never finish it," she said. "In my life, what have I ever done right?"

The Flora Chadwick Academy, located in Southeastern Massachusetts, was a prep school designed to "inspire confidence, encourage robust mental growth through small classes and individual attention." We called the dean of admissions. *The diverse student body, a tradition of excellence in orthodox academic areas going back one hundred and four years, and attention given to the needs of every individual,* it read in the catalog, *makes it a perfect choice for that special student.* It seemed the right answer. The school year—which began two weeks after the public schools'— had already begun, but the dean of admissions agreed to meet with us. This was a school geared for anomalous situations, and the dean was used to hearing about the short-circuited lives of modern adolescents, roads not well traveled.

My mother called the night Peter drove Ellery up there to start her career in boarding school as a special student, and I could barely speak to her. I lay on my bed in my darkened bedroom holding Ellery's toy monkey and felt as if the sweet juice of my life had been drained right out of me. That night I dreamed of snow and cried out Peter's name again and again. I finally stood at my bedroom window and looked at the dark and snowless street and tried to imagine how I could have changed it all.

Peter threatened to follow through with legal action if Ess tried to contact either of the girls again. Got his lawyer to send off a severe letter to "Salvatore DiBuono and family," on official stationery. There was no response, although once, when I was pulling my car out of the garage, I saw Ess's black, dented van drive by the house, caught sight of the blue-mirror glasses, the glint of an earring, and—something new—a baseball cap, visor in back, hiding the military haircut. I saw the van slow down, saw his head swivel in the direction of our house. I remembered how he'd swaggered into our yard, the way his mouth stopped in midsmile, his wise-cracking, bulldozing brashness. Then I saw him again, standing in the fluorescent light outside his family's house, his arm around Ellery, and—for only the shortest flicker of a moment—imagined his spirit shrunken, the swagger gone, his soul permanently stunted. I felt sorry for him until I saw the van turn the corner. There it sped up, whizzed around the curve, took off, the way Ess would whiz ahead—after kneeling in a darkened confessional, shedding a tear perhaps, murmuring a penance—speed off, without looking back, in whatever direction his life took him.

It was the week after Christmas. Ellery and I were dressed and ready, eye on *Jeopardy!* in the bedroom, but

Claudia was still in the bathroom, having been delayed by the usual assortment of telephone calls. She'd been hoping for a call from Kevin Bevan, home for the holidays, who had sent her a Christmas card saying he hoped to see her and wishing her a Joyeux Noel. The silver-turquoise ring was not back on her finger, though. So far, no Kevin, but calls had come from someone named Damon. "Is that Stephanie's brother?" I asked.

"Are you *serious,* Mommy? Stephanie's brother's name is *Todd.* Todd is skiing in Gstaad. This is Damon. Damon works at the Pet Pit. Don't you remember when we took Dumpling down there to buy a collar with a bell? He was the one who kept calling him Dimples?"

"Damon is short," Ellery said.

"Not really. He's taller than I am. Anyway, height doesn't matter."

"You always felt it was revelant before," Ellery said.

"Relevant, dear."

"Relevant. Anyways. One minute you say one thing, Claudia, and the next thing you say something else."

"Girls, please."

"Okay, Mommy. Okay, okay. *Pas de* sweat. The truth is, he's a very intelligent person. He's gotten me to quit smoking. He showed me some pictures of sick lungs like you wouldn't believe. And he's into archaeology. He was telling me about the excavations of Pompeii and Herculaneum. They found whole cities buried under the ash of volcanic eruption from Mount Vesuvius. And in 1983 they found fossil jawbones in Kenya that were eighteen million years old."

"Wow," Ellery said. "Was that B.C., or what?"

Claudia rolled her eyes. "So, it doesn't matter if he's short. He's interesting."

"You said you'd never go out with someone under six feet. You said that about three months ago, Claudia."

"I never said that."

"You did!"

"Okay, so I'm changing. Now I want a boy with a brain bigger than a pinto bean. Okay? Am I allowed to change?"

"You always said—"

"Ellery, will you give it up!"

"Girls, please! Let's have peace. Your father will be here any minute."

We were all going to the club in honor of Claudia's birthday, which was not for another two and a half weeks, but would be celebrated tonight, while Ellery was home from school.

So far, she had adjusted well to Flora Chadwick Academy, had a new friend, her roommate, who suffered from seasonal affective disorder, and had to sit under a fluorescent light for several hours every day. Another Chadwick friend had never lived in one place more than six months, and went into cyclical depressions, had once tied a plastic bag over her head in a suicide attempt. "It's not like Crandall Junior High," Ellery said, and she pushed up the tip of her nose with her finger, ". . . but hey, it's okay. I got to read the invocation at the tree-lighting ceremony and you know what? I'm going to learn the saxophone like Ess's sister"—her voice dropped; we ignored the reference—"and play in the marching band at all the games. And guess what? They're building stables. Next semester, I'm going back to horseback riding! It's like I feel I'm someone who *is* someone at Chadwick. People don't care what happened to you before you got there, it's like here and now that's important. I don't have to try so fucking hard. And, I mean, I'm not always keeping up with everybody. It seems like at Chadwick some people are trying to keep up with *me*." She pushed her hair back with the fingers of both hands, fluffed it up and out, and the gold cuff bracelet Ess had given Claudia—now a gift to Ellery from her sister—caught the light as it slid down her arm.

In our weekly telephone conversations, we never mentioned the abortion, never spoke of Ess. When I looked into my daughter's eyes now, I thought I saw shadows there that I hadn't seen before. But that is subjective, and after all, we'd spent quite a jolly Christmas with my mother, the girls and I—no shadows in Delray—had flown down for four days of palm trees and poinsettia, and Rudy's honey-basted goose, white chocolate mousse, and the beach. Except for a few bad moments, once when my sister called and began asking questions and then when my mother badgered me to tell her everything, it was a sunny, unreal, temporary diversion, a different sort of Christmas, a holiday with less sting than any we would spend without Daddy in Crandall.

Peter had gone off to Two Bunch Palms Spa out West, not with his mother, who was off on a Pacific cruise, trying to recover from the judge's defection. Darley blamed us, specifically me, for his departure, because the judge had begun to cool very quickly after he got wind of our scandal and had recently been seen in Rowayton with a woman who breeds Irish wolfhounds. And who else could the Countess blame but the undersupervisor? "He's a public figure," Darley had said, in our last (strained) telephone conversation, "with a flawless reputation. He has standards, he's a Republican . . . he served on the *ethics* committee when they were investigating corruption in the state government . . . he's been to the *White House*"—she began to cry—"during the Nixon administration. And his sister was sending him those newspaper clips and—and whispering in his ear. About, about our family. Our—our *stained, disgraced* family. So, who could blame him for taking up with that dog woman?"

* * *

Claudia sat up front with her father. Ellery and I in back. Ellery had a new permanent and, despite the Countess's anguish, a Dubonnet velvet jacket Darley had found it in her heart to send for Christmas before departing for her port of embarkation in San Francisco. The wine color seemed to cast a flattering glow, or perhaps I imagined the newly robust pink cheeks in my anxiousness to look for positive signs of health and recovery. If only Ellery could gain a few pounds, round out those severe, sad features. If only I could hear her laugh—not just smile, as she had when she'd jumped the waves in Florida last week, not just let out a short sound of amusement, but really let go, the way I remembered she once used to—when was that? It seemed so long ago, a time when there never seemed to be a minute of peace—the phone, the fights, the pounding footsteps and slamming doors that blitzed through the days when I took fun for granted.

Claudia had surprised everyone by getting most of her hair cut off. "I have to get used to it, sweetie," Peter said, as she climbed into the seat of birthday honor next to him. He'd bought a new digital camera, and snapped the birthday girl on the front step. I sat next to Ellery in the backseat, making small talk with my husband. It was as if I'd stepped into a video someone was making of our lives, that we had a script I had to stick to: "Was the weather good in California?" "Is Dr. Wu working out?" "What's happening with the Greavy Scholarship Fund?" and so on. He asked about Annie, the Bergins, and Dumpling. Finally, the more personal, the loaded, the poignant: "How are you doing, Libby?" when the girls bounded ahead as we made our way into the clubhouse. Meaning, "without me."

"Okay. And you, Peter?"

"Doing all right," he said, but he was subdued and inaccessible. I felt he wanted to say something but couldn't get it out. Peter wasn't doing okay, and neither was I, and that was how I felt, going off to the club to celebrate Claudia's seventeenth birthday, as if I were—we all were—withering. Our top-notch family, in bankruptcy.

We walked through the dining room, our elegant retinue, all eyes on Claudia in Gap Christmas red, whose new haircut, severe, dramatic, different, made heads turn and voices lower. Since there were no more copious curls through which to push her fingers, her hands stayed at her sides, in her lap, or on her knife and fork, throughout dinner. And she talked about driving lessons ("At last!"), her new cashmere sweater set from Daddy (he'd been told that she had enough watches, but not enough sweaters, "hint, hint"), her "miserable geeky stiff of a math teacher," "the dweeb with killer breath" next to her in French, and Damon. She ignored the new busboy, although it was clear he was ogling her. And then, she talked about archaeology, segued into anthropology, mentioned she'd like to go to Bath to see the Temple of Sulis Minerva, intended to read Marcel Mauss and Margaret Mead. She felt fossils were fascinating, did Peter visit the La Brea Tar Pits when he was in California? Did we realize human beings' ancestors appeared on earth five million years before Christ? And human beings date back 92,000 years?

Peter and I looked at each other, in sort of unspoken astonishment. And listened in dazzled bewilderment as our older daughter described a book she'd read about natural disasters, the volcano eruption near Crete in the seventeenth century BC, which gave rise to the legend of Atlantis. "I've taken out a book on Mount Etna. Did you know it's Greek for 'I burn'? I'm sort of turned on by ancient history. And in honor of my father, the doctor, medical treatments they used long ago. Daddy, did you know that people who lived in the tenth century had *measles*?''

Mary Frances O'Connell stopped at the table to remark that the girls looked more beautiful than ever. She put a hand on Ellery's shoulder and gave it a squeeze, a message no one could possibly miss. ''We're happy to see you all back,'' she said pointedly, omitting ''together.'' She had heard about us, of course—everyone had—but knew enough about club protocol to never, ever bring up anything she knew, except behind our backs. Peter told me he had no intention of allowing himself to feel awkward in his own club because of gossip, which would run out of gas faster than a punctured tank. He didn't care what the commodore or anyone had to say, or whether there were whispers left and right when we walked through the clubhouse. He said there wasn't a person in this dining room who did not have a demerit or two, a secret sin. He told Ellery that whenever she felt uncomfortable, she should lift her chin up a quarter of an inch and fix a little smile on her lips. ''Mona Lisa has her secret. You have yours.''

''What's hers?''

''*Mon Dieu,* is she for real?'' Claudia moaned.

When the cake came out, Peter said nothing to the Madonna-like waitress. Everyone all around us joined in singing ''Happy Birthday'' and Claudia took a deep breath and blew out all the candles and there was a little round of applause. ''I've never gotten them all out at once, never,'' Ellery remarked, and Peter put his hand over hers on the table.

''Ellery is too hard on Ellery, sweetie.'' Then he looked over the cake at me and in a voice that was a bronchitic low register, he said, ''I have to say something.''

''Oh, God,'' Claudia said, ''Not again! Does it have to be now?''

"Yes, now."

"And here?"

"Here and now. You see, girls? A golden opportunity. It's been there between your mother and me, a tight, bloody knot. All these years."

"Peter, do the girls have to hear this?"

"A knot I could never undo."

I stared at a little rewoven patch in the tablecloth. "Peter."

"I want them to hear this."

"I don't want to hear this." Claudia was shaking her head vehemently.

I pushed back my chair and got up. "Not here, Peter, goddamn it, not now."

"People are looking, Mommy!" Claudia was clutching her fork as if it could jump out of her hand. "Please sit down, Mommy!"

"I don't want you to ruin Claudia's birthday." I was firm, strong. Standing my ground.

Peter lowered his voice. "Please sit down, Libby. Please."

I hesitated.

"I'm not going to ruin anyone's birthday. No scenes. I promise. Still sober, see?"

"Peter—please." I sat down.

"Libby, I have to say it now, or it'll be too late. I've been thinking about this since I left. All these years—you saw everything that happened, from that day to this, as a repercussion. An aftereffect. All our lives a sequel to that day of the blizzard in March. Everything to do, from the moment she was born, with Ellery. Mea culpa."

"What's mea culpa?" Ellery looked from one to the other anxiously.

"My fault," Claudia said.

"Is that French?"

Claudia's eyes rolled. "Ellery, are you for real? It's Latin."

"Then how do you know it?"

I finished off the water in my glass, gulping fast, as if someone might take it away any minute.

"And you know I love you both. So help me God. Are you listening, girls?"

The girls looked at each other.

"Did you hear me?"

They both nodded solemnly.

"See, Libby, you've never—you wouldn't, no matter what—tear that page out of your mind's calendar. You've never let it go. Terrified of the crazy, guzzling monster I used to be! You never really trusted me again."

I looked up at the chandelier so I wouldn't have to look at him. I would practice restraint in the middle of Claudia's slicing a piece of cake for her sister, the piece with the red candy raspberry and a chocolate leaf. I took hold of the edge of the table and held tight, finally lowered my eyes to the level of the liquid green eyes of our navigator, met his gaze head on.

"For Christ's sake, Libby, please, God, can't you finally rewind and erase?"

I had to wait while the waitress filled our coffee cups, explained they'd just made a fresh pot of decaf, asked if cream was all right or did we need milk? I had to wait while she circled the table and asked Ellery if she wanted another soda while we were having our coffee.

When she'd finally moved off, I'd calmed down. I was breathing nicely again.

Peter got icing on the sleeve of his jacket when he reached for my hand across the table. "Why is it so easy to talk to patients and so hard to talk to you?" The twitch came and went. It wasn't very noticeable; it was just Peter, and I suppose I was finally getting used to it.

"*Mon Dieu!* Would you *puleese*? I'm going to freak! Everybody is *looking* at us!" Claudia whispered through her teeth, putting down the cake knife.

"Daddy, you got icing on your sleeve." Ellery was taking her napkin and wiping it off nervously.

Now I was looking at my husband's bow tie. I didn't want to embarrass Claudia and Ellery with red rabbit eyes, tissues, a club dining room crying jag. For someone who'd rarely shed a tear in her adult life, I had recently turned into being on the verge of waterworks on an almost daily basis.

In my imagination the club dining room seemed to hush, conversations died all around, the chandeliers dimmed, the plate-glass windows steamed up, and for a moment Crandall, Connecticut—and the world—receded. When I reached for my purse to get a tissue, just in case, I knocked over my empty water glass. Ellery grabbed the two little ice cubes that had hopped onto the tablecloth.

"I am so embarrassed! Everybody is fucking *looking* at us." Claudia shook her head in exasperation as the busboy sped over with a water pitcher. A moment later she pulled her fingers through what was left of her hair, picked up the cake knife, and continued slicing her birthday cake.

*Love is difficult*—I imagined the words written on parchment and found in a hundred years in our attic, along with our antiques and a copy of *Southern Connecticut Life*, the paper yellowing and curling with age, but the script indelible. This was our story, not bigger than life, but maybe just life. Not always, and never consistently, but it's true I loved them all desperately, sometimes Peter most of all.

And I had the last word, finally. "I forgive you, Peter," I said.

## ABOUT THE AUTHOR

TWO DAUGHTERS is Marlene Fanta Shyer's fifth novel. She has also written ten books for children, a play, and a memoir, coauthored with her son, Christopher Shyer. In addition, over one hundred of her short stories and articles have been published in women's magazines, and most recently she has been writing about her travels here and abroad. The mother of three grown children, Marlene divides her time between her homes in New York City and Westchester County. You can visit her Web site at www.Marleneshyer.com.

# More Women's Fiction From Kensington

| | | |
|---|---|---|
| **__Beyond the Promise**<br>by Barbara Bickmore | **1-57566-329-5** | **$6.99**US/**$8.50**CAN |
| **__Cha Cha Cha**<br>by Jane Heller | **0-8217-5895-0** | **$5.99**US/**$7.50**CAN |
| **__Chesapeake Song**<br>by Brenda Lane Richardson | **0-7860-0304-9** | **$5.99**US/**$7.50**CAN |
| **__Come into My Parlor**<br>by Marilyn Campbell | **0-7860-0399-5** | **$5.99**US/**$7.50**CAN |
| **__The Last Good Night**<br>by Emily Listfield | **1-57566-354-6** | **$5.99**US/**$7.50**CAN |
| **__River Without End**<br>by Pamela Jekel | **1-57566-307-4** | **$6.50**US/**$8.00**CAN |
| **__An Uncommon Woman**<br>by Julie Ellis | **1-57566-122-5** | **$5.99**US/**$7.50**CAN |

---

Call toll free **1-888-345-BOOK** to order by phone or use this coupon to order by mail.

Name______________________________

Address____________________________

City_______________ State ___________ Zip__________

Please send me the books that I have checked above.

I am enclosing $__________

Plus postage and handling* $__________

Sales tax (in New York and Tennessee) $__________

Total amount enclosed $__________

*Add $2.50 for the first book and $.50 for each additional book. Send check or money order (no cash or CODs) to: **Kensington Publishing Corp., 850 Third Avenue, New York, NY 10022**

Prices and numbers subject to change without notice.

All orders subject to availability.

Check out our website at **www.kensingtonbooks.com.**